OF MAN AND SUPERWOMAN

Han felt misgivings. Consider: a girl alone on a long voyage. a *ler* adolescent, no less, and hence, by human standards, highly sexual in her behavior, which in her society was normal and expected. But she was also a trained killer of a discipline that was feared even on *ler* worlds.

He looked at her again: she appeared relaxed, feminine, tender. Yet he knew very well that she could probably take on every person in the room and leave them submissive, maimed or mangled. She would be the human equivalent of a perfect gymnast, armed with something like karate and kung-fu, and expert in the use of all weapons "which do not leave the hand," as the *ler* put it.

Alone, Han realized, he could probably not overpower her even with a beam rifle. . . .

Yet he would have to be alone with this sensual girl for the length and breadth of the galaxy—and Han was male and all huma . . . .

THE WARRIORS OF DAWN

M. A. Foster

DAW BOOKS, INC.
DONALD A. WOLLHEIM, PUBLISHER

1301 Avenue of the Americas
New York, N. Y.   10019

Dedication:
FOR MATTHEW

FIRST PRINTING, JANUARY 1975

3 4 5 6 7 8 9

PRINTED IN U.S.A.

Part I

CHALCEDON

I

———◆———

"*A ler called Maidenjir, of the period when they were still on Earth, is reputed to have said, 'Fools think that everything must have a name and so apply themselves, forgetting that at the completion of their activity, the Universe will end. Now shall we speak of last words?' This has its roots in the curious ler doctrine of ignorance (facts are finite, but ignorance is as boundless as the Universe) and in their concepts of person and number theory. But more than one human scholar has seen in this an interesting parallel to the ancient Hindu belief that if one repeated the name of Shiva, Lord of Destruction, often enough, He would open His eye and destroy the world.*"

—*Roderigo's Apocrypha*

In the early history of one particular planet, Seabright, human colonists came and broke the ground for a new world's development, and built a port town of tarpaper shacks, warehouses, dumps and shabby repair depots. Likewise, they thoughtfully installed brothels, gambling dens, beer halls, and filled the city up with a raw new world's drunks, entrepreneurs, derelicts and whores. It was a vast running sore, and they named it "Boomtown," taking precedent

7

from many hasty towns which had sprung up before on other worlds.

But Boomtown, of course, like all things, changed with time; it was renewed, urban and otherwise, rebuilt, scraped over, moved several miles down the coast, moved back, burned, and built again after being shaken into ruins by earthquakes. Now, Han reflected, enjoying the bright morning light playing among the apartment balconies, it was perhaps more resort than anything else, with "minor government center" trailing in second place. Tourists swam in the clear water of the bay, around which the city curved in a sophisticated embrace, hoping to find artifacts and old coins. The Boomtowners made it beautiful and they moved part of the government to it, but they retained the awful name out of a bizarre sense of humor and a sense of the power of habit: the name was several thousand years old and every attempt to change it had ended in failure.

As with every city worth the name, yokels arrived daily out of the hinterlands seeking adventure and fame. They found neither. Boomtown was now lazy, bright, lovely, seductive . . . and people woke late of mornings, as Han Keeling ruefully thought in reference to himself as well. He finished his bun and coffee, paid the waiter, and departed the half-empty sidewalk café, knowing well enough that he was already late.

As he walked towards the top of Middlehill, in the direction of an unpretentious residence and office building, he reviewed what he knew about his appointment, which was little enough.

He was an apprentice Trader, almost finished with the trade guild's finishing school. He was in his mid-twenties, sound of mind and body, and a moderate success with the lazy, teasing secretaries of Boomtown. And he had been told by the Master Trader that if he wanted an interesting and undescribed assignment, he could report to a certain building on Middlehill and once there, go to room 900 at a certain time, and press on from there. Press on! That was the guild's overworked motto. Press on; in the face of dire calamities, fires, cannibals, slavers, economic "readjustments" and accidents. Indeed. But in this case, if he took the job and completed it successfully, he would get his Trader's papers, and his license.

And of course, he was late. Han quickened his step, and so doing, caught a glance from a passing, brightly dressed girl, apparently on her way to work. She wore a flowerprint gauzy dress that floated around her, suggesting curves as it swirled from her motions in the clear morning air. He surreptitiously checked his reflection in a shop window: slim, elegant, knowledgeable, competent, relaxed. So he thought. The figure that covertly glanced back at him in the reflection was dark of hair, smooth of face, with features which a more critical observer might have described as being slightly too sharp, too well defined. But he was not a critical observer; he saw the reflection as being somewhat taller than average, and dressed fashionably enough after the tastes of the times.

He arrived at the building and went in, without passing any checkpoints or observers he could see. At the door of room 900, he paused before entering and reviewed his excuses for being late. He was sure, however, that little would be made of it, if anything, for everyone in Boomtown was always late; to be early or precisely on time was considered slightly vulgar, in bad taste. He knocked, and entered, through an old-fashioned door which swung open rather than sliding.

The room inside was brightly lit by the morning light streaming in over the terrace; there was no other illumination. Beyond, the blue sea, Steelsheen Ocean, rolled and played, throwing quick flashes of sparkling light and sudden glimpses of whitecaps. The room itself was a large one, floored with natural stone. Instead of the expected furniture, there were planters scattered about, some containing miniature trees which, by their gnarled appearance, were very old and carefully tended. But the decor of the room went far beyond mere mannerism; there was something delicate and natural about it, a difference one could sense below the level of direct perception. It was a ler room.

There were nine people in the room, obviously waiting for him, because as he entered, they began settling themselves at a low table on the terrace proper. Four were humans, which Han could distinguish by their colorful Boomtown clothes and gestures of impatience. The remaining five were ler, which he could distinguish by their slightly smaller stature and homespun robes. There was an almost total absence of decoration on any of the robes, which Han recognized as an indication of high status.

A florid, heavy-set human approached Han and introduced himself as one Yekeb Hetrus, regional coordinator. The other humans introduced themselves in turn; Darius Villacampo,

Nuri Ormancioglu, and Thaddeusz Marebus. No other titles
or positions were referenced; this caused Han to become
more attentive. That they would not mention titles indicated
that they were either very high or very low. He decided that
they were high. Most likely Union Security people, who
were reputed to be a closemouthed lot in any circumstances.

The ler were more interesting, if for no other reason than
that they were rare and strange in this part of space. And as
he had often heard, he could not distinguish at first sight
whether they were male or female. In a certain way,
they looked like, disturbingly like, slender, graceful children
with slight signs of age and maturity beginning to show on
some of their faces. They were all rather uniform in height;
Han guessed they would all be around just over five feet.

Han knew very well that ler were human-derived, the
result of an early atomic-era program to accelerate human
evolution. The theory had entailed DNA manipulation and
a reliance on a magic-number hypothesis analogous to the
early approaches to quantum mechanics; to continue the
analogy, they had been reaching for the next stable junction
on the "magic number" grid. The project had no sooner
reached its goal than it was attacked from without, by humans who felt genetics was oriented to the environment, and
by the specimens themselves, who had stabilized and formed
a culture of their own. After several hundred years of uneasy
relations between ten billion humans and several thousand
ler, the ler had discovered a faster-than-light drive, built a
spaceship in secret, and departed. Before they left, however,
the world government of the day had become dependent on
them to supply the necessary technological input to keep an
overconsumptive culture afloat far beyond its years. Naturally, when the ler left Earth, there was a "readjustment."
Humans had called them ungrateful, and were terrified of
the implications of an advanced human type in their midst.
The ler were not competitive, were terrified of human numbers, and wanted to be left alone. That was ancient history.
Since that period, they had mutually colonized a large volume
of space, the humans expanding spinwards along the ga-
lactic disc, and the ler antispinwards.

Still, Han experienced something akin to awe, as they
introduced themselves. Neither race had ever found any
other intelligent life in the worlds they had discovered, by
now, some forty worlds. There were traces here and there,
an occasional undecipherable artifact, but no aliens. So, in

the popular mind, they had become, to each other, the alien race.

The first introduced itself as Defterdhar Srith. Han knew enough basics from school days to recognize the last "name" as not a surname, but an honorific that indicated that the individual concerned was a female past the age of fertility. She was as quiet and self-possessed as one of the large stones that stood here and there about the terrace. The second and third were, respectively Yalvarkoy and Lenkurian Haoren, insiblings to each other. Han looked closer. Male and female. The fourth was dark, rather saturnine and quiet, but with bright, animated eyes. He did not speak, but instead stood quietly with his hands in his sleeves.

The fifth, and closest to Han of the group around the table, was at second glance a female, and a young one at that. In fact, she was, as he looked and listened more closely, much younger than the other ler present. She gave her name as Liszendir Srith-Karen. Han's suspicions were confirmed: the ler girl was young, in their terms still an adolescent, although he could not guess her age at all. She might have been sixteen standard or twenty-eight. Their adolescence went up to thirty standard. Somehow, subtly, he became aware of her not as a member of a race near man and derived from him, but as a young girl. She had plain, clear features of no particular distinction; her hair was short and pale brown, almost uncolored in its neutral tone, cropped off artlessly neat about ear level. It was straight and extremely fine in texture.

Her manner suggested something unfathomable and contradictory: an apprentice sage; a tomboy. She had a small, delicate nose and a broad, generous mouth. She was not a beauty in human terms of reference, but at the same time, she was attractive in a clean and direct way. Her eyes, however, were the most noticable feature of her face; they were large and gray, and the pupil almost filled up the whole eye, except for corners of white. A faint yellow ring exactly divided the inner and outer iris. Han looked away from them. They were intense, knowing eyes. He looked at Lenkurian, the other young ler female present. Yes. There was some difference. Han could catch a hint of it; Liszendir was much better-looking than the other.

At this point, Hetrus made some introductory remarks, and then indicated that they were to listen to a recording. which he initiated by pressing a concealed switch. The recording started, identifying itself as a Union Security tape, subject, an interrogation, and circumstance, the statement of one Trader Edo Efrem, Master Trader. Han did not recognize the name at all, and assumed that Efrem was probably not of the Seabright system, but from some planet further out.

The interrogation recorded by the tape went as follows:

—Proceed, Trader Efrem.

—Very well. As I said before, I had headed outwards towards Chalcedon to do a little trading and see how things were. None of us get out that far on the edge very often, so I was sure I could sell a load of primitive toolstuff I had picked up deep inside as a . . . ah . . . a speculation, so to speak. I arrived at night, so of course one couldn't see very much. We set the bazaar up and waited for morning. But nobody came. I sent my Crew Chief into the local area to see if he could stir anyone up. Much later, he returned with a handful of people. To my surprise, of both kinds. In fact, I hadn't made a voyage to Chalcedon before, and I didn't know . . .

—Yes. We know about that aspect of Chalcedon. Go on.

—Well, to make a longer story shorter, they had been raided. Now, we all hear tales, of course, but we rarely ever see any hard and fast evidence. But they had gotten it there, all right. Later, I flew around the planet, and it was all over. Destruction everywhere. Some of the craters were still hot. Apparently, they came in, shot the place up, looted and took captives. They stayed about a month, and then abruptly left. Incredible damage. I unloaded as much as I could afford and beat it back here as fast as possible.

—Did you hear a description of the raiders?

—Yes, and that was what bothered me. It didn't make good sense. Both kinds of people on the planet described them as 'ler barbarians.' They all had their hair either shaven off, or done up in plumes and crests. They wore loincloths and many had tattoos. And they were definitely ler.

—They were sure?

—Absolutely. Both kinds said so.

—What about captives?

—From what we could make out, only a few ler were taken, but quite a few humans. At first, the locals thought that the purpose in mind was ransom, but when more time passed and nothing was heard, slave-taking seemed the more probable. It was pretty strange, though; the raiders only

appeared to take certain types of people. Perhaps "types" isn't the right word. They used a ler word which means something like "subrace" or "one who has a tribal characteristic." They did not seem to pick according to any known standard of beauty or utility. Now that's what bothered me. You hear tales, of course, but slavers and raiders? Besides, as far as I know, nobody has ever known ler to do anything even remotely like that. They fight well enough when the occasion demands, but they aren't aggressive.

—Did anyone know what kind of weapons the raiders used? Or what their ship looked like?

—No, to both. Nobody saw what caused the craters. And nobody saw the ship close. Some saw it above, at night, but all they could see were some lights. It was a terror raid, simple. There isn't anything on Chalcedon except a few mines and farms. There are no defended places or anything like that. No concentration of wealth.

—Any indications of where they came from?

—The survivors said that the raiders called themselves "The Warriors of Dawn." But that could mean anything. Every planet has dawns; plenty of them, too. No. Nobody knew. But I would guess, as did everyone else on the planet, that they came from somewhere further out.

—What language did they speak?

—The ler on Chalcedon said that it was a very distorted form of their "Singlespeech," barely understandable. There were words mixed in that no one could identify.

Hetrus turned the reproducer off. After a moment, he spoke, slowly and at length.

"This tape has been primarily for the benefit of you two young people, Han and Liszendir. The rest of us have already heard it. Likewise, the history you are about to hear. It is well known to some of us, but probably not to you.

"You already know that the ler originated as an experiment in forced human evolution on Earth. After they fled Earth, many years later, they founded a world they called Kenten—'firsthome.' No contact was made for many more years, partly out of inability and partly out of mistrust. When contact was made, it began an unpleasant period, which was a shame to both our peoples. The Great Compromise ended all that, with humans expanding spinwards and ler anti-spinwards. New worlds would be, as discovered, for one or the other. Disagreements would be kept local. This worked for more years.

"No provision was made in the cases of inwards and outwards. Inwards, there has been some rare skirmishing, but nothing of any great importance. Outwards, however, it has been completely peaceful. Towards the edge, at the farthest known habitable world, the guiding councils of both decided to dual-colonize one world; to see if perhaps the rent in our fabric could be mended. To date, we have been successful—on Chalcedon."

As Hetrus paused, Lenkurian broke in. She seemed impatient, and spoke in a whispering, breathless voice which seemed so quiet it hardly sounded at all; yet curiously, it carried effortlessly to all parts of the terrace.

"When we heard this report, naturally we were interested. Note that the raiders were apparently ler, but of no origin anyone could determine, and of decidedly abnormal behavior. This caused some strain among our senior governing bodies. So we urgently wish to look further into this matter."

Hetrus continued, "Naturally, we wish it to appear innocent. We know in fact almost nothing, and we do not know if the area is under observation. That is why you two were suggested. Han is waiting for an assignment; Liszendir is likewise unoccupied at this time, and can be considered to be making her journeying for her skill, her 'tranzhidh.' "

The girl nodded approval at the alien use of a ler word.

Hetrus said, "You need not feel particularly gifted. Others would have perhaps been better; but you two were readily available. Neither of you has family responsibilities at this time, and you are not likely to develop any attachment to each other beyond the business at hand. We have provided a ship, an armed cutter, and some goods to suggest traders. You will voyage to Chalcedon and pursue the matter further. Efrem was in a hurry to leave; you need not, and may follow it as far as it leads. Your skills complement one another's admirably."

Han and Liszendir looked at each other. As if she anticipated the question in his mind, she said quietly, with a subtle undertone of belligerence, "I am Liszendir, an adolescent of Karen Braid, infertile, *Nerh* or elder outsibling, unwoven. You would say unpromised and unattached, I believe. My age in standard is twenty-six."

Han felt immediately put on guard by the frankness, which, he reminded himself, was not so much a personality

trait of the girl herself, but a cultural trait they all shared in
in various degree. Still, it seemed that as she spoke, she had
deliberately dropped the little femininity he could perceive,
and become something different. Something fey, wild, tomboy. Aggressive. He wondered just what her skill was. And
if she could turn on her femininity as easily as she turned it
off.

Han asked her, "I am Han Keeling, male, unattached,
Srith-Karen Liszendir. May I ask what your skill is?"

"You may. I am a violet adept of the Karen school of
infighting."

Han nodded politely. He felt misgivings by the score
creep up the back of his neck. Consider: a girl alone on a
long voyage. A ler adolescent, no less, and hence, by human
standards, highly sexual in her behavior, which in her society
was normal and expected. All that was pleasant enough. But
a trained killer of a discipline that was feared even on ler
worlds. He looked at her again; she appeared relaxed,
feminine, tender. Her skin was pale and very smooth. Yet
he knew very well that she could probably take on every
person in the room and leave them, at her choice, submissive,
maimed or mangled beyond recognition. She would be the
human equivalent of a perfect gymnast, armed with something like karate and kung-fu, and expert in the use of all
weapons "which do not leave the hand," as the ler put it.
They had moral objections to that, at least.

Han had heard tales. They were not for him to verify.
Alone, he realized, he could probably not overpower her
even with a beam rifle: she would be too fast. He resolved
to leave her strictly alone. She noted his appraisal through
his facial movements.

"That is good, Han. You know what I am. So there will be
no problem. I accept."

One of the continuing reasons why humans and ler
avoid each other revolved around the sexual issue. One concept intimate with evolution was neoteny, an extended im-
maturity. The ler had gotten a heavy dose of it, and so to
human eyes retained the beauty of youth well into middle
age. But of course the attraction did not flow both ways.
They saw humans as "ancestral primitives" and wanted
nothing to do with them in any way that even suggested a
sexual relationship. There were other strains as well. Ler
were infertile until their adolescence ended around age thirty,
but their sex drive started at the beginning of adolescence,

around age ten. They were encouraged to enjoy their bodies without restraint, and since they were infertile, even incest was permitted. Humans, on the other hand, were more restrained by necessity. Lastly, even if there had ever been love between two of different kinds, it would have had no yield: the cross between ler and human would not even produce offspring. The original project had gone that far.

Cultural differences had grown alongside physical ones. To humans, ler society seemed too agricultural, static, and oversexed to the point of madness. To ler, human society seemed mechanistic and overhurried. Methods of aggression differed, also. A ler dealt with his or her fellows directly, or ignored them. If the issue came to a fight, then so be it. But they regarded any weapon which left the hand with horror, and by extension, any practice that avoided direct involvement. Lastly, the ler birthrate was low, and so all adults were expected to share in childbearing to their limit. Humans used every form of birth control known and it still wasn't enough to keep overcrowding at bay on some worlds.

So Han knew without thinking about it very deeply that he would not be able to play sex-games with the girl, Liszendir. Very well. He could match her in his skill, which was in bargaining, piloting, machinery. He thought, with rueful complacence, that she did not know anything there. They did not train their children for general purposes, but to a particular role, which went with the family, the "braid" willy-nilly.

"I accept also," Han added.

Hetrus nodded, in conformity with the others. "Fine, fine, sure you'll work well together. Now. You can leave at your convenience, although we would prefer it to be as soon as possible. The ship is ready at the spaceport, already cleared. It is set up to be human-financed and ler-registered. It is called by a ler name, *Pallenber*, which means, I am told, 'pearly bow wave.' Just notify the departure controller when you are ready."

Liszendir arose with no ceremony. "I am prepared now. Let it be done and finished."

Han also got to his feet. He thought on the name. Yes, that sounded nice, poetic, bringing visions to mind of sailing ships on a blue sea, with brightly colored sails. Yes, indeed. But it didn't take a linguist to devise, out of those same roots, a name somewhat like "Bone in his teeth," which referred to warships bent on destruction. But he said, "I will need to get some things, make some arrangements."

Hetrus interposed, "No need, my boy, no need at all. You have everything you need already aboard the ship. The Master Trader of Boomtown will take care of all arrangements, your papers, your affairs. We advise discretion and deliberation in most things, and they are good practices. However, in this case I am sure you will understand . . ."

"In other words, get going," Han interrupted.

"In a hasty word, which implies no diminution of good will, yes."

"Well, then. I suppose that since this is the case, then I can go now, too. I would as well see it finished." He directed the last at Liszendir, who either failed to notice, or pretended not to.

Preparing to leave, the ler group arose quietly and began their departures with no ceremony whatsoever. Hetrus and the remainder of the humans, Ormancioglu, Marebus and Villacampo, paused by the terrace rail to speak privately about some matter which seemed to occupy their full attentions. Han and Liszendir looked at each other coolly and critically for a moment, then started for the door. Liszendir went through the door first, apparently within her own frame of reference already broken with the group and its business in the room. However, by the door Han turned to the quiet ler who had not given his name.

"I beg your pardon, sir," he began quietly, although no one was near them within earshot, "what ever became of the trader Efrem? And what was your name? I don't believe I caught it . . ."

"Efrem is here in Boomtown, Han Keeling." From the timbre of the voice, Han guessed that the creature was male, although from appearance alone, it was even more ambiguous than the normal ler. The voice also seemed curiously resonated and accented, although he thought no more of this than considering the possibility that the ler could have come from some very remote world. The creature continued, "Efrem feared murder, and decided to retire on a generous pension. You may well guess that his cooperation came at a price. But what he had, he sold. You need not worry that he left something out. There would be no point at all in your seeing him. None at all."

"Well, fine enough. Am I being impolite in asking the name, committing some breach of etiquette?"

"No, no. Not at all. Pantankan Tlanh at your service. And may I be fit to assist you in any way that you require."

He had answered in a soft fashion which left Han with the impression that he was being played with. There was something hidden and devious in the expressionless face, some quality which was not present, say, on Liszendir's, however haughty she might have been. Something he wanted to probe. But there was no time for it. Pantankan was headed for the stairwell, now retained only for emergencies. Liszendir was waiting in the lift with an expression of utter boredom on her face.

Han walked to the lift, and joined the girl. The sliding doors closed and they were alone. They avoided looking directly at one another. Yet something was gnawing deeply at Han, and it was something which wouldn't keep quiet long. They reached the ground floor and started out of the building. Liszendir started out confidently in the general direction of the underground tube to the spaceport.

Han looked about in the midmorning crowd to see if they were being noticed, which would be only relative since the ler girl would stand out in her self-conscious plainness here in Boomtown greatly; the ler came here only rarely. He slowed, stopped, and motioned to her to come closer. She did, but with some impatience and annoyance.

He said to her, "I think before we leave, we should stop off and have a little chat with Efrem. We've got time, and it may give us some ideas on what exactly we're looking for."

"I see no need of it," she replied. "We were told the essence of the facts. Besides that, we hardly know where to look for him."

"I can't believe you see it as all that simple," Han said, with some of his own annoyance. "But however it seems to you, I'm going. The dark ler who didn't speak during the meeting said Efrem was here. In Boomtown. I suspect you can't fly the ship by yourself, so I ask you to accompany me to his quarters. You will prefer it to a boring wait at the ship."

"Really? You think I could not force you here on the street? You are very foolish, or dangerously brave. It is true that I could not fly it, nor do I wish to learn. But you would be happy, perhaps overjoyed, to do it for me, should I exert a minor effort which would surely go unnoticed by these barbarians."

Han looked about helplessly. He had not intended to goad

her, or excite her temper. But he believed what she said. Perhaps guarded by a platoon of snipers concealed on the roofs and balconies at all points of the compass, he might have had a chance. But they were not present. Therefore he decided to try to reason with her. Ler were reputedly logical folk.

"As you say. But there is a thing I am uncertain on, which I must know before we go on. Will you allow this?"

"Go on. But we waste time."

"All of your names mean something, yes? They are not just meaningless sounds, a label? And you recognize the significance of each name?"

"It is so. We do not call ourselves by numbers, or by letters that fulfill the same purpose."

"What does Pantankan mean?"

"That is foolish. It is not a name. It can't be. As a symbol, it means, I think, what you would call an alphabet. You say the old names of your first two letters. We say the first three. Panh. Tanh. Kanh. P. T. K."

"That's all it means?"

"All and only. To my knowledge, that trisyllable is not to be used for a name."

"Well, that is what the dark ler told me his name was. Could he have been joking?"

"No. Names are not joking matters."

"He made it a point to say that Efrem was here, but that we would learn no more by seeing him."

"Did he say this before any of us?"

"No. We were alone, by the door. You were waiting in the lift. Did he give his name to your people, before I got there?"

"No. He did not. We would not ask, if he preferred silence. A name, in some ways, in our system, is . . . private. But. Never mind. I agree. I see the rat in the grain. Yes, we shall go and see this Efrem. But by my lead. There is a trap here, I think." She said the last with something almost approaching friendliness, or camaraderie.

" 'Alphabet' wants us to go there."

"I think not. It seems baited for you. I should not have been interested, and you should have been ignorant enough to fail to tell me, or if you had, fail to convince me. No. I am sure now; the trap is for you. Good work! You are sharper than I would have given you credit for!"

"Thanks." Han added, "Just what I needed." He hoped

this shallow foray into sarcasm would not set her off again; but she only gave him a cool glance in return.

The public telescanner catalogue, to their surprise, indeed listed one such Edo Efrem; and the address was not far away. Han at first wanted to call him, but Liszendir urged caution and deviousness. He agreed, and so they set out by round-about ways which he knew. Along the way, Liszendir made a running commentary on the disadvantages of human cities, but as she did, she also pointed out strategic locations should street fighting ever be required. It was a subject she seemed ferociously knowledgeable in. Han felt he was no sissy, but all the same, he shuddered, invisibly, he hoped, at some of the things she calmly suggested.

When they arrived at the building where Efrem was reputed to live, she paused thoughtfully. She asked, after a moment, "If you were going to visit someone in one of these hives, how would you go about it?"

"Through the front door and to the lift. Then to the apartment, and stand before the door and state who you are. If anyone answers, you go in."

"Are there stairs?"

"Yes."

"Then we will use them."

Inside the building, at the floor they wanted, the third, she cautioned Han, "Ring the bell from the side, from as far as you can reach. Then step back. I will hold you."

Han did as she asked, extending his hand to hers. She grasped it, firmly and directly. He felt a sudden shock: it was a soft, cool, feminine hand of no apparent great strength. The double thumbs, one of each side of her rather narrow hand, locked around his wrist in a peculiar grip. There seemed to be no real restraint in the grip, but he knew instinctively that he could not be pulled free of her.

Han rang the bell. A pleasant voice from within said, "Please enter," and the door slid open noiselessly. Han leaned further forward, but Liszendir pulled him back, none too gently. He looked at her; she was making a gesture with her hand and her face . . . she put her finger to her lips, pointed to both eyes, then to her forehead, and then made a rotary motion with the finger. Han recognized the crude sign language. She was saying, "Be silent, watch, and learn."

Liszendir moved around Han to come nearer the door, carefully lay flat on the floor, and *undulated*—there was no

other word to describe the motion she made—into the doorway. Then she half raised, and made a peculiar motion upwards with her free hand. Immediately, from within the
room, there sounded a faint hiss, which ended virtually
instantly with a low *thunk* in the corridor wall behind her.
Han started forward, but she said, in a low voice, "No. Stay
where you are!" Some long minutes passed. Liszendir lay
very still, as flat as a rug. Then there was another *hiss-
thunk*. The girl gained her feet in one flowing, smooth motion, and darted into the room. A moment later Han heard
her voice from within, "It's fixed now. You can come in."

He went into the room cautiously. Liszendir was standing
opposite the door, holding a pistol of unfamiliar type. It
looked like a pistol, but like no one Han had ever seen before.
It was molded in one piece, of some dark and apparently
heavy metal, and as he approached, could be heard to be
hissing quietly to itself. The barrel was long and very slender,
while the handle or butt flared into a bulge shaped somewhat
like a shoe. To the side of the room lay a corpse.

Liszendir said, "This is a devilish thing. The gun was set
in a triggering mechanism keyed by the door. There was a
timer; there was no radar or sonics I could find." She
indicated the muzzle. There was a tiny hole in it. "I have disarmed it. It uses highly compressed gas to fire rifled slivers,
probably made of a material which will dissolve in the body.
The slivers would also contain poison and a coagulant for the
wound. They are terrible things, but luckily for both you and
me, weapons like this do not have a great range."

She opened the magazine expertly, and removed gingerly
a tiny, glistening needle of some transparent material. She
handled it carefully, putting the needle down on a shelf to
look at it. Han reached for it, but she stopped him.

"Some things like this are hollow. This one does not seem
so. If that is true, the whole needle is poison and may be
activated by handling."

He nodded agreement, then turned to the body.

"No," she said. "It may be trapped. We can learn nothing
from it. We can call the police from the ship, although we
should call Hetrus. But let us leave here, quickly. I have
danger-sense. This room is loaded with traps."

They left the room cautiously. Han picked up the strange
little pistol where Liszendir had dropped it.

"Can this thing be recharged?"

"Oh, yes. The reservoir I bled off is the secondary one,

the one that powers the firing chamber. The main reservoir is still almost full."

"I thought I'd take it with us. We may have need for it."

"You may. Do not ask me to touch it again. I will explain after we have boarded the ship. But not now! We must move fast. Someone wanted at least for you to come to this room, perhaps to be killed, perhaps to be caught and accused."

Han agreed, and pocketing the deadly little gun, hurriedly left the apartment.

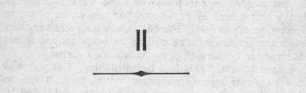

"The sage knows more than four seasons; the Fool says that the four of which his calendar speaks are of no importance."

—Ler saying, attr. to Garlendadh Tlanh.

Liszendir was tense during their trip to the spaceport, and did not fully relax, or reach a state which appeared to be relaxation, until they were actually on the ship, the *Pallenber,* and well into space. Indeed, she had gone over the ship with extreme care, looking carefully for snares, traps and miscellaneous tracers, bugs and the like. After a few days, she pronounced the *Pallenber* free of all such devices. Han agreed, although privately, he reflected that such an absence might in itself be curious in the light of the events which had occurred just before they left.

In the meantime, he had also been busy, counting and checking their provisions, the ostensible trade goods, the state of the weapons carried aboard the ship. He had also been engaged in several commnet conversations with Hetrus over

the matter of the body in the apartment (which had indeed
proved to be that of Efrem), the possible trap and the
identity of the unknown fifth ler. Hetrus was definitely interested, and was pursuing matters with a great amount
of bureaucratic zeal, but at least up to this point, he had
uncovered nothing. The ler he had contacted knew no more
than he did.

Among these jobs, they entered matrix overspace, set the
course and settled down to routine. They set up shifts, so
that one of them would always be awake. Liszendir did not
enjoy being responsible for the ship while Han was asleep,
but she accepted the training he gave her stoically and
agreed to awaken him immediately should an emergency
occur. He didn't expect one, but at the same time he saw
no lack of virtue in a little caution.

He wondered what it would be like if she should have to
wake him up in an emergency. Would she pitch him out
of his hammock in some artful way, so that he would perform some odd pervulsion of motion before he hit the deck?
No, he thought. To imagine that was silly. More soberly,
he suspected that she would not use her "skill" without good
reason or provocation, in line with other, similar disciplines
which had appeared from time to time among humans. No.
She would be completely inhibited during normal situations
by a complex code, or if one preferred, a set of rules
of engagement. Such creatures would be incredibly dangerous
turned loose in society without some inhibitions of that nature.

After several days, however, he found out. He had fallen
out of sleep early, for some reason, and was just lying in his
hammock, drifting, imagining, half-asleep. Then he became
aware that without his noticing it, a presence had entered his cabin and was watching him, silently. He lay
quietly, waiting. After what seemed to him as an almost
eternal passage of time, she leaned forward and touched
him gently on the shoulder. As she did, he caught the tiniest
shred of her scent, which was her own and not perfume;
it was heady, rather grassy, with some sharp, but very faint,
undertones.

He nodded, pretending that he had been asleep, and got
up, hoping that she would not see that he was pretending.

"Is it time already?"

"No. I woke you early. After a few days of this, I am

bored and lonely and need some talk, some interaction. We
are not used to solitude. Do you mind?"

"No, no; not at all. I feel much the same way. But I
did not wish to offend you by forcing anything you did not
want." The last was a barb at her early haughtiness. If she
noticed it, she gave no sign.

"I understand. We are not all that different. Good, then.
I will wait for you in the control room."

She turned and departed, as silently as she had come.
Han wondered at that. At first, during the busy first days, he
had not noticed, but as the time they had been alone together on the ship increased, he began to notice, more and
more, the silence and grace with which she moved. It looked
effortless, flowing like water in a stream, but he knew with
the logical part of his mind that a thousand years or more
of tradition and training went into that uncanny movement.

His thoughts strayed further. She was in no way he could
identify like the girls he had known, chased, loved in short
and desultory affairs which were the norm for Boomtown
society. She was curved and feminine, true enough, now that
he had time to notice, but the shape was all subtlety, suggestion, hint. He thought, almost like a riddle, whose question was at too fine a focus to be put exactly into words he
knew. The shapeless robe she wore, a standard ler garment,
was a concealer which revealed, and contributed in no
small way to the growing sense of eroticism that he felt.
He was sure that to ler eyes, she was young, agile, pretty
and extremely desirable. And of course, easily attainable,
with no qualms on either side. But to him, it was a different
matter.

That, he shut off, abruptly. He strongly suspected that he
would be able to cherish no hopes in that area. He didn't
even know if anything would be possible between them,
emotionally or physically. Ler adolescent eroticism was well
known among humans, yet at the same time, there were few
tales of any adventures between the two. And such tales as
were, were invariably structured like the vulgar stories of
little boys, whose imaginations so easily outstripped reality,
and even probability.

Still, even after thousands of years, the ler were remarkably casual about dalliance; or for that matter, about re-
fusals. Oddly enough, all their myths seemed to revolve
around the efforts of individuals; nowhere was love or passion about it featured in even a major role.

So Han dressed, depilated his beard, and went to the control room. The forward part of the room, which was the largest on the ship, was not a window, but a converter screen which passed a real-space view even when the ship was in any one of the matrix overspaces. Moreover, it was tunable over a wide range of frequencies. It was now fully open, tuned to the slightly broader response characteristics of the ler eye. The only light in the control room came from this screen and from the instruments; outside, with no apparent barrier between them, lay the deeps of starry darkness, drifting visibly at the corners of the screen. Liszendir sat quietly in the pilot's chair and looked out on the spectacle. If she noticed Han enter, she gave no sign.

"Have you traveled space before?" he asked, trying to start a conversation. He knew very well that she had, because there were no ler anywhere near Seabright.

"Oh, yes, many times. But never with such a view as this," she replied, almost cheerfully. After a short pause, she continued.

"This is not new, it is just the endlessness of it which both attracts me and disturbs me at the same time. There is more here than all of us together can ever know. Here, I become receptive to the reality of my own insignificance."

Han agreed, but only in part. He did not understand why she should become so pensive over the immensity, and implied infinitude, of space. It really didn't matter whether you were on a planetary surface or not, you were still a finite creature working and striving, or just coasting with the current, in infinite systems. But he replied, "Yes, it does prompt that feeling. I know it well. Still, we must do what we will measured by what we are able to do."

"Yes, like the sea. At my home, on Kenten, our *yos*, where the braid lives, is beside a body of salt water, a narrow bay of the sea that connects up in the west with the ocean. All around are mountains, some wild and rugged, some terraced with gardens and orchards, other *yosas*, towns, towers. I used to watch the sea before the garden for hours. The waves, the play of light, the changeable winds and that timelessness which is great time, *kfandrir,* passing, greater than our lives. The sea said to me, 'I was here, reposed, filling the basins of my will, gathered, caressed by the wind, loved by the light, before ler came to this planet; and when they have gone, I will still be here.' The waves, such little things, mock us in their infinitude; I look here outwards in my shift and I see the same words."

Again she became silent, and resumed looking at the darkness immense and the spotted glory of the far stars. Han tried to imagine the depth of the picture of her home she had painted. He could not. He knew about ler "family" structure and how it dominated their society, but he had no insight into it, *how* it was.

The ler "family" structure, the so-called "braid," was dictated by their low birthrate, which rarely produced more than two offspring per bred female during the fertile period, which ran roughly from age thirty to forty. But other elements played important roles: the long, infertile adolescence with its high sex-drive tended to make individuals independent and solitary by nature. The short, fertile period with its long gestation periods, eighteen months. And their original low numbers, with the associated small gene pool. On Earth they had had several family models to emulate in their early period, but they had liked none of them. So they invented a structure which would widen the gene pool, use the birthrate to the fullest, and provide an organism for raising children. But it was not, like human models, a hereditary chain, a bloodline, but a social procedure which wove their society together in a complex fashion.

Basically, the braid originated with a male and female of the same ages, at fertility. They would mate, hopefully producing a child, who would be the *nerh,* or elder outsibling. At age thirty-five standard, the two would select and recruit second mates for each other, and remate. Each pair would produce a child, who would be called *toorh,* insiblings. After that, the inductees would mate and produce a last child, called *thes,* or younger outsibling. All lived under one roof, together.

"At *their* fertility, the insiblings, who were not blood-related to each other, having separate parents, would weave and become the nucleus of the next braid generation. The *nerh* and the *thes* would weave into other braids as afterparents. So each child-generation would be distributed into three braids. This process kept the genetic pool wide and actually prevented inbreeding and the establishment of racial traits.

As soon as the insiblings had woven, the parents of the old braid would leave and go their own way, leaving the house and everything that went with it in the hands of the new generation. They were then considered free of all responsibility and could do as they would. Some stayed together, some went off on their own.

That was *what* it was, but few humans, if any, had any feel for *how* it was, as it was completely at variance with the way humans, with variations, structured their families. At times, on various planets, some enterprising humans would set up analogues of the ler braids. But they never lasted very long. The strains were too great, emotionally, sexually, and particularly in the matter of property. And in the fact that, after all, the braid was a mechanism for making full use of fertility. Used with humans, it was like throwing gasoline on a fire.

Han said, "Tell me about your family, your braid. Your friends. What you did at the school. I suspect that you know more of the way I live than I of your way."

She turned back to him. "Not necessarily so. You know I am *Nerh.* I am now at a point in my life when for all practical purposes school is over, but I am not quite old enough to be invited to weave as aftermother with another braid. I was head of house, with the other children of my generation, probably much like an older sister in your terms, but with more authority. Still, it was a waning authority. My insiblings were Dherlinjan and Follirian. They pay attention to me, but they know very well that all they have to do is wait. In your society, eldest gets all. In ours, the insiblings get everything—house, title, braid name. Even the parents leave when the insiblings become fertile."

"Where do you go? Do they put you out in the cold?"

"Oh, no." She laughed in a low tone, quietly. It was the first time he had heard her laugh. It was a relaxed, pleasant sound. "As for me, or like me, by then I would already have woven. The *thes* stays at home until they are chosen. But the parents—they are elders, then. They are free; they can do anything they want. They have gender, but no sex. So they are completely free. Some go off in small groups, you would say communes, although it is not exactly like that. Others go into government or business. Still others become *mnath,* the wise. They live alone, rarely in pairs, in the hills and forests."

"Don't the adults of the old generation stay together?"

"Yes, sometimes, they do. But as often as not they don't. There is no rule and people do as they please. With the Karen, it is tradition that the insiblings stay and teach at the school, which belongs to the braid. Sometimes the after-

parents, who were outsiblings before weaving, stay as well.
But our braid is an old one and such traditions are meaningful to us. But the elders do not live in the *Yos*. That is forbidden. This way, a *yos* need only be of such a size, so
everyone has much of the same size of house. That dis-
courages vanity."

Han was surprised at the insights he gained from her. He
had always thought of ler weaving as something either akin
to marriage, or sanctioned cohabitation. It was neither, and
apparently was regulated more strictly than either. He was,
however, still dissatisfied. "Well, that sounds nice, but what
about rich and poor? Don't the rich have bigger houses? Or
don't you have rich and poor? And who runs the government?"

She answered easily. Liszendir either ignored sarcasm, or
did not recognize it. "Oh, yes, we have rich and poor. But
you think in terms of family, and inheritance. With us, it is
the braid that is rich or poor. For the rest, all you take
when you leave, outsibling or elder, are some personal
things, clothes and the like. We know that possessions en-
slave. And it is the same with land. The property one owns
is where one works or lives. No more. Nothing else. Some
elders become very rich and powerful. But when they
terminate, all that they have made goes back into the common treasury. All of it.

"And as for the government, you know that braids are
set for certain roles. One bakes bread, another builds
houses, another performs still another function in the community. So it is with the government; a certain braid runs
it, others perform supporting roles within it. You met
Yalvarkoy and Lenkurian Haoren? They are also from Kenten, and they are what you might call 'a braid which is
responsible for the ministry of the interior.' But our governments are small. We restrain ourselves, so that we do
not have to call on someone else to do it for us. And the
way to outlaw complex, weighty governments, is to outlaw
preconditions which lead to complex problems."

"That doesn't sound very free."

"Well, in the matter of running the government, no. But
our government leaves us alone."

"You said self-restraint. I must ask if some are not so
restrained?"

"Yes. Some are. And that is where the school comes in.
We Karens are something like what you would call police

and judges at the same time. Our law is equivalence. We are as prone to dishonesty as any folk, I suppose, so I am trained in ler law and in many degrees of violence. And in philosophy, for only the wise may judge, and only the gentle command violence." At the last, Liszendir slipped into a peculiar kind of measured speech, almost as if she were chanting.

"Or, 'An eye for an eye, a tooth for a tooth'?"

"Or in some cases, the money equivalent."

"Then you know a lot about ler society."

"Yes. Would you like a recitation?" She laughed. "I can recite the *Book of the Law,* the *Way of the Wise,* the *Fourteen Sages' Commentaries,* and if you desire, all the names of my insibling chain back *zhan* generations. That number is the second power of fourteen to you, and has the same significance as your one hundred."

Han laughed back at her. "Anything else?"

Liszendir sat pensively for a moment. Then she brightened and said, "If we had a very long voyage, I could also teach you Singlespeech, which is our everyday language. You could not learn Multispeech, but I am a master of both modes, *one to many* and *many to one,* and could at least tell you about it. I could also teach you sliding numbers, which you would find useful."

"Sliding numbers?"

"We do not have a fixed number base, like your tenbase or the one your machines use, two-base. We use many, as fits the situation. We are non-Aristotelians: hence to us, reality cannot be categorized into any fixed number of states. So we use many bases; theoretically, we could use any number as a base, but we restrict ourselves to bases which are twice a prime number, such as, in decimals, base of six, which we call childsway, or base ten, which we discourage, or base fourteen. There are many others. Base ninety-four, or another which uses most of the wordroots of Singlespeech for numbers in its unity sequence."

"Why not ten and two, like us?"

"Two reasons. To program non-Aristotelianism into all, and to prevent children from counting on their fingers. We have five digits, just like you; but we make them go abstract from the first—it makes things easier later on."

She held her hand out for him to see. It was a graceful, strong hand, smooth and finely shaped. It was very similar to a normal human hand, except that the palm was nar-

rower, and the little finger had separated and moved back,
like a smaller thumb. It was opposable, just like a thumb,
and in the matter of writing, ler were not "handed," but
wrote with either hand, holding the pen with either thumb.
She wore no rings of any kind. The nails were pink, plain,
and clipped off short and neat. The only distinguishing mark
of any kind was a small tattoo at the base of the inner
thumb, suggestive of the ancient chinese symbol of Yang
and Yin.

Han asked, "What is that mark?"

"That is the badge of my skill."

"That is very similar to an ancient symbol of old Earth.
Chinese. Did your firstfolk model on them?"

"Yes. Some things. The best example is language. Our
Singlespeech was modeled on theirs, but in phonetic root
building only. We did not imitate their grammar or sounds.
Each Singlespeech root has three parts—leading consonant,
middle vowel, and final consonant. Within the rules, every
combination has four meanings. But only that far. We used
old English for the phonetics, for we lived in a country
where it was spoken. And we did not like using tones. In
that way, we modeled much on their ideas, but we used
different materials. It is that way in other areas."

Han started to interrupt, but Liszendir went on. "And
especially we borrowed from them the lesson of change.
They knew change and permutation well, and that all things
end. All that begins must end, and all that is, must be something else. They were called backward, yet their society
lasted on Earth much longer than the ones of those who
trusted in stone and metal and illusions of changelessness.
Who hoped they would live forever."

Han arose from his chair, went to the kitchen unit and
programmed it, and then returned. Then they talked about
humans. Han felt at a disadvantage here, since he lacked
the continuity with his ancestors which Liszendir seemed to
have. Here was a puzzle: ler society seemed static, old-
fashioned, primitive, tribal. Yet they assimilated some forms
of technology with no apparent effort and seemed to suffer
no cultural shock from those newer ingredients. And as a
group, they showed little change in time or space. They
were remarkably homogeneous; ler from different planets
spoke the same language and held the same social structures
in common. Humans were changeable, divergent.

Of his own forebears, Han only knew back to his father's grandfather, who had come to Boomtown from somewhere else and become a trader. Beyond that, he only knew that the great-grandfather had supposedly come from Thersing V. What had members of the family been before that? What difference did it make?

He saw, in Liszendir, a girl of such basic culture, that, having learned basics from her, he could reasonably expect to find the same motivations in another ler from any place. The individual would be different, just like humans, but there seemed to be much less of a range. One human was easy and tolerant; the next might be a bigot of the most intolerant sort. But to her, she could not hope to have the same assurances: every human she met would be different.

Religion was another area where there was a deep rift between their mutual comprehensions. He described human practices in this area in great detail, hoping by conversational trade to elicit some description of ler practices out of her. As always, the ruling classes of human society were more or less agnostic, paying lip service to whatever cult happened to be active in their area at the time. This was one human constant that ran unbroken all the way back to Gilgamesh. The deeds remained the same, and only the excuses were changed to protect the innocent. And as in all other areas, human society varied in religion in both time and space.

But of ler religion or lack thereof, men knew little or nothing. Some savants averred that there was indirect evidence of this or that structure; but upon more sober examination, these theories seemed to revolve more upon the prejudices of the author than on the practices of the subject. Nor could Han get any information out of Liszendir: she was curiously reticent to discuss the subject, and avoided questions with great dexterity. The only positive statement he could get out of her was in reference to the projectile weapon they had found set for them in Efrem's apartment. She was definitive in her distaste for it; apparently projectile weapons of any kind were ritually unclean to her. He remembered that she had handled it with the greatest reluctance, and when he asked her now further about this, she said little. She had shuddered, and said sadly, "No ler would touch the filthy thing. And especially no Karen." She made a curious gesture with her left hand, the one that bore the yang-and-yin mark. That was all he could get out of her.

As they ate, the talk drifted towards sexual topics. It was an area Han did not really want to come up, but he felt it was almost inevitable; a certain tension was rising between them, and here was its obvious source. Han was no beginner, and was not particularly bashful, or ashamed of the things he had done. Yet he was reticent to talk at length about his past adventures. However, the girl was not restrained in the least, and became more animated as she discussed this aspect of their lives in detail. The kitchen delivered its work, and they sat down to eat together.

For a time, they traded some relatively innocent stories back and forth. But it became clear that here was a very great difference between them.

She said, "I am surprised at only one thing about your way—that you wait so long. You are concerned first about your identity, then later, sometimes after you have become parents, with sex. It is just the reverse with us. We do not worry so much about our identity until after we have become parents.

"I will tell you how it was with me, not to satisfy your curiosity so much as to work something out in my own mind. You see, for us, I was somewhat late in getting the idea. As children, we are very free—we can do as we want, and curiosity about the body is not discouraged. And in good weather, we do not wear clothes. So as a child, a *hazh*, that is a pre-adolescent child, you see young people, adolescents, *didhas*, playing body-games with each other all the time; no one goes to a great deal of trouble to hide. But you do not have any interest in it—it's silly, you know? But one day it isn't silly any more and you want to do it."

She stopped for a moment, as if she were reaching for a memory, savoring it, weighing it to determine its exact substance. She smiled weakly. "As I said, I was late. All of my friends the same age were all crazy about this new thing they had discovered they could do with each other. But I didn't seem to understand why it was so important. So one day we were swimming, not far from my *yos*. It was very warm. And a boy I knew, Fithgwinjir, very pretty, took me to the beach, holding my hand. I felt very strange. I saw he was different, ready. But all I felt was expectation. He said, 'Liszen, let's do it together, now.' That was the first time anyone had ever called me a love name. We only use the first syllable of our names when we are children. Two when you are adolescent. And later, three. I told him I didn't know how. He told me he would show me. We kissed, and then we lay down together in the warm sand. The others, some looked, and some didn't. It wasn't important to them. Just *madhainimoni,* 'they who are making love to each other.' But it was very important to me. I felt turned inside out. And I loved Fithgwin, of course.

"Afterwards, I wanted to talk to someone, but I knew the other children would laugh; they were way ahead of me. It wasn't new to them. I was ten. They had been at it for months, some a year. My insiblings were about five, so they knew nothing, and my *thes,* Vindhermaz, he was just a baby. So I told my foremother, my *madh.* She was very happy— she was worried I would be retarded.

"But I learned fast. At first it's like that. Play. Fun. Something to do. Then you fall in love, over and over again. You begin spending nights with your love at each other's houses. Then you have group parties together. But by your late teens you are settling down, playing at more adult games, hoping you will be chosen to start a new braid as *shartoorh,* honorary insiblings. That is very wonderful, because that is the only time you can pick who your mate will be. That is what we all dream about before we are woven.

"So. Now. The present. Wendyorlei was my last lover. We were living together, schoolmates, in a *yos* which was not presently being used. We felt the same way: we hoped we could stay together and be chosen. But we did not have a great love. Yes, we cared, we were loving-kind to each other, but we still wandered, too. We had other lovers, and as is custom, we did not hide them from each other. That is training for when you are woven—there can be no jealousy in the *yos.* None. You learn to erase it before you weave.

"School finished. Wendyor was needed at his home, which was across the mountains. We were waiting for something. And I heard of this, and so came. I harbor no illusions. I will never see him again close within my arms." She took a very deep breath.

Han told her a parallel tale, the story of his adventures in love, the ones he had felt like they were the last thing in the world. And the others, which had been just fun. But he admitted that he had started much later, and couldn't come near her in quantity.

She said, "Well, I approve, of course. And I understand

why you are so cautious. We are not fertile—it is just fun, with no price except the one you pay with your heart. But you do not have that room to move about in. A mistake, and your life is out of control, yes?"

"Yes," was all Han could say.

"Now. Your name is very close to the form of a ler name. It is easy for me to call you 'Han,' but hard in another. The single syllable reminds me of a child, but there is nothing childish about you. Also, the child name ends. And I do not know how to handle that."

"I would be less than honest if I said that I had not found you desirable, even with our differences," Han said, after some hesitation.

Liszendir had finished eating. She leaned back in the chair, stretched gracefully, and her face took on a coyness, an arch flirtatious look which Han found unbearable. She had, in an instant, become beautiful in the soft light of the instruments and the stars. He could not turn away the thoughts he had of that smooth, completely hairless body under the homespun robe.

She said, in a soft voice he had never before heard her use, and which matched perfectly a face which had become mysteriously lovely, the broad mouth soft and generous, "Yes. I see, and I have felt some of the same with you. It frightens me, for I know very well that physically we are compatible; yet it is said that such things are not to be done, and with wisdom, for our endurance is different from yours. We can do it many times. So it is not to be done: but you are male and not unattractive, even if you are too hairy." She laughed shortly, and then became pensive and sober again.

After a long, silent moment, she said, quietly, "You must not touch me when we are in this mood. The urge to couple in ler is very strong, more intense than to you, until we are no longer fertile. I have not made love for some time and my need is great. And you and I should not do this thing, Han."

As she finished, she rose and turned away. "It is now your turn at the watch. I will do my exercises and sleep." She started towards the passageway door.

Han said, just as she paused at the door to go through it, "By the way, you never told me the meaning of your name."

She looked back, startled. "You do not know what you ask. But it is no secret. It means, literally, 'velvet-brushed-night.' A 'liszendir' is a special kind of sky . . . it is when the night sky is very clear, like there was no air in it, but streaked with very fine, high cirrus clouds, filmy, lit only by starlight. It is normally a winter sky, although we rarely see it in summer."

Han, mystified, shrugged. "Well, that's progress, at least. Now we know each other better."

Liszendir looked unfathomable. She made a gesture of negation. "There is no progress. There is only change." She vanished through the door.

III

---◆---

> "There is no such thing as a doctrine, a theory, or an idea which lacks the capacity and the ability to imprison the mind.
>
> —The Fourteen
> Sages' Commentaries, v 1, ch 3, Suntrev 15

The remainder of their journey to Chalcedon passed in what Han would later think of as courteous silence. Yet, there was something unfinished between them, something unresolved, which in other circumstances might have posed no problem at all.

Han, amused and bemused by his own reactions to his growing appreciation of Liszendir's intense sexuality, consoled himself and, so he thought, made things easier for her, by growing a fine full beard. Beards were not, as a general rule, very common in more settled areas, but it was a habit indulged in occasionally by most traders. At first, it grew slowly, but soon it was coming in with fine speed, and an increasingly silky texture. It grew in dark, darker than his dark-brown hair, and he was pleased with it, and spent considerable time training it.

Liszendir disapproved, as he had hoped; her race grew no beards. In fact, they had no body hair whatsoever below the eyebrows, a fact which disturbed him somewhat whenever he let his thoughts stray in the direction of a possible liaison with the ler girl. Would it be like making love to a child? No, on second thought, he doubted that very much, watching her wise and knowing eyes, the way she walked.

In turn, she made all attempts to be businesslike and completely unsexual. It did not work, completely, for as she observed, such a thing was like a rabbit pretending that he did not really like greens. She had never had to repress it before, and admitted that indeed it was a fine exercise in the art of self-control. Han agreed. Self-control, indeed.

To pass the time, he taught her how to fly the ship. He argued the necessity of this through the logic that there could be an occasion when they would need someone to fly the *Pallenber* while the other operated the weapons, of which they had a considerable variety. And he knew very well that she would not use those weapons unless at the utmost extremity. According to the ship's papers they carried, the *Pallenber* was listed as an armed merchantman; Han knew this as a euphemism for "privateer." He knew well enough that such things were done, but they had been unheard-of in his portion of space for many a year.

As they worked—which went slowly, for she seemed to have a rather low degree of mechanical competence—he asked her how the ler fought wars, if they had any among themselves. He could not see how they could fight a war, without using weapons that leave the hand.

She answered, "We have wars, enough for anyone's taste. 'Once through a ler war and you become a pacifist,' so the saying goes. But we have our disagreements, and if it comes to a resolution by force, then so be it. All participate. But we fight over issues which can be seen in front of you. Immediate things. I suppose you would call them light-infantry actions. But for all that, they are rare. Another difference from humans is the fact that our sense of territoriality is much weaker than yours. It was considered a disadvantage to those who were trying to breed us at the first. And we do not fight over things like politics and religion. Those kinds of things mean that the fighting goes far beyond the battlefield, where such things should be settled."

So when there was a war to be fought, they took up knives and swords, shields, bludgeons, hammers and morningstars, and set upon one another with all the skill they could muster. After the issue had been settled, the combatants retired from the field, the winners took what they had been fighting for, or against, and the losers consoled themselves. After all, in losing, they did not lose everything.

But they were not pacifists, and it was true that ler were not particularly unaggressive. Fights between two were not uncommon, and brawls in taverns or on the street were known. But they did not resort to weapons which left the hand, whatever the level of conflict, however many pursued it. A ler who did that would be instantly lynched, then and there, by his fellows. It was the only unappealable death penalty they had.

And for all that they were opposed to their use, they were not blind to the uses of projectile weapons. They extended their penalty to anyone who used them; and since the penalty was eradication without quarter, few ever considered it. They had developed the perfect defense against interplanetary war; try to bomb a ler planet, and they activated a device which caused your sun to go nova. Then they went after your ships and tore them apart with grapples. If anyone should survive to the surface, they were met in turn by a horde which had removed all restraints. They would not give up, and they would not stop until the entire invasion force was in shreds, literally torn apart.

In trade for teaching her how to fly the ship, Liszendir offered to teach Han a few basic moves and falls, so he would, as she put it, "be able to look after yourself in close quarters." The instruction went smoothly, but it developed that Han had the same lacks in motor coordination that she had in mechanics. He appreciated what she taught him, but he ached for days afterwards with sore muscles. And the body contact disturbed them both more than either of them would openly admit.

"Liszendir, do boys and girls train together in your school?"

"Indeed. Together. We make few distinctions according to gender or sex," she said with some amusement.

"Well, aren't they stimulated by the close physical contact."

"Certainly. They train in the elementary part, the first six years, nude. They have to learn basics by seeing muscles. Feeling them. And if they have a problem, why they just go off to a corner, or to the bushes, and satisfy themselves. Why not? You humans allow your students breaks for needs they have. So do we. But in the more advanced parts of training, they learn self-control."

But after a few attempts to instruct Han in some of the finer points, she pronounced him, for the time being, a hopeless case. But when she said it, she was smiling. And Han had done better than either he or Liszendir had imagined he would have.

In the meantime, Han consulted the instruments and announced the end of their journey to be near. The star which was primary to Chalcedon was drawing near. Soon, they would be back on the ground again, to see first-hand the evidence of the "Warriors of Dawn."

They made a festive occasion of their last meal together while the *Pallenber* remained in matrix overspace, decorating the control room, and setting what pretended to be an elegant service for two at the control panels below the view of space transmitted into the ship by the huge screen. They sat, and ate, in relative quiet, each savoring the better parts of what had happened since they set out on this trip to the edge of known space.

As they finished, Liszendir asked, "Can we see Chalcedon's star in this?"

"Of course. It's been aimed at that point since we started. Here. I'll show you." He depressed a small button on the panel: immediately two lines, finer than the thinnest hair, appeared on the view, one horizontal, the other vertical. The screen display suggested the illusion that the fine silver lines had been impressed upon space itself. At the point where they intersected, a single star waited, seemingly nearer than the millions of other points.

"It's still too far away from us to show a disc, just yet. And we'll drop out of overspace before it gets an appreciable one. But there it is, nonetheless."

"Could we see Chalcedon with this?"

"Not as it's set now. It will only process objects of a certain angular diameter when it's set in this mode; that's why the background looks black. We have to get closer and be in our normal space."

Liszendir became quiet again and resumed staring at the screen. Ler ships, for all their sophistication of drive systems, were worse than primitive when it came to sensory receptors. In the particular matrix they used, there was nothing to see; in normal space, the crew and passengers looked out on the universe through nothing more exotic than quartz panes, heavy and ground optically flat. Their pilots sat way up on top of the great rounded bells they called ships, in a little cupola, and flew the huge things *manually*.

So this view was particularly impressive to her. She had spent most of her waking hours here in the control room, looking through the viewscreen that looked like a huge picture window.

Something was nagging Han from the screen; a suggestion of movement. But as he looked, he could see nothing more than the drifting points of the stars. Then he would look away, and his peripheral vision would start acting up again. The more he thought about it, the longer he recalled having noticed it. Still, try as he would, he could actually see nothing. Trying to catch it by watching along the edges of his peripheral vision, as last he became sure. There was a motion. But what?

"Liszendir, do you see anything moving in the screen?"

"Moving? No. But the image has been disturbed all along. Could you not see it? I thought it was something in the equipment, and that you knew about it. It looks to me as if I was seeing this image under water, and I was directly above the surface, looking down into it. Ripples move across the surface from a point, but nothing I can see is making them."

"Hm." Han, muttering to himself, blanked out the screen, and put its computer through a self-check routine. In a few minutes the screen came back on, no different than before. He asked her, "Is it still there?"

"Yes."

"Where is the point the ripples seem to be coming from?"

"At the crosshairs. The star of Chalcedon."

Han reached into the console and produced a great heavy manual, which listed characteristics of known stars. He thumbed through the manual for a time, and then spoke. "According to this, Chalcedon's star is AVILA 1381 indexed, a normal GO yellow star of median age, securely on the main sequence, no abnormalities whatsoever. If that ripple is a real effect, and not an error in the display, I would expect some kind of gravity abnormality in the system, there. Like a very sick star, or perhaps a neutron star that had wandered into the area. But the star is listed here as a perfect example of a star that's right, not wrong, and wandering neutron stars have a very low probability of being captured by such a system. They almost always move across a system in hyperbolic orbits. Granted, if it was a wide pass and a shallow hyperbola, we might see some effect as long as this trip—even longer, if we had the really fancy instruments the colonial survey uses. But that's just guessing. Besides, AVILA 1381 is not so massive it couldn't be moved about by a neutron star in orbit. We've got detectors for that kind of wobbles, and ours hasn't uttered a peep the whole trip. It's not impossible, of course. Any event always has a probability of plus zero—that's old science. And it's been months since anyone's been out this way from the interior. But . . ."

Liszendir interrupted him, "It's stopped!"

"Just like that?"

"Yes. Quick. While you were talking. In the center, and the last ripples fled to the edge. The image is quiet now."

Han got up, and consulted several instruments. He also ran the computer through some computations. He looked up. "Whatever was causing it is not in the star."

They both became quiet and thoughtful. During the entire trip, they both had been guilty of thinking of the trip as nothing more than a quick flight to the edge to gather a few facts; an excursion, as it were. Now the possibility had loomed that there was more here than met the eye. The tape Hetrus had played had not mentioned any such ripple effect, or any effect that could stop suddenly. Of course, there were reasonable explanations—Efrem's ship didn't have modern detection, and coming back he would have been aimed away from Chalcedon and its star. Ships had rearward screens, but it was a universal superstition among traders to the effect that it was bad luck to look back. Etc. Etc. But where Han and Liszendir had felt on sure ground, well within the known, before, they now felt the touch of the unknown. Han retained his apprehensions within himself. In civilization, the universe was tame and well-behaved. Here . . .

Liszendir was not so quiet. After a moment, she said, "When we were at that meeting, back at Boomtown, before you came, I had a few words with Lenkurian, in multi-speech. She told me then that she thought that however it seemed to Efrem, here was no simple raid for loot or slaves. It smelled of deliberate provocation from an unknown source. That and more. There is darkness and evil off Chalcedon, and a mind that has weighed things to a nicety. And the warriors? If the worst of our suspicions are true . . ."

"What?"

"We *know* nothing. Only suspect. But if half of it is true, I shudder to face the Warriors. But let me tell you a story. When the first ler ship left old Earth, it was many stops before they found a suitable world. But they did eventually find one. That was Kenten. It wasn't long after they landed that two factions developed. One desired to stay and build our culture like we wanted it to be on the new world. And later, others. We knew so little about ourselves then—for hundreds of years we had been buried in an established human culture. And like all buried minorities, we defined much of our own natures in reference to human terms. But there were others, of different opinions. The main other faction, led by a female named Sanjirmil, wished to go on, and more . . ."

"I have heard of Sanjirmil. In your histories, or at least the ones I have heard, she winds up being something like a cross between Lucretia Borgia, Lilith, and perhaps Rosa Luxemburg thrown in for good measure."

"So it was. I have seen holograms of her. She had a beauty that was terrible, like a wild animal. But there was a great disagreement. It almost broke us. We thought that the two factions would lock each other in a death-grip, and in a couple of generations, along would come the earthmen to gather up the ruins. But in the end, when the elders thought the matter was settled, Sanjirmil and her braid, the Klaren, or 'flyers,' and their adherents stole our one spaceship and departed. In those days whole braids flew the ship. We thought it would work better. The Klaren had been woven years before any of them were fertile, just for our flight from Earth, and they were more disciplined in working together than any ler should ever be. And Sanjirmil, while not actually the pilot herself, but the navigator or astrogator, was also f—" Liszendir cut herself off in mid word, before anything recognizable got out.

Han caught it. "F——"? He said, "What were you going to say she was?"

"Nothing." Liszendir answered sullenly. "It is," she added, apparently deciding to brazen it out, "something I cannot tell you. You are not ler. You would not understand. You must forget that I ever started to say anything else." She waited a moment, to see if Han was going to pursue the topic. He didn't.

"So. On that ship were incredible weapons. Things we would see today with horror. And projectile weapons were just the beginning of it. Vile things! And they were never heard from again. We have always assumed, perhaps you might say, 'hoped,' that they crashed somewhere. Or went to another galaxy, as they had said that they wanted to do. That would have been almost as welcome. But nobody knows. There is a whole cycle of legends about them."

"So since the Warriors of Dawn seemed to be ler . . ."

"Ler they are, make no mistake. Your people suppose as mine, that the general hominid shape goes with intelligence as fangs go with carnivores and horns with grazers. But look at you and me, Han. We are ultimately of the same soil, the same planet. Ler and human, for all the obvious differences you and I know so well now, we are perilously close. You and I were picked for this trip because we have the same blood type—we can give each other transfusions! Did you know that?"

"May I use the term 'Kfandrir' as an oath?"

"It is impertinent and irreverent, but I understand."

"I had no idea . . ."

"Neither did I. But it is true. One of your four types and one of our two are compatible. Even so, we could couple if we were very foolish, but nothing would come of it, even if I were as fertile as you are now. But you know the shape is different for us in details. So aliens would be upright, have a head, arms, legs, and all that goes with those things. But they could also be very different. But the witnesses Efrem talked with described precise details."

"But that was some time ago, wasn't it? The original crew would have been dead for years . . ."

"Yes. Thousands of years, many thousands. Sanjirmil and the rest are of the fourth century, atomic. And their children's children."

"Even if this is true, which I don't believe—it isn't any more probable than . . . Oh. I see. Exact details. It would be difficult to arrange those kinds of coincidence, wouldn't it?"

"Especially for ler. We were *artificially* bred in the first generation. I do not know if we could even occur in a completely unguided sequence. But as we say, 'Never mind where I came from, I'm here now, for love or hate.' We're organic enough now. But we control our race! Who knows what they have done! On Earth before we left, they were restless and impatient with braids. And they wanted to stay and fight. On Kenten, they wanted to go further and conquer the galaxy. No, I do not know, and neither does anyone else, if the Warriors are the descendants of Sanjirmil. But I hope they are not. You have your race-fears, Han; and I have mine. The *klarkinnen* are one of them: the 'children of the flyers.' "

"And we are approaching Chalcedon," he reminded her after a moment. "How are they living there, humans and ler? Together, or in separate communities, or countries, or what?"

"I cannot imagine such a thing." It was her only answer. Nor would she say any more about her suspicions during the short remainder of the voyage to Chalcedon. Only hours remained.

Han expected to be met off Chalcedon with suspicion and requests for detailed identifications, what with the recent raid; they were bound to be suspicious. But as they approached the planet, there was no response on any frequency. Nor were they being tracked by any detection system which used electromagnetic waves. Liszendir was unconcerned. She thought that if you came to someone's house, and there were no lights, you could at least knock on the door. They couldn't see you otherwise in the deeps of night.

Han, however, was inclined to look at things in detail before doing anything rash. So they let the preliminary orbit they had established carry them around to the night side. There, it was more informative, but only slightly more active. With the screen at full magnification, and the instruments at maximum gain, they could see and hear the signs of a civilization in its early technological stages: illuminated towns below on the surface; some light radio traffic, most of it point-to-point, for Chalcedon didn't have much of an ionosphere; and also in the radio bands, faint popping or tapping sounds which indicated internal-combustion engines.

But after several passes around the planet, which was about ten thousand miles in diameter, they believed what the ship's senses told them: Chalcedon was early in the colonization stage, and only one continent was inhabited to any degree. And not being near any known line of commerce, the locals below were proceeding at their own rate, which was the slow-time of almost complete isolation. They decided to land at what their charts indicated to be the capital city.

As they settled to their landing site, which was an open field some distance from the capital, they were neither hailed nor intercepted. It gave Han an eerie feeling; they had flown over the city, which was not large, so he knew whoever lived in it could see him, but they didn't seem to care. He had been trained for space flight in an area where ships were monitored every instant. But with no one to tell him not to, he hovered momentarily, then settled and grounded the ship. They shut it down, and debarked to an empty field. Apparently there were no customs procedures either. So they locked the ship and started walking in the direction of the capital, which could be easily found by noting a plume of dust above the trees.

As they walked down a dusty road which did not seem to be heavily traveled, he said, "It gives me a strange feeling to come as far as we have, all to walk down a country road at noon, as if we'd never even seen a spaceship. And so unprotected! You'd think they would be alert as bees after someone robbed the hive."

Liszendir answered by flinging off her soft boots and turning a cartwheel in the road. Then she dusted herself off, retrieved her boots, but did not put them on, and said, "I care only now that I have honest earth under my feet again."

As she walked on, barefoot, Han noticed her feet; like the hands, here also was a divergence from the human original. There were four toes, instead of five, and they were short. The ball of the foot was wider, in proportion, but back toward the heel, it was more slender. It was a foot that was a degree more adapted to walking rather than holding. Her footprints in the dust of the road showed that she put little weight on the heel.

They walked for some distance before they saw anyone, although there were signs of settled life all around them—

cultivated fields, some grazing animals of recognizable shape but curious detail, an occasional house in the distance. In fact, they were almost to the capital itself when they saw, coming down the road towards them, two persons who waved from the distance. On closer sight, the two resolved into a human and a ler, both male, and seemingly over-worked to the point of exhaustion. The human, tall and gaunt, introduced himself as Ardemor Hilf, the mayor of the Capital. He apologized for the name—they never had taken the trouble to name it, so it was called simply "the Capital." The ler with him appeared to be a somewhat overweight elder with long hair woven into a single braid. He called himself Hath'ingar.

Hath'ingar was not bashful. Immediately he said, "And never mind all that *tlanh* and *srith* crap. We scarcely have the time here, especially now, to be civil enough to shout 'Hey, you' at one another."

Hilf stayed only long enough to find out who they were and what they had in mind. Then he took his leave, asking Hath'ingar to see after them. The shorter ler patted Hilf familiarly on the shoulder and told him to be off. Then he turned to Han and Liszendir.

"I'm the deputy mayor, here and now. Before that, I was an honest farmer north of here, growing radishes." He dis-played strong, callused hands. "When we were raided, the Capital was struck quite bad; so I wanted to come down here to see what I could do. I was drafted. But what we have done is not enough." He gestured at the roiling dust clouds. "Not enough."

Liszendir waited quietly, somewhat startled by Hath'in-gar's brusque manners coupled with some startlingly human habits. He, in turn, favored her with an evil leer almost as obvious as an expression on a stage performer. "Ah, were I thirty years younger! A young civilized ler adolescent girl, ripe as a berry and body-knowledgeable as a professor of erotic arts! And all-atravel with this young primate, eh?" He dug her rudely in the ribs. But immediately he returned, mercurially, to his previous mood, a blend of fatigue, melan-choly and overwork. There was a large amount of meaning in these gestures, but neither Han nor Liszendir could de-termine if it, any of it, was the meaning they were looking for.

"Well. The unwoven rascals, the shaven-headed apes, at the least left us with a tavern." And motioning them to follow, he led the way towards a shabby wooden hut which apparently served the neighborhood as a beer hall. At this hour, most of the patrons were away, as he explained, stepping down into cool darkness. The floor of the establishment was of packed earth and gave off an aroma redolent of wet ground and old beer. Liszendir fastidiously put her boots back on before venturing completely into the dive. After securing a single pot of ale from behind the bar, where a human woman slept soundly, snoring faintly, Hath'ingar led them to one of the cleaner tables and invited them to be seated. He took a healthy swig of the brew, wiped his lips, sat the pot down, and waited.

Han began, "We are traders, financed by a group on Kenten. I heard of your plight, here on Chalcedon, and so set out as soon as Liszendir and I could get free of Trader Efrem. Do you remember him?"

"Ah, yes. Efrem. The rascal, a first-class robber and for all I know, a bugger as well. Such was his disposition towards money, at any rate. He was almost as hard to endure as the robbers, but by some shrewd trading we did manage to get some good stuff out of him before he headed back to civilization."

"Why did he leave, then? For money? He told us he wanted to get off Chalcedon to get some credits for some things he dropped off for free." Han fabricated as he went along.

"I'd expect such a tale of Efrem. No, we paid hard cash for the goods we bought, platinum, thorium and gold bullion, if you please, and a hard bargain it was, too. No, indeed. He left because we were going to put him to work here. I'll wager he's swanking it now at some human-planet resort town, right in the very jaws of civilization."

"No. He's dead. Somebody murdered him the day we left."

Hath'ingar raised an eyebrow, which, as Han observed, was singed. "Murder, now, was it? Hm. I'm sorry to hear it. He robbed us, Efrem did, true enough, but I would not have deemed it a life's-worth, even before the Kenten judicistrators." Here, he turned to Liszendir. "And you, my lady, do you not speak as well?"

She answered, seemingly in a retort, but the language was not anything Han had ever heard before. It seemed to be a singsong clipped dialect. One of the Multispeech modes, he thought. But before she could get very far, the deputy spread his hands, palm outwards, in a gesture of negation.

"None of that, here. We all speak Common alike, here on Chalcedon, or do now, at any rate." He looked oddly disturbed by the incident. "We have all had to pitch in here. There was a lot of mistrust. And the Warriors were ler." He made a small pause, and added, as an afterthought, "And may they couple with scavengers."

Liszendir said, "I came to see. I heard of this voyage, and being *nerh*, I was superfluous to both parents and insiblings. I am to learn trade, and could not have a better opportunity. We suspected that Efrem had been murdered for his money, which was never found, and that being so considerable and a probable motive, another could be made. We," she gestured at Han, "are temporary partners. I own half, and answer for the registry of our ship." Han was astounded. A liar as well. But he watched her closely. He did not know if she was suspicious of this strange creature before them, or was merely being cautious.

Hath'ingar quaffed another mouthful of the sour ale and passed the jug to Liszendir. She sniffed at it, dubiously, then sipped daintily. She turned aside, sneezed quickly like a cat, and made a wry face. Then she passed the jug to Han, who was thirsty and accepted with relish, guzzling gratefully.

"Well, well," said the deputy mayor. "What won't we have next, out here on the frontier? But I suppose we'll see more of this as time goes on. But it was not so when I was a young buck." He became serious. "But I understand all too well about your outsiblingdom, your *nergan*. In my own braid I was *thes*. Here on Chalcedon. And a fine lot I got. 'Hewer of Wood and Drawer of Water,' so I believe the ancient human tale has it. So I ran away from the *yos* and found some boon comrades of these parts, and we started up our own braid. I was forefather, and those were certainly the days. Myself, and Kadhrilnan, Jovdanshir and Merdulian, so we were; tried and true! But I digress. You must tell me more."

They replied that the first thing they needed was a place to stay while they were arranging for sales. It had been a long voyage out to Chalcedon, and they were tired of the ship. They realized that housing was probably scarce because of the raid, so they would take anything reasonable. After that, the local merchants could come and they could start trading in earnest. Hath'ingar agreed, and arose to leave, saying he was off to see what could be found. Then they were alone in the beer hall.

Han and Liszendir sat alone, except for the snoring woman, who was still behind the bar, and said nothing to disturb the cool darkness or their thoughts. They were also thinking about disposing of the ostensible trade goods, for they certainly would have to keep up a front here.

He asked her, half joking, half serious, "What's the matter with the ale? Don't you drink?"

She made another wry face. "We are as fond of our tipple as the next, although we fear spirit greatly. Our tolerance to it is lower than yours. But this stuff! It is terrible! It is stumpwater! Ugh." She returned to her musing, and Han did not disturb her again.

Presently Hath'ingar returned, bearing a key ostentatiously, which seemed to be of dubious appearance for locking doors. Still, a room was a room, and they followed him out of the beer hall without protest or comment.

Outside, the light of day had mutated somewhat to an air of afternoon; shadows were lengthening. For the first time, Han began to look around him at the world on which they had landed. Notwithstanding the considerable destruction caused by the raid, Chalcedon, or at least this part of it, appeared to be a relaxed and lovely place. It seemed to be a rather flat world, with clear air which faded gradually into the blues of distance, marked with no hills or mountains, but with gently rolling ridges. He observed as much to Liszendir, who agreed. Her own world, Kenten, had no really high mountains, but it was hilly and precipitous all over. Hath'ingar, hearing the remark, spoke somewhat boastingly on the charms of Chalcedon.

"Ah, yes. You notice the fine afternoon sun slants, the openness, the quiet, the grace of the feather-trees." He pointed towards an exquisitely tall tree nearby of great charm. It had a smooth, off-white bark, hanging boughs, and long drooping cascades of shiny, scimitar-shaped leaves. A pungent, aromatic odor wafted from it, which teased the sense of smell rather than offending it. Han looked again; it was tall, over three hundred feet. As his eye became more accustomed to the background, he saw more of the feather-trees, scattered here and there. Some of them appeared to be even taller.

"You marvel? But Chalcedon is a quiet world. No great

winds, storms, earthquakes. And we have no seasons as we have a regular orbit and virtually no axial tilt. So the trees grow tall. Of course, I find it too quiet, too orderly, if you know what I mean; but never mind that. A mild climate, and plenty of wealth, all for a little harmless grubbing. But how I ramble on! Here we are!"

They rounded the tall feather-tree, under which huddled a small wooden house of dilapidated rustic appeal. It looked abandoned and rather dusty, but at the same time sturdy and solid. Liszendir observed quietly to Han that it was not to her taste, but that it would do if that was all there was. There was no ceremony: Hath'ingar, on hearing her comment, handed her the key, announced he was off to gather in the local merchants, and departed.

As he left, from the distance, his voice drifted to them; "I will bring them here at dark, on the very instant." He gave a great flourish, and faded into the dusts of the road.

The little house was very dirty, so they were first occupied with cleaning it up so they could bear to stay in it. It seemed to have stood empty for years. Thus they spent the long Chalcedon afternoon. When Liszendir asked Han how long the day was in standard hours, he was forced to admit that he had neglected to look it up, or reset his variable-rate watch to conform to the rate of local time, but he could recall something like thirty standard hours. Towards evening, after they had finished as much as they were going to do, Liszendir went out for food to last them at least a few days.

After a while, she returned, waking Han up from the nap he was taking on the front porch. She had bread, sausages, cheeses and smoked meats, plus a few fruits. She brought the provisions in the house, and as soon as it was laid out, they both fell to it. It had been a long day and they were both starved, Liszendir especially. Her metabolism ran at a higher rate than Han's. Soon after they had satisfied the most immediate part of their appetite, she began talking again, in a low voice.

"While I was out, I rummaged around to see what I could find out. Believe me, I have been cautious! There is something going on here I cannot measure; and the ler here are very strange—like none I have ever seen before. It is a beautiful and prosperous world, all over very much like this around here, so they say, but it abounds with the oddest rumors."

She reflected on something for a moment, and then continued, "I was unable to ever get any kind of description of the weapons used by the Warriors. Nobody seems to know. They always used the same pattern—bombardment from the air, then they would come in. But the explosions! All people knew was there would be a tremendous explosion, followed by a crater. You are deep in these things; what kind of device could do that with no warning? Others spoke of streaks in the sky afterwards, and fireballs. It is all very confusing to me."

Han thought for a moment. "I don't know. Except for the craters, it sounds like coherent-radiation beams, lasers or masers, at any rate outside the frequency response of either ler or human eyes. On the other hand, beams don't leave impact craters. And they start fires. We detected no gross radioactivity when we landed, I checked it for that reason. If we had some reading, there, it would tell us something, too. Total conversion at distance? I doubt it. TCD has been demonstrated theoretically, but it's the devil to control in the real world. And I rule TCD out for the same reason I rule out nuclear weapons—we'd see evidence of fallout, which you always get with the kind of ground burst that leaves a crater. And we'd also see flash burns on the buildings and a lot of people. None of that. It completely baffles me. But whatever it is, they must have a lot of control over it."

"It is true that very few were killed. They avoided the residential areas entirely."

"So they were not strategically destroying supplies, or killing people, but making an impression."

"I agree, Han. But for what?"

"For the captives."

"Yes. Efrem said, only humans of a certain kind, and a few ler as well. But those were at random, or so it seemed."

"So we don't know any more?"

"Not really. But I know what I heard at the market: they think the Warriors haven't left, that they're lying off-planet somewhere, perhaps hoping to ambush a battlecraft when it comes in."

"Did they cite any evidence to support that?"

"No. But they all seemed sure. And they were scared."

But however it was, they were given no more time to speculate on the problem that evening, for the sun had finally set, AVILA 1381 moving infinitely slow across the wavy horizon in a slow demonstration of old gold. And Hath'ingar was in the yard under the feather-tree with an unruly crowd of local merchants, just as he had promised earlier.

During the remainder of the long night, until quite late, past midnight, they argued and haggled, made proposals and counterproposals, some of which were met with derisive laughter, some with hoots of scorn. And they wheedled, extolled, told various atrocity stories, and rarely made a deal. It seemed to Han that if Efrem had had to put up with much of this, he got out well. The merchants of Chalcedon were hard-nosed, unyielding, and taletellers of incredible abilities. He used all the tricks he had learned and practiced at the Traders' Academy in Boomtown; he sulked, he threatened, he made allusions to parents, he looked disdainfully over his nose, hoping he had the professional sneer just right, and he seemingly ignored the horrendous fates of, so it appeared, thousands of women and children who were simultaneously ravished, singly and multiply, violated, buggered and burned many times over. Liszendir said nothing, beyond the disclaimer of looking after her interests. But Han could tell now that he could read some of her facial expressions that his performance must be having some effect—she winced from time to time.

One thing became clear, as they digested the meat out of all the stories they heard. The people on Chalcedon had indeed had their wits scared out of them, but all things considered, they had gotten off remarkably well. Very few had actually been killed or injured. And the stories confirmed that the Warriors took only certain types of humans with them, and they were not picking at random; they knew their business well, and knew exactly what they were looking for. After several sessions of small talk during impasses in the haggling, Han was able to determine that, for instance, the Warriors had cleaned the Capital district completely out of any shape below a certain age; also, those with the odd combination of blond hair and dark complexions. In other groups or classifications they had been more selective, seemingly picking by individuals.

One of the merchants said, "Oh, absolutely, absolutely." He waved his hand around in a limp-wrist maneuver which

Han, despite a great deal of tolerance, found personally disturbing. "The Warriors would arrange the people in a line, and then groups of threes of them would come along, prodding and poking, for all the world as if they were at a livestock auction. But you could see some order in it; they —that is, the threes—were each looking for a certain type. By type, I mean the degree of likeness that you see among people in a large crowd, or when you see a stranger and he reminds you of someone you knew before. Someone has said that basically there are only about a hundred kinds of combinations of face and build, you know. They were not interested in sex, nor in beauty, but in youth; they assembled great wads of uglies as readily as any other standard, or so it seemed to me. Then they would visit each other's groups of prisoners and crow over the size of the take. The ler folk here said they were speaking Single-speech, but it was very distorted, and with a lot of special terminology thrown in. *We* couldn't understand a word of it. And of course they were proud as peacocks over what they had gotten, every one of them."

Another merchant, this one dour, short, fat and more to the point, said, "They all went around in threes. Some of these groups had all male members, some all female, some both. And each threesome acted as if they thought their fellow triples were clods of the worst sort. The local ler they took were also arranged into threes as they herded them off. After that, which they encouraged us all to come to, they climbed in several bulky personnel carriers and departed for their ship; I hear they ransacked other parts as well. After they were done, they threw around a few bombards for good measure, and left Chalcedon."

But no one had any idea as to the nature of the "bombards." The one which had struck the Capital had arrived with no warning at all: a bright explosion, a loud noise, and the ground rang like a gong. Afterwards, some held that they had seen a vapor trail to the zenith, and they heard thunder in the air. But even these were unsure. Whatever it was, it did something to iron and steel. No compass had worked right in the area since the attack. And the effect was strongest near the crater. Magnetic bombs to disrupt computers? Such things were known; yet use of such an expensive weapon was unlikely in a place that didn't have a single computer more elaborate than an abacus. Chalcedon was a frontier planet: they didn't have an excess of data to worry about.

Other than that, they learned no more during the night of haggling and trading. And finally, everybody began to run down, so Han and Liszendir closed the trading off, tallied up the deals which had already been made, and promised to deliver on the morrow, should trucks or wagons arrive at the ship to carry it off. The arrangements were made, and the locals left. And Han and Liszendir collapsed into the nearest thing resembling a bed and slept immediately.

The morning came, clear and limpid as water from an ancient village well. The feather-tree was on the east side of the house, but the sudden light woke them up, and after a quick breakfast, they walked back to the field where they had landed the ship. There, a great disorderly crowd had already gathered. During the remainder of the long morning of Chalcedon, Han and the girl supervised unloading and loading of the goods they had taken in exchange.

By noon the greater part of the work had been done, and they were left in the midst of a colossal mess. Piles of boxes, crates and trash. The field had been rutted and gouged by wheel, track and hoof. The *Pallenber* was coated with a fine patina of dust.

Hath'ingar now approached from the last truckload to depart. He was as grimy as the rest of them had been, but he seemed indefatigable and curious.

"Ah, now, all done, a profit made, and so you leave our stricken parts. What's this? Weapons bays?" he added in surprise, pointing at some suspicious protuberances in the smooth line of the hull.

"Yes, weapons," Han answered. "We thought it best to come prepared for the worst—for all we knew, we very well could have met the Warriors coming out here. Or even more ordinary raiders. Such things are not unlikely even in this age. It had been said back there that this was why Efrem left in such a rush—he feared for his life."

"Well, so be it," Hath'ingar replied evenly. "Still, it did him no good, did it? Everyone goes at his time and to music, some to gay lover's tunes, some to heroic marches and flourishes, and others to dirges. But all go!"

It sounded strange and alien in Han's ears. Even stranger was Liszendir's reply, which she made shyly in her own tongue: *"Si-tasi maharalo al-tenzhidh."* Then she translated for Han's benefit: "Thus endures the way of the world." There was no response from Hath'ingar.

There was a pause, as if no one knew quite what to say. Then Hath'ingar spoke, "Now where will you be off to?"

Han answered, "We thought that we would fly over to the west coast of this continent. Our maps are probably very much out of date, but they show a large city there. It seemed to be large, so was probably hit; they will be needing some goods as well."

"Yes. That would be Libreville. So they are in need. In fact, I have heard that they were bombed out pretty badly and have left the city. But I know of other settled places all over which do have needs. I assure you I'll be no trouble, but I could show you where the places are. You can conclude your affairs sooner and be on your way."

Liszendir had already entered the ship. Han looked long at the ler elder below, on the ground. After a time, he said, somewhat against his nagging better judgment, "Good enough. Come on up."

Han stayed on the ladder to see if Hath'ingar needed any help climbing up the high ladder to the entry port. He didn't; in fact, Han was surprised to note that Hath'ingar climbed the ladder with a great deal more agility and style than he had himself. He credited it to good physical conditioning and forgot it. The two of them entered the ship.

Once aboard the ship and in the control room, Hath'ingar wandered around, looking at everything, seemingly amazed and very appreciative. "An absolute paragon," he enthused. "Indeed, superior workmanship, fine stuff! Is this ship a ler or a human work?"

"Human," Han answered, as he was settling down in the pilot's chair. Liszendir sat down beside him, as he observed, with an odd motion that suggested uneasiness. Han felt it, too, but he couldn't pinpoint the source.

They lifted off and retracted the landing legs. Han thought that they would not be going very far, so he did not set a course for an orbit, but selected a lower altitude for a powered cruise. After he had done so, he turned around. "Now where to, Hath'ingar?" There was no answer. The overweight elder had disappeared. "Well," he said in Liszendir's general direction, "He's probably gone looking for the convenience."

At that moment Hath'ingar reappeared, but this time, he

was not dressed in the traditional ler overrobe; he was naked except for a loincloth with long, brightly decorated ends, and in place of the gray, long braided hair of an elder was a glossy, shaven pate. On his bare, hairless chest was an elaborate tattoo illustrating a titanic battle between two peculiar beasts, neither of which Han had ever heard of before. Nor was he as old as Han had previously thought. Han groaned aloud; Hath'ingar held a gun exactly like the one which Liszendir had disarmed in Efrem's room back in Boomtown. Where was that one? Han groaned again. If it was not the one in Hath'ingar's hand, it was secured in a locker, which was directly behind Hath'ingar. It might as well have been back in Efrem's room, for all the good it could do them now. And the figure across the room: he was still overweight, but the fat was the dynamic fat of great strength. The erstwhile deptuy mayor waited poised, standing expectantly on the balls of his feet.

"Yes. Tricked," he said. Liszendir moved to regain her feet. Hath'ingar continued, "Now without delay and no tricks, set a course for the two gas giants of this system. They are in conjunction, now, opposite the main fields of the galaxy. There we will rendezvous with my warriors."

"Your warriors?" Han wished to stall for time, although he did not honestly know what he would do with any gained. Below, Chalcedon was receding slowly, turning beneath them to the east as they flew north and west. If one looked well, one could already see a slight curve to the horizon, barely perceptible.

"Yes. I am hetman of the outer horde. Now move slowly. This gun fires slivers of a most unpleasant substance. And though its effects are swift, it takes consciousness last. I am expert with it as well as with other arts. Do not, either of you, think you can outmove me."

Han glanced out of the corner of his eye at Liszendir. It was hardly visible, but it seemed as if every muscle in her body was working invisibly under the robe, warming up for use. Her jaw muscles clenched and flexed slightly, an eerie sight on the face which Han had seen once or twice in its full beauty of amorous interest, or perhaps recollection. Who could know? Ler had fully eidetic memories.

As Hath'ingar took a preparatory step towards them, she shouted one word, "Move!" and performed an incredible maneuver. Han let himself fall to the deck, rolling, just as she had shown him. Effortlessly she leaped straight up, apparently without flexing her knees, leaving the soft boots behind as she rose. At the overhead, she was upside down and leaving the robe behind; using her legs to carom herself, she left the robe behind and sailed across the control room to Hath'ingar, or whoever, or *whatever* he was. Han gaped in astonishment at the naked white form: she had done that in a full 1G field. He was still rolling when he heard the puff of the gun. He felt nothing.

Hath'ingar could not bring the gun up to bear on her and avoid her at the same time. He elected to avoid, diving forward in a motion which looked clumsy, but which Han knew wasn't. But he retained the gun.

There commenced a scene Han could not follow. Afterwards, all he would be able to remember was the blurred speed of fast motion, move and countermove. The two of them moved with blinding speed. Occasionally the forms would meet, and there would be a quick flurry of activity, sharp grapples and attempted holds. Neither succeeded. And Hath'ingar still retained the gun. Liszendir moved back and forth across the control room in a dizzy white loom of motion. Han saw that she was deliberately preventing Hath'ingar from taking aim at her or even tracking her motion; and with an extra person in the room, it was for the time threat enough to keep things at a stalemate. Then they came together again. This time something happened, and then Hath'ingar bolted out of the control room. Han caught a glimpse of him as he left; he had been trying to fire off one more shot, which went wild. His right ear had been pulped.

She locked the door and stood before him, naked, shiny with sweat and panting heavily. "Got him one good lick, but he's tough! And the shave-topped ape got away from me! Damn it! Damn him!" It was the first time Han had seen her angry. She was angry with herself.

She asked, peremptorily, "Do you have a way out of the ship?"

"Yes. Life rafts. In the locker behind the pilot's chair. Should be five or six."

"Then get into one and get off!"

"Liszendir, I . . ."

"No! Do as I tell you! Against him alone, I have an even chance, and I can fly the ship if I have to. I learned. I remember. He is too much for you with what you know now. You only have hostage value. If he gets you we are beaten. I am not degrading you—I am trying to save you. I must kill

him. He used a projectile weapon against us. I can only
succeed alone: he is extremely dangerous—you do not know
how much."

"He's got that gun, Liszendir . . ."

"Never mind that. I can beat that as long as there is only
one of him. So if I win, I will fly the ship back. If he wins
there will be no back—for either of us. I am doing this for
you for my own bad reasons. It is wrong, it is forbidden,
it is not for us ever—but I care and you must not be caught
by him. Now go! I must get him, soon. I am in *bandastash*
—high anger flow. It gives me speed and strength, but I
cannot keep it long: it costs terribly." She pressed her cheek
against his, briefly. It was burning hot.

Han saw she was right, but to give up the ship? No. It
was the only way, bad as it seemed. He remembered a
thing she had said when she had been teaching him simple
holds: *If you cannot give up the ground upon which you
fight, in order to win, then you have lost already.* He
opened the locker and climbed into one of the rafts, ready for
launching. As he pulled the airshield over himself, she
reached in and touched his face, very tenderly. She said,
"If I am successful, I will come to you in the mountains
north of the capital, near the ridge with two pinnacles
we could see from there. If not, farewell and remember me.
Your name means 'last.' " She slammed the lid violently
and ejected him.

There was a moment of vertigo, as he felt the switch
from the artificial gravity of the *Pallenber* to the real gravity
of the planet Chalcedon. Then he could see the ship, falling
upwards away from him. Suddenly, it jerked off westwards
at tremendous speed. The sled functioned automatically,
and began its descent. It seemed slow, but Han knew that
was only an illusion of the distance he was above the planetary surface. He looked down to the surface below, blue-
green and brown, mottled with white puffs of clouds which
did not tear into streaks. Chalcedon did not have rapidly
moving major weather systems. It was the last he saw. The
automatics took over, and he lost his consciousness to
G-forces and a special gas, released just to keep the passenger quiet; it had been assumed by the builders of this
kind of raft that for a person to witness his own fall from
orbit or suborbital distance would itself be fatal in the
absence of injury. They were, of course, right. Han knew
nothing.

IV

"*Once upon a time, on Chalcedon where men and ler both lived in relative peace, a certain human rushed to the hut in the crags of Klislangir Tlanh, a very old and wise ler, who was considered by many to be a holy man. The human, a mere boy, bore a message that said Klislangir's insibling Werverthin Srith had just died, wishing him well. The sage continued to study the sunset clouds. Finally, he said, 'I am also grieved to see these lovely clouds that will be no more with the night and its clearing.' The human, one Roderigo, ejaculated, 'What? How can you be so callous as to talk about clouds at a time like this? The lady, alsrith, had lived with you from birth, almost, and for years after the next generation were home in the yos.' The sage answered, 'It is exactly for those realizations into the meaning of sorrow that I am called wise.' He turned away and did not speak again that day. In that instant, Roderigo looked at the clouds also and was illuminated. He returned to his home, disposed of all his goods, and became a disciple of Klislangir Tlanh. In later years he was accounted wise as any ler holy man.*"

—*The Chalcedon Apocrypha*

"*One alone in the wilderness is never bored, nor does he feel the despair of a meaningless job—to the contrary, everything is invested with mean-*
58

*ing, some of it dire, indeed; but in the heart of
a great city that tramples the stars themselves
underfoot, one needs ceaseless entertainment to
distract him from the knowledge of his vileness,
which lies about him, everywhere. The herb of our
cure is a bitter one, but gnaw it we will."*

—*Roderigo*

Standard life rafts were required on all spaceships, and few flouted this regulation. They were intended to be used near a planetary body, or as a refuge in deep space until such time as one could be rescued. Near a body of certain mass, they worked automatically. All during space flight, men of both kinds had compared space to the sea, and indeed the comparison was valid in all ways except in the scale: space dwarfed all the water seas that ever had been, were, would be, could be. And its shores were infinitely more perilous than the shores of the wildest seas. Therefore, the standard life raft. It was designed first to get its passenger through that surf and those perilous reefs of an unpowered landing from orbit. They were neither kind, nor comfortable; but they worked.

Han awoke, knowing nothing, and aching at every point he could imagine as belonging to him; and some whose ownership could have been debated. He tried to move, but immediately felt his motion arrested. He felt a quick flash of panic, but then he remembered. He stopped, and rested for a moment, thinking. Through the transparent shield, he could see that he had landed in a wooded area, and it was deep dusk, almost dark. Vents in the raft were bleeding fresh air in. He slept. Sometime later he awoke, and it was completely dark; stars were shining through the branches. Now he remembered the opening sequence, and after a few fumbles, was able to stagger away from the coffinlike life raft. The air was cool with night, and the forest was silent.

Traders, like everyone else, were schooled for a variety of reasons: tradition, someone having excess money and wishing to keep it, whatever came, out of the hands of functionaries, or society wanting to have an excuse to civilize its children. But perhaps best of all was the reason that traders had to be both shrewd and prepared for any-

thing. And Han had, on the whole, been a good student at
the Traders' Academy, although he had played their mer-
cantile trading game with a vigor that earned disapproval.
Also, he reflected, he had been evaluated as having "spent
too much time with the girls." But he remembered well.

Paraleimon Kardikas in *The Survivor's Manual: If you
ever crash, no matter if it's in your own yard, STOP. DO
NOTHING. Remember first who you are. How you got
there. Trust no impression, make no identifications. The survivor is Adam, but he is an Adam who does not know if he
has fallen into Eden or Hell.*

Han sat to the side of the raft on a fallen tree in the
dark, remembering. The flight, the ship, Liszendir. And so,
here he was, somewhere on Chalcedon. That was excellent—
at least he knew which planet he was on. And with no
food, no money and no equipment. No, that wasn't true.
He had some basics in the raft, and some survival tools—
wire, sawblades, a knife. A water distillery, for drink and for
the basic food concentrate. He got up, went to the raft, and
removed the survival pack. Now what?

Kardikas: *Travel at night wherever possible, for lights
are visible. But great strangers by day. Get the lay of the
land.*

Han could not see very well or very far in the dense
woods. He knew he was on a slight slope, so, leaving the
raft, he walked quietly through the darkness until he found
the top of the low hill he was on. Through gaps in the trees
he could see stars, outlines of more distant hills, darker
places where valleys were. He performed several turns about
the hill; he could see nothing—no lights, no smoke, no
indication anyone but he walked the surface of Chalcedon.
He didn't even know directions. But he waited. He could
find out. It would take time, but he had plenty of that.

He marked groups of bright stars near the horizon, making a game of naming new constellations, which also helped
cheer him up. He gave them fanciful names, some obscene,
but he also noted very carefully both the shapes of the
groups, and where they were in relation to his subjective
landmarks, and their shadows—tree-shapes, rocks, peculiar
horizon lines. He did not wait for a moon—Chalcedon
didn't have a moon either.

Time passed slowly on Chalcedon, but after a time, what
his watch said was several standard hours, he looked at the
sky around the horizon again. Some of his constellations had

sunk below the edge of the ground. Others had risen high in
the night sky. Still others had moved more to one side or
another. From his efforts and waiting, now he could determine the position of celestial north: it was higher towards
the zenith than he had thought it would be. He was far
to the north of the Capital, which was closer to the equator. And he knew which way was east, west, and south, even
if he did not know how far their flight had offset them. He
suspected he was somewhat to the west, also.

There was no way to go, then, but southwestwards. Han
gathered up the pack, put it on, and set out, picking his way
cautiously through the quiet darkness. He kept his knife out,
at the ready; he did not know much about the native animal
life of the planet, which was an object lesson he would
never forget. If he ever got the chance to use such knowledge
again.

He walked through an empty land for days, until he lost
count of them. Chalcedon was not a flat planet; it had a
surface which undulated gently, sometimes more hilly, sometimes more flat, but never quite attaining real hills, or a
plain. He crossed rivers, was rained upon, and walked, in a
routine which soon evolved into two sessions each day:
predawn to forenoon, rest, late afternoon to early night,
rest. He found that walking as he was doing, he could not
accommodate himself to the long day-cycle of Chalcedon.
He was able to refine his measurement of the day; it was
almost thirty-two standard hours long. And it did not vary.
He could not estimate how far he walked, either; there
were no landmarks visible for more than a few miles in any
direction. One of the hills or ridges looked very much like
another.

He saw no animals, although rarely, at night, he heard
cries from far away. He was not being tracked—the cries
were never the same, except in their suggestion of endless
emptiness. Nor did he see birds; apparently there were none
on the planet, a fact which disappointed him. He knew the
fruits were edible, that was one fact about Chalcedon which
helped him along: it was one of the kindest worlds in the
universe, without poison plants of any kind. Those he ate,
adding his food concentrate, which he ate stoically, because
it tasted terrible, and he purified water by the side of
streams. And walked on, avoiding the thoughts he might
have had about what he would do when he got somewhere.

Han had stopped for the night, more tired than usual from climbing among rocky terrain all day. His place this night was in a dense grove of fragrant trees down in a narrow valley. So for a long time he did not notice that one part of the sky on the horizon was ever so slightly glowing. Much later, taking a turn around the patch of woods as he always did, just as a precaution, he noticed the glow. It had been too many days, and he was too tired to feel any excitement; besides he did not believe it was anything more than some natural phenomenon. He retrieved his pack, and wearily climbed to the top of the ridge.

At the top, he looked down into a broad, flat valley, so wide he could not make out the far side, even with his newly used and practiced night vision. But that was not really what he was looking at. There were lights in the valley—weak, to be sure, but lights, like windows shining into the darkness. Not just one, either—many, as if of a small community. It was the most beautiful sight he could ever remember seeing. Forgetting his fatigue, he started out down the slope towards the lights, practicing the story he would tell, with all parts clear except how many days he had walked.

As he drew nearer to the lights, a process that seemed interminable, probably since the clear air distorted distances for him, he first grew suspicious, and then disappointed. One by one, the lights went out, except one group which seemed to belong to a house. Han had hoped for a human settlement, but apparently this was going to be a ler village; he could catch an occasional glimpse of the suggestion of shape of the houses—and humans did not live in low, rambling ellipsoids. The braid houses they called the *yos*. As he drew nearer, he could see that it was a thriving little community—there were well-tilled fields on all sides, barns, sheds, houses, now mostly dark. But it was isolated—there were no power lines, no beam towers, and beyond the narrow paths beside the fields, no roads. The paths were marked only by hoofprints and footprints, footprints that showed, even in the dark, four toe marks and hardly any weight on the narrow heel.

Han guessed that just about everyone would be asleep by now. Ler liked sleep, and normally went to bed soon after dark, even in their civilized places. Here, they probably worked hard during the long day and would never stay up late. Still, though, it was late, yet the lights were just going off. Only one *yos* was still well lit, and it seemed to be making up for all the rest of the village. He was close enough now to hear voices in the dark. Voices! They were faint, and what he could hear of them was in a strange and alien language—ler Singlespeech—but they filled him with joy. He suppressed an urge to shout, and continued on.

Presently he stood before the well-lit house, or *yos*. Han knew about their peculiar custom of living in a dwelling without angles—but he didn't know why they preferred them. The barns and sheds seemed angular enough. He had never seen a *yos* except in pictures. It looked just like descriptions he had heard—a random collection of flattened ellipsoids, following the contour of the ground, each "room" mounted on its own pedestal, a foot or so off the ground. He wondered, how did one announce oneself? Did one step up to the door and knock? There was no door on this particular *yos*, but a woven curtain. Perhaps one stood in the yard and crowed like a rooster. He felt giddy, drunk with fatigue and a longing to be with people again.

The problem solved itself. Out of the *yos* came an oldster, with long, white hair. The person stopped, looked incredulously at Han for a moment, and then, quite coolly, considering the circumstances, spoke to him. Han didn't understand a word of it. It was indeed ler Singlespeech. He shook his head in what he hoped the creature—he couldn't tell if it was a man or a woman, the usual ler apparent sexlessness being even more ambiguous from aging, as was also the case with humans—would understand him to mean that he couldn't understand what he or she or it was saying. He started to speak, but the oldster interrupted him, saying something and pointing at the ground. It seemed to mean, "Wait here." Then it darted back into the *yos*. Han waited.

Presently a younger one appeared at the door, cast a quick look about the yard, and disappeared. In a moment, it returned. Han identified it as a young girl, mature, fertile, for she was carrying an infant which she nursed. Then the creature spoke.

"Yes? What will you do here?" Han felt a certain sense of unreality. The voice was unmistakably male. He felt an edge of something like lunacy, remembering, idiotically, the words of a character in a written novel of the classical period: *If you think you're going crazy, it means you aren't.* He decided to answer anyway.

"I am Han Keeling. Trader and spaceman. There was an

accident and I was ejected from the ship. I landed north of here, many days, I don't know how many. I would ask your hospitality and assistance if you have any to give." It was the longest speech he had made in many days. His voice sounded strange to his ears.

"I am Dardenglir. You must excuse us for acting so odd, but we are very far out here and we see few humans. Hardly any of us even know Common: this is an old village and most of us have been here several generations. I am not from here by birth, but my own village is hardly less isolated. But of course we will help. What do you need?"

"Food. A few days' rest. And directions. I am trying to get back to the general area of the Capital."

"I understand. It will be easy. Will you accept our, house, here?" The words sounded peculiar. "We are crowded now, for there was a birth tonight, and we have stayed up overlate, celebrating. But we have room, and there is food, warmth, people. We can find a place."

"I accept gratefully, Dardenglir."

"Then come in." He did not wait, but turned and vanished back into the house. Han could hear him speaking inside. He followed, climbed the stairs, and went in, through the curtain, which in Chalcedon's mild climate seemed to be all the protection they needed from the elements.

Inside, the room was circular in plan, and a wide shelf went all around it, except where round holes interrupted the curve, and except for an area to his left, where a raised platform served as a hearth, smoking outwards through a hooded vent into the ceiling. There were candles, lanterns, and people. They were strange to him, but he felt the same as all survivors—they were people. He blinked in the light.

While one of them gathered up some food, apparently from the party which had been going on, Dardenglir introduced them all. There were two infants, one small girl-child, four adults, and four older ones. It was the whole braid—past, present, and future. And there was no mistake, Dardenglir was male. But Han kept quiet.

Indeed it was a birth celebration. One of the females had apparently given birth this night, for she lay back on some cushions, bare, and her face was flushed and happy, while the infant nuzzled at her breast. Han noticed the cord was still attached. They looked at Han with more curiosity than he felt to them, while Dardenglir spoke rapidly, in Multi-speech. Then they all smiled. They waved at the hearth.

"Eat, drink. Be happy with us. There is a trough in the yard for washing and you can sleep in there, to your right."

Han nodded with what he hoped was a polite gesture, and gratefully did as he had been asked. He ate, went out and washed in icy water, returned, and with a gesture, crawled into a dark, smaller space; there he found, eventually, something soft, like a blanket, and pulling it over himself, he slept, deeply.

He awoke. Alone. There was light in the room, another smaller ellipsoid; the light came through translucent windows which had the appearance of cloudy stained glass. Han reached over and touched one: it felt rougher than glass—it was rock, ground down to translucency and polished, travertine or alabaster, he thought. The effect was one of warmth and beauty, even though he could see no way to open them. How did they get circulation? He looked around, and finally saw that there was a vent in the domed ceiling very much like the one over the hearth, only smaller. The whole "room" was a bed, apparently. All around were quilts and cushions, neatly folded, seemingly placed at random. No one was in the room except Han. The surface underfoot was yielding, but not soft. Like everything else he had seen since he had entered, everything seemed to be handmade. He wondered about the unopenable windows, as they obviously did not have, and would not want, any kind of air-conditioning equipment. But perhaps they looked at houses, especially in this mild climate, as being more shelter than fortress or castle; if you wanted to see outside, why you could go outside and perceive it totally.

He crawled out into the larger room, which served as entry, common room, and kitchen all in one. It was also empty, but cleaned and straightened from the night before. He listened, trying to determine if anyone was in the house. There was no sense of presence in the house at all, although he was aware of voices outside. He hesitated. Han felt his beard, which had become unkempt during the long walk. And they would not have anything to trim it with, probably. He wondered how he looked to them, if Liszendir had thought him "too angular, too hairy." Proportions all different. Still, they had been both generous and kind.

He went to the front and pushed the curtain-flap aside.

The *yos* was, he now saw in daylight, situated on a low hill. Not far away, a clear stream made water noises with restraint and probity, commenting on the site, the village, the clear air. A wooden trough conducted water to a point near the house, where it collected in a large wooden tub. The overflow was led back to the stream by a similar wooden trough. At the place where the used water rejoined the stream, he could see a small naked girl-child, about four years old in human terms, playing, making little dams, which she would then subtly damage and watch the penned water flow out and overcome the dam. She looked up and saw Han. She looked at him directly, unafraid, but with a certain amount of wide-eyed wonder. She stopped playing, and shyly approached the steps, coming up to Han to touch his beard. Then she laughed, and abruptly ran off, calling to someone in a gay, musical voice.

Presently Dardenglir, the ler Han had met the night before, arrived, still with the infant slung under his arm. Yes, he had been right: it was definitely a male person. Now that he had been around Liszendir for a while, he could sense differences—the walk, the hips, the general carriage. Dardenglir greeted Han courteously.

"The sun is up, friend, and now so are you. That is a good thing."

"I don't know how to begin to thank you . . ."

"Not at all. We have very few visitors here. The last human visitor we had built a large edifice on yon hill." Han turned to look. There was no edifice, nor were there signs one had ever been there. He looked back to Dardenglir, smiling. "So you see it as it is. Even ler do not come so far often. And we are easy—all we ask in return are a few tales, and a hand in the fields."

"The fields part I can do, but what kind of tales?"

"Events. What occurs in the wide world."

"Oh, those kinds of tales. Well, I can tell a few, but I doubt if many will understand my words."

"No matter there. I will translate. And if you stay long enough, I will teach you Singlespeech and you can tell it yourself. But right now, you and I are the only speakers of Common in the village. I am grateful for the practice—it has been a long time. I grow rusty, here in Ghazh'in."

Han came down from the steps into the yard. "Where are the rest?"

"Here, there. Tanzernan, she who gave birth last evening,

is today visiting with the insiblings of her old braid. She was *thes,* there. Today she has something special for them. She and I are *korh* and *dazh,* you would say 'aftermother and afterfather." I wove with Pethmirian, who was *madh,* foremother. This is ours. She is out in the field today. Bazh'ingil repairs a cart yonder, by the barn. Do you know much about us?"

"Only basics. I know no ler well, except . . . but never mind."

"You saw you came in the midst of a party. It was not only a birth we were celebrating, but the continuation of this *Klanh,* this braid. We now have our next insibling generation, boy and girl. The little one who likes your beard is Himverlin, of Bazh'ingil and Pethmirian. She is *nerh,* but for all that, she is a shy one."

"I understand. What happens if both are of the same sex?"

"With the *nerh,* it is pure chance, but from then on, it is partly determined. By our interactions. I don't know the word . . ."

"Pheronomes? Chemical traces, like hormones that carry messages among individuals?"

"That is how it works, but it is not perfect. If the *toorh* are both of the same sex, then the braid ends. They have to weave with others, like outsiblings. Even if we can find another braid in the same straits, with insiblings of opposite sex, ours and theirs both end. The four start new braids, with new names. But not so for us, now."

"So I see."

"It is good, then. Now, what of you?"

Han did not answer immediately. And of him, what indeed? What of the ship, the mission, Liszendir? A sudden pang passed through him.

"Well, I have a long tale to tell, indeed. I may ask more than I answer."

"Aha!" exclaimed Dardenglir. "I see you are an apprentice *mnathman* of the ler."

Sage or *wise man.* "No, certainly not. Why would you think that?"

"Because it is always the part of the wise to ask, not to answer; is that not why they are wise?" He smiled. Han felt like an idiot. Here he was, a cultured and educated member of a technological culture, a civilization which stretched across twenty-five planets or so, human worlds. Yet this farmer with an infant in his arms could disarm him in an instant. He realized better now why humans avoided ler, even though they were graceful, even beautiful creatures, man's own kind, and peaceable in addition. It was disturbing. So, he thought, might have felt some poor Neanderthaler who had wandered into a Cro-magnon tribe's camp, in the Ice Ages of prehistoric Europe.

"No. I am not a sage, of the ler or anybody else. As a fact, I feel somewhat like a fool. But never mind; you will hear all, when all of you are gathered together. And for the answers, and the help, I will freely offer what work I can do and what I can learn."

"Gladly, with the answers, such as we have. And work? There is plenty of that."

So in the morning of the long Chalcedon day, Han went to work at simple agricultural tasks. He spent the day with Pethmirian out in the field, picking beans and filling a small cart, which they pulled along the rows behind them. She showed him how to do it, shaking her head sadly when he displayed his one-thumbed hand. Her hands flew among the vines like small birds. But he learned.

Towards evening, a shower blew up, moving lazily and deliberately after the manner of all Chalcedon weather, so Han and Pethmirian repaired to a shed, joining Bazh'ingil, where they spent the remainder of the day shelling the beans they had picked. Occasionally Dardenglir would drop in and talk for a while; then he would be gone again. As the afternoon rain slowly evolved into the deep blues of night, gradually everyone drifted to the water trough, where, with a great deal of splashing and whooping, everyone stripped to the skin and washed, bodies, clothes, everything. Han joined in; he was not bashful, but he was slightly embarrassed because nude, the differences between the two peoples became the most noticeable.

Dardenglir had presided over the preparation and serving of supper, a performance which bothered Han a little until he recalled that they carried sexual equality to what even the most rabid partisans of equality of the human sexes would call extremes. And in direct reverse from human models, ler became more equal in sexual roles as they became more primitive. They believed it with conviction; Han already knew that one of their most solid beliefs was in the convergence of function through evolution. Not ler, nor their successors in a million years, but perhaps after three or four more evolutionary generations, it would arrive where both sexes would be completely undifferentiated, even as far as bearing children. Sex would then be a function purely of individualism, and not of gender.

After everyone had eaten, they began talking. Dardenglir told Han a few anecdotes about ler. With his eye for minute expressional details, he had noted Han's surprise at his nursing of the infant. His explanation was that from the appearance of mammals, males had carried vestigial nipples and glands to go with them. It had been suspected that adding function to those glands had been a subroutine of the basic DNA developmental program which occurred very late in the sequence, and that their structure worked very well for them because it shared the work of caring for the young child.

From the far corner, Tanzernan, the girl who had given birth the night before, said something and giggled. Dardenglir translated it into "Man-milk makes the children mean!" From the opposite side came a taciturn remark from Bazh'ingil. It was translated, "But it makes the boys better lovers later on." All of them, including Han, laughed at this exchange.

Han began to notice another facet of them, besides their sense of humor; there was considerable difference between individuals, even though there was a great deal of cultural conformity. Bazh'ingil and Pethmirian were more alike, as might be expected, as they were the insiblings of the old braid. But even there there was difference: both were quiet and reserved, but Bazh'ingil kept just below the surface a rude sense of humor which Pethmirian lacked. She was small, dark, and hardly ever spoke. But for all that there was a lot of thought behind her eyes. Dardenglir was smooth as warm oil, crafty as a snake. Wise and alert. Back in civilization, Han could easily visualize him as a diplomat, and one to watch constantly. Tanzernan was bright and pretty, a kind of sprite, who was always, it seemed, laughing about something. During the day, he had discovered that she was something of a practical joker as well.

So he told them his story, leaving nothing out, including the development of an odd attachment between himself and Liszendir. As they listened, they asked question after question, curious as children. When they had asked him everything they could think of, and resumed gazing at the fire

with their large-pupiled eyes, then he began asking his
questions. About the raids, the Warriors, and which was the
best way to get to the mountain with two pinnacles north of
the Capital.

They knew nothing new. The raids had been nowhere near
the remote community of Ghazh'in. They had heard tales,
seen lights in the sky, noticed more meteors than was usual
during the raids. But that was all they knew.

They knew about the pinnacles Han had mentioned;
indeed, it was a major landmark on a planet which had little
variation of local relief from place to place. It was about
two weeks, in their computation, to the southeast, which
meant in his reference twenty-eight days. Han explained
why he felt he needed to go there. They all scoffed it off,
and Dardenglir explained why.

"There is nothing there, no habited place, no town, no
village. Nobody lives in those hills. How would you eat? And
if the girl Liszendir succeeds, she will come in the ship—
and not finding you will begin looking. She will eventually
hear of the visitor at Ghazh'in; wanderers will have spread
the tale. So she will come here for you. So you should stay
here with us until she comes. At any rate it would be dangerous for you to return to the Capital."

Han did not like to admit the possibility, but nevertheless
he asked the question anyway, feeling deep misgivings as he
did. "And what if she failed?"

Bazh'ingil answered, and it was translated. He spoke seriously and earnestly. "If she fails then you are no more than
a colonist, like us. Ships call at Chalcedon"—which he
pronounced as *Chal-sedh-donn*—"but seldom. Face truth
and grow strong from it; you are stranded on the beach. If
this is so, then we will go over to the nearest human village
and find you a nice girl of weaving age, of your own sort,
and you can move out here. There is plenty of room—raise
children and beans! There are worse things."

Han could not answer him. It was a future he had neither
considered nor had he wanted to consider. Now it was late,
and there was quiet throughout the *yos*. One by one, they
drifted off to sleep, cleaning up after supper as they went,
casually but thoroughly. There seemed to be great liberty
about who slept with whom, and they appeared to be unconcerned. Bed had no sexual connotation to them, not when
lovemaking was condoned even in public. And here in the
yos, they certainly knew who could mate with whom. It

would be Dardenglir's and Tanzernan's turn next. Han wound up with the little girl, Himverlin, curled up in his arms. She liked his beard, and was soft and warm, but she kicked and poked mercilessly in her sleep.

So Han entered the cycle of daily life among an isolated farm community of ler. Remote, steeped in what they called wise ignorance, they gently but firmly taught him, unceasingly and patiently. The days went slow and hard at first, but then one began to merge into another. The umbilical cord which still bound Tanzernan and her child finally became nonfunctional and separated; that was one of their peculiar adaptations, too. And Han waited for the coming of Liszendir and the ship, but with each day, it receded a little further off, like a lake drying up, desiccating in a desert.

They were especially insistent on his learning ler Singlespeech, and constantly worked on him. Han found that very hard at first, but it soon began to start coming through for him, in short bursts and flashes. It was a strange language; it was completely regular, without any form of special expressions, but that was not so surprising, considering that it was, in origin, an artificial language.

The grammar was complex—involving a case-declension system for nouns and adjectives, and a highly elaborate system of interacting voices, moods and tenses in the verbs, but its regularity helped greatly. But something else about it troubled Han as he was learning it, and continued to for a long time thereafter. Each word root had one syllable, and was composed of one or two consonants, plus a vowel, plus an end-consonant. There were about fourteen thousand of these roots, each pronounceable combination being used. But each root carried at least four meanings, and there was no way to distinguish which of the four was being used—it all depended on context, which was maddening until you could follow the context. That gave them a one-syllable basic vocabulary of somewhere in the vicinity of 55,000 *basic* words. When you started figuring in two-syllable and three-syllable words, the numbers of possible words became astronomical in a hurry. He could sense a system behind the allocation of meanings, how each of the four was related to the others and the root itself, but he could not grasp the concept, and they seemed curiously reticent to explain that. They told him he didn't need to know that.

All he could figure out of this hidden order was that

Liszendir's name, as she had translated it when he had asked, was related to fire in some curious way, and *hanh,* meaning "last," was related somehow to water. He told them of this conversation, and they called him, from then on, *Sanhan,* like a nickname. Water-last. And there were four words which did not have four meanings, but only one each, about which there seemed to revolve some deep secret which they would not share: *Panh,* fire; *Tanh,* earth; *Kanh,* air; and *Sanh,* water. It sounded vaguely like some type of alchemy, but Han knew little enough about that, so he did not pursue it further.

In Ghazh'in, there was little need for written material, so Han saw little of the way Singlespeech was written. After one glance at a book Dardenglir had brought with him, he wanted nothing to do with it; it seemed each root was written with only one basic character, to which were attached diacritical marks above, for the vowel, and below, for the end-consonant. Han had seen samples of ancient Chinese—it looked like a simplified form of that, even though it was not ideograms, but a true spelling script.

As he learned, he worked with them, doing the thousand chores and tasks that life on a farm required. And except for his concern for Liszendir, he found that he rather liked the life: it was natural, spontaneous, unhurried and unconcerned. But with all the good points it had, he knew very well that he was an alien among them and could not stay forever. And he missed his own kind. And love and sex. Each night, the flashing bare bodies at the water trough did not help.

He did not know how many days had passed, but it was a large number. He had reached the point where he needed almost no help from Dardenglir to talk with them. But Liszendir had not appeared. So he told them that he felt that it was time to leave, much as he hated it. He would go with Dardenglir and Bazh'ingil to the regional market and there try to make his way back to his own world and time. Despite what they had said earlier about finding him a "nice girl for weaving," they were honest. They congratulated him for a wise decision, good for him and themselves as well. But they offered him a share of the profits from the sale of their produce, in which he had helped greatly. At first he refused, but after a time, he gave in, and they began making preparations to leave.

Not so many days later, at sunrise, Han, Dardenglir and

Bazh'ingil loaded and boarded a long, heavy wagon, and after many goodbyes, departed the village of Ghazh'in. The wagon was hitched to a team of four animals who resembled overweight alpacas. They called them *drif*, but Han understood that this was a purely local name—the beasts were common on most agritultural worlds and had been spread because of their adaptability. They followed a narrow, pale road winding over the rolling landscape. It was the only road into or out of Ghazh'in.

The three of them took turns driving, while one slept, and one kept the watch as a lookout. This perplexed Han until Bazh'ingil told him stories about miscellaneous ghosts, bandits and ravenous predators which could be encountered. But during the trip, they saw no more than Han had seen on his walk to Ghazh'in from the place where his life raft had landed. Furtive suggestions of movement in the dark —an occasional wailing cry. Nothing more. The land was empty. Whatever one could say about Chalcedon, it certainly had plenty of room, room enough for many people.

Finally, on the fifth day, they arrived at the market town, a place which the ler of Ghazh'in called Hovzhar, but which Dardenglir told Han was actually an old human town which had been called Hobb's Bazaar. It was now mostly ler. They named places with two syllables with the same persistence they named themselves with three. He asked if it had ever had a ler name. It had not. They were content to call it by a worn-down form of the old human name, which they had all along.

Hobb's Bazaar was a sizable community of both peoples, now mostly ler, which served an extensive hinterland as a trade center and depot for farm produce. Dardenglir was animated and excited. "Back to civilization," he cried, pounding the plank seat of the wagon with the palm of his hand. Bazh'ingil, taciturn as ever, expected to be cheated and pronounced anathemas on all, indiscriminately, of the region. "A vile lot of rascals and thieves," was all Han could get out of him. Bazh'ingil, rather short and stocky for a ler, contrived to look as short and belligerent and uncouth as he could as they were driving through the streets of the town.

To Han's eyes, Hobb's Bazaar was quaint and old-fashioned. It was a wooden town with high, angular buildings, most of which had high, peaked roofs, apparently for decoration, since the region had no snow or heavy rains.

The streets were made of cobblestones, mostly poorly laid, and everything was painted in bright and clashing colors.

But inhabited by thieves or not, they were able to dispose of their goods with a tidy profit, Han helping, haggling in his new found gift of Singlespeech, even if it was still shaky and accented. He had made mincemeat of a couple of merchants, who were very uncomfortable, being accustomed to fleecing the farmers of the local area. By the evening, they had cleared out the wagon and partially filled it again with supplies to go back, and all three of them were feeling expansive and generous.

Dividing up the profits, of which there was a considerable sum left over, they offered Han half, to his surprise. At first he refused, arguing in fairness for fifths, but they reminded him that in ler usage, the braid was a single entity, a "person," and its share could not be divided. Moreover, their half was much larger than they had expected to get. So, in the end, Han agreed, and they repaired to an outdoor restaurant where something was being roasted whole over a sumptuous smoky wood fire, which filled the whole town with the odor of woodsmoke and roast mingled. Meat! Han could not remember the last time he had eaten a nice greasy roast. Ler farmers did not eat much meat, not because they were vegetarians, but because square foot for square foot, they could develop and raise vegetable protein more efficiently. But it seemed years, although a logical part of his mind said that he had been on Chalcedon only a few months, perhaps half a standard year.

The three of them loaded up plates, took tankards of fresh ale, and sat down at a rickety table to eat and enlarge upon the day's profits. The evening went through its slow blue and purple evolutions, at the measured pace of Chalcedon, and they ate on, refilling their tankards from time to time. They were in the latter stages of the last bits of roast when Han noticed a motion, a figure, out of the corner of his eye. He looked, through the dust and gathering darkness. It was Liszendir.

He got up quickly, and excusing himself, walked quickly towards her. She seemed disoriented, and as he came closer to her he could see that she was bedraggled, dusty and thin. She also carried her arms in a peculiar way, gingerly, as if she were carrying hot coals, or hot potatoes, or perhaps very delicate flowers. She did not see Han at all until he was almost upon her. Ignoring the stares of the crowd and the

amazement on the faces of Dardenglir and Bazh'ingil. he
touched her shoulder and opened his arms to her. She fell
into them, grasping Han with a strong. steady grip which
did not relax for a long time. She buried her face in his chest
and clung to him like a child. After a long time, she released
her grip and stood back. Her eyes were red, but there were
no tears in them. They did not speak.

Han led her to the table, where they immediately made a
place for her, sending the potboy off for another platter of
roast. While she ate, Han performed the introductions; she
started slow, as if she had never seen food before, but as
the long evening wore into night, she progressed slowly but
steadily through three servings of roast, two plates of vege-
tables, and three tankards of ale. She did not talk, but only
nodded politely at an occasional remark, and now and then
raised an eyebrows at Han's use of her language.

At last she finished. The four of them made some small
talk for a little while, but not too long thereafter the two
from Ghazh'in admitted that they had to leave for bed, so
they could get an early start back tomorrow. After all,
with only two driving. it was a longer way back. So in the
end, Han and Liszendir were alone again. She sat very still,
staring into nothing, immersed deep within her own thoughts.
Her eyes drooped, and finally closed; she relaxed in the
crude chair. Han paid the bill, picked her up, and carried her
to the inn. She was as light as a feather.

Liszendir slept for three days, in a deep sleep which displayed no hint at all of any struggles or remembrances she
might be replaying. While she slept, Han cleaned her up
and doctored her scratches and bruises as well as he was
able, with the advice and guidance of a cranky herbalist who
operated a nostrum shop next to the inn. Slowly, the color
came back to her skin, and the tone to her muscles. On the
evening of the third day she woke up. She said nothing for a
long time, staring out the window which ran narrowly from
floor to ceiling, watching the square below under an overcast
sky, where human and ler haggled and strove for advantage
just as they had days, years before. It was a scene ten thousand years old. Finally she spoke.

"You can see for yourself that I failed, and cost us the
ship."

"To tell the truth, I was more concerned with you than I
was with the ship. I had given up hope."

"You are kind. But it is so, nevertheless. And he will

be back. If so, then we are captured; if not, we remain stranded. And I have lost some of myself, as well."

She held her hands up. The wrists were still swollen, out of alignment. Han felt something bitter worming its corrosive way through his emotions; both wrists had been broken.

"Yes. As you see."

She was silent again for a time. But she began to talk, slowly, hesitantly, and so gradually the tale unfolded. She was reluctant to tell it all, but it all came out anyway. After she had ejected Han, she had gone hunting for Hath'ingar; he had been elusive, and had kept his distance well, apparently trying to set up an ambush. But she had caught him, and for a time gotten the gun away from him, but in doing so, she would not use it, and it was then that he had caught her and broken her wrists. By superhuman effort, she had gotten away from him, but she knew she was as good as finished. With all her abilities, she had just barely had the edge on Hath'ingar—now the advantage had fallen to him. The first chance she got, she made her escape the same way Han had left, using the life raft. He let her get away. He didn't care. He knew she could not survive.

But she did survive. She had landed somewhere far to the west, in completely uninhabited lands, wide prairies. The food concentrate in the raft made her ill, from some trace element present or not present. So she started hunting. It had been a problem at first, with two useless hands, but somehow she managed. Worms. Grubs. Small animals. Berries. Leaves. Finally, she had come to an isolated settlement, where, surprisingly enough, word had drifted in that a spaceman had crashed and taken up living in a tiny village called Ghazh'in. She had not waited, but started out immediately, moving cross-country to cut time down to size. By the time she had gotten as far as Hobb's Bazaar, she had just about reached the end of her endurance. She estimated that she had walked sixteen hundred miles across the planet. The wild food had made her sick, too, but she had kept it down. She had to.

Finally she said, "I don't know any more. I learned no more from Hath'ingar, if that is indeed his real name. He sneered at mine, so I think the name he gave us is false. But for now we have failed. And if it is at all possible, we must get off this planet; people know you and I live. He will come back, he said so, and he will hunt us to the ends of the universe." It was the first time Han had seen her admit defeat, or fear.

She lifted the bedcovers gingerly and looked down at her bare body. She was scrubbed clean, and the scratches and scrapes she had come to know so well had been started on the way to being healed. Some were already disappearing, although she would bear some of those fine scars to the end of her days.

"You did this? You?"

"Yes. You had a much harder time of it than I did. And you needed care. Better by me, strange as I am to you, than with strangers, or so I thought you might think. There is much I don't understand about the way your people think, but I know much more now than I did when I saw you last." He spoke now in her language, and then, halting and stumbling over the odd and cabalistic way the four meanings lay within the single roots, he told her his story, all he had done and learned at Ghazh'in. At last, he finished.

"You have seen much, learned much, penetrated far into us, here. That, at least, is not for nothing. And though your accent is barbarous, worse than Hath'ingar's when his mask was off, it sounds sweet to my ear." She reached to him and embraced him, holding him tightly to her for a long time. Han felt embarrassed, confused by this sudden display of emotion, so uncharacteristic of her. She had apparently become completely unhinged during her long walk.

She sensed his thoughts. "I was alone, absolutely alone. I have never been alone in my life before. I saw visions sometimes, I could not tell if I were remembering or seeing something new. Old lovers, friends. You. I was confused. And so I finally find you, here, and you are not the proper human any more, but you speak to me in Singlespeech, *poor kenjureith,* and heal me as would the most intimate bodyfriend. Only one more event between us and I will have to tell you my body-name, something I have never told anyone outside my braid."

He let her run out of steam, and she gradually fell into a pensive silence once again. Han got up from his place beside her where he had been sitting, and after a quick rummaging through an ancient and much-used wardrobe, produced a new overrobe he had bought for her, which was embroidered with designs in vines and flowers according to the bucolic tastes of the region.

"I know it's not your style, Liszendir, but I thought

something like this might attract less attention, as we traveled. People would probably take you for a native. As if a pair like us could not but attract attention, even if we were dressed in grain sacks."

She threw her head back and laughed aloud. Then she shut it off, abruptly. She was herself again, certain, brash. "So now what of us?"

"I'm not sure at all. I do know there is little likelihood we will get off Chalcedon in the near future, possibly in the conceivable future. The *Pallenber* was the first ship since Efrem's, and his was the first in ten years. Chalcedon is very far off the normal lanes. And if the Warriors don't come back, we can count on being stuck here. Until you are fertile."

"Like that?"

"Yes. I had thought to head for the hill of the two pinnacles, where we were to meet. We could try to get some money and wait for the first ship. But we could not go to the Capital for any period of time . . ."

"No. 'One rat, another,' goes the proverb. And so it is. We can't wait for a ship in the Capital. But why not the hills. There is no better way, at least until we feel the pressure of time on me."

"And if nothing comes, Liszendir?" He did not finish. He knew very well what would happen. They would have to go their own ways, the ways of their people; and something undefined was taking shape between them.

"I know," It was all she said.

V

―――◆―――

"Events follow definite trends each according to its nature. Things are distinguished from one another in definite classes. In this way change and transformation become manifest."

—Hsi Tz'u Chuan, *I Ching,* Introduction.

Han and Liszendir stayed in the inn at Hobb's Bazaar for only a few more days, until she had begun to recover her strength, at least enough to travel. During the long walk, her wrists had started healing, but they had not been reset properly, and so, although they were regaining their function again, especially with the enforced rest Han was insisting on, she would bear the mark of their disalignment the rest of her life. Liszendir offered no more intimacies, and Han cautiously avoided any situations likely to produce them.

When she announced she was ready, together they took the money Han had made and bought up a store of provisions and a pack beast, a *drif,* similar to the ones of the team which had pulled the wagon to Hobb's Bazaar. This one was slightly smaller, however, and it definitely possessed a livelier personality than either of those in the team.

Neither Liszendir nor Han were particularly knowledgeable with animals; but with much trying, they eventually got it to behave more or less as they wanted, all to the general entertainment of the stablemaster and his louts and hangers-on. After the initial trying session, they led it through the streets with a light bit and halter. Liszendir favored the *drif* with an evil leer, then turned to Han in resigned disgust.

"One thing is certain: if all else fails, we can at least eat the intractable beast!" At the tone of her remarks, which he sensed was not completely to his advantage, the *drif* raised a ragged eyebrow, lowered an ear, and thereupon seemed to behave with slightly more decorum. Liszendir was unimpressed; she continued to glare at it from time to time. She was still hungry. Han grimaced and added, for emphasis, a few remarks of his own.

"And on the hoof might even be more effective. Then it can serve both ways!" He also leered at it meaningfully. "If we can find any meat at all under this fluff." He poked experimentally in the general area of the ribs. The creature was covered with a fine rich pelt of light tan-brown color.

Despite Han's suspicions, however, the *drif* did have meat under the soft fur, and for all its seeming fragility, would carry a huge load without complaint. In fact, it misbehaved only when it had no load.

Thus they set out for the hills to the southeast, where they had originally intended to meet. Curiously, Liszendir was reluctant, when it came to it, to leave Hobb's Bazaar; but she admitted readily the wisdom of it. The two of them together attracted too much attention, too much curiosity. It was true that ler and human both lived in peace on Chalcedon; but they did not yet cohabit. Han and Liszendir were not intimate, but they had been together, and he noted that a new side of her personality had appeared since they had gotten back together, after she had wandered, dazed, into the market. She was more relaxed, less peremptory, less standoffish. Sometimes she could be as charming as a child, innocently affectionate, and full of unexpected turns of thought and word. She was not the only one changing; he was noticing changes in himself as well.

Along the empty road to the south and east, they passed few travelers. An occasional wagon, a herd of *drif* being driven by country louts who gaped in astonishment at them, and at anything else which happened to pass. As they walked, Han outlined his plan.

"We cannot live in the Capital. We both agree there is a high probability of spies. Yet we must live somewhere within reach until a ship comes in. We could farm, I suppose, but I know neither you nor I are knowledgeable. I have thought that if we can find a deposit in the hills, we could pan for gold or other stuff. It has no great value here, but it could support us — we could make short trips to the edge of the city for food supplies."

"And what if no ship ever comes?" she asked, looking intently at Han.

He did not answer her for a long time, even though he knew the answer well enough. Finally he spoke.

"If all else fails, then I suppose you will have to weave here, within a few years." They did not speak again for some time.

At last the ground began to rise above the gentle ups and downs of the Chalcedon landscape. After that, which had taken many days of travel to reach, it was not long before they sighted the two pinnacles they were looking for. The last time they had seen them, it had been from the city; that now seemed years ago; time was distorted on this world of long days and no seasons. Long ago, Han had disposed of his chronometer, which was set to standard time. The one with a variable rate setting for spacefarers who might land on many different worlds was far behind, somewhere with the *Pallenber*, wherever it was.

They turned off the road and climbed the hill towards the outcrops, looking for a suitable site. To their surprise, they found soon a small abandoned cabin, human in style, but sturdy and comfortable. Nearby was a shallow stream of clear sweet water tumbling over a sandy bed in which gleamed specks of gold. Nearby were remains of industry— rotted chutes and spillways, pans and shovels; the owner was long gone.

Han speculated that the owner had been one of the original settlers, a fellow who had come up to the pinnacles alone to pan for gold. He had hit upon a rich field. But gold was common on the planet, and so had no real value anywhere except at the port, and even then only when ships came in. So what would, anywhere else, have been instant riches, became only a source of isolation. And eventually, perhaps many years later, he became sick, and with no one near, died. Liszendir agreed with the scenario, but added another thought.

"I do not worry he will return. These tools, structures, and so forth show evidence of long time upon them. He left or died long ago. It only underlines how little we know— that we do not know how long Chalcedon has been settled. I have been guilty of making the assumption that it was only in the last few years, but it appears roots here go deeper than we thought."

"Yes. And as you see that, I see that it may have been long enough for the ler settlers at the isolated village of Ghazh'in to abandon Common as a working language. That would mean that they did not teach it to the children, not that they forgot, because I know your memories work differently from ours. They would not forget, but they might not pass it on."

"You open doors of speculations into which I do not care to look, less walk through."

"But I do not, having the disregard for personal welfare which characterizes us ancestral primates. No, I am not aiming that at you. But consider: Chalcedon has been kept a secret. And we were sent out here, untold, as if it was just next door. I know technology shrinks distances, but this is too far. Now: Hetrus was chief, for the humans, at that meeting. Who was boss for the ler? Not you, you are an adolescent, you have no standing or status to speak for society until you have been woven and given birth. Not Yalvarkoy or Lenkurian Haoren, either, although they may have known. That other one we can discount as a spy from somewhere else, who wanted us killed. So who is left? Defterdhar Srith the elder. Who is she and what does she know?"

"Defterdhar Srith is very old and wise, but more than that I know little of her. She is not of the braid of those who assume responsibility for Kanten. She has a reputation of being one who will ultimately be called among the wise. Some call her *diskenosi mnathman*—the fifteenth sage. There are only fourteen."

"But as you suggest, we can open the door, but we cannot go into it very far."

"No. Possibilities, possibilities."

They spent the next few days in making the little cabin habitable. The cleaning was easy. Repair they managed by cannibalizing superfluous parts of the cabin and the sheds attached to it. For recreation, they made little side trips, exploring the area around the cabin. It was during one of these explorations that Liszendir found a skeleton, far up the stream, near its source, which was a tiny spring trickling water out of a cleft in the rock. She examined the bones carefully, and pronounced the skeleton a human one, from the structure of the hands and jaw. Ler did not have wisdom teeth. Han was not superstitious, but he felt uncomfortable in the presence of this reminder of mortality. But to the contrary, Liszendir called it a good omen, and immediately became noticeably more animated and personable. Han was mystified at her behavior.

She said, "No, no, this is not bad! This is a good sign, a good omen. I have been looking for something to lend depth to this place. Tone. This is very good! I will explain."

He agreed to listen, suspecting that he was in for another long explanation. Han was beginning to suspect that the reason why ler society was so static was that all their energy went into producing the next generation and keeping it stable for the future.

She continued, "You know about us now, that when you have woven, had your children, and raised them, you are free and often go off on your own. Many become solitaries. So the person, alone, feels this end near—then he goes out, alone, doing what we call *tsanziraf*, cure-seeking. Sometimes it heals and you know you were wrong—it was not yet time. Other times it brings the end. At any rate, it solves the problem. There is much wild land on ler worlds, and *tsanziraf* must be in the wild. So when you terminate on one, you lie where you fall. We do not dispose of the dead—they dispose of themselves. Perhaps I should not tell you so much—this is high religion. But it is so; just so. The body returns to the earth. To find skeletons in the wild is a good omen because it means that someone was there, fulfilled."

"But that's a human skeleton, not ler. For all we know he wasn't at peace, or even satisfied; hell, he was probably scared half out of his wits."

She dismissed his objections with an airy wave. "No matter, no matter. So it was a human, the prospector? Think— such a one would have to be at some peace with himself to travel space and then walk out here all alone. I know gold lures, but it does not change nature, however much we might wish it so. Could you do this? You will say no and give me a thousand rationalizations; you are young, you wish company, mates, lovers, make a living after the lights of your own kind. I know because I feel exactly the same way. I would not come out here. I cannot live alone." For a moment she stopped, and became pensive, abstracted. Then she continued again. "Even now, I should be making

the first tentative steps toward seeking insiblings. And at
fertility, weave and bear children. But him, now. So he
was probably greedy. So he was disappointed. But if he
stayed, I know he would have eventually seen within—
humans can do it too, the only difference between us there
is that you have to want it more than we do. Otherwise he
would not have stayed, and ended his days in the city
yonder, hiding from himself with other old people."

But they had to admit that, omen or not, the place possessed a wild beauty all its own. The cabin was situated
about two-thirds of the way up a rocky defile which ran
parallel with the line of the ridge. At the top were the two
pinnacles which could be seen on the horizon from the
Capital. There were trees all around, in some places becoming thickets, and the stream wound through the defile,
saying the things streams felt important to say—comments
about humus and rock, rain and long days of sun and
shadow. The sunlights played among the heights, and down
in the plains below, cloud shadows prowled over the land
in the slow and measured way of Chalcedon weather. In
the defile, there was a breeze most of the time. And from
the pinnacles, the view was uncommonly magnificent for a
planet with such generally low relief. True, it was a lonely,
isolated place, but it was quiet, conducive to thought, and
the morning light slanting into it from the east was lovely.

After a few days of living and working together, things
slowed down to the point where they realized that they
had now a certain problem between them: they were now
too close to each other, both in physical proximity, due to
the close confines of the cabin and their common fate since
arriving on Chalcedon, and in a certain emotional sense,
which both of them felt apprehension about exploring. One
night, after supper, the day they had finished arranging the
cabin to suit them, they fell into a discussion about this.

Han started it by admitting that he found their closeness
more disturbing now than when they had been together on
the ship. She only laughed, teasing and provoking him.

"How so? In Ghazh'in you lived for months with ler,
fertile ler. But they neither molested you nor buggered you
in your sleep!"

"You know it's not the same with us."

"Ah, now. That I know. All too well." After that, she
lapsed into a serious, brooding silence. But he wanted her to

talk, and seriously. Something had been bothering her since he had known her, something about ler which she could not or would not express. So he tried to steer her to more openness by asking about herself, her people. He had learned much at Ghazh'in, but not so much he could do without her insights. She cooperated, and opened up as he had never seen before.

He began, "I have always thought of ler as just something like another race or culture of men; distant enough so that we could not crossbreed, of course, but like that, nothing more."

"No. It is not like that at all. We are different in more ways than you know. You see it as a cultural difference—and that it is, but there is much more underlying it. Your people have forgotten how it began, but we never do."

She continued, "Look at your own kind. You have the comfort of ignorance about your origins. You have the option of following evolution, and the unknowable part of science, or otherwise believing in creation myths that aren't scientific, but at least they cover everything. The first is a process only, in which no instant of time is more significant than the other, the latter significance without process. Either way, you arise of primal chaos. Ah, but we cannot delude ourselves with either. We were *made*. A product, like a new kind of screwdriver. To bring a race into the universe with no more thought than designing bathroom fixtures! Your scientists were playing with truly cosmic laws, more lunatic than a child playing with a nuclear weapon trigger. Pragmatism! Experimentation! And in almost total ignorance!" She grew agitated, angry.

"So, Han, we know they wanted to see if they could breed the supermen they had always dreamed of. So they played with human DNA, they arranged matings. They raised whole generations in laboratories under accelerated growth, creatures who never saw consciousness, may the *One* blight them with eternal senility. Now I tell you that evolution is both multiplex and multifarious. Common is awkward here, but I know an ancient Russian word that fits perfect: *raznoöbrazny*—of various features. But nobody knows all its laws, all its realities. Not humans, not ler. So when finally the coherent form appeared, it was just like magic to them—actions and incantations. They had reached the next stage of self-resonance. Like music. The next half-tone. Without knowing anything about chromatic scales.

Better, the next chord. Or like physics—the next stable element. Magic, magic. I shudder at what they played with in their arrogance. But they were happy and so made many. They knew how. And they raised us in little camps. But the Firstborn knew what was going on—they could see with intuition better, so they knew. So they isolated themselves in tribalism, studied primitivity. They *were* primitive. You had ten thousand years to design a culture to fit you—we had to leap from creation into the second century atomic without so much as a wiggle. Out of nothing, they made a culture for us.

"Then the humans found out that they could not crossbreed with us. They had attained the superman very well, but it could never do them any good! Supreme irony! They reached for the impossible, and got it—but they couldn't use it! And they realized one truth, that it was like *Homo sapiens* and its relatives in the far past. Different. Maybe not higher or better. Just different. Six thousand of us, with a low birthrate, so low that if we weeded ourselves in the interest of stability of our genetic line, it took us generations to recover our numbers. And on a planet of fifteen billion humans. So they used us, until many years later we escaped.

"So it is true we have abilities you do not: you make much of eidetic memory, but with retaining everything comes the problem of what to do with it—so we also have the ability to forget. And it is not like what you call forgetting. With you it is misplacement, not loss. With us, it is loss, completely. And when we edit, we have to be so careful, because one slip and you have lost everything. Of course, there can be no torture—because you cannot scare a secret out of someone who can forget everything, even that he exists. We have better vision, because light has the broadest bandwidth of all natural sensors; two extra colors at each end of your spectrum and eight wavelength receivers instead of three.

"But liabilities, Han. We have no special night vision. That is why we turn in with the end of day—we have only color vision at night, and it's less sensitive at low levels. And what about the low birthrate and short fertility, timed like one of the animals in the field? It is said that this is one of the laws of evolution—that the higher the form, the more consciousness it has and the less instinct, the lower the birthrate . . . and everything else, too, our size, our hands. Or the appearance of youth you envy us for. Yes, we know about that. It is only neoteny, the retention and expansion of youthful characteristics, supplanting more mature ones. And the sex of adolescence. They gave it to us on purpose and not for our pleasure—it was so we would be so obsessed with it that we would have little time for anything else. And so it is sweet, body-love, but we never can confuse it with anything else, anything more than that. It is casual, everyday, mildly affectionate. Love is rare.

"You want to know how it is? I will tell you: it is twenty years of fun, pleasure, intense feelings, but fruitless, fruitless. But we fear fertility, because it is more than fun then, we almost have no choice. That is why all the elaboration with structure—it is too powerful to be treated any other way. Why do you think we would make something as complicated as a braid if we did not have good reason? It is to retain some vestige of control over who shall be born and what we shall look like after instinct has run its course. And that is why it does not last for life, too. We would not design such a thing for the exercise of intellectual curiosity.

"You did not see this with the ones you visited with. The insiblings of that braid, Bazh'ingil and Pethmirian, were already becoming infertile. For the others, they were waiting for it to start up again—it would be a year or two before Tanzernan becomes fertile again. She and Dardenglir—they may like each other, as *people*, they may hate each other; it will make no difference, none whatsoever. The desire overcomes everything. The insiblings will not envy them, they will pity them, for they had all their lives to get used to one another; those two outsiblings are relative strangers, and what they will do is beyond their control. Have you not wondered that our elders live alone, when they can? They do so out of choice, not necessity, and they are *grateful* for it."

"But, Liszendir, what about one's loves before weaving? Why not weave with them? And what happens after the weaving is done? What then? Glad to be alone or not, do they wander in the woods and wrestle with desires like fasting anchorites?"

She laughed, shortly, an unpleasant sound. It was a laugh, but there was no humor in it. "Were it so. But it is not. Each step forward in evolution, however halting, however sidewards, means that each process becomes fractionally more finished. For us this means that when fertility is over, all of us undergo something related to menopause, like human females. But all of us. Males alike. And ours is more finished: when it is done, we do not want sex, nor do we have the ability to have it."

She was near tears, as close as he had ever seen her. Not anger, not hurt, but realizations of finality. "We call it the sadness. Why? Because we can remember so well, the exact degree. Eidetic memory can also be a curse. We have no subconscious. So we remember it all, not impressions and composites and special significances. Exact scenes, just as they occurred. This is how I have kept myself from you. I simply remember others. You see only the sex. The fun. The irresponsibility. But how we pay later. Think of how it must be: you have a lover, with whom you have shared body-love for many years, you feel the deep kindness for each other. Then you are woven and you are separated. Insiblings pick you—you do not say no to them without good reason. And when you see your lover again, years after, you are free but the two of you can do nothing except remember how it was. It is painful.

"But for insiblings it is worse. *Nerh* and *thes* are encouraged to roam, to wander, to sleep around. After all, they have to weave with strangers. But insiblings cannot; they grow into one another. We do not forbid sex at home, no taboos, but come what may, they have to stay together. And since they are the same age, they compete and fight constantly."

"You didn't answer why not just do like we do, two by two?"

"Because our genes are unstable. We cannot risk ever developing even a recognizable family trait. It could lead to races, subraces, special populations. Each species has a unique rate of mutation. Artificially developed breeds have very high rates. And we have such a one."

"I didn't know . . ."

"It is a marvel that all do not autoforget into oblivion. Some do. But it is rare. But not unknown."

She fell into silence. Outside, it had become quite dark, and Han could see her face dimly lit, in the darkness. He knew, now, he could see more of her than she could of him, although she could probably track him accurately enough by scent and sound. Far away, in the trees and rocks, some unknown animal bayed at the stars. Liszendir sighed, once, very deeply.

"And so we come to us. You have spoken of desire to me but your acts have spoken deeper. And I am adolescent, hungry for love. In my eyes you are too close to the wild, too angular, but not unlovely. And you have been kind, knowing. All that has passed makes me feel something deep I know I cannot handle so easily. But nothing can come of it. We have no future. Do you not see it?"

He could not answer, immediately. It was far too close to his very thoughts at that moment. He knew a deep secret about himself—he had changed from the "easy come, easy go" attitude he had held about love. Fun, play. Not so. It was deadly serious. And for them, there was another difficulty.

He said, "Is it also true that your love-acts last longer than ours?"

"You needn't be tactful. It is true. Longer and more often. Both ler sexes have multiple capacity. So it is cruel for you and me to be around each other. What could we do, save that you burn out my heart, and I burn out your interest in love-play."

It expressed what he felt perfectly. And it was a dilemma he could not answer. He felt a tension in the small cabin, a need for some kind of action; it was as close as they had ever come to what had always lain between them, so close that it fit the old saying perfectly: "If it had been a snake it would have bitten them." Both. But he got up, and began to gather the pots and bowls up from supper. As he busied himself around the cabin, Liszendir vanished outside; shortly, he could hear her splashing in the stream.

By the time he had finished, she was returning, wearing a fresh robe, to hang the old one out to dry on the porch. Han left then to go to the stream and wash. There, the icy water chilled him, but only the skin. The old wives' tales were no more true here than they were about anything else. It did nothing to a deeper fire that was burning inside him. The night was unusually cool. Scrubbed, Han climbed to the top of the broken rock of the nearer pinnacle and looked out on the plains to the south. Far in the distance, a thunderstorm was being born, moving invisibly, already rivaling the weak lights of the Capital, glory without effort, rearing above the dark, silent, enduring plains. In the low winds of Chalcedon it might stay in that place for hours. Han watched

it flicker for a while, too far away for the thunder to reach
him, and then, with a deep sigh, climbed down and returned to the cabin.

He entered the cabin, catching a trace of the odor of
clean female, a warm, grassy scent that was intoxicating.
He did not hesitate nor edit what he felt.

"Liszendir? . . ." He waited a moment, then asked, softly,
"Liszen . . ." Her love name sounded strange as he said it.

A bundle of quilts in the corner opened itself, to reveal
a pale form in the darkness.

She said only, "I have been waiting for you to say that."
There was a softness in the voice he had never heard before.

"Liszen, let us take what happiness we can as we have it."

He touched the still form, the smooth pale skin. It was
cool, like the night air, but underneath there was fire. She
said something softly, breathing the words; they were words
he did not understand at all: Multispeech. He didn't understand the words, as he knelt beside her, his knee touching
her thigh, but he knew their message; they were sad, tender,
loving, passionate—all at once.

He felt the desire take him, loosing his grips on reality.
Her face, close and pale, gleamed in the dark like a lantern,
all afire. How could he ever have seen her as plain, tom-
boyish? She was lovely, utterly feminine. Before he went
completely under, he had time for one last sane question,
which he remembered asking, idiotically, like the popular
song tunes you can't get out of your head, for the rest of his
life.

"Do you kiss?" He still wondered if they had taboos.

She answered with a sudden fluid movement. Han was
unable to speak coherently for a very long time. Darkness
closed over him, removing every reality except one. Darkness and fire.

From that night on, they entered a totally new dimension in their relationship. Within their new framework, they
had no guideposts, no knowledge of how to act with one
another. Only emotion and appetites; so they pursued the
deep needs they felt, mingling them well with a growing
deeper emotion. Time ceased. Han saw the sun of Chalcedon,
AVILA 1381, rise and set. It meant nothing. They ate. They
slept. They made love. Liszendir was inexhaustible. Han was
not; he kept going as long as he could, but at last, he could

do no more. He collapsed in a state of complete exhaustion.

He did not know how long his final sleep was; he only knew that it was morning when he awoke. Or was it? Perhaps it was evening. Han had heard of people who could tell the difference in a strange place just by the tone of the air, but he had never been able to do it. Dazed, he tried to remember which side of the cabin got the morning sunlight. He couldn't. After a time that seemed like centuries, the shadows fractionally lengthened. The light dimmed ever so slightly. He felt warmth beside him. Liszendir was curled in his arms, breathing deeply. Sensing his movements, she awoke also. Her eyes were clear and bright. She stretched, smiling; Han ached, feeling her muscles move under her skin. It seemed she had voluntary control of muscles he didn't even know people had. They did not speak: what was there that could be said now between them in words?

So it endured for a time that never seemed to have an end. They spoke little, they explained no more, they recited no histories, they explored no speculations. They lost count of the days. They dismissed them with a laugh. They were, as Liszendir put it, "locked into the present. There is no more past, no more future; no more *me* and *thee*." They took a full measure of delight in the smallest, most ordinary things they did, and she took to going about during the warmth of the day completely bare. Han grew to appreciate deeply the firm, compact, pale body; everything about her was subtle, economical, graceful. To his eyes, she resembled in build more a human of oriental race, but the face and hair were different, and in the cool air of early morning, her skin was pale ivory, shadowed and flushed with pink.

She did not demand. They both knew she could easily outendure Han in what they were doing; so she conserved him, saved him. And teased, provoked, and tormented him.

They ran out of food. Han collected a few things together, loaded the *drif*, and journeyed over the plains to the outskirts of the city and traded what in Boomtown would have been a fortune in gold dust for a few more weeks. He returned to the pinnacles without learning any more about the Warriors, and he and Liszendir resumed again where they left off.

Very gradually, they began to talk again; at first it was just short anecdotes out of the past, shallow remembrances, but soon they began to flesh out the problem they shared again.

It was a warm night, with a thinning overcast which had served to keep the heat of the day in longer than usual. They sat by the stream, close together, arms around each other, and talked. Liszendir spoke first.

"Now it is different with us, you call me by my love-name, Liszen, or by my body-name, Izedi. That is good: it is your right and my pleasure. This has been a lovely time in my life. But there is no sign that any ship will ever come, so you know that this must end as we have foretold."

"I had hoped to forget, Izedi." He used the body-name more and more, now. It was a special thing, certain letters extracted in order out of her full-name, which could only be used according to ler custom by someone who had deep body-ties to the one so named.

"And I also, dear Han. But my body does not. Will not. With it I cannot pretend. Already I can sense the beginning of some changes; small things, true, but changes. Now time remains to us, good years, if we wish. And I do wish it—with all my heart."

"I know nothing else we can do but stay here and pass the days as we have done, as long as we can."

She spoke hesitantly, shyly. "The closer in time we come to my fertility, the less I will want you—what we do will not be enough to fill the emptiness, do you know that? But never mind. Listen: sometimes in late adolescence this very thing that we know happens to ler couples, too. So they make a vow, a promise, to return to each other, after weaving, bearing and raising, knowing that when it does come, it will be unlike it was before to them. Some promise, many fail. But will you consider this thing?"

"What?"

"That wherever you are, I will come to you again after everything is done. Would you accept me then as I will be? We will not be able to do it, then. No more *dhainaz*."

"What about your people, your ways, your own plans? You would give all that up for the hope of something forty years away?"

"Indeed I would. What is our living for except to be happy? Only fools think life is all duty. For the body, I can do nothing about that, but all the rest, the culture, the special things . . . they are just mannerisms. I can learn more." She took a deep breath, looked at Han closely.

"There is much you do not know yet, much I want to tell you, but I can't, yet. But I can tell you this, now. Each of us has a sign. Mine is fire, and it is associated with the will. With will comes the ease to make mistakes, to go against. I do it, thus."

He thought long about this. It was one thing to promise for a love that could be fulfilled now; another to say, one part now, another part in forty years. Who could know what the future could bring? But he remembered the things they had said and done, the still white form in the dark of the cabin, the graceful figure walking bare in the stream, shining with water, the soft, short, silky hair.

"Yes. It is strange to me, stranger than all we have done. But I will see it in the end, if I can."

"Good. Then I will come to you. You will be traveling among the stars, trading, but I will know when it is finished for me, on whatever planet I live on then, Kenten or Chalcedon." The stream before them rambled on in its unending discourse, as they fell into silence again.

After a time, Han arose and went up to the pinnacles, to look out over the land and think about how it would be then, when they were much older. As he came to the top of the ridge by the broken rocks, he looked to the south, and felt ice in his heart. There were lights over the area of the city, lights which moved together, slowly. A bulk darker than darkness lay behind them; and Han knew that it could be only one thing.

He stood for a long time, looking at the lights of a huge ship, one in the darkness whose true size could not be guessed. Liszendir, noticing his long absence, joined him quietly, so that he did not know she was there until he felt her warm hip pressed against his. She said nothing, but she looked at the lights for as long as he had.

Finally she spoke, bitterly. "There is a ship."

"I don't believe it will be going the way we want, Liszen."

"No. But we may yet ride it."

"Do you think they will hunt for us?"

"I know it with the same certainty that I know we cannot escape them. And even if I were whole in my wrists again, and you were armed to the teeth, it would be nothing against the numbers they must have in that thing."

As if in answer to what Liszendir had said, the cluster of lights began to move, slowly gaining altitude, moving north, towards them. Han saw the movement, and started violently. Liszendir watched for a moment, and then laid her hand on his arm.

"Not tonight. They can't see us from that thing. They will come later." The dark mass and lights moved into the clouds overhead. But they could still see some of the lights. It moved majestically northwards, and then disappeared.

She motioned to him. "Run the *drif* off; he will fare. And come inside with me. We will have one more night, at least."

Han half expected not to wake up again. Thinking it very well might prove to be their last time together, they had outdone themselves; she had been exquisite, delicious. He yearned to take her again, but he knew as he awoke that he could not. He left her, warm and half-sleeping, and started out of the house to the stream. He was only a few feet from the cabin when he became aware of an incongruity in the now-familiar landscape. He looked again. It was Hath'ingar. And many more. The *Pallenber*, unmarked and undamaged, had been grounded and sat placidly, somewhat down the defile, shining in the early morning sunlight. He looked back to the cabin, hesitantly. Liszendir stood in the doorway, looking quietly out on the scene in the dooryard.

Hath'ingar broke the silence. "Bravo, bravo! You see the wisdom of inaction! You cannot run, you cannot fight. There is hope in no direction. And of course no one else will come. You must wish to know how I came here so easily. It is simple. No magic, no powerful instruments. Just good ears. I heard her say to you on the ship that she would meet you here. So I came here also. I agree with you—you have excellent taste: this is indeed a fine place."

Han was steady. "What do you want of us?"

"Really, little enough to fear. I am revenged for my ear, as you and she doubtless know by now. In other circumstances I would be tempted to seek more, but she is a highly trained fighter and much more valuable than the petty satisfactions of personal pique. We have many uses for such as her on Dawn."

Liszendir said plainly, "I will not aid you. I will autoforget before then, and you can treat the remainder as you will." It was a good threat. Total autoforgetting would erase her personality. The body would respond, but Liszendir

would no longer be in it. Han felt a deadness inside. Yes—
she would be beyond the reach of pain. And pleasure.

"I think not. Your pet, here. You would not see him
treated unkindly? So none of us would. You can escape inwards, but he can't. So by certain arts, if it came to that,
he would remember you forever, and us, of course. And
little else. But let us not descend to such a level. Besides, I
wish you no bizarrity. You, Liszendir, will breed and teach
the Warriors. No indignity. Share and share alike. Leave
these four-bred weaklings. The Warriors will engulf them all
in time."

Han asked, "What about me, Hath'ingar?"

"You have a certain value. You appear to be close to
the, let me see, ah, yes, the Mnar-geseniz type, and doubtless
capable mechanically. I have no interest myself in that
breed, you understand this is nothing personal, but I can
sell or trade you on Dawn. Who knows? If you two conduct yourselves respectfully, I may even sell you to her,"
he said, gesturing at Liszendir. "If she can afford my price.
You, Han are a trader. So am I, in my very own small way."

Han saw motion out of the corner of his eye: the ship of
the Warriors was returning from the north, bulking over the
horizon. As it came closer, Han realized that its size was far
beyond any artifact he had ever seen before. It was truly
colossal, a great fat rounded shape, somewhat conical. He
could not accurately guess its real size; it distorted scale
and measure in its immensity. Accompanying it was an
orbiting swarm of irregular blocks, each one following its
own circular path generally in the horizontal plane. Han
looked again. The blocks were apparently meteorites. One
passed under the approaching ship, passing near the ground
and a landmark Han had become familiar with. He was
impressed. That one appeared to be a good half-mile in
diameter.

Hath'ingar said, "You marvel at our ship and its toys?
That is good! Those are our weapons. They need no fuses,
no tricky timers, no magic juggling of atoms. Just good
old iron, the warrior's tool. When we need persuasion, one
goes out, to gain momentum, and back, using planetary
gravity in part. If we shoot from high over the planet, it is
even better: then we can speed them up so that they act
like real meteors when they impact. One of those beauties,
so employed, will leave a beautiful clean crater, about a

hundred miles across and several miles deep, say, a score or so. No escape, no hiding, no fortifying. And no defense.

"We expect," he continued, "to move inwards shortly and indulge ourselves to the great disadvantage of so-called civilized humankind and four-by ler. The latter we will liberate from their effeminate enervating philosophy, and the former we will own. We need more ships, but I am sure you can see we could do the task with just one."

Liszendir said calmly, "The ler will not cooperate with such a scheme."

"Then we will obliterate them. They will cease to be. And as for your nova-detonator, we know about it and fear it not. How shall you aim at a star whose location is unknown, and whose inhabitants have already left?"

From the bulk of the Warrior's ship looming nearby, as if to lend weight to Hath'ingar's words, a shuttlecraft emerged, at first looking tiny against the enormous, pitted mass. But as it approached, Han could see it was almost as large as his own ship. His and Liszendir's, the one they had lost.

Without further expostulation, Hath'ingar herded them into the shuttle as soon as it landed. Inside, they lost all view of the outside, for there were no windows or screens in the section in which they were housed. After a short, rough flight, they stopped. Then Han was herded off to one part of the large ship, while Liszendir, well guarded, was marched off another way.

He eventually found himself in a small, padded cell, which was, though secure enough, not especially harsh. It was fully equipped. The door closed. Han was immediately knocked off of his feet by a whole series of tremendous lurches. After some minutes, the violent motion stopped, or rather, subsided to the point where he could sit or stand upright. He guessed they were on their way.

Part II

DAWN

VI

―――――――◆―――――――

"Desire arises of the face and not of the body or any of its parts."

—Fellirian Deren

"Love is a thing whose degree of intensity is directly proportional to the degree of strangeness of the partners."
—Leskormai Srith (*The Tenth Sage*)

"We all interpret the new in terms of the old and are thus comforted or terrified, as the case may be. But the error to which we are prey does not lie in the area of misidentification, so much as it does in the area of scale. One may identify essentially correctly, say, for example, that an object is a mountain, and yet get the scale so wrong that the identity must be questioned. It is true that a ripple is in fact a wave, but very small ones are not of importance except to a weather-seer, medium-size ones a type of beauty, and large ones a great danger."

—The Survivor's Manual

For a certain time, Han knew nothing. The food was insipid, but self-dispensing at regular intervals from a slot in the wall, and it kept him alive and well without apparent ill effect. There seemed to be a bit more than he needed or could stomach; Han suspected that the rate of dispens-

ing had been designed for creatures with a higher caloric
requirement than humans. Namely, ler. It made sense to
him; they were slightly smaller than humans, and seemed to
eat more, or so he had noticed from observing Liszendir.
He remembered achingly the heat of her body. He suspected their normal temperature was higher, also. But he
ate the pellets, stuffing the remainder in his pockets in
case he should get hungry, which seemed remote.

Days passed, or perhaps it was weeks. Han had no way
to mark time, and all attempts he made to gather an idea
by timing his own body functions, breathing and heartbeat,
seemed to make the time stretch alarmingly long. So he
stopped that. The cell was lit, and the light stayed on, without relief. He knew very well the danger to his mind in
such an environment, but he did not think they had intended
it that way. Now and then, at irregular intervals, groups of
Warriors would come by to look in on him; they always
came in threes, and like all ler Han had met so far, mini-
mized sex differences as far as was possible. But Efrem had
heard correctly—they were a barbaric-looking lot. Some
were tattooed, males and females alike, and all wore their
hair in various odd configurations, plumes, queues, bristles,
fuzzes and indescribable concoctions. None of them spoke.

Han began playing a game with himself, to retain his
sanity. He called it, "See how much you can learn about a
ship from the sounds you can hear from its brig." It wasn't
particularly long before a definite idea began to creep into,
and then dominate, his mind. But when it came fully out
in the open, he was astounded. It came in a flood: this
ship, this colossal fortress that hurled meteors for weapons,
and was certainly capable of wrecking an entire planet,
was old and in an advanced state of decay and disrepair.
Only extreme and clever maintenance had kept it alive as
long as it had. How old was it? He had no idea; hundreds
of years, perhaps thousands. He half-recalled Liszendir's tale
about that ler rebel, Sanjirmil. The Klarkinnen. Yes. He
stopped pondering and listened.

The ship groaned and vibrated constantly, and occasionally lurched uncontrollably. Han fingered the padding material; it was new stuff, of course. This whole section seemed
new, or recently rebuilt and refurbished; and any ship would
show some modifications across time. But the material,
rather crudely woven, did not make him feel any better

about the ship. The creaking and groaning went on, and increased ominously.

He had also noted another distressing symptom: the air vent system only worked sometimes. Now and then the air in the cell would become stale, and at other times, it would develop peculiar odors. And these symptoms also seemed to become worse as time passed at its unknowable pace. Han began to grow apprehensive. Finally the lurching, shuddering, and discoordinations reached a climax. Then silence.

Not too long after the silence came, to Han's surprise, Liszendir appeared at the cell-door window, looked in, and opened the door. She had a large bag slung over her shoulder, he guessed, filled with the food concentrate pellets, and in addition had brought with her an ancient crossbow and a quiver of darts. It had to be for him. A crossbow? In a spaceship? But he took it, gratefully. The first thing he did was to cock the weapon, using an obvious foot-strap, and load it with one of the crude but deadly-looking iron darts. Liszendir was smiling, unhurt, and not even busy-looking.

"Come on! No talk, now. You won't believe it, but I really think that we can get out of this thing. We're on Dawn."

A single guard appeared in a corner of the corridor, looking confused and harried. As he or she—Han couldn't tell—caught sight of them, he shot it deftly without hesitation. The plumed Warrior sank to the floor, and the only sound it made in dying was a small groan, which apparently went unnoticed. Liszendir gave Han a look which he could not quite interpret—as if she approved of the action, but not the methodology. But she had brought him the weapon, so she intended that he use it, even though she wouldn't.

Han recocked and reloaded the arbalest, thinking dire thoughts about men who designed single-shot weapons of any sort, and hurried off down the corridor with Liszendir. She led the way through a series of tubes and halls until they were at a shuttle craft, either the one which had brought them to the ship, or one just like it.

She asked, "Can you fly it?"

"I don't know. Damn! All the controls are for hands with two thumbs, and the labels are in their characters."

"That is old writing. We used to use that system long ago. I can read it. Let's see . . . ah, this one, it says *hovgoroz*. Even the right verb form. Do you remember *hovgoroz* from your language lessons?"

"To go out. Verb of motion. Easy." He pushed the button, having an afterthought that the word could also mean escape, and in that case, how did the mechanism work? He did not want to be pitched into space again. But no, it was the right interpretation. Before them, a section of the wall opened, as a section of the shuttlecraft wall suddenly became transparent before them.

Liszendir was still puzzling out the indicators and controls. Finally she pointed to some levers and knurled wheels, half-sunk in the console. "This one for speed. This one, this stick, for attitude. This one controls vector. And this, this silly little furry button, is what activates it." She pushed that one herself.

"Hang on," said Han. There was no sound, but the shuttle craft rose smoothly, hovering. Han pressed the levers in combination. The craft gave a great bound for the portal opening, slewing sideways as it did. They barely missed colliding with the portal edge. Finally, Han got it figured out, which motions he had to make for pitch, roll and yaw, synchronized with velocity. Liszendir was busy holding on, and Han was busy with controlling the craft. By the time they had time to look out at the world, they were well outside the warship, falling out and away from its bulky mass. The controls were impossible to handle correctly; they were tiny, but their effects were great. The craft responded immediately, as if it had no inertia of its own. Han reasoned that this was a power effect, not one of unified field, as if they had had that, they would have not felt their own inertia in the cabin.

They had fallen into a world of harsh, piercing bright light. The shuttlecraft was flying above a great plain, flat as a table top. Han got a quick glimpse of the ground. To one side a sandy riverbed meandered, bordered by a darker growth, which appeared to be trees. He couldn't tell. The distance was too great. The sky was cloudless, and a brilliant, electric blue, almost violet color he had never seen before. The sun was stark white with a tinge of blue, powerfully and painfully bright, and objects cast razor shadows, so sharp they seemed dangerous, as if they would have cut one if one had fallen on them. It was impossible to tell what time of day it was, morning or afternoon. Behind them bulked the ship, its orbiting meteors grounded on the plain below, still and unmoving. In the distance, seemingly not so far, jagged mountains reared. Near? He looked again. The lowest peaks in front of the range, and the lower saddles between them, were streaked with cirrus. Near? They were a great distance away. He revised his estimates of their size; they must be enormous.

Liszendir said, gloating, "We had to land for repairs. The ship is falling apart. They couldn't even make it to their own country after we made planetfall—that is several thousand miles away, on the other side. We had to land, to adjust the drivers. No sooner had they stopped, than these people came rushing over the plain and attacked the ship. They are using chemical rockets and cannon, and the like. And they have done some damage! It seemed to be light, just chips off this hulk, but it made the Warriors *mad!* You should have seen them! They all sallied out to fight like a crowd of maniacs. They were actually worried about their monster. Look below!"

Han looked below to the plains. There was fighting there, and figures rushed madly about, smiting and being smitten. He could not distinguish figures into factions from altitude, but the action seemed lively and vicious. Groups on foot strove against groups mounted on animals of some indeterminate sort.

As they increased the distance between the warship and themselves, Han asked, "So we're on Dawn?"

"Yes. I think their country is behind the ship relative to us. This area is considered no man's land, under partial control. They either can't subdue it, or they think it isn't worth the trouble. Those are humans down there attacking, not ler. The Warriors used some term for them—it was *klesh.* Part of it—I didn't understand the adjective. *Klesh* is what we call a domesticated animal."

Han looked again. There was a puff of black smoke, perhaps from a cart or carriage. Seconds later he could see a small explosion on the underside of the warship, now well behind them. This was answered by green flares from the upper part of the large ship.

"That's the recall signal!" Liszendir exclaimed. Below, the groups began to disengage, some of the tiny figures scurrying back to assembly points, where shuttles from the warship were already arriving. And farther out, the meteors began to stir in their landing spots, at first rocking back and forth, wobbling unsteadily. Then, one by one, the smaller ones first, they began lurching off, rolling and bouncing as they went, leaving huge gouges on the plain and shedding chunks of themselves as they attained flight. Short bursts of dazzling light came from the ship; if the bursts were from weapons, they were singularly ineffective.

Liszendir said, "For sure, we've got to hurry, now. They don't know yet that you and I are gone. They left me in the control room with three guards. A mistake. Now they are reduced by three." She chuckled to herself and smiled, baring her teeth in a gesture of hostility. "One person can't fly that monster by himself; it takes a whole crew, all over the ship. Otherwise, I would have stolen it while they were out and dropped some of their own eggs on them."

"I thought your wrists couldn't take stress. And I thought you wouldn't use anything that left the hand for a weapon."

"Well, for the first, I still have elbows, knees, feet and heels. And forearms are almost as good. And as for the other, when that beast Hath'ingar shot at me and you, he removed any restraint I might have. It is open season on them now for me. I can commit atrocities if required." She smiled with evident satisfaction. Han found it chilling.

Their speed increased. Han was gradually descending in altitude as they drew away. Liszendir was watching the warship in the rear screen. Han asked her, "Can you find anything on this shuttle that looks like it might be a power source?"

"No. Nor have I felt any since we started. Do they have stuff that good, and they can't fix that ship?"

"I doubt it. I think these shuttles run off beamed power from the big ship. Probably a high-power microwave, using part of the echo from the shuttle to align itself. If this is true, we are going to run out of power in a few minutes, when the big one gets going."

"Ah! You may be right. The big one is moving now, off the ground and away, towards their own country. And one of their rocks . . . Han, it spiraled upwards right out of sight!"

"Well, we can't go any faster; I've got it on full power, now. If the ship is moving, we won't get far anyway."

"They're going to drop one of those rocks. Yes, the attackers are scattering, too. They know!"

But their speed did not increase; on the contrary, it slowed appreciably and steadily, as the big ship drew away from them. Han said, over his shoulder. "Speed dropping now, and the controls feel mushy. Inverse square rule, power drops off. And the atmosphere may attenuate the beam signal strength, too." He brought the shuttle lower as fast as he could, now. He didn't know what would happen when the power went off for good. They seemed to crawl over the plains, now visible as being covered with a kind of grassy plant cover, golden in the harsh bright light. Time crawled, became infinitesimal in its pace.

He looked around at the rear screen Liszendir was watching. The big ship was still visible, but it was now far away and at some altitude, receding fast. But it was still good; as long as it was in sight they still had a chance. Ahead of them, in their path, rose a grassy rise, a ridge line. The plains were not absolutely flat. They would probably make it.

"I'm going to drop us behind those hills in front. If their aim is good with those meteors, we should be fairly safe there."

"They claimed to me that it was quite good, decreasing with speed, of course. Within ten miles of the target point for this kind of shot."

"Good. Now be ready. We may crash, after we drop behind the hills. It will cut off the signal."

In the rear screen, the ground rose as they put the ridge line between themselves and the big warship, now almost out of sight, fading in very distant haze, not in apparent size. The warship dropped below the apparent horizon. Instantly, the control panel in the front went completely dead, and the shuttle dropped sickeningly in free fall, then braked, none too gently. They felt themselves gripped by a sudden force field, that faded even as they noticed it. Automatics. Then they fell free another few feet, and impacted. Han and Liszendir were shaken up and dazed, but there seemed to be no injuries.

Liszendir looked up, glassy-eyed, from the floor. "What now? Can we run?"

"Won't do us any good. Just get free of the shuttle. It may roll about. Lie on the ground. Roll into a ball."

They helped each other up, and climbed out of the shuttle. It did not seem to be damaged in any way, other than some dents, which might have been there before. They ran a short distance, threw themselves on the ground, rolled up into balls, and waited. They didn't wait long. There was a single bright flash from the zenith, followed instantly by a lurid quick glare near the point over the hill where the warship had been. Then they heard the shriek of rending air, and then a titanic sound that could not be described. The earth shook violently, opening small cracks all around them. Dust rose and hung in the air, close to the ground.

Han looked up. "Now we wait for debris to fall. Keep an eye out. Chunks could come this far."

Liszendir got to her feet, looking into the sky, with an expression of disgust on her face. "That was truly obscene."

"I know. It's a projectile weapon. I feel horror, too, even though I have no prohibitions such as yours."

"It is ultimate sin. I have seen evil."

Han got to his feet, and started for the hill. "Come on. I want to see what it did. Maybe someone made it."

She was obstinate. "No. I will not look. Go. I will wait. After all, where do I have to go?"

Han started out for the top of the hill they had sheltered behind. It took a good half-run to get there. The clear air distorted distances even more than on Chalcedon. At the top of the rise, he stood panting and out of breath, gazing out on a scene of utter destruction. He felt dizzy. The air was very thin, he thought, too thin. He sat down, laboring for breath.

Below, where the plains had stretched unmarked, yellow and clean, there was a crater. A large one. A huge cloud of dust and dirt obscured the impact zone and the crater, so he could not see fine details. Streaks radiated away from the crater, for several miles. The grass was on fire in places. He tried to guess the distance. He could not. The thin air gave no hint of depth. There were no marks by which he could judge. Guessing, he estimated about fifty miles. They were lucky. The projectile had probably been solid nickel-iron, a third of a cubic mile perhaps in volume, moving at higher than orbital speeds. They were indeed fortunate. Nothing moved, back on the plains.

He returned to where Liszendir sat, with a puzzled look on her face, mingled with a trace of pain and fear. She had rifled the shuttle while he had been gone, and had the food bag with her. And the crossbow. And some blankets from one of the shuttle lockers. For the time, they would have some shelter and food.

She spoke, as he came up, in a whisper. "Han, what are our chances now? You are the survivor, not me. I did it once, but it was by guess and I almost died of it. What is this place like? Where do we go?"

He answered, "I don't know." Then he took a long look around them. The land was nearly featureless and flat, except toward the hill that had saved them, and in the direction of the mountains. The distant mountains stood quietly as Han inspected their outlines. Distant, deep blue with distance. They were high, high, even if they were only ten miles away. And he knew they were farther. He tested the air, glanced sideways towards the sun.

"Without instruments, an atlas, knowledge? I know now only what my senses tell me. That is little enough." He jumped up and down experimentally. "The gravity feels about right—about a little higher than a standard G, maybe 1.1 G. But the air is very thin."

"Yes. I noticed. I am not breathing well at all."

"This seems like a high plateau. Feels like around thirteen thousand to fifteen thousand feet, but with a higher oxygen content. Altiplano. *Kadhyal* to you, if you have any on Kenten. It will get cold at night. We can also expect altitude sickness, headaches, earaches, maybe vomiting. Respiratory bleeding. We will have to get off this plain to survive. I can see no way out, but towards the mountains. There may be a gap, or a canyon. But notice the snow on them. It only goes up so far. Above that, it's naked rock. Those clouds you see on the lowest peaks and saddles are cirrus. They are high-altitude clouds—35,000 feet, in a gravity and an atmosphere near standard. Here, higher gravity, thicker atmosphere, I don't have any idea. But they are very far away, and they are much higher than us. Miles higher. They may go up to sixty, seventy thousand feet equivalent. Higher. I know we cannot cross them on foot. But that way is our only chance. Mountains that high and that rough more often than not have a trough behind them, if they have a plain high up in front, like this. Continental edge. There should be a sea behind them." He finished. He wanted to say more, but he couldn't. He was out of breath.

Liszendir gazed at the mountains for a long time. She shaded her eyes, peering intently. "Yes, you are right. They are far away—many days for us. But I agree—it is the most reasonable way to start. I do not fancy walking out on that plain, not after the meteor. But notice how the sun moves. Already it is getting on into afternoon, and when we landed it seemed near noon. The day here must be very short. You can almost see the sun move."

"Don't look at it! That blue tinge means ultraviolet. We can get a vicious sunburn, especially you. And it will burn your eyes out."

Resignedly, they covered themselves as well as they could, and, gathering up their few possessions, they started walking.

"Walk slowly, Liszendir. Breathe deeply. We can't hurry."

She smiled back at him. "Who's hurrying?" She spoke cheerily, defiantly, but it was with effort. Han began to worry, it might be hard on her. He did not know how tolerant ler were to altitude. But he knew one thing about them. They never lived in extremely high places. Yes. It could be very hard on her.

Nightfall was as abrupt as a door slamming, and they had not gotten very far by the time that it happened. And Liszendir had developed a headache. In the mountain wall ahead, Han had picked out a saddle, a notch in the gargantuan wall, which had a peculiar, easily recognizable shape, for reference. He wanted to see what kind of progress they were making, if any.

They found some water. It was a murky trickling spring, with no apparent source, and the water sank back into the ground no great distance away. Han smelled it, tasted it gingerly, and looked all around the area for slimes and iridescent deposits. There were none. They drank at its meager output for hours.

The light behind the mountain wall across the world went to an indescribable color, a burning pearl-blue that hurt the eyes, then dimmed, darkened; and went out. After eating the food-concentrate pellets without enthusiasm, and without conversation, they made a shallow pit in the ground, and in it, partially covered and wrapped around each other for warmth and comfort, they settled in for the night. Liszendir was suffering. She gasped for air in deep breaths which were constant effort. Han enclosed her in his arms. He was feeling bad himself, extraordinarily tired, for no more than they had done; but it was not as bad as he had expected. The oxygen content must be high.

The stars came out, shining with unusual brilliance and clarity, although even at the zenith, they sparkled and flickered like stars close to the horizon on more normal planets. Yes. A heavy, thick atmosphere, low in water vapor, high in oxygen. But they were utterly strange, and after the gentle, kindly nights of Chalcedon, hostile in their strangeness. And it was cold. He had been right—the temperature did indeed drop fast.

They did not sleep well; nobody does with altitude sickness. The cold and the discomfort. Han was almost glad to see the sky brighten in the east after a short, seemingly too short, night. The sky first turned, without warning, so it seemed, a hot pearl color, then burning, then the piercing sun again. It was quick, brutal. He now understood why they called this planet "Dawn." It *was* beautiful, in a hard way, like the glint of fire on blued steel. The temperature began warming up before the sun had completely cleared the flat horizon in the east. The foot of the mountains was masked in darkness.

Liszendir was awake. She looked feverish and bedraggled, and admitted to little sleep either. The thin air was a slow torment. But stoically and quietly, they picked up their things and pressed on through the short day, west, straight for the mountains.

Several times during the day they felt earthquakes; not severe ones, but large enough to notice. Liszendir noticed them, but said nothing. Han told her, "These mountains ahead, the high plateau, the earthquakes. We must be near the continental edge. If we can make it to the mountains, there must be a way through them, a gorge or canyon. On the other side, the altitude will drop down to something nearer sea level. There will be lower country on the other side, and maybe an ocean. All worlds have drifting continents—that's what piles mountains up like those, it's the only thing that could pile them up that high and that regularly north to south. The only thing that differs on various worlds is the rate at which they move around."

She nodded. She had heard and understood. They walked on.

The mountains grew no bigger, not even by a little bit, and Han revised upwards his estimates of their altitudes, and the distances he and Liszendir would have yet to walk. They stopped early, too tired to continue until actual darkness. There was no water at this place; they ate listlessly and curled up together against the coming cold. Han took one last look around the featureless plains, and at the mountains. The sun was just dropping behind them.

To the right, or north, of the notch he had marked the
day before. Not a lot, not a great distance, but enough to be
noticeable, and he knew that they could not have moved so
far to the side of their route, north or south, to make that
much of a difference. It was disturbing, but the answer was
not apparent, so he filed the fact away, and lapsed into
fitful sleep.

Then there was the short night; which was followed by
another day, which was very much like the one previous,
clear and unmarked by weather of any sort. And another.
And another. At first, it only became important whether
they had water when they stopped for the night, but even
this faded. They stopped talking. They ceased to notice any
differences at all.

But there was a difference, as the days passed endlessly
and monotonously. The mountains were coming closer, and
the plains were beginning to undulate in rolling hills; it was
hard for them to go up the gentle slopes, but pure pleasure
going down the western slopes, even though there was one
more just like it just ahead, and just a little higher.

They rationed the tasteless pellets as well as they could,
for neither one of them could visualize even the hungriest
man bolting them down in an abandon of hunger. Yet, as
well as they stretched them out, they knew they were drawing on their reserves, and Liszendir was showing severe
weight loss; her face was becoming drawn and haggard, and
Han thought she looked more worn than when she had
stumbled into the market at Hobb's Bazaar. Hobb's Bazaar.
It seemed years, ages in the past, in another time, remote as
childhood, meaningless. The numbers of the days were meaningless as well—and the only realities were the amount of
food concentrate remaining in the bag, and the distance to
the mountains, which was now growing less, at last. Each
evening, the violet shadows rising from the bases reached
them sooner, earlier. And the sun was moving daily to the
right, the north. Han's mind was fogged. He knew that movement was significant, but somehow the connection always
seemed just out of reach. The significance grew into
suspicion, still unformed. He could not put it into words,
but something deeper knew and told him that they must get
off that plain and down; they were casting shadows at noon,
shadows that fell to the south, and every day, they were a
little longer, at noon. The earthquakes grew stronger and

more frequent. And the mountains gleamed above them, now dominating the western half of the horizon, giant fangs raised skywards in a terrible rictus of defiance.

At the end of the next day, they came, quietly and un-dramatically, to an enormous gash in the earth, which they did not see until they were almost upon it. The other side faded away into the violet haze of the evening shadows of the mountains, and could not clearly be made out. The far side merged into the tumbles of the foothills, imperceptibly. And below them it went down and down from the gentle break at the rim, the air growing misty toward the bottom, where they thought they could see the suggestion of a silver river, wearing away at the stone. They stood in the short twilight on the rim, looking down into the depths; the river, if there was one, seemed to flow to the south and the gorge seemed to trend back toward the mountains, although they could see no hint of break in the wall above them. Like everything else on Dawn, the gorge exceeded anything in their experience in sheer size. It matched the mountains well in scale.

Liszendir looked downwards with shining eyes. "Air, that's what I need. If I could just breathe again, I could go down there and die in peace." Her voice was a croak.

Han added, "And I as well. It will be enough, if we can just get down there." His voice sounded even stranger to him.

They started down immediately not willing to spend even another night on the terrible high, cold plains. But despite the apparent gentleness of the upper slopes, the going down was not easy, for the distances were deceiving; and the slope soon became steeper. In the dark, under the stars, and for the first time with a restricted horizon, they stopped.

Their distance per day dropped to almost nothing, but they moved steadily downwards. Each day the rim to the east rose higher, and the air grew fractionally denser and warmer, easier to breathe, and each night the shadows came earlier. And still they crawled down, down, making slow progress. But one thing had improved—they had water all the time, fresh water dripping from springs in the rocks. With water they could stretch the food concentrate even further. But it was showing on them. Han was gaunt and skeletal, but Liszendir was worse; and what bothered Han even more, now that he could think better in the denser air, was something he had noticed the last day, although he had dim recollections of it starting back on the high plains: Liszendir was starting to hallucinate and talk to herself.

They ate the last of the Warrior's food concentrate. There was enough for both of them to stretch two days, or eat it all and go as far as they could. They ate it all and threw the bag away, laughing. And far from being sad, they felt, as they ate, the closest thing to joy they had known since Chalcedon. And after they had eaten, Liszendir seemed to return to her senses. It was good—she had been babbling most of the afternoon about castles and the thirsty eye.

"So, Han, here we eat our last. Now how far can we go?"

"If we were in good shape, about three days' worth, but as we are, I'd guess no more than two, to amount to anything."

She looked around, "So here is where it will end, our most amazing thing, something no others know. I do not fear it. Look around us, look at this."

Han did as she asked, and in the swift evening fading light, the buttes and buttresses of the gorge reared above them, sizable mountains in their own rights. Now the high range was out of sight behind the western rim. Han was thankful for that, for he had felt daunted and humbled in the sight of those naked, high rocks. No human, nor any other conceivable creature, would ever walk those passes, climb those peaks, "because they were there" or for any other reason. There was no air. They towered miles above the high plains, higher than any mountains Han had ever seen or viewed pictures of.

Liszendir began again, not waiting for him to reply. "You cannot see it, but I can. There is far-violet in the deep shadows, *nefalo perhos 'em spanhrun*. The rocks, the river below. This is a place of giants in the earth, heroes, *reison*, cold, relentless, cruel beauty. I have journeyed far to see this." She seemed entranced by the spectacle, like a child again, he thought. She looks death and termination in the face and says, "How lovely. Look at the view." Han saw only oblivion and darkness forever. Pain and cold and the big sleep.

Night fell and they slept. In the morning, which was coming later and later, they picked up what they had left, the blankets and the crossbow, and continued on their way down. They saw nothing to give them hope. There were plants, now, fairly common, but they looked suspicious, and neither one of them wanted to eat them. And they were wrong about two days' travel. He knew that they could not go any farther than they got this night. And as the night closed about them, she went far ahead of him, pushing what was left of her strength to the uttermost. In the last light, he saw her far below, her face shining with joy. Joy? It was probably, he thought, a combination of fear and hysteria, which he was feeling himself. And exhaustion and starvation. Yes, perhaps she was right—it was better to face it this way, than to meet it cringing.

She was waiting for him by a large boulder, her face full of happiness. Han hesitated to join her, fearing her insanity, if that was what it was. But she did nothing more irrational than falling into his arms and pulling him down in the shelter of the rock. Not for love, for they were long past the strength to accomplish it, even a part, but for comfort against the night they knew was coming for them. She cuddled against him like a small child, and later, semiconscious, she began talking in her sleep. It was Multispeech again, and went on at a steady pace for a long time, the voice, now soft, whispering next to him, saying many things simultaneously that he would never know. She would not stop for long. He looked at her face before he went to sleep; it was very thin, drawn and worn, but she was smiling as she talked, happy, even rapturous. She probably did not expect to wake up. Neither did Han. He stroked her hair, and went to sleep.

But they did wake up the next morning, early, with the first light. They arose listlessly, silently. This would be the last day, absolutely. He felt he could not walk another step. Once more they gathered up their blankets, more for the reassurance of ritual than for any other reason, and automatically started around the boulder.

Before them spread not another interminable slope down, but a large, level terrace stretching parallel to the river, still far below. And not fifty paces from them was a house. A rude stone house, with thin blue smoke rising slowly out of the chimney. Lights within the house glowed yellow in the deep blues and violets, overlain by the nude pearl sky overhead, of the morning of the planet Dawn. A chill was in the air.

He looked at Liszendir. Tears were streaming down her thin cheeks, and as he watched, she slowly folded up and sank to the ground. He picked her up; she was light, hardly a burden at all, a mere collection of bones. He knew. She had been starving, so he could get the lesser amount he needed. And he knew why she had been so carefree the last day. Carrying the small load, Han started for the house, but he only made it as far as the gate of the dooryard before he, too, sank down. The owner, much to his surprise, found them there about an hour later, as he was making his morning rounds.

The farmer was human, and had a wife and two daughters, big strapping homely girls, all of which Han noticed very little. He ate, and he slept. And ate and slept some more. He heard voices speaking ler Singlespeech, or a version of it. It was far away, and it meant nothing. He slept deeply.

He finally awoke, clearheaded, to find Liszendir, thin but recovering, sitting on the floor beside his pallet. It seemed to be noon of some day, a day he didn't know, but he knew one thing. He was recovered. He looked at her, seeing that she had been waiting for him to wake up.

She asked, "Are you feeling better now? I can tell you that I am."

He nodded. She was fleshing out again, but the experience they had been through had molded and eroded and rebuilt in her a new, sober and more thoughtful beauty. Whatever her age-status was in ler glandular terms, she was now neither adolescent nor tomboy, the intriguing ambisexual creature he had met in Boomtown, and loved on Chalcedon. Her eyes reflected the electric blue of the light of the sky.

"I think you will have trouble talking to them for a while. They speak only Singlespeech, but it has changed even more than the version the Warriors use, and at first, even I had trouble with it. But humans! That is what amazes me. Han, I really must admit to prejudice and wonder why your people persist in speaking such irregular and redundant languages. Even when given a regular language, they contrive to make it irregular."

"Are they friendly?"

"Yes, friendly enough, although you will possibly think them rather close-mouthed. I have told them that we escaped the Warriors and walked here from a great battle scene miles to the east, up on the plateau. Better that than the truth. It is all they can handle, and even what I gave them is a lot. They distrust me some, because I am ler, they can see that. But my hair and the way I let it fall straight has convinced them at least that I am not a Warrior. We are heroes, to have walked so far."

"You look beautiful."

She looked away sharply for a moment, as if the remark pained her. Then she turned back. "We can also get down the gorge, on the river. It gets low in this season, and they say that they raft down after the harvest. And if we will stay and help them, they will take us when they go to market. Guess where it is? On the other side of the mountains! The gorge does go through."

She looked back outside again, as if searching for a reminder for some knotty problem. "There is something very strange, here," she said at last. "I hear echoes of the proper words for seasons in his speech, but they have additives which distort them terribly, more than any other part of the language. If my ears do not lie to me, I understand from him that there are eight seasons on this planet. Two winters every year. I have never heard of the like. How could that be? Would the high mountains cause it?"

Han suddenly sat upright. It was what he had been waiting to hear, the missing piece that fit the puzzle of the swift sun drifting to the north so fast. "What season is it now?"

"North, or short winter is coming. This is little autumn."

"What happens in short winter?"

"It will get dark, but not as long as long winter, which they fear."

"Now I know. I suspected when we were up on the plateau, walking, but it didn't make sense to me then. I have heard of planets like this one, but all the known ones are out of the habitable zone for our kind of life forms. They are called uranoid planets, after the first one discovered, back in the old Earth system. Remember Chalcedon? It had no seasons because it had a regular orbit and no axial tilt. This planet has an extreme tilt; its plane of rotation is closer to perpendicular to the plane of orbit. It means that from the ground, the sun will be over the poles once during the year for each pole. The polar regions overlap the tropics. It will be a strange place with a stranger climate. Probably the only thing that makes it livable is the presence of high mountains, high enough to block mass circulation of the atmosphere with the rotational direction."

"The days are already shorter, and the sun is more to the north than when we were walking."

"Right. Here, they have eight seasons, four when the sun

is to the north, four when it goes to the south. At the poles, it would be even stranger: if we were there, we would see the sun rise, spiraling around the horizon, and then it would climb to the zenith, or near it, still spiraling. It would wiggle around overhead for a while, and then start spiraling back down. Then it would get dark for a long time, three-quarters of the year. And cold. It must be hellish at the poles."

"How?'

"Temperature. At the poles, once the sun rises, it stays risen and in a day, illuminates every object from all sides. It probably gets hot enough on the surface to melt lead in the polar summer, and in the long dark winter, cold enough to freeze some gases out of the air."

"Yes! He said that. I did not understand; I thought it was the language. He said that the air freezes in places and falls to the ground."

Han thought some more, then asked, "And how far is it to the ocean?"

"More problems for you to figure out. He said that there wasn't such a thing anywhere near here. He didn't even know the word. He used the old word for pond or lake, or so I thought. I corrected him, and he said not that, but a lake, and he waved his arms around to show me how big. Not very big at all. A salt lake, very far down and very hot in the summer. There are salt deposits all around, and it sometimes boils. They go there and get salt in other seasons. But he had never heard of an ocean."

"That is curious."

"However it is, over the mountains are people. Plenty of them, too many for him. Human and ler, both. But while he was telling me all about the region, thinking I'm from a far country, the whole time he was talking about the ler, not once did he mention the four parents, the four children. They marry by twos, human style. Except for the Warriors, whom he fears greatly. They do something else, and it isn't by fours. He didn't know what. The word for 'braid' does not even exist on this planet."

Han didn't know what to make of that, either. He got up from the pallet, dressed, and started out to meet the farmer. As he did, he looked down at his body, now still thin from their hard trek across the high plateau. He was clean. He looked at Liszendir. She smiled.

"I pay my debts." It was the only thing she said, all she ever said about it.

The farmer and his family were indeed friendly, if some-what reserved, but they balanced their suspicions of Han and Liszendir with their admiration and awe of their exploit of walking across the bare high plains. He himself had heard that people lived up on the plateau, but he had never seen any direct evidence of it; as far as he knew, the air was too thin for people to live in it. Han and Liszendir agreed with him. The farmer also thought that perhaps the plains were the abode of ghosts and various dire spirits, although Han could not be sure just what he meant; his language was sketchy to begin with, and Han's command of it was none too good. So, after the local accent, the peculiar usages, the irregularized grammar and the changed phonemes, the ambiguity of the resultant idea in Han's mind was indeed high.

But he had been right about the course of the sun of Dawn through the heavens; it did go to the very pole, or very close to it. Of course, no one had actually seen the polar summer—only from the edges, where some mining was done. And in the winters the poles were far worse. The farmer said that once, during south-winter, on a trip north, he had actually seen a fall of dry snow, luckily from the inside of a snug cabin. He was terrified of it, and Han did not blame him; those temperatures were nothing to face with bravado and a hairy chest. A space suit would be more appropriate.

There were small freeholds all along the gorge, usually in places where large natural terraces had been formed, and they were all completely independent, free of tax and over-lord alike. No flags flew in the gorge, no armies marched. Only scattered farm families, making a precarious living between the dangers of wandering nomads, who infested the lower gorge, the cold of the winter, which was more severe on this side of the mountains, and the unknown of the high plains. On the other side, however, the density of population went up; there was even a city, Leilas, which the farmer regarded as the very nadir of corruption. There was another range west of the large mountains, separated from them by a trough, which was extensively cultivated. The river had cut a low point through the trough as well as the rocks, and the trough actually had two arms, south and north, which rose gradually away from the great river. The lower parts were generally human, and were ruled from Leilas, while the upper parts were mostly ler, and were ruled from, it was reputed, castles perched high up in the farthest reaches of the troughs.

As the description of Dawn went on, Han was disappointed by the news. It was a primitive society, more feudal than anything else. And in addition, the natives had to put up with an impossible climate which kept them constantly at bay, and an incredible geography, which kept them isolated and ignorant. To the farmer's knowledge, there were no oceans or seas—just lakes. Dawn consisted of vast, rearing mountain ranges, which were separated by huge sinks, or high plateaus. Earthquakes were common, in fact, so common that Han could feel very slight tremors almost constantly. The difference was not between earthquake and no-earthquake; it was between a greater intensity or a lesser. He tried to visualize the kind of imbalances in the crust which would produce mountains like these. He couldn't. And besides all that, the specter of the Warriors hung over everything.

Years would pass with no incidents, and the memory of the Warriors would be forgotten. Then they would come again, to sift the people. They never took many, but they always took some. Naturally, they were never seen again. They generally left the ler of the higher troughs alone. He knew them well, and called them by a curious name: firstfolk. Even Liszendir derived a wry amusement from that.

No one had any idea about the size of the planet, or anything in the area of astrophysics. They thought the world was flat. Han did not question him too deeply on this subject, knowing that sometimes questions revealed more about the questioner than answers about the answerer, and he did not want to get involved in any kind of religious dispute. A flat world! Archeoforteans! He thought wryly that the theologians of Dawn would have evolved an interesting cosmology to explain the erratic path, or even surrealistic path, their sun followed through the heavens.

Han and Liszendir, for their part, agreed to stay and help with the harvest, and further, help him dispose of it for the best price in Leilas. Han identified himself as a merchant by trade, and vowed to obtain the best possible price. The farmer, in turn, agreed to transport them downriver in several tendays, depending upon the harvest and the weather.

Liszendir asked him how they returned from Leilas. He told her that they took their pack animals with them, loaded them in Leilas with the things they needed, and walked back, up the gorge. By the time they got back, it would be in the first half of north-winter, but it was not so bad, and gave them time to prepare for the rigors of the half-year darkness of south-winter. From the times he mentioned, Han hazarded a guess, in Common, to Liszendir, that they were somewhere around thirty degrees north in latitude. The information was not particularly important. They had nowhere to go.

VII

"This is not the real world. The real world is Yar, a great place of bright cities, towers, magic, fertile ground and gentle rains. For our sins, we were banished and cast forth to Limbo, which is here, by Hoth the Sun-God, and here we expiate the sins of our ancestors. We do not know today what those sins were; they must have been terrible, however, for such a punishment to come to an entire people. It is said that they cannot be described with words. So, we are here. The dual hells are nearby, and convenient. One is located in Uttermost North, the other in Uttermost South. Those of excessive passions are cast into the North, where Hoth visits them with fire. The cold-blooded go to the South, where Hoth visits them with cold unimaginable. The Firstfolk maintain the purity of the Word, and the Warriors dispose of the impure in thought and heretics, chiefly from among the young, who are prone to harbor resentments. Those are judged, and sent to the appropriate destination. The Warriors live in the

*lower heavens, but they follow the orders of
Hoth, who goes to all parts of the rocky world,
who sees all and judges that we may be deemed
fit to return someday to Yar the Beautiful, Yar
the Kind."*

    —The story of creation, as told to
    Liszendir Srith-Karen by Narman Daskin,
    the farmer of the gorge.

*"It is only when one has somewhere to go that
it becomes manifestly important to know precisely where one is."*

            —Cannialin Srith-Moren, woven Deren

The raft, made from boles of light, spongy timbers from
the slopes of the gorge, made its clumsy way down the great
river, piled high with bales of produce, grains, legumes, and
tubers of several sorts. Besides them, there were others on
the river as well; Han had seen them pass, just as heavily
loaded, poled and steered by crews of dour men who spoke
little greeting as they passed the shoals below the farmer's
house. Mostly, they spoke no greeting at all.

Narman Daskin, the farmer, stood lookout at whichever
end happened to be the front at that time. His two daughters,
Uzar Rahintira and Pelki Rahintira, worked broad sweeps at
the end which happened to be facing rearwards, back upstream. Han and Liszendir wielded poles in the middle. The
way was surprisingly smooth, free for the most part of rocks
and rapids.

Pelki had explained why. "The south-spring flood-thaw
sweeps the lower gorge clean of rocks and gravels; they all
flow down with the great waters and collect in a great wad
below Leilas, down on the salt flats by the bitter lake." So
had spoken the younger daughter, the more personable one.
The older one, Uzar, was a heavy-set, brooding girl who was
no beauty and who said little, even in the way of routine
pleasantries. Pelki was no less homely, but she evidenced
considerably more animation, and at times almost approached plainness. Han was not deceived. Neither was a
prize.

Liszendir had thought that Pelki's half-hopeful flirting at

Han had been interesting and had so informed him, to his general discomfort. As for him and Liszendir, he felt a certain confusion about their relationship, as it seemed to be for the present; their intimacy had been dormant, secondary for a time. It might come into flower again, and then it might not. She, for her part, was not avoiding him, but on the contrary, had become closer, more confiding, more affectionate, relaxed. The haughty Liszendir he had met at Boomtown had entirely vanished, but the replacement Liszendir was still full of unknowns, perhaps more than before. All this was true, yet it was also true that she had withdrawn into herself in an odd way Han could not quite discern.

From the other side of the raft, she observed, in Common, "If all else fails, at the least you could probably marry Pelki."

Han replied in the same tongue, "Well, I don't want to, not now nor any other time I can imagine. Not that I would care to choose if driven to begging, but she can't be the most exciting woman on Dawn, in looks, and besides that, she's dumb."

Liszendir laughed. "So I thought it would be. Really, Han, I agree also. I was just teasing you." She shifted the subject. "You know they have a strange custom in these parts, for all I know, all over Dawn with the humans here: they do not have family names—just proper names and a patronymic for boys or a matronymic for girls. Boys are regarded as the yield of the father, girls of the mother."

Han stayed on the subject of Pelki. "Why would you wish such a thing of me? If that is all the choice I have I may not want a mate."

"No reason. You may as well have one, for if I stay here very long, I won't be able to have one."

"Well, do without, then," he said, half-irritably.

"Oh, it's not so simple as that," she replied, rather impishly. "Besides the strength of the drive, unless I conceive within a certain time after the onset of fertility, which means even if you and I stay together, I have another problem. If I don't conceive, my reproductive system will shut itself down."

"You mean you will become sexless."

"Yes. Permanently. Just like after-fertility. It is a modification performed upon us by the firstborn, before they destroyed all the means of how to engineer such genetic changes, and the records. Its purpose has been to prevent obvious failures and grotesques from passing bad genes on.

Use it or lose it, you know? All it takes is about half a year."

"Well, that shouldn't worry you now. If I understood your standard age correctly at Boomtown, we've got years yet before we have to worry about that. I hope we can either get off this planet, or find you a partner of the ler, before then."

"In normal circumstances that would be so. But here, the short day-cycle has been acting to speed me up, to fit its cycle. You, too. You and I have started sleeping Dawn hours the last few days. It doesn't seem to have any effect on you, but it could very well bring my fertility sooner."

Han looked away, at the dark water. He could not answer her unspoken question.

Now on the great river they slept and poled, poled and slept. There was, according to Narman, need for haste.

"Notice the sun! It is well to the north, now. Darkness incarnate rises out of the south. The days are short; soon will come the cold. The upper waters freeze, the lower ones dry up. Then the river is not passable. It is only now that it is in the whole year."

The whole family agreed that there was more to it than simple failure to reach Leilas. The lower gorge, particularly where it had dug across the mountains, was infested with bandits and vagabonds of dubious origin. These feared the river and all moving water, so as long as the travelers were securely on the river and moving, all would be well. It was if they were to become stranded that they would have cause to worry. It had happened before. The goods were stolen, and the passengers eaten, so tales had it.

Han looked about suspiciously. He could see no evidence of habitation of any kind. The river whispered quietly with chilling power, moving swiftly through a vertical trench cut into solid rock, tormented layer upon layer of deeply metamorphosed basement rock. Distorted and tormented, crushed, folded and fused.

Pelki said, from the back of the raft, "They live high up. Above the cliffs. They lower themselves down on ropes, after the lookouts tell them someone is stranded."

"Well, why don't they bother you on the way back? Isn't that just as dangerous?"

"They are inexplicable people. They disappear after the last boat."

Han asked, "Where do they go?"

"Who knows? Never in memory have they molested a homeward trek. Perhaps they have taboos. Perhaps they are demons who fear the dark."

The raft grated ominously along its bottom, lurching slightly, pausing, then freeing itself. Pelki's eyes rolled in a sudden spasm of fear. She pointed ahead. Sure enough, there was a figure hanging down into the deep vertical part of the gorge in a flimsy contraption of ropes and slings. Han could not tell if it were human or ler, at the distance. Han drew his crossbow, cocked it, and waited as they drifted closer to the figure. As they came within range, he aimed carefully and shot at the figure. The first bolt missed, and the creature began screaming imprecations downwards to the raft, and instructions upwards to comrades out of sight behind the rim. The sling-and-rope contraption moved upwards fractionally. Han cocked and fired again. This time he hit the creature in the back, and he released his grip and fell backwards into the river with a wailing cry of despair. Faintly, from above, invisible, they heard answering calls of woe, hoots of disappointment. The echoes rang eerily down on the hard rocks and smooth river surfaces, bounding and rebounding. They saw them no more. The creature who had fallen had apparently vanished below the surface instantly.

For the rest of the journey, there was no more trouble. Han and Liszendir spent the days, when they were not poling, leaning against a bale, napping, watching scenery. There was not much to see; the gorge cut off all sight of the uplands whatsoever, as it wound through the complex, meandering trench it had cut through the mountains. All they could see were the various textures and colors of rocks, and patches of blue sky above, now flecked with clouds increasingly often. Sometimes it grew darker, independently of the time of day or apparent weather: they suspected then they were passing through a particularly deep part. But down at the bottom of the gorge, on the great river the air was humid and mild. When they crossed infrequent patches of sunlight, it felt almost hot. And so the days passed.

Finally they emerged from the deep defile and floated on stiller waters. They still were in a deep canyon, but they inferred from the lightening of the air and the sky that they were on the lake above Leilas. The sky above their heads was no longer oppressed by deep blue shadows, except in morning. They were on the west side of the mountain barrier. The lake was shallow and very muddy, its bottom vague and sticky when found. They poled and rowed westwards, seemingly getting nowhere.

On the fourth day on the lake, with the air very light and noticeably cooler, they sighted an elaborate dock area on the water, slightly to the right of their course. Behind it, bare bluffs rose, capped by a rosy, smoky haze. Han asked Narman if that was Leilas.

"No. Leilas is up on the bluffs, out of sight. The fume exudes from their kitchens and shops. What you see below, here, on the water, are only the docks. We will sell everything there, on the water. Porterage costs too much! Let them haul it up the slope! That which you see is smoke from the great city—they cannot move it down on the water because of the floods when the sun comes back from his visit to the hell of the south."

They began to pole towards the floating docks with more energy. Han watched Liszendir as she worked at her pole, setting it from the fore part of the raft, walking with it, leaning into it all the way to the back, and then deftly snatching it back out of the lake-bottom muck. He looked at the daughters, Uzar and Pelki. All three were female, yet there was some quality about Liszendir not shared by the other two. For the moment, it escaped him. Then, suddenly, he had it. The image came into sharp focus. The difference was that Liszendir seemed, somehow, "more finished" than the other two. He blanked the image of the ler girl from his mind, and strained to see the other two girls as he might have seen them in a situation with only humans. Yes. Uzar became just plain, and Pelki became, with some work, almost attractive in a heavy, rawboned way. Capable and competent. That fit very well with talk he had heard. More finished.

As he watched Liszendir, he saw something else as well he had suspected, but had half-feared to let surface. Now she was allowing her hair to grow longer, as the short style was a mark of adolescence. But he remembered how it had been a straight fall, parted in the middle, to the ears, styleless and sexless, just like any other adolescent. But he could not confuse her with a male figure by any stretch of the imagination. It was as if as the cultural differences between the sexes fell away, the innate differences that had been there all along came into full play; as if clothes and hair style keyed to sexes obscured the issue, rather than dramatizing it as he had always thought, as all of the humans he knew thought. People said that if boys and girls wore their hair alike and wore the same clothes, how could you tell them apart? But the boys and girls never seemed to have any trouble; they knew. And now Han knew, too. The quaint culturalisms of the ler now glared with harsh realities humans feared, knowing themselves almost as well as the ler knew themselves, but not quite as ready to admit it, or what they saw, within.

Liszendir now caught her hair up at the neck, with her characteristic nonchalance, with a piece of string borrowed from one of the bales, but it hung down her back with a grace that could not have been attained with the finest silk. She noticed he was watching her, and turned to him, easing off on the pole.

"I have a riddle for you, since you seem so thoughtful today. Are you ready? I want to know how running water of no greater depth than we have seen can cut a gorge across a range of mountains miles high."

Han laughed. "You, a philosopher, ask me? Does not water conquer all by its humility that seeks out the low places, and does not elevate itself?"

"A *mnathman*, indeed! Dardenglir was right about you Han! You must cast off these delusions about riches and become a holy man. We cannot make you ler, but you are ready to learn secrets. Where did you find that?"

He laughed again. "I retire to certain caves in the required season, and by sheer mental effort, deduce the secrets of earth and water, of red and black, of man and woman."

She laughed and corrected him. "*Tlanman* and *srithman*, do you not mean? Male-person and female-person?"

"No. Man and woman. I have to confine my efforts to us *hyunmanon*, the old people, lest I suffer a spasm, as if from eating too much roast *drif*. Ah, me! How I wish we had eaten the rascal before Hath'ingar caught up with us and carted us off to this vegetarian place. No, I will answer, Liszendir. I think the reason for the river cutting through the mountains lies in the floods they mentioned in the summer, when the sun returns from the south. When the sun is at the one pole, at the other pole an icecap develops, which melts all at once. The water has to go somewhere, and if the pole is high ground . . . I think the river is older than the mountains, and kept cutting down as they were raised up, slicing each summer through what had been built up the year before. All their water here comes at once. And as it ebbs, the smaller particles and silts get dropped here in the lake, renewed every year; that is why the lake is so muddy."

Narman had been following this closely, despite the language barrier, which was as hard for him as for Han and Liszendir. But he caught the particulars, and nodded enthusiastically. "Yes. The river scours out the gorge every year, just like that. But the mountains are cut by it for punishment, because they aspired to be sky, therefore they are cut and tormented by water, which multiplies into a terrible force. It is like women."

Han and Liszendir respectfully agreed. They had accepted Narman's orthodoxy without comment.

They were appreciably closer to the docks, now, and were able to ease up on the poling somewhat. Han found himself anticipating the city, however it was. He had not seen one since they had departed Boomtown. He did not count Hobb's Bazaar as a city by any stretch of the imagination. To hear Narman describe Leilas, it must be the veritable navel of the world, a wonder to equal the storied ancient cities of old Earth. Cosmopolitan, fleshpot, center of commerce and culture; he waited for the experience. But Liszendir only looked suspiciously at the haze above the bluffs, and an occasional visible chimney-pot, or tower, and shook her head. She had been skeptical all along about Leilas, and the few remarks she had made were not enthusiastic.

They moored the raft to a floating pier, and immediately were set upon, boarded, hounded and invaded, by as rascally a gang of hagglers and potential cutthroats as Han had ever set eyes on. The selling of the crop commenced immediately, with no introductions or formalities; and no quarter asked—or given. He was hard put even to keep the shirt on his back, and in fact got a substantial offer for Liszendir's shift, if she would be so good as to step behind yon bale and remove it. It ended late at night, and began again the next day, before the east had become decently light. By the end of the second day, everything was sold, a few items stolen, and they had a bit of money to split up between them. If you could call it money: it was currency only in Leilas.

They went up the bluffs to the town, with only the pack animals left, and some clothes. There, before the walls of Leilas, they made their farewells, and they were short ones. Narman was in a hurry, and they had caught sight of some other gorge farmers getting ready to be outfitted for the trip back upriver. The long walk. It was all understandable, since they saw each other once a year. Han and Liszendir took their share, and after watching the group for a moment, entered the city.

In its own terms, Leilas probably was a very great city, with no rivals within traveling distance. And to the locals, it very likely seemed to be the very center of the planet Dawn. They knew of no other city at all. But to Han it was a living text out of the far past, long before spaceflight. As they wandered through the narrow, dusty streets, they saw no weapons more advanced than crossbows, and at that inferior to the one he carried, now disassembled. The sewage disposal system was nothing more than a series of noisome ditches and stone channels, some covered with boards which might be rotten or not, as determined by whether they would support weight or not, which ran through the streets in the general direction of the lake. This was fairly intelligent, as the lake got flushed out yearly, but if it ever missed a year, this city on the north shore would change, or move. It would have to, for even in its prosperity, it was a place of incredible density of smells, odors, gusts, and miscellaneous stenches.

No street was straight, nor long, nor did there seem to be any organization to it at all. Houses, inns, shops, villas behind walls, and slums all lay tooth and jowl together. But it did seem to be the center of a flourishing trade, which was natural enough, considering the size of the hinterland it must serve. The river upstream, the broad trough valleys north and south, and some large territory westwards, down on the flats, around the salt pits. But however prosperous it was, it was not the metropolis Han had expected; rather, he guessed that Leilas had a population of perhaps thirty thousand, if that many.

Liszendir's only comment during their first day was, "They have fallen far, here." And she said it with genuine sadness in her voice. They saw a few ler about, on the streets, in shops, but they did not attempt to contact them. Han saw that Liszendir did not want to, and even he could detect some difference, but exactly what it was could not be discerned. He only knew that they were not the same as Liszendir. To her, the difference must be a glaring, especially since ler were not, as a rule, strange no matter where they came from. For the first time in her life, she was seeing strangers, citizens of another country, and it disturbed her.

After much looking, inspection, and searches which ended, as often as not, in some blind alley, they finally located an inn, which was surprisingly comfortable inside, in contrast with its outside, which resembled a dungeon, complete with stained and streaked walls, and heavy bars on the windows. "For security from burglars and footpads!" exclaimed the owner. The inn was called the Haze of the West, and was an eccentric, stucco, blocky, rambling structure which seemed to have grown together out of several buildings over the course of many years. Han and Liszendir secured a set of small rooms overlooking a pleasant courtyard, with balcony, for which they paid extra, and, wonder of wonders, not running water but a wood-fired bath, which cost nothing. The rooms were plain, but late in the day, the evening lights and shadows played along the undecorated whitewashed walls with great charm.

Liszendir was most excited about a real bath, so they arranged to have water put in the tank on the roof by the potboy, and a load of firewood brought up. While she busied herself with making the fire up, Han told her to take her time and use all the water, and he would go out to the public baths down the alley. He wanted to look around some, anyway, he said. Then they could go out and try to find something decent to eat.

When he returned a few hours later, he found Liszendir fast asleep on the small bed, a fresh shift on, her face scrubbed and rosy. The only light in the room came from a candle, still burning beside the window. Outside, it was quiet. Leilas went to bed early, however its reputation was. If they went to fleshpots, they did not go late at night. She woke up as he came in, awake instantly.

"Did you enjoy yourself while I was out?"

"You will never know! I have not had a hot bath, a real bath, in years, so it seemed. I went to sleep in the tub. But now I am ready for whatever Dawn can hand out. Bring it on! We have outraged probability on all sides." Then, "So here we are in great Leilas! Leilas, the pearl of Dawn. Now, what?"

She sat up on her elbows, a motion which tensed her collarbones, and cast shadows on her skin in the soft light.

"I went around, trying to get an idea of what we can do here. It isn't much. About all we can hope to do in Leilas is find out more about Dawn, and then we should try to get up to the ler communities in the upper trough. North is as

good as any other. Reputedly, higher up, there are ler countries. I don't know what we will find there. Maybe nothing."

"Maybe nothing. I agree, but it is still better than sitting
still here in Leilas. The ler I have seen do not look like much,
and they may be no better high up. But there is nothing
here—this city is tenth-century preatomic, at least."

"Yes. Maybe worse. And it looks old, you know, like it's
been this way, just like we see it, for a long time. They
aren't going to build a spaceship tomorrow in the next alley."

She shook her head. "I see. Now tell me, Han. What you
want to do. Yourself, not us. Really."

He sat on the edge of the bed, and reflected quietly for a
long time, looking at the candle. Finally, he said, "I want to
try to get back, of course. But if I can't do that, then I
suppose live as good a life as I can, here, if nowhere else.
I want to return to my own world, my own people. I want
to try to steal our ship back from them; but they are all the
way around the planet, and for all we know, by the time we
could get there, they could just as well be off somewhere.
But I have no other."

"What did you find out about Dawn?"

"Not much. There are geographers and astrologers, which
is what passes for erudition and enlightenment. We will have
to find out where we are in relation to where the country of
the Warriors is, and then see if we can get there from here.
And as for the upland ler . . . I don't know. All we can do is
go and ask."

"Ah. So then, we should begin tomorrow. Our money is
short."

She arose from the bed, walked around it quietly, and
stood by the window for a while. Han blew the candle out,
and joined her there.

"There is another matter, Liszen . . ." he said, expectantly.

She shrugged her shoulders and let the shift fall to the
floor, her eyes shining. "I thought you would never ask
again," she said softly. "Tell me, body-love, what is your
wish?"

He slipped out of his clothes as well. "That I could, this
night, go all over your body, like a man with no teeth or
arms or spoon eating a bowl of warm applesauce." It
sounded odd in his ears, but he knew by now from her that
it was what she would have expected to hear from a lover
of her own kind. She smiled at him, and shivered, deliciously.

He moved closer to the girl, smelling her hair, filling himself with the scent as if he would never know it again, touching her cool skin. They turned, as one, and lay down on the small bed together, every sense wide open, even conscious of the rough blanket. They did not sleep for a long time, but neither did they bother to go out for supper. Supper could wait. This couldn't.

The next day they slept late, but as soon as they were up and around they set out through the streets of Leilas to see what hard information they could find out about Dawn. If it was anywhere to be had, it would be here.

There were no books, they soon found out, except in the lockers of collectors and certain religious establishments; the printing press hadn't been invented on Dawn, or had been forgotten, much the same thing. Nor were there anything like schools, where you could go and ask a ridiculous question like, what is the geography of this planet? Nor were there maps; the general outlines of the areas around Leilas were known to all, the gorge, the troughs, the mountains, and the flats west of the lake. All areas beyond that would have been marked "unexplored," and left conspicuously blank. So in the end, they were reduced to visiting astrologers and soothsayers, prophets and religious savants, adding together what information they each contributed, and sorting out the suggestions of fact later on, back in the inn.

Han was particularly frustrated with the lack of knowledge about Dawn, evident on the streets of Leilas. Sorting out their information, which Liszendir had memorized as she heard it, he complained in some heat about the general ignorance of the area. Liszendir was unconcerned, which made Han all the more agitated and impatient.

"I want to know, how are these people ever going to do anything without schools, knowledge?"

"Those things don't really matter. People always learn what they have to, what is appropriate to their environment. Han, you grew up in a culture which has schools for general purpose and schools for every conceivable subclassification of data, but they do not as a rule spread knowledge or wisdom—just assemblies of data. As you have them, schools work on your society just like the differentiating fashions in clothes your sexes use, and hair styles as well—they obscure the innate differences, muddy them, make everyone equal, but it is the equality of a facade. People really are different from one another. And schools obscure the only kinds of knowledge worth knowing."

Han remained unconvinced. "Well, how do people learn to do anything unless they get some instruction? And what about your school, the one your braid operates—isn't that a school?"

"I have two examples for you. One, human and ler children learn to speak whatever language is native to their area, without school, at home, with playmates, with other adults in the area. At first their phonemes are unclear, their grammar is primitive, but they learn because they must communicate, and by the time they are adults, they do passing well enough. Sending them to school has only one effect—it makes them dishonest, for at school, they say what the instructor wants them to say, and when they leave, they go on talking the way they always did. Second, recall your own world, Seabright. It is a world of small continents and extensive seas and oceans. Winds blow over the water, and so sailing is still common there, even though you have powered ships for work. What is the difference between those sailing ships and ones which preatomic men sailed upon the salt seas of old Earth ten thousand standard years ago? And what did those sailors know about the physics of gases and liquids, principles of flow, drag, lift, coefficients of friction? Nothing. But they could see a smooth object moves easier than a rough one, and an elongated shape better than a blocky one. So they made boats, and held up sheets to catch the wind."

He retorted, heatedly, "Yes, and they lived with ignorance and superstition for thousands of years as well."

"Every age is superstitious, no more, nor less, than any other, your and my age, as well as in the ancient histories of old Earth." She answered back amicably, as if speaking to an errant child. "Han, knowledge is just like a mathematical notation of a number and a part, what do you call them?

"Decimals? Where you symbolize the fraction by successive repetitions of the number base, after a point which cuts off the whole number?"

"Yes. We have the same thing in our numbers. Very well, let me use your system, ten base. You have a number, yes, which is not divisable by whole numbers evenly—it has a part left over. So you keep after it, you say, 'I've got to know exactly what this quantity is,' and so keep dividing, dividing. But it doesn't end, it just keeps on going, and each new digit is unexpected. You discover, but for every one you derive, you know there is another one waiting for the operation in the next place."

"You mean irrational numbers?"

"Yes. And what do you call things like this? Irrational! Yet they are the very symbols of the universe, the very heart of what rationality it has. So, knowledge is just like that—you can derive as many places as you please, the next one is just as unknown as was the first, and there is no end to it. Do you understand me? There is no such thing as exact knowledge."

She waited a moment to see if he was following her. "And so we do not have what you would call public schools which teach things the child can and should learn on his own. The only people who learn in schools are the dumb. But we do have other things, where you learn a particular discipline, an art. Do you know that? Ler do not have science, we have arts only. We have physicists, chemists, mathematicians, as many as humans, but they practice *arts*, they learn discipline, and they do not play with abstractions. It is things like that which brought the ler into being in the first place.

"In my school, the place of the Karens, we take the child only when it becomes adolescent, sexed. What do we teach? We teach philosophy, knowledge of the body. How do we start? We make them sit down and learn about themselves, about nature. The first year, all they do is look, at waves in the sea, streams, leaves, small animals. We have a saying: 'To learn calligraphy, leave pen and ink at home, for calligraphy does not consist of pen, brush, and ink, but of what is within the calligrapher.' Or you will say, 'I wish to learn how to paint pictures of nude humans,' and ler as well, for all I know. So you gather up all kinds of surfaces upon which you will paint, you arm yourself with brushes, knives, various sorts of paints, you spend years learning about these things, and all this time you have not learned anything about the body, that irrational surface which you will represent, or how you may feel about it. And to treat it well, you will have to love it and be at peace with yourself. So you come to a ler school for painting pictures, and the teacher will say, 'Now, you take all those brushes and things and we will go and have a nice bonfire with them, perhaps cook something over them, because what I will teach you is not of brushes and techniques, but of the subject, for if you do not know it, you will never represent it.' You say, 'Oh, but I want to paint! He will reply, 'We can get to that later, perhaps.' So I know how to fight, hand-to-hand, I am trained, I am an adept. I did not get this way by learning about tensile strengths of bone, compressibilities of skin and tissue, about weights and forces. I learned by thinking, exercising, making love with my fellow students, dancing, and other things. You look to the side of a star when you wish to see it, yes?"

"Does that help us, here?"

"Yes. We do what we can, with such style as we can muster."

But they discovered there wasn't very much they could do, alone on a strange and primitive world. The locals of Leilas knew very little about conditions elsewhere on the planet—they thought that the world was flat, and that the sun moved, and that earthquakes were caused by the carrier of the world, a primitive reptile called a *khashet*, which occasionally stumbled or itched. The poles were hells for sinners, unknowable and unapproachable, and the middle latitudes scourged by two winters a year. West of Leilas the desert started, and as far as they knew, it was endless. The mountains marched far to the north and south, and the only break in their great ramparts was the gorge, cut by the great river, which led to the "freecountries."

Geography was against them. The country of the Warriors was somewhere around the curve of the planet, probably at least 12,000 miles away, and to get there, they would have to walk, braving the winters, short but hard, and physical conditions which had brought civilization on Dawn to a standstill, to its knees. Who could cross mountains on foot whose *passes* were at the pressure equivalent of 20,000 feet altitude; who could cross high plains such as they had landed on the edge of when they escaped the Warriors; or cross desert sinks where water boiled when the sun was overhead?

Nor could they join trade expeditions, pilgrimages, or the like. Outside local areas, there was no travel on Dawn. It was rumored that there were other settled places, lands, cities. The Warriors, for example, were reputed to live in a very large country. But nobody went there, unless the Warriors came to get him in their ship. So people were stagnant on Dawn, barely holding their own, ever so slowly becoming steadily more crude as the years marched on.

And from what they could determine, Dawn as a planet was in an early phase of the evolution of life; there was no

animal life native to the planet more complex than things
intermediate between reptiles and amphibians, and the plants,
save some things which were obviously imported, were no
better. It was a world, young and raw, on which its own
mammalian life forms were somewhere three hundred million years in the future. If the primary didn't go nova first.

And the Warriors had Han and Liszendir's ship, and their
own. These were the only two spacefaring craft on the whole
planet, and in fact were the only long-distance craft of any
kind on the whole world. Thousands of leagues lay between
them and the ship. They could do little. Before they went to
sleep, they slid into each other's arms, and made a slow, exploratory kind of love, again. And then slept, daring to
hope for no more than that, for the present.

On the morning, they bought a small pack animal similar
to a burro, and loaded it down with food and provisions, on
which they spent most of their money. Han suspected that
the ancestors of the little animal had arrived with the people. They left the inn, the Haze of the West, with sadness, for
if what they had learned had been hard to bear, the peace
and rest they had known within its walls had been welcome
to them, a quiet time they had enjoyed deeply. The last of
the money went for a short sword for Han and a dainty,
but effective-looking, knife with a leaf-shaped blade for
Liszendir. With all of their things stowed on the pack
animal, they departed Leilas through the north gate for the
country of the upper trough.

As they left the city and began climbing up the gentle but
steady slope, they looked back briefly at the great city,
or what passed for one on Dawn. The wall around it was
neither high, well fortified, nor continuous, being broken in
places by time in two winters a year. They may have
needed it once; that was many years ago, judging from the
condition of the wall. Behind the wall, the irregular, rambling city spread itself out in the harsh sunlight, and as they
got farther away from it, blended into the background of
rock, mud, and sparse vegetation like some natural growth
of dun-colored moss, or perhaps an odd type of lichen.

They faced to the north and began walking in earnest. On
their right, they could see full on the harrowing mountains
which rimmed the high plateau to the east; they went up, up,
first snow-covered on the lower slopes and peaks, then naked
rock, and still higher, the terrible broken summits whose

highest points stood glaring over the planet from a height above ninety per cent of Dawn's atmosphere. To the west, their left, there was another range, lower, and from all appearances, mostly volcanic. No vent was erupting at present, although several peaks trailed thin streamers of smoke from their summits. And although the west range was lower, it still was too high to be passable. Once away from the city, they looked out on a bleak, harsh landscape, lit by a piercing sun, that was not a lot better than the view they had seen from the high plains.

In Leilas, Han and Liszendir had been in a relatively warm climate, low down close to the river. During the day it was decently warm, cooling off only at night. But as they gained altitude walking up the north trough, the air cooled noticeably, and began taking on the unmistakable colors of autumn. They were not walking fast enough to keep up with the sun of Dawn on its journey north to the pole. A steady wind began blowing from behind them up the trough, whose end lay over the horizon, out of sight. As each day passed, the sun made smaller circles in the northern sky, and in the south the darkness grew. It became colder.

Human forms of buildings, particular styles of houses and outbuildings, ways of cultivating land, began to give way to ler forms, gradually, then predominantly, then finally completely. The houses were not the ellipsoids of the ler familiar now to both Han and Liszendir alike, but smallish stone houses of two stories, each with what appeared to be a watchtower attached to it. By the time they had reached ler country, the weather had finally turned sour, and rain and cold were common. They met fewer and fewer travelers on the road, which grew more and more narrow. They were both beginning to feel like fools. The few ler who would talk to them were worthless for their purposes—and they seemed even more ignorant and benighted than the humans of Leilas and its outlying areas. Liszendir pronounced them hopeless, fidgeting with frustration. They were not the people she was looking for.

On a night of a wild storm of either very wet snow, or half-congealed rain, they could not be sure which, they reached the top of the trough. In the darkness and wind, they would not have noticed, except for the fact that as they were looking for a place to shelter, Han saw that the sluggish creek they had been partially following no longer flowed south, but northwards. North, there was a hint of

greater darkness than there had been before. They had no
idea how far they had walked; only many days, perhaps
twenty, in the worsening weather. In the dark and storm,
they finally managed to discover an abandoned shed, and
just as they were moving into it, it started snowing. Inside
the shed, they were protected only from the wind, not the
cold. They looked outside several times, but it grew no better. Without any comment, they resigned themselves, and
curled up together in their blankets, unspeaking and unmoving. They were beaten, most of the food was gone, and
there was nothing left to do but start back for Leilas.

In the morning, Han went out to see to their few remaining packs of food. Inside, it had been cold, but as he stepped
through the door of the shed, the air bit at his face with
a new vigor he had not felt yet on Dawn. It was a portent of
what would come with colder weather. He looked about in
the dim, north-autumnal light leaking over the mountains.
There had been a fair amount of snowfall during the
night, and most of it had drifted in the winds; but for the
while, it was all they were going to get. The sky was absolutely clear, deep violet-blue, through which an occasional
star could still be seen. Eastwards, the mountains reared
high above them, casting deep shadows. The south lay in a
hazy darkness, and to the west, the other range looked
hardly less forbidding, though at the least the west range
had snow on its summits. It was unhuman, wild, fierce
beauty. He stood in the cold morning air for a moment
and looked out over the rocky, desolate scene. They were
at the high point of the trough, and there was nothing
there, absolutely nothing.

Something far away, on the edge of the west-range, caught
his eye; something moving. He looked closer. He couldn't
make it out. He looked away from it, then back. Yes, now
he could, but just barely. It was a building, the same color
as the dark, andesitic rock of the volcanic mountains to the
west, now not yet out of the shadow of the higher mountains eastwards. The moving part which had caught his eye
seemed to be smoke, a thin wisp of smoke which dissipated
quickly. It was too far to tell what it was. But there was
smoke! Somebody did live here, high up on the hard crest
of the world Dawn.

Han went back into the shed, hurriedly, and woke Liszendir. As he gathered their things together, she went out-

side to look at it herself, the dark, smoking building. She came back in, shivering. But she agreed. They set out for it immediately.

The distance was greater than they might have guessed, for neither Han nor Liszendir had learned to guess distances accurately, either on Chalcedon or on Dawn, but there was another element—the drifted snow, which had fallen the night before. It slowed their pace from a walk to a crawl, and for hours they seemingly made no progress at all. But they did close some of the distance, and as they drew closer, they could see the smoke more definitely, and they could also see the shape of the building better. They were not particularly encouraged by what they saw: it was apparently a castle or fortress, of grim black rock. The sun finally cleared the mountains and shone on it from the northeast, illuminating it with a stab of harsh light. They could see it clearly, although it was still miles away: a castle, with pennants or flags visible above the higher parts. Whatever it represented, someone lived there, and they were home.

It took the greater part of the short day for them to reach it through the snowdrifts, but at twilight, with the light fading swiftly, they stood before its gates. The gates were closed. Nor did it appear to either of them that they had been opened for a long time. Another dead end. Small, stunted trees grew in patches of windblown dirt which had collected in the lintels. In exasperation, Han walked up to the gates and pounded on them with the hilt of his sword. Liszendir watched for a moment, then raised her voice, calling out loudly. They expected no answer; to pound on the door and shout was better than nothing. But in a few moments, lights and faces appeared at the top of the walls. The light failed, and all that was left of the daylight was a hesitant, trembling pearly color in the northwest. In a few moments they were directed around to the other side, and there, through a small door in the walls, which would have been near-invisible even in full daylight, they were let in, pack animal and all, and shown to a room for the night.

Inside, it was very much as Han had expected it to be; he had been a reader of medieval romances as a young child. A nobleman's castle was exactly what it was, but one without the spendor of the ones in ancient tales. It was run-down and dirty, and fading hangings of no distinction, past or present, many frayed and tattered, covered the bleak stone of the inner walls. Shabby watchmen and ser-

vants passed on errands of seeming urgency, as shoddily
decorated as the walls. It was a cheerless, ugly place, cold
and damp.

"I can't believe ler would live up here to begin with, but
if they were crazy enough to, they surely would not live
in a pile like this," Han observed to Liszendir, as they
washed in the cold room one of the servants, a human, had
set aside for them.

"It is certainly beyond me, but after talking to some of
those we met along the way up here, I should not be too
surprised at anything we'd see. Brr!" She shivered, goose-
pimples popping out all over her skin, which Han was scrub-
bing at that moment vigorously. Then she continued, "But
why a fortress? People build fortresses when they expect attack, but from whom? This would not even be worthy of
the notice of the Warriors, either for its strength, or how
many could hide in it, for it is too small." Han could not
answer her question.

They were even colder after washing. Han searched the
small room, which was filled with shelves and closets along
the walls, until he found some rough blankets. Then they
lay down together on the small, hard bed, which creaked
ominously as they both put their weight on it, and curled
closely around each other, primarily for warmth. Soon, the
fatigue of the day and the warmth of their bodies began
acting on them, and they drifted off, asleep without realizing it.

They were woken sometime later, they did not know how
long, by a major-domo with a leer, who announced through
the opened door that the lord of Aving Hold would be
pleased to have their company at dinner. He spoke with a
cynical air which chilled Han to the bone.

Without speaking, they got up, dressed, and began following the major-domo, who had respectfully waited outside.
He conducted them through a bewildering array of portals,
drafty hallways, junctions, nodes, nexi. Sometimes they
passed rooms and halls where there were lights, voices, the
sense of the presence of many people. Other times they
seemed to go through parts of the castle which had been
abandoned; doors stood ajar on darkened rooms whose only
inhabitants were piles of trash, stacks of wooden fagots,
dust, as glimpsed in the quick light of a sputtering oil lantern borne by the servant. It was to Han an eerie, fey, dangerous place, perhaps the most perilous they had entered
yet on their journey. If Liszendir felt any of the same appre-

hensions, she gave no sign, spoke no word; she was totally absorbed in gathering sensory impressions of the castle. After what seemed to be an interminable walk, they finally arrived at a grand hall, or what would pass for one in this hulk. It was decorated and lighted in a semblance of gaiety, of celebration, but Han mentioned to Liszendir that it was generally as shabby as the rest of the castle, and that he hoped at least the food might be a little better. She smiled weakly back at him and nodded.

Once inside, they were seated before ornate place settings at a large octagonal table. There was a fire in the fireplace to one side, candles and lamps all around, and to the other side, what appeared to be a platform, as if for musicians, or entertainers, a stage. Some of the servants were busy there at this very moment, arranging chairs, moving other articles, cleaning and dusting, all with great haste and urgency. They were soon interrupted, to their general annoyance, by the arrival of a troupe of musicians, who carried instruments the likes of which were completely foreign to Han. The instruments were all of the stringed-instrument family, handmade in fine style, but their bows were complex mechanical devices, which used battery power, apparently, to drive belts of bowstrings or little pluckers. The musicians settled themselves into an order of seating known to them, activated their electric bows, and commenced playing, without introduction or hesitation. There was no conductor. They all seemed to play together without effort. The motors concealed in the handles of the bows made a very fine whirring noise, which, oddly enough, seemed to fit into the music very well, particularly when certain of them varied its speed for a particular passage.

Something jarred Han's perceptions about the musicians. They all seemed to be humans, well enough, he could see that from the configuration of the hands, if by nothing else, yet they themselves bore a striking resemblance to one another, almost as if they were members of a family. He watched them closely. No. Not a family, something else. He had seen shows put on by families of entertainers before. Family members had features which differed a certain amount, but their expressions were similar. These resembled one another rather more closely, but the effect of likeness was distorted, broken up, by a great variance in expressions and mannerisms among the individual members. This latter impression was very strong, so that they did not appear to be a family group at all.

But however much the performers looked like one another, their instruments varied greatly, almost impossibly, in an astonishing array of shapes and materials, woods and metals and hides and other unrecognizable materials, and they produced an even more astonishing variety of sounds, seemingly every possible vibration, harmony, squeak, overtone, resonance, microtone, slide, drone and gasp. There were no drums; the rhythm seemed to be implied, rather than directly stated. Liszendir listened intently to the music, and after a moment, pronounced it to be of ler origin in musical structure, but highly mannered and in her opinion, far gone into artistic decadence.

Han laughed to himself and said to her, "You have been many things to me since Boomtown, but I hardly suspected you were an art critic, too."

She looked at him incredulously for a moment, then laughed herself. "Of course you wouldn't know. But I am, indeed. You see, for us it is the reverse of your human way of doing things. We have a word in Singlespeech which means a person who does nothing but make art of one medium or another. This word is also a slang or popular word for what you would probably call a freeloader, if my Common is correct. We regard art as the province of all, and the profession of none. And as for myself, a special curriculum of art was included in my training as an integral part. Performance and criticism, both. I am trained in many media, senses and limbs. You know that there is an art for each sense. So then: I know symbols and visual methodolgy, music, poetry, as well as dance, mime, and other forms which have no parallel with humans. My degree of accomplishment varies somewhat, for we all are not equally competent in all ways of expressing ourselves, which is a truism with which you are doubtless familiar. I do three things: ler poetry, in which I am known in a minor way on Kenten; in painting, which I do well enough, but am not known, and do not wish to be, being one of the leaf-painters . . ."

"Do you mean painting on leaves?"

"No. Pictures of leaves and branches. It is an ancient discipline of concentration and form. And the other is music. I play an instrument which makes sound with a reed and you control the pitch with fingerholes and pads. You would say woodwind, although the *tsonh* has no exact parallel to anything you would know. It is double-reed, but like the bassoon, only higher in pitch, like a female voice, alto. Yes. An alto bassoon. It is about so big . . ." And she made a gesture with her hands. "I have been in some public concerts, although none of them have brought me fame as the world's greatest *tsonh*-player. Still, I was neither booed nor hissed. Sometimes I play alone, sometimes with backgrounds, and with groups which play all together and then apart."

Han sat back in his chair, dumbfounded. He tried to imagine Liszendir playing her instrument, the soft, full mouth, which kissed so well, intent, drawn, tightly gripping a double reed, concentration on her face. He gave up. It could not be visualized.

She watched his face, carefully reading expressions. An impish, fey look flashed across her face. "Aha! You think I work hard at it, that I make wrinkles in my face. Not so. I like to play very much, it is very relaxing, transporting, I do not live in this world then. It feels *good,* it is not work. But I have to admit to you that however much I like it, the *tsonh,* I do not play it so well as I write poetry, or so is the opinion of those on Kenten who have seen me do both. So, for art, I shall be a poet, I suppose. But I do know music, too. That is why I say what I do about these."

She would have said more, and Han would have let her. It was completely incongruous, that they should have had the escapes and adventures they had had, and be sitting in the hall of some unknown character, with the future, even as close as the next minute, being completely blank, blurred, unknown, and be calmly discussing music; amazing. But that added spice to it. But they were interrupted, not by an addition of something, but by a deletion. The music had stopped. The silence was dead and empty after the rich texture of sound that had filled the background of their perceptions. It was broken now only by the whirring of a few electric bows, as apparently some of the musicians had forgotten to deactivate them when they stopped playing. The others glared at the clumsy offenders, obviously novices, and the tardy musicians silenced their bows. The whisper of hair on little pulley wheels stopped.

The cynical majordomo they had met before marched into the room with an odd attitude which suggested equal measures of insubordination and abasement, coming to a halt at the head of the table, where he announced in a stentorian, grating voice, "The Lord of Aving Hold and his honored guests!" Then he departed. Han stood up, as did Liszendir.

Two figures emerged from behind a curtain and strolled up to the table, smiling and very obviously pleased with themselves. They were both ler, where the servants had all been human, and Han and Liszendir knew them both. The short, bald one was Hath'ingar. The taller one was the very same elder ler who had told Han in Boomtown that his name was "alphabet." He wore a black overrobe trimmed with silver, and underneath a simple shirt laced up at the neck, tightly. But when they spoke, it was Hath'ingar who spoke first, while the other waited, respectfully. He was, whatever he was here, as "Lord of Aving Hold", subordinate to Hath'ingar, completely. It was a very bad development, and all they could do for the present was to look at one another in astonishment, just as they had been doing since they recognized the identity of their hosts.

VIII

———◆———

"The direction of the aim of evolution is toward the production, or creation, of autonomous creatures who will be able to alter their structure to fit the environment, and pass that structure on, by conscious choice: Homometamorphosis. 'People,' as we define them, human and ler, are as yet intermediary in this matter of relationship with the environment. We are not even wise enough to visualize how such a creature might make such a decision, or what it would seem like in our evaluation of decisions."

—Al Tvanskorosi Ktav, The Doomsday Book, Pendermnav Tlanh

"Well met, well met again, and the third time pays for all!" Hath'ingar exclaimed with great cordiality. "Be seated, eat, indulge and enjoy yourselves! Aving's cooks are the best on this side of Dawn, or so travelers and other rogues tell me. Well? Go on, fall to it! There is no trap and no trick." He sat himself down and began to eat, with great gusto and an air of appreciation and satisfaction. The tall one, Aving, signaled to the musicians to play, and they began, immediately commencing a relaxed air.

Han and Liszendir sat down, stupefied. Han looked at the ler girl. She sat still, as if paralyzed, staring at the pair across the table. He leaned toward her and said, "Eat, Liszen. We have endured enough of that clabber he calls food concentrate on the ship, and because of him we have both starved, more than once. So take it." She looked down at her plate as if it were some strange implement about which she knew nothing, could know nothing. Then she blinked, and began to eat.

"Excellent, excellent advice. After all, why face the future hungry, whatever it may become? We all need well-padded bellies against the cold and circumstances, and besides, we have much to say to one another, and what better time than over a friendly meal?" Hath'ingar was completely at ease, the very image of a perfect, jovial host.

Liszendir looked up, sharply, eyes flashing. "I cannot imagine what we could ever have to say to each other."

"No?" His amazement seemed sincere, a genuine expression of puzzlement. "Ah, but there is much indeed. Indeed and indeed! But I have been remiss in my duties as host. Let me introduce my friend here, Aving. And my real name, which you may use, no titles, please, is Hatha." Han caught a flicker of motion out of the corner of his eye, from Liszendir, at the mention of the stranger's real name, Aving. Something about a name, about words, about Singlespeech, which was the universal language of Dawn, which was phonetically completely regular, even as used by the Warriors or the humans on Dawn. Aving! Of course! No word or name in Singlespeech ended in two consonants, even-ng. It was a trait they had noticed in the speech of the family they had known in the gorge, and in the people of Leilas. Now he had it, and he could see Liszendir had it, too. But what was the reason? In a language which allowed no exceptions, the one exception they had seen flared like a beacon, but its brightness obscured the reason behind it. But Hatha-Hath'ingar was continuing. He had not noticed. " . . . Aving is here to keep an eye on things in this district, this area around and about Leilas. The castle deters the locals from prying into affairs which are beyond their scope, and which will not only remain so, but withdraw to increasing distances. When you arrived, here of all places, Aving remembered, and so notified me. I came from the home countries of the Warriors, flying your ship, if you please, and may I say that it is as fine and responsive as a passionate adolescent girl. Why you would come here is beyond me, but now that you are here . . ."

Han tried to betray no confidences at the remark about adolescent girls, but some movement, some grimace, gave him away. Of course. The remark had been designed to do just that.

"Ah, yes. So I see. Yes, I am aware of the interesting liaison you two have formed along the way, have been for some time. How do I know? By reading body language. Han, yours shouts to one who is an adept in such reading, but I hardly need to turn to shouts, when even Liszendir, with her training, which appears to be extensive, cannot silence her own. And it tells me far more, and in greater detail, even though it is muted." Han turned to look at her. He knew the gestures, the ways people acted to one another, but he was no reader of the language of gesture, except in a very primitive way. And what did Liszendir really feel?

She answered Hatha, calmly, coldly, "So much I admit, which is my problem alone, and which I shall solve under the law in the proper season for such things."

"Poof and pah. We are not concerned in the least degree with the strictures of the fours. We have overthrown such bucolic botchery, and have substituted in its place a truly noble concept—one which recognizes the true evolutionary status and duties of our people. So, Liszendir, do you wish toys for the body? Then take them. It is your right. And when you are finished, then cast them out in the trash, or if you feel charitable, give them to the poor in used condition. I care not. I am elder phase, and do not envy or resent your simple gratifications, when I have a greater one, the itch for power."

Han interrupted, "We can discuss toys another time, but you live under a misconception if you still believe that nonsense about supermen. Hatha, it has long been proved that the ler are not *hyperanthropoi*, but *alloanthropoi*, not super-men but other-men."

"So we shall see in time, shall we not."

Liszendir, always to the point, asked, "So what are your plans for us, now that you have us again?"

"A good question—a good answer. First: you both are now beyond punishment, and I have absolutely none in mind. For you, Liszendir, an honored place with the horde. And for you, Han, also honor. You will teach us about your drive system. As you now know, we do have problems with our drive, with the great ship, now called *Hammerhand*. It is old, but it has also been rebuilt, in a hurry, and there are other technical problems as well. I know you are not a technician, but you know enough to be of great use. Both of you have shown extraordinary skill in escaping me twice, and we can certainly use the mental workings behind such exploits. Also observe: you have survived to walk to Aving's castle, which is a feat no native could imagine, and one no Warrior, un-fortunately, would attempt. And not only survived, but pros-pered, as you wished. Ah, yes, we need that greatly, more than little revenges."

Aving added, "It will not be all work, of course—there is compensation, according to the degree of service you are able to perform. Both of you will have choice of mates as well. For you, girl, the meaning must be clear—you will be fertile soon. There are Warriors in plenty, as many as you want. And for you, Han, you do not have the faintest idea of what we have to buy your cooperation. None whatsoever. But I will hint. You see, we are engaged in a great program for humankind, one which you would never have been able to do for yourself. We are domesticating humans, cultivating them for their potentialities as the farmer grows and selects his varieties of grains. For all the long generational times, humans are as plastic as wax, as changeable as weather. Some will be livestock, others for creatures of burden, others for technicians, still others for amusing pets, just for the exercise in control of shape and color. I know humans keep pets, but ler never have. So we remedy still another lack. And like the small carnivores humans are so fond of, we shall also take our pets with us to hitherto unknown heights of luxury, and shape them into forms, sizes and colors never imagined by them, just like humans have done with their animals and pets."

Han asked, "Is this a new idea, or is it an old one?"

Hatha answered, "It is as old as time, and actually can be traced back to human beginnings."

Liszendir commented, "I am surprised you go on this path, so easily. You violate many wise principles, many things which are not opinions, but insights into reality. I am well grounded in these. People, and I include ler in that term, are low in efficiency as loadbearers, and as food they are hopelessly inefficient. Because a creature is high in evolutionary position does not mean it falls in a usable position in the chain of ecology. We have found many planets, and on every one where there was indigenous mammalian life, in its seas there were whales. Whales do not eat other whales —they live on the simplest foods available. Whalebone whales, the majority, live on beds of floating plankton, the simplest sea life. We take this lesson of success for our own."

"It is not a course I, Hatha, chose, but one chosen by the firstborn, many years ago. Besides, the lesson is meaningless for us: there are no seas on Dawn, and certainly no whales."

"So the person of the city, lacking words in his language for natural forms of terrain, imagines that such things do not exist, and that he can imagine glaciers in the equatorial deserts, or put horns on a tiger. Are you of the blood of Sanjirmil?"

"We are indeed descended of the line of the great foremother. The humans we took later. We intercepted, by accident, a colonial ship. Some we began domesticating immediately, others were strewn over the face of Dawn, to grow wild. They could endure greater extremes that we could. This was long ago, and is counted matter of legend. Myth has it, it was done in the time of Sanjirmil, although there are those among us who reason that it was several generations later, on the basis of old tales. What difference does it make?"

"Only that these people survive in an environment beyond you."

Han asked, "What becomes of us if we refuse your offer?"

"I will personally give you a sack of grain and escort you to the door, from which you may fare as you will. Yes, both of you—the girl alike. I wish to woo you, not dispose of you. Disposal is easy, and an easy thing is a cheap thing. Is it not so, trader? Who will work for a cup of sand, and who will buy it with hard-earned coin? So refuse and go your way: I can afford to be generous. But consider—you cannot leave Dawn, for I have the only two spaceships within many a year of space. You cannot stir the locals up, human or ler of these parts. They do not care. They will kill you for heretics if you persist with your wild tales. Survival here is enough: and without our assistance, they would soon be back to grubbing roots on the plains and living in caves. And for yourselves; you know very well what is going to happen to Liszendir. Now she will cohabit with you, you will be lovers, you will do all the things to each other that such do. But once her fertility commences, she will either leave you, or come to hate you. It is a cruel time. So you will spend your lives for nothing. Do so. I will, as I said, show you to the door with a sack of grain. Walk back to Leilas and squat in the streets and void like the beasts."

He paused, to let it sink in, and went on further. "And as for the ship which was yours . . . in time we will puzzle it out. We have other resources, and some fine domesticated minds we can direct to it. We are not in a hurry."

"At least you do no discredit to the firstborn by annulling that principle." Liszendir spoke with some heat.

Han felt a chill of despair and disgust pass over him. Hatha had drawn a cruelly accurate picture, one which was not attractive in any aspect of it. They had a choice, but it was no choice at all.

Liszendir said, "All this sounds very well, of course; very well thought out. Crude, but possibly workable. But I have many questions to ask."

"And answers you shall have!"

Han could not mistake the gloating in Hatha's voice. That he expected. But Liszendir, fishing for something with this monster? There was no mistake, he had heard a distinct element of curiosity in her voice, of interest. Could she actually be interested in working for him? He looked over to her, watching her face intently, carefully. He could not read her face. Han felt another chill, a sinking sensation, a vertigo. What of her loyalties? Han felt all of the certainties he had known in the past, their past, turn into mud, hot wax, to slump and run, permutate into new shapes, shapes of disturbing outline. He looked at her again. The face he knew well now was no longer lovely, child-plain, charming, promising adventure. It was blank, vacant, the face of a statue, despite the movement that was in it; her thoughts were elsewhere.

He saw no longer the lover, but an alien female of completely incomprehensible motivations, and possibilities.

There was a lull in the conversation, during which Han kept glancing at Liszendir, trying to read some intent, or pattern, in her face. There was none visible to him. The face was stony, distant, abstract, where before, even when it had been disagreeable, it had been involved, concerned. She blankly watched the musicians, the guards, Aving and Hatha, the table setting. Aving and Hatha were now in the process of having a polite but intricate argument. Aving might very well be the subordinate, but he clearly considered himself knowledgeable in some area over and beyond any knowledge Hatha might have. Han could not follow it: they were using an arcane technical language, more involuted than the hair-splitting of theologians, and even if he had known the subject, the language alone would have been enough to bog him down. Liszendir appeared not to be interested.

The argument concluded, or so it seemed. The results seemed as inconclusive as the subject had been incomprehensible. Aving signaled to the musicians. Some, according to no order Han could discern, stopped playing, deactivated their instruments, and departed, as the others continued playing, without pause or hesitation. From a side hall behind Aving, others appeared, bearing even stranger musical artifacts. These new instruments were powered, as had been the first ones, but these had small compressors driving air into a bladder, whose pressure was valved out through tubes of various configurations, some controlling pitch through finger-holes, others by pads and levers, others by slides, and still others by valves. Some appeared to utilize bizarre combinations of all four controls. The new arrivals, who had the same general appearance as the first group, family yet not-family, settled in their places and began playing their ornate, overdecorated instruments, entering the stream of sound effortlessly. Han listened to it for a minute, but gave it up—it gave him a headache to try to sense order in the alien music, although he could, by straining, catch evanescent hints, suggestions, outlines which faded as swiftly in his perceptions as they had come. He stopped trying; its seeming simplicity concealed an underlying order which stupefied the mind.

Aving noticed that he was trying to listen to it. He said, conversationally, "I see you appreciate the music. This type they are playing now is very special—it has been patterned so that it avoids the persistence of memory of melody, which is a special feature of the human-type brain. Oddly enough, the musicians cannot learn it as you might learn some tune—they have to memorize the parts and play by rote, which detracts from the flavor of the performance, don't you think?"

Han politely agreed. Hatha took notice of them again. When he spoke, it was with an air of great confidence.

"I did not mean to imply earlier that you two had an unlimited sphere of decision and freedom of action. Ah, to choose, to steer one's own course: that is a privilege given to few, the high and the mighty. As we proceed down through the lower strata of society, naturally we find that such moments of choice become fewer and fewer. Now you, Han, have no class at the moment and hence no span of choice at all, as an integral part of your person. But I have much choice-span, and will, as we say, lend you a bit of mine, temporarily, for this issue. So: join the horde or go to Leilas, or at any rate, outwards out the out-gate, as we say. Binary, the very system you humans have tied yourself up in such knots over. The choice does not extend beyond that point of time, although in theory, you will doubtless accrue some choice of your own in either case, more perhaps in Leilas. Liszendir inherently has a bit more, because she is of the people and has reproductive potential; but in essence it is so little more than yours that the distinction is academic. However, I wish to make the distinction that hers is partially an inherent part of her potential class, even though at this time, it is of necessity rather low."

So they attached importance to the degree of choice one had, rather than material things, or money, as an indicator, or was it result, of class. Perhaps that had been the substance of that argument they had been having—Hatha's speech suggested quasi-religious overtones as he had been outlining the matter. Han said to Hatha, after this reflection, "I see what you mean, and cannot question your framework, because I do not entirely understand it. Yet, such as I see of this thing about choice, I do not agree entirely, because studies have shown that in human society the head of the organization most often has the least freedom, that freedom decreases as one moves upwards. But we see the ultimate in freedom as absence of responsibility, the vagabond who has only the primal concerns of his body to worry about—sleep, food, warmth. Apparently, you see ultimate freedom residing in the top, in something like an autocrat."

"An interesting point you bring up. I had not thought you quite so perceptive. And I should like to pursue this, as well as any other insights you may have. Yet, regretfully, I must use persuasion here, and remind you that you are embedded in my system, like it or not, be it intrinsically right or wrong. As matters stand, if I averred that the sky was made of stone, and had the power to treat with it as if it were so, you would be compelled by reason to agree, at least provisionally, would you not? So then! Make your choice! Choose carefully. You will have no further opportunity such as this."

Han looked away from Hatha, considering. As he did, he noticed something very peculiar: Aving, who had been ignoring them, was listening to the music with rapt attention, as if he were following it, note for note, melodic line for line. Han looked at the musicians. They were concentrating, deep in thought as they played. They could not play it by ear, but Aving could, apparently, follow it. He put his attention back to the matter at hand—go with Hatha or back to Leilas. He looked at each path carefully. Leilas was tempting, because it was away from the horde, the Warriors. And it was free, or at least so it seemed. But the freedom was meaningless. He would stay in Leilas forever. The other was repugnant, but in it was the hope that he could somehow get close to the ship, the *Pallenber,* once again. And to the little deadly gun which hopefully was still located in the locker at the back of the control room. And if he could learn how to activate it. . . .

"I have decided, Hatha. I will go with you, although for what it is worth, I am not overjoyed at it."

Liszendir said, tonelessly, "And myself as well." It was short, decisive, with no hints of feelings, hopes, plans.

The music played on. The new instruments produced sounds of great complexity and perhaps even charm, full of harmonics, overtones, resonances. They seemed to be more like woodwinds than anything else with which Han was familiar, which might go far to explain why Liszendir seemed so interested in the music. But there were disturbing suggestions of other kinds of instrument as well, and many things unknown to Han.

Liszendir asked, "I'm interested in one thing: why did you first try to capture us on Chalcedon? I mean, you yourself. Why not just send a crew of subordinates?"

"For one, there was no one else there. A spy needs to operate effectively, a great deal of choice, so of necessity he must be high in class. For what we were doing on Chalcedon, and why, the class level required was approximately that of myself. I was there to observe, and if possible, guide the reaction, if any, into proper courses. Efrem, you know? He did not come. We caught him lurking off-planet, the dirty little profiteer, waiting until we were done with the place. He planned to do some ravaging on his own. So we took him on a little tour, gave him a bag of money, and sent him on his way, to spread tales back in your Union area."

Han exclaimed, "So you had Efrem murdered, so he couldn't tell the truth!"

Hatha answered, thoughtfully, "No, in fact I had nothing to do with that. You surprised me with the news, if it was true."

"It was true enough. I saw the body, and there was . . ." Han was interrupted by a powerful kick under the table, of which above its surface there had been no indication. It was from Liszendir. He stopped. He had intended to say that Aving had been on Seabright, at the time, but she did not want him to say it. Aving noticed nothing. He was caught up entirely in the flow of the music.

Hatha noticed the pause, but apparently gave no thought to it. He continued, "So I was there, waiting for the reaction. You two took me by surprise, but the size of your expedition convinced me that we were either dealing with timidity, or subtlety so vast that it could not be distinguished from the former. A bully attacks two cowards; one cringes, and says, 'I am a coward!' The other cringes just the same, but he says, 'I am only waiting for time to strike.' But both cringe, you know? So subtlety dissolves into just another tawdry excuse. I thought first to catch you because I assumed high class, by a system of reckoning similar to mine. You were alone, you had choice, thus you were important, key people. Later events convinced me of my error. I saw that you two were most expendable, low pieces of no value at all, except as sensors for a greater, more cautious organism, whose real strength I had no idea of, even after I had seen you. I do not know, even now, and will have to make some more exploratory moves. Do not be so swift to take offense, for that was not my final evaluation. So I then thought, 'Capable, resourceful, but cheaply spent, withal.' Not so. In resource and adaptability alone, you both are more than a match for any of my line Warriors—were they of like disposition and patterns of thought, we could have had the Union long ago.

So now, after many corrections of course, I feel I am arriving at last closer to the course that is true, the one which will lead me to the answers I want."

She answered back, "There are indeed answers which we ourselves do not know. But since we join you, rest assured there are some areas we are only too anxious to communicate—when we find the answers, ourselves. Now. What do you do in place of weaving, the four-by-four way? That has bothered me since I have been on this terrible planet."

"You are wise, Liszendir, but not so wise that convention blocks the view of the horizon for you just as it does for others. But that is an interesting question, which I shall answer. We have several systems. When we first came here, there was great dissatisfaction with weaving in fours. It was held to be reactionary, antiprogressive, stultifying. Many held the four-by-four weaving responsible for the lack of enthusiasm of the old majority for the dreams of Sanjirmil. They refused adventure. So we applied ourselves to the problem, and devised a most interesting system. But first we went back to the old way and married, human-style."

"You should have known that that would produce subracial traits shortly."

"So it did, and rather more quickly than we had anticipated, a curious fact, a difference in rate which we have not yet explained. You can turn your efforts to that one, in addition to other things I will have you do. But soon a dominant tribe established itself, and established the new order. Now, we regarded couples as low-class, a human thing, and the weaving of fours as wrong. So we made up the triad system, which has parts of both in it, and which, being more complex, fits our view of ourselves."

Han interjected, "May I not appear so argumentative, but my people think that higher-order forms do not necessarily exhibit more complex features in all things."

Liszendir said quickly, before Hatha could answer, "I don't understand. Triads?"

"Thus. On Dawn, all society is divided into classes. The several types of humans, wild and otherwise, occupy the lower order. For the ler, there is a further division. The lower ler who are not Warriors continue to arrange their families in human fashion. The upper classes, in adolescent years, arrange themselves into threes, more or less randomly, although we ensure that all types of triads have equal numbers according to whom they will mate with. We call the threesomes oversexes."

"Oversexes?"

"There are three persons in each triad-oversex. They may not have sex with each other. Only with an oversex group of opposite gender. With three individuals, and two base sexes, there are eight possible arrangements of order, which divide into four types—three of one, three of the other, or two which are two-thirds male or female. Of course, the pure triads form the highest classes."

"I see. *Khmadh!*" The word Liszendir used appeared to be an obscenity, but if it was, it had no effect on either Hatha or Aving. It was equally meaningless to Han, who had no idea what it referred to. He had never heard it before. But he could see one effect of the triads right away: it would reintroduce and keep reinforced sex-specific behavior. He could also make a reasonable guess that the predominantly female oversexes would be the ones which would raise the children. Probably in isolation from the adults, in a subculture world of their own. But it made a sort of sense: a punished child grows up into a punisher, and one who is pushed into seeing his own age group as a special category of people will be a separator as an adult. With the main population of ler, of which Liszendir was a part, they obliterated cultural differences between the sexes to bring each sex up to its full contribution; they would apply similar processes to the difference between child and adult, with the seemingly contradictory result that the child would be more child, the adult more truly adult, than if imposed differences, with commercial origins, were grafted on them. But the Warriors had carried the other extreme further than anyone else. They probably would show a corresponding degree of aberrations. Han did not reason this out in linear fashion; it came to him all at once, as he thought of it, "sideways." He felt proud of it—he had learned more than just language, or even the expressions of love, from Liszendir.

Hatha added, "Such oversexes, once formed, last until the members die. For example, I now stand alone because the other two members of my triad have been killed in battles."

"Let me guess," she said. "Your triad was all male."

"Indeed."

"It figures." She looked at Aving. "And him?"

Aving replied, "Of the highest of the lower ler. But have

no fears—our order is flexible. My offspring have joined the
Warriors as good triadists."

"Please tell me no more. I must digest this new order, to
see what sort of place I might have in it."

Hatha said, "Good enough. You will see more on the morrow."

Han felt impatient, anxious to get going. "Why tomorrow?
Why not now?"

"Nothing mysterious. It simply is late, and I have been flying all day. I will need to be alert, with both of you aboard
tomorrow. So, then. Liszendir's choice: do you desire to be
apart this night, or together?"

"Together." Again Han thought; the old decisiveness. No
hesitation, no second thoughts.

"So be it, then," said Aving, and made a gesture to the
musicians, who stopped abruptly, in midstatement, as it
were. The majordomo came forward, from an alcove to the
rear of the hall, waited respectfully. Aving and Hatha arose
and departed immediately. The servant motioned to Han and
Liszendir. Without words, they followed him back through
the winding, confused halls, back to the room where they
had rested before. The only change was a welcome one;
the room was warm and comfortable, where before it had
been cold. The door closed behind them, clicked shut,
snapped locked with a heavy, definitive sound. They were
locked in.

Han realized as he became acclimated to the warm room
that he was tired. He began undressing as Liszendir was
turning out the lights, small lamps that used some aromatic
oil. With darkness in the room, they could see a high, tiny
window they had not noticed before; through it, dim, frosty
starlight came into the room. His eyes recovered before hers,
but not before he heard a rustling sound, and then felt the
warm, smooth body beside him on the small bed.

He half-turned away from her, and asked, "Can you really see anything we can do? Or do you hope to join these
creatures? I can't bring myself to call them people."

She did not answer immediately, but to his surprise, curled
around him, over his body, sensuously, erotically, with a
sinuous motion he knew well now. Only this time there was
something extra in it, an extra component. It definitely had
an effect, and it was more unbearable, feeling her so close,
smelling the scent of her hair. She brushed her face close to
Han's ear, began murmuring something in a soft, lascivious

voice he could hardly make out, who ever listened to those exact words, anyway. But then he did listen.

"Listen to me closely. We can talk no other way now, and I must be sure you know what I do, now. So listen. I am sure, by instinct, that we will be watched as long as we are together." It was clashing, discord; the tone of the words, their rhythm, volume, all carried the timeless messages of lovers since the beginning of time. But the words themselves, they came across to him like spears of ice out of a warm, wet fog. They glittered like diamonds. He couldn't tell if this effect was subjective, imagined, or an intended one. But it confused and chilled him. The soft voice with the hard words continued, ignoring his vague motions of escape.

"Do not suspect me now of race loyalty! I owe you more, body-love, than to any of these apes, despite any likeness which may be in reality or illusion between our hands. A hand is only as good as what it holds, and the use to which it is put, two thumbs or one. Or none, if there are such. But there is no other way—we must go with him! You acted perfectly, there. In Leilas there is only futility, filth and superstition. I will tell you about us, first. So you will understand all that I do. Completely. Consider that in Common, your people still have only two words to cover what happened to us—love and sex. And the word 'love' only rhymes with two or three other words, neither of which can be a noun. In singlespeech, we have almost four hundred words to cover various kinds of love and desire. And every word in Single-speech has over a hundred rhymes! Love, Hate—they are of no more significance than white and black, and the universe is filled with shades of grey and a full spectrum of color. So. Somehow, we have made between us, for my part, what we call *hodh*. It does not translate. But of it come deep emotions, and choices far beyond sex and loneliness. I did not give you my body out of weakness or lust. Fool! I am trained to deny the first, and the second I can banish by nothing more complex than full-remembering. It is just like before."

The tone of voice was amorous, hypnotic, lascivious. But the words! Han felt as if he was in the grip of some master witch, who could distort reality at will, with just words! They were savage, burning like fire, like swords and daggers. He groaned.

"I understand. Your perceptive field will not take the contradiction, the strain; you hear what my skin says, the tone of voice, and the words. You cannot take much of it, for it will tear your mind apart. You are fortunate I do not use Multispeech on you, it would be faster, if you could understand it. Even for us, this is hard, and this is where multichannel speech had its roots. This is *perdeskris*, Doublespeech. Now listen.

"I suspected that Hatha from the beginning, but I hesitated, did not act, and so much of all this is my fault. You already know why we keep a wide gene pool through the *klanh*, the braid. To abandon that system is to open the door to chaos. Mutations, freaks, who knows—all of which much faster than with you. Remember, we were made. So that beast in there will finish by destroying both humans and ler—the former through conquest, the latter by accident and negligence. We have to stop him. Quarantine Dawn. And to do that we have to act loyal, get close.

"There is more. Hatha did not know Aving had been offplanet. Keep that to ourselves; he already has an excuse ready, and Hatha will believe Aving, for the present. And you know as well as I do that Aving is not ler. He only looks like one. That may be cosmetics. He was listening, most carelessly, to the music he said neither human nor ler could follow. You saw, too! And he has been careless with his name—it is probably his real one. It ends in -ng, like no word of anybody's Singlespeech. And we must look into this higher-than-expected rate of race-forming he spoke about. If it was enough to pass into folklore, then there is something here on Dawn causing it. Something perilous to ler, perhaps to humans.

"I have guessed what is coming for you and me when we get to the place where the country of the Warriors lies. Now I must ask you: if what has passed between us had happened back in civilization, with ler planets close by, or we had stayed on Chalcedon, at my fertility, would you have helped me to weave into a nice braid? Would you?" He nodded. "And so would I for you. So will we both, if we get the chance. But from now on it will be hard for us, for there are things I must do, and things you must do as well if we are to survive. This is more dangerous than when we were up on the plains. So perhaps tomorrow, perhaps even tonight, I will do and say cruel things. You must act and commit yourself as if I were no more. And soon it will be so anyway, because of fertility. So. You must do as I tell you. A test is coming. And tonight, you must reject me. Yes! You will do it! Now!"

He felt numbed, befogged, incapable of action. How long had she had him in that net of words? He looked to the small window. The same stars were visible in it, he remembered them well. Not more than a few minutes. But he remembered her instructions. Resisting her was hard at first, but slowly, he began to master, to override what his emotions and body were telling him. He pushed Liszendir away.

"No."

"But this is the last night for us."

"No. Do your worst. But I will not be a toy for you, while I see my own kind sold into slavery or worse."

Liszendir moved away, a motion of rejection, but in the faint starlight leaking into the room through the high, tiny window, he could see that she was winking at him. He ached. In the weak light he could also see her shoulders gleaming in the starlight. She pushed him over to one side.

"Very well. But I will sleep here. I am cold. Move over."

Han moved over and made room for her, and she settled into the small bed beside him. They did not speak again.

Han could not sleep, although soon he noticed that Liszendir's breathing had become deep and regular. He had not had time to reflect, time to foresee, since before Chalcedon; actions had been required, and actions were taken. Decisions had been necessary, and were made, to the best which could be expected under the circumstances. The method she had used to pass on this last bit of mutual planning had stirred all that up, brought it all to the surface, and moreover brought their relationship into sharp focus. Sleep was impossible; his mind was humming, busy, remembering, projecting.

All that she had said since they had been together had been so close to what he had been thinking himself that he had accepted it as they went along, putting the categorizations she outlined into the framework about such relations as he knew, his past. Now he saw that such a system had been totally inadequate to the task. Perhaps if he had been more experienced in affairs, instead of occasional encounters, which, for all their fun and sensual enjoyment, did not involve the participants very deeply, it might have worked, with some adjustments. But it was not so. Liszendir had been a completely new level of experience for him, and it would have been so even if she had been a human girl, and utterly conventional. But of course the first did not apply, and hence the second also went out the window, however conventional she might have been strictly within her own ler reference. But even after allowing all that, and recognizing the change in attitudes within himself, he could see still another problem area, and its secondary position in time could not obscure its primal position in importance. For a long time, he had been immersed in an alien surround, notwithstanding the fact that so much of ler ideas was seemingly familiar, as if the shapes were the same, but the colors different. That was not so, either. They had been in a survival relationship, in which they had had to learn to support and depend upon each other; they had become lovers. Was that because of the needs of their survival, or was it additional to it? He could not resolve that one, lying here in a strange room of an alien castle on the planet Dawn.

He felt deeply towards Liszendir still, undiminished. But at this point, the human and the ler view were coming into contradiction. His basic ideas told him that he should stick with her, whatever happened. Semper fidelis! But hers told her, and he was becoming increasingly aware of the ler idea that what they had made had reached a level from which there could be no denial. Circumstances might require other commitments, other liaisons, perhaps forever, but those things could not change the uniqueness they had known. As she saw it, then, necessity was necessity, and one had to weave. Liszendir would not take on the human outlook here, so hers would have to apply to him as well: because of what she had called their *hodh,* they would now make the supreme effort, the final gift, and find weaving partners for each other. If they could get back to civilization, even Chalcedon, then she would expect him to assume this role, which in other circumstances would be done partly by her, partly by the old braid generation. And what was more significant, she would take it on herself to do the same for him. It was a difficult attitude to accept, but it was clearly coming, at the greatest time they could hope for, within a few years, two or three, perhaps four. He had seen this coming, for Liszendir, since Chalcedon; what was difficult for him to absorb was that she saw the same thing clearly on the way ahead for him as well. The import of Aving's remarks, added to her words of a few moments ago, now became clearer; he would be exposed to human girls again, of unknown shapes and sizes, and there was a high probability that he would be offered one, to keep, as an enticement. If he could think like Hatha and the Warriors, that would be easy—take it, and use it. But through his deep experience with Liszendir, such an act would be untenable—he would assume even more responsibility for the enticement than he had for Liszendir.

He thought, for a moment, about something she had said to him, on Chalcedon, as they were having a mild argument about comparative philosophy: "Han, you humans build your systems of categorization of reality, your sand-sifters, as we call them, - *praldwar*, upon assumptions which you provisionally say are rock-hard, and then you stagger up onto them, blinking and gasping, like some lungfish on a flat rock. But in the ways of looking at reality, we are chaoticists, we return to the water. There is nothing stable, except the striving of life to impress its will upon the universe contrary to the direction of the flow of entropy."

To her, all living things, and many nonliving things, were individuals and deserving of respect. This was revealed by the language; symbols had one or two syllables, but *names* had three or four. She had said, "It is not practical, of course, to name them all, but when we are learning this principle, we are always instructed to look out upon the waves of the sea. 'See those waves?' says the teacher. 'Every one of them has a name, all that you can see, and all of them, all the way around the world, that you cannot see, will never see, *can* never see. We lump them all together, we say these are waves, but you should never let the convenience of that act of categorization blind you to the greater fact of the individuality of each one of them.' " So he thought of girls' bodies—sweet things, delightful. But there was nothing casual, nothing light whatsoever, in the things that passed between male and female, and that was the reality of it—not the excuses one told oneself to hide the early blunders one made upon others.

He saw the result of all these things coming. And, oddly enough, his new appreciation of how they fit together gave him a sense of complete relaxation, and he went to sleep immediately. His last thought was not verbal, but imagic: he felt an odd sense of accomplishment, but whether it was from a long-term change in himself, or what he had seen this night, he could not tell. It wasn't important, anyway.

They were awakened before dawn the next morning by the same leering head-servant, who escorted them back to the large hall where they had dined the night before. There

Hatha met them in great good humor, speaking in a most friendly manner, especially to Liszendir, and even offering her a place at the table. Han watched his actions closely, and after a few moments, was sure that she had been basically right; by some method, they had indeed been observed last night. There was subtle knowledge showing in Hatha's behavior. That was good for them, for it meant that he was starting to read things wrong. For a very short moment it flashed through Han's mind that perhaps it was he who was reading Liszendir wrong, that here was subtle double game-playing. But no, it blew away, vanished. She was not that subtle, but rather the opposite, direct and uncomplicated; and if she had wanted to dispense with Han, she could do it easily enough by a virtually unlimited number of methods. Now, if only Hatha would continue to read things wrongly, and if he and Liszendir could continue to play the charade out until they got close enough to move. If. If.

For his part, Han did not join in the breakfast discussion, but attempted to appear sullen, uncooperative, broken and resigned. Hatha spent scant attention on him, and apparently satisfied any suspicions he might have had early; thereafter he paid only cursory attention, if any at all. Hatha and Liszendir made a lot of inconsequential small talk, which underneath its bland exterior was really quite transparently interrogation. And of a high order, as well, skillfully professional. Hatha seemed to be trying to gather information primarily about Union ler attitudes and weapons, using a peculiar indirect approach, as subtle as the music had been the night before. But she gave nothing away, avoiding the interrogation easily enough, sidestepping the cautious, fencing approaches. Liszendir was a slippery fish who could make herself smaller than the meshes of the net being used to catch her. As he watched this performance, Han could not avoid evaluating the girl in a new light, much as he had been doing since they had met; a continuous process of re-evaluation. Hatha was obviously capable and alert, sharpened by decades of experience gained in the exercise of power, and in the effort to climb to those heights; Liszendir was, in her terms, not yet adult, but through an accumulated and passed-on store of wisdom, and training, she was, on the whole, almost a match for the leader of the Dawn expeditionary forces, by herself.

Everyone seemed to be finished with breakfast. Hatha

looked around impatiently, then gestured peremptorily, which caused the immediate appearance of three of the triads, nine warriors in all. They were all young, younger than either Han or Liszendir, but they seemed confident and dangerous, fanatics accustomed to instant obedience. Moreover, they were armed with several kinds of weapons, some of which Han recognized, and some he did not.

"Naturally," Hatha mentioned with a very courteous manner, "to the intelligent, the obvious never need be explained. Why explain such things—it is like explaining a good poem, or perhaps a well-constructed joke; the explanation takes the impact of recognition away." It would have been a good allusion if addressed solely to humans; but to Liszendir, and Han as well, now that he was also a speaker of Singlespeech, it was doubly pointed. Because every word-root had four meanings, and because the basic roots were "saturated," every pronounceable combination within the rules *was* a true root, with the resultant possibilities of confusion and misidentification, Singlespeech abounded with puns, "jokes," double and triple entendre, and from what Han had gleaned from Liszendir, the poetry was even worse, with severe syntactical compression and odd literary references to add to the confusion. Get the point, indeed. He thought Hatha might be overobvious. To the girl, the attempt at "subtlety" would be as brazen as a raucous shout in a quiet and secluded grove deep in the forest.

Hatha continued, "I do not wish to be troubled or disturbed by further futile attempts or false bravado. So. Han, you will fly the little ship. Now that I know something of how to operate it, doubtless primitive in technique by your standards, I can observe you to judge if you are performing correctly. I am sure you are able to cause the ship to perform some pervulsion detrimental to us all, but hardly one which will incapacitate ten of us, and yet leave you and Liszendir standing, or should I say, operable."

"I understand very well. It shall proceed as you wish."

They left the hall with no further ceremony, and went to the place where the ship had been grounded through another winding and dark passageway. After the close, dense darkness, their sudden emergence into the stark, clear openness of Dawn was something of a shock. It was early morning, and the north-autumn light was all around them. The sun was now low in the northeast, just clearing the far ramparts of the high and naked summits of the larger eastern range. The air was still, transparent as spring water, full of blues and violets. For Dawn, it was cloudy, with planes and swathes of layered clouds all over the sky, lightening toward steely grey and hints of pearl in the north, darkening into rich, deep blues and violet and darker tones in the south, which now was severely darkened. Han tried to imagine what the extreme of winter would look like from this point; the sun would describe shorter arcs across the northern sky, would move closer to the northern horizon, and would finally disappear, leaving behind only a vague northern glow which would dim and brighten daily. An eerie blue twilight, lit from the north, not the west, and overhead, the stars would shine. The South would be almost completely dark. He looked around, to remember the impression; it was unspeakably beautiful, the shifting planes of the sky, the piercing bright sun, the shadows and tones of the mountains, the spatters of snow left from the storm of two days ago. And the ship was there, too, grounded on a spur of rock. It, too, was beautiful. As they walked towards it, the ground underfoot crunched with frost. Before they entered the *Pallenber,* Han paused by the foot of the ladder, gazing out at the colossal mountains to the east one more time.

Hatha noticed. "You approve, you appreciate! That is good, very good! As for the natives of this Leilas district, they haven't the wit; they are terrified of them. They imagine them the abode of demons." Han could well believe the tale. Who else could live among those torn and rended surfaces than demons and malevolent spirits. Dawn had its beauty, but it was a terrible beauty which daunted and humbled and cast fears, rather than a beauty which reassured, comforted. Hatha went on, "We call those mountains the Wall Around the World. Technically, it is a misnomer, for they reach north and south only about two-thirds of the half-circumference. As far as I know, there is nothing like them anywhere else, on Dawn or on any other planet. They are so high that they break up the circulation of air, which is actually a help, for if they, and others similar to them, did not break it up, Dawn would be quite uninhabitable. I assure you it would not be so lovely here if the winds followed their natural bent—they would blow with truly hellish velocity. And they tell me that the mountains are still growing!"

They climbed up the ladder, and entered the *Pallenber.* As they filed into the control room, Han expected to feel at home, reassured. But he didn't; he felt profoundly strange, like some wild tribesman out of the bush, suddenly thrown into a room full of incomprehensible machines. The triad guarding him was watching him very closely. He did not think now was the best time; if they were expecting anything, it would be now. Later was better, if he could get the chance again. But he knew it would be better to wait for a better opportunity than act in a situation where there was little or no hope.

Han went through the sequence of activating the ship, slowly, carefully. When it was fully operable, he turned to Hatha and said, "We're ready."

"Good. Go simply—straight across. I had thought that perhaps we might take a grand tour, but on reconsideration, I think it might be better if we waited for that. Call it a reward, if you will, for good behavior. So, now; proceed!" He turned to the guards, who crowded the control room, and said something to them which Han did not exactly follow. He didn't need to; the meaning was transparently clear from the situational context. It most likely had been something like "Kill them at the slightest pretext." Han turned to the controls, but then turned back to Hatha.

"Wait. You can fly this kind of ship manually, if you want, but the most common practice is to set it up for automatics. It requires less energy of the ship, and definitely less of the pilot. But I can't insert a course until I know data about the planet—size, mass, reference points for arbitrary latitudes and longitudes."

"I don't have any of that information. We don't use those . . . what you called them. And size is of no matter. When we want to go anywhere, we just get up high enough to clear obstacles, and go there." For the first time, Hatha seemed genuinely perplexed.

"I can rise vertically, calibrate my altitude, and determine the size and mass from measured G force and angular diameter. Then if you tell me which direction you want to go, I can put it in. By your leave?"

"Of course, of course. Up, then down again. Fly the course in the fringes of the atmosphere; just enough to clear the peaks. There are no other mountains between us and the homeland of the Warriors." He now seemed not only uncomfortable, but actually embarassed. Why?

"Done."

Han enabled the drive, and the ship rose vertically until the planet lay below them, mostly dark and shaded, the terminator curiously slewed in respect to the rotation. In the far south, the land was covered by a mist or fog, which grew steadily denser and thicker in the direction of the pole. At the northern edges, nearer the equator, the cover graduated into ragged pieces, shreds and tatters of clouds moving up out of the cold parts of Dawn. Han steadied the ship, and began taking his measurements. Dawn was, as it turned out, quite large, even larger than Chalcedon, which was oversized, as habitable planets went. There was something else notable on all the instrument readings, but it was ambiguous in one sense, so for the time he kept it to himself. Finished, he informed Hatha that he was ready to take the course he indicated, which Hatha gave him, in vague terms. Han thought he knew what Hatha meant, and inserted the course.

The ship then dropped back down to approximately the level of the highest peaks. Han stared at the maser altimeter: it was indicating 75,000 feet above the top of the trough! He put the course into activate, and sat back, work done until it would be time to pick a landing site. Hatha looked impressed, and Han told him, "There is no need to fly it yourself, manually, in a gravity well. Besides, it wastes energy. You just set up a suborbital path and the ship flies itself along the minimum energy curve. Energy is low for lift, so all you get is thrust."

Hatha looked even more impressed. It occurred to Han that the reason for this must lie in the fact that he had flown the *Pallenber* from the land of the Warriors to Aving's castle manually, not even knowing about orbits, or the ability of the ship to follow them automatically, once commanded. But he had already flown space, in a ship of his own! What kind of energy were these idiots playing with? But he did not follow these speculations very far, for they were moving slowly now, crossing the high mountains, the Wall Around the World. The screen was showing titan naked summits so close it seemed that they could reach out and touch them. The effect was deceptive: the peaks they were looking at were miles away, and it was only their size and, at this altitude, the lack of atmosphere which lent them the impression of nearness. Han looked again; they had the same general appearance as free-floating asteroids he had seen. Over them, on the far side of the range, was the sun. Above them, the sky showed totally black, except for a pearly-blue band close to the horizon in the north. Below, the land on the far side of the mountains was a dull gold-brown color.

The high plains rolled beneath them, as their speed increased. They moved, and pushed the mountains back into the west. Han looked down onto the bare, apparently featureless surface. He supposed that he was looking at the same general area over which he and Liszendir had walked with such difficulty only a few months ago. But he could not make out any feature. Even the crater was invisible, at least so far as they had seen. The altimeter showed a decrease in altitude from the reading they had taken over Aving's castle. But this was apparent altitude, distance to the ship, not reference altitude above an oceanic level. It was higher than Aving's castle, as he already suspected very well. And they had walked over that surface. A blemish, a mark, drifted into view from his right, somewhat more to the south than he had expected. It was the crater, and there was the line of brush they had seen from the grounded warship. He could not see anything else.

"Hatha, when did you notice we were gone from your ship, when we first landed here?"

"Actually, quite soon. I suspected something when I came into the control room on my ship and found the young lady, here, gone, and the guards, ah, incapacitated. Permanently. I fear that out of gun range, I shall have to keep her under guard by many. She is more docile now, but for a while I thought that it would come to removing all her extremities, in order to keep her safe without doubt, and even with that drastic step, one might not be completely sure." He nodded politely towards Liszendir. "Correct, dear?" She smiled sweetly in reply, a facial gesture which really did not resemble a smile as all. Under the circumstances, it was thoroughly unpleasant.

Han turned back to the main screen. Ahead was new country. Below the ship, the land grew hazy, masked by a layer of thicker air, to which the altimeter agreed that the land was indeed lowering slowly in altitude. Some geography began to be visible on the face of the barren plains, and cloud formations could be seen. Ancient traces, mere rock colorings now, showed where mountains had been once, and sluggish lakes and rivers crawled over the surface. The lakes resembled nothing so much as the roots of tuberous plants, or perhaps curious organisms which might have anchored themselves to a sea-bottom, and fed in the upper waters.

After a time, Han saw, slightly to the right and south of their course, the object he had been looking for. It was near the terminator of approaching night. The trip had indeed taken only about an hour, but now they were on the other side of the world, and winter night was coming. The object was visible, even from suborbital distances, or perhaps it disturbed the weather enough so that was the visible part of it. But whichever it was, there was the ship of the Warriors, a visible bump on the surface of Dawn. As they drew closer to it, they could see that what they had first sighted was the weather it produced, for they could see it more clearly, and observed that it trailed streamers of cloud downstream of its bulk, the shreds and tatters blown away from the cloud masses by the prevailing winds out of the south. A lenticular formation with at least ten layers they could see domed over it, and the overcloud picked up fragments of the pearly light out of the north and spread the iridescent second light all over the area where the warship had been grounded. Han revised his estimates of the size of the warship upwards. He turned to Hatha.

"How do you ground that monster, and keep it in one piece in a gravity well?"

"Easy, easy. We simply never turn it off!"

"Never?"

"Never. At least not since the great ship was rebuilt and refitted, altered from its old role to fit its new one."

Liszendir had been silent the whole trip. But now, as they approached closer to the dreaded oversize warship, she became attentive and alert. She interrupted, "Is that the ler starship, the first one ever built, which left old Earth so many years ago?"

"Yes. The same. Although it is much changed; the old interior is completely gutted and filled with machinery. It takes a lot of it to be able to move those rocks and control their motion at a distance. The exterior you see is not the old shell, either; the outside part had to be enlarged as well. I must admit that its size is somewhat a problem to us, for as Han has probably guessed already, if we deactivated it while it was grounded, it would collapse under its own weight. Perhaps we could turn it off in space, above the surface, but there, we need its stress-field, because it will not hold air without it. It leaks."

"Hatha, we are finally being detected. When we land, may my first task be the chastising of your detection operators? We've come well within striking distance, and before they even knew we were coming. I hate to embarrass them, but don't you think you need some cover?"

"No. There is no one to watch for. Look at the sky! When you are on the other side of Dawn, by Aving's castle, that part of the planet is pointed to the main part of the galaxy. But over here, we look out, in winter, on the utter void. Look!"

Han looked in the upper part of the screen. The stars were indeed few, and the few which were in the field were generally rather bright, as if they were all nearer stars.

"You look, you see, and perhaps therefrom understand; there is no one to be looking for. You people back in regions where the stars cluster thick as mudsprouts after a rain could have no idea. Out here on the edge there is nothing. It is farther than you think from here to Chalcedon, and even Chalcedon is considered far out towards the void."

"Well, I'm no militarist, by any means, and don't intend to be; what I say is just opinion, unexpert, subjective. I do know that we haven't found intelligent alien life forms yet. Yet. But the people occupy a very small part of the galaxy, even considering exploration efforts. And were there anyone about in these parts, they could certainly come and go unnoticed, doing as they pleased. And your ship, from space, is a sitting duck. A fish in a barrel. Wide open to attack. Anyone coming in here with half-good detection, or better kinds of gear, such as we have on here, would have you before you ever knew they were in the system. At the least, you need an off-planet watch. And if you can rebuild that warship, surely it's within your resources to build a couple of orbital forts—have them up, on watch, from alternating polar orbits."

"Our capabilities are not for your speculation."

"No?" Han felt a slight prickle of the sense of danger, but it was not particularly strong. He could go on a little further. "Well, I assumed that I was now, per our decision, working for you, and my contribution was to be knowledge. That goes further than just building and operating weapon systems. I know that one does not build ballistic missiles and use them for crop-dusting! And there is more about this

system you should know. For instance, when I raised the
ship to take the measurements, back at the castle, I got a
very curious reading—as if I were picking up traces of an
anomaly somewhere in this system, like another spaceship,
but with its drives masked or in some kind of standby condition. And it was so well shielded that I couldn't get a
location on it. The energy flux was too low to be resolved
from one detection position. To find it accurately, I'd have
to take readings from several positions. You can increase
the effective resolution power of any sensor system, mechanical, electronic, or logical, if you move it around; it
acts as if it were the same size as the area you move it
around in, if you synchronize all your readings. But I had
time for only one scan of the system, so all I can tell you
now is that there is an anomalous, unexplained neutrino
source in your system."

Hatha said lamely, "That must be the *Hammerhand* you
are picking up."

"No. Your warship isn't an anomaly, it's a beacon! Now,
this ship has good instruments, but not the best there are.
But even on this ship, with some looking, I alone could
pick up your warship from as far away as the far side of
Chalcedon. With both Dawn and Chalcedon between us and
shielding you. A trained operator, which I am not, and
good detection, really good equipment—why, your ship
leaks so bad, they could probably pick you up and track
your movements from old Earth. And that's with the drives
shut down! Just sitting there. I can imagine what kind of
emissions that thing puts out under battle speeds. You're
lucky all of you haven't been fried by now, if not sterilized."

Hatha was not to be daunted by suspicions. He asked,
"Well, what about a hot gas giant? We have one in this
system, a huge gas planet, with an unusually high temperature, much higher than others in other systems we have
visited. It presently is on the other side of the sun, but most
of the time it is very visible."

"No. Gas giants, even hot ones, don't emit radiation like
that. If you get anything out of them, it's infrared, and nothing any more involved than that. What I'm talking about is
stellar interior stuff, or spaceship drives and power sources.
That star out there puts out more than its share to suit me.
And your ship is sitting there, blazing like a bonfire to the
right kind of instruments. Unless the high-pressure dual
source is causing a malfunction in the detection gear itself,

I would have to say there is still another source here, hiding under the output of the other two sources. I am not sure we could locate it, even using spread detection."

"Land there. Before the *Hammerhand*. We will discuss this later."

Han did as Hatha had directed, moving the *Pallenber* down, settling close to the *Hammerhand*. Indeed they had not turned it off! It sat there, happily emitting across the whole spectrum, drowning out half his detection instruments from anything else. No, you certainly could not ignore it. But he kept his other thoughts about the ship to himself. The first time Hatha tried to run that thing up against a proper defense system, or went into battle with real armed ships, they'd carve him up like steaks at a banquet! Worse. At the first direct hit, it would probably explode, and, overpowered as it was, would probably blight a whole system before it was through. The Warriors were wild and brave, he granted them that, like so many peoples of the past who thought that they had the ultimate weapon. But there was no ultimate in weapons, ever, and when you matched power for power, the superiority vanished like a candle flame in a high wind. A man with a knife could terrorize a man without one, but what if the one threatened suddenly revealed a pistol, even one of the old projectile-hurlers? Or revealed himself to be a master swordsman? Or was a Liszendir—a master of hand combat? She wouldn't even blink at a knife.

As they landed, Han could see an emblem painted on the side of the ship, in a place set aside just for that. It showed a pictorial image of a giant mailed fist smashing a proud tower, while all about played lightnings, and over all a huge red eye glared. Below the tower, its inhabitants leaping out or falling, waited a horrible fanged mouth, the very jaws of hell. It reminded him of something, he could not remember . . . wait, yes he could, too. Tarot cards! The ancient divination still hung on, on the fringes, for science had no such hope of explaining the whole. They considered science a success when it worked well on one of the parts. Han had seen them, the cards, once, and had felt disturbed, threatened by those emblems out of the far past. They mocked the familiar things he knew, they suggested, "all this grubbing after facts means nothing! We knew in the dawn of history, and we know now." The image on the warship was very similar to the trump card of "The Tower." And that was a card of singularly bad import. To carry it as emblem was even worse. Han looked over to Liszendir, for he knew that most ler dabbled in their own form of Tarot, one with a different underlying numerical base, but a Tarot just the same. She did not notice his glance: she was too busy looking at the insignia herself, and the look on her face was not one to reassure the superstitious, or even mildly questioning.

Still, as he settled the ship on its extended landing legs, he looked at the warship next to them and marveled. There it sat, a flying wreck, yet it towered over the world, even the world of Dawn, from the ground view. Void of space! It must have been several miles tall, close to seven or eight, and something near the same dimension in diameter at its widest part, closer to the ground. And according to Hatha, most of it was machinery!

Liszendir was pursuing another angle. "Hatha, you say that you used the old shell to build upon. Do you still use the old drive system that was originally built into the ship?"

"I have no idea. I suppose so. I do not trouble myself with mere mechanics. I command troops, forces—for that one needs to know how to command."

The fatal error so many would-be overlords made, Han thought. By denying that they had to know anything except leadership and command, they made themselves prey to kingmakers who had spent their lives learning the specialty of command and influence. And so fell into the sordid tangles of palace intrigues and political maneuvering, wasting time, wasting their underlings, wasting themselves and in the end doing nothing except becoming addicted to luxuries, which were fed them by the kingmakers, gladly. Pomp distracts from the matters at hand. And that which distracts is a drug, regardless of the container in which it is packaged.

Liszendir was continuing, "I was just thinking. We abandoned that drive system long ago. We sold it to the humans, but they found something in it which we had missed. Say what you will about the old people! They are persistent, and they fill in outlines. The old drive system, the way it was, used a dimensional lattice which was strange and very dangerous to use. That was why we abandoned it. And why the humans changed it. I am not technical, I do not understand such things. It worked fine for us, so history says, from old Earth to Kenten. They knew no problem or danger."

Hatha reflected a moment, then said, "There has been no danger or odd problems I know of. None has been spoken of, outside of certain legends, which I discount. We are as prey to fancies as anyone else, I suppose."

Han was thinking about the ancient conquerors out of history. Mostly of the period when people, human and ler, were planetbound to one world; conquerors were few in space, because even with matrix overspace drive, the distances were just too large, the communications stretched too far, the materiel tonnages too great. So what could this situation here on Dawn be compared to? Tamerlane with nuclear weapons? Hitler with spaceships? Or Darius the Usurper with those odd machines which used fluid dynamic lift, Bernoulli's principle, to support them as they moved through the atmosphere, what was the word—yes, airplanes. Yes. But give them only the devices, vastly oversimplifying them so the users would never be able to build more on their own, or repair the ones they had. When they were used up, there would be no more, and any reaction generated by the mixing-up of cultures would be self-limiting. Teach them only the rudiments, and make sure they wouldn't theorize. But these people on Dawn were ler! They should have been hunch-theorists of great power. What had been happening here? Whatever it was, it was neither simple nor completely recent, but a vast enigma which had deep roots in the past, perhaps all the way back to the half-legendary Sanjirmil.

But he was allowed no more time to speculate. Hatha motioned to him. "Shut it down, now. We will leave."

Han ran through the shutdown sequence with ill-concealed reluctance. Then he got up out of the pilot's chair, and went with the party out into the evening.

Outside, in the open, the bulk of the *Hammerhand* was even more impressive, especially standing comparatively next to it. Or perhaps one might better say "oppressive." It towered over them, a vast, pitted, sculptured mass wreathed in clouds; and doubtless crowned with lightning in the proper season. The shuttles lay on the ground before it, arranged in a neat row. And the meteors with which it fought lay all about in careless profusion, quarter-mile blocks of nickel-iron, streaked with heavy rust from long immersion in a corrosive, oxygen-rich atmosphere. Han hoped that nobody on Dawn relied upon compasses, because they would clearly be useless—all that iron would

disrupt compasses for a thousand miles around. But of
course they wouldn't—only oceanic or sea peoples used
magnetic iron. On Dawn, they navigated from one landmark
to the next. But they could have. When he had taken his
measurements, he had seen that Dawn had an enormous
magnetic field, the highest level he had ever seen. It would
have to; otherwise, that hot star which was the primary
would fry them with charged particles. That would indeed
play hob with the unstable ler genes. Yes, and . . . he
choked it off for now. He had to see more.

Han turned from his observation of the warship to lower
levels, around the ground level. Of course, they were farther
south, and therefore winter was somewhat more advanced.
It was cold. All around in the gathering darkness, the low
sun in the north flashed its slanting, pearly light over tents,
sheds, and miscellaneous buildings scattered all over the
plains, as far as Han could see, without limit. There seemed
no end to it. It was a city, but it was not a city. Rather, it
was a large and unorganized assembly of people, in a place,
for no other apparent reason than that they had to have
a place, and this one seemed as good as any other. An
unurban city in which one could virtually disappear overnight, if one were ler. He didn't know about how humans
might fare.

Hatha echoed his thoughts somewhat. "We sojourn here
on the Pannona Plains. When we tire of a site, we move on,
sometimes a great distance, sometimes only a few miles.
Some go with the ship, while the less favored walk. And of
course, we have permanent settlements all around this part
of Dawn. There is a lake on the other side of the warship,
and we like it here. This area is where our heart is."

"I cannot fail to be moved by the sight of all this," Han
commented, genuinely impressed.

Few people of either sort were about, visible in the
evening dusks and glooms and blue and purple shadows
cast everywhere by the slanting sunlight, waning fast, and
the buildings scattered randomly all over. Han thought it
was probably because of the cold, and the fact that they
had arrived somewhere near local suppertime, although for
him it was only an hour or two downstream from breakfast,
and still morning. As he looked, he could make out a few
figures, seemingly Warriors, but none of them were close
enough for it to make any real difference. They walked
through the cold over to the rather nondescript front of an

unimpressive building, whose size and extent was masked by the front surface and the dark. Inside, it turned out to be a sort of combination state residence, guardhouse and administrative center, and seemed to have no limits towards the rear of it that Han could determine. It was surprisingly comfortable, if rather spartan in decor and furnishings.

"These," Hatha said, with a sweeping motion by one arm, "are my personal quarters. We will settle you two temporarily in the vicinity, and later, see to something more permanent."

"Do you rule all this camp?" Asked Liszendir.

"No. By no means. I fall under the high triad. I am . . . what you might call something comparable to a minister of foreign affairs. Ha! That has been my role all along, but in fact, until a few years ago, I didn't have much of a job."

Hatha led the way into a small parlor, or sitting room, and, making a motion, signaled the guards to depart, which they did, silently. Han suspected that wherever they went, it was not far, and that should Hatha want them back, the slightest sound would bring the same bunch back, erupting out of the very doorjambs. Hatha settled himself down in an armchair. Han and Liszendir remained standing.

"Now, we shall, as you say, get down to business. Sit. Be comfortable, relaxed, and at your ease. I am aware that the overall circumstances of your . . . ah, service, are perhaps not to your highest expectations and ambitions. But then, what circumstances are, for any of us in this troubled universe of chagrin and tears? We do what we can, myself no less than you, despite appearances that deceive us one and all. So then! To work! We have arrangements to make, tasks to be determined."

Liszendir sat down in another overstuffed chair. "I see one thing. If you expect me to teach infighting of any degree to all these people, I will be a very ancient elder when I am finished."

"Ah, not so at all! Not all, but only an elite. I should hope that you can complete most of your work within a year."

"Even so, I hope not all by myself. I should think the best way would be to train trainers first, and then set them to work on the others. It would proceed faster."

"You have no idea how small the group is. It is very well within your scope. And what you have is a very dangerous weapon, do you know? So we do not want such secrets widespread. No, no. A small group. I will bring them to you, and I will respect any evaluations of them you care to pass on. If they are not suitable, then so state! I am most definitely a believer in the privileges of rank, but then who, having rank, says otherwise? Only those who lack it despise it! But I also believe strongly in the recommendations of experts and professionals. Friendship and personal favors —now, they are fine things in small scale, in the home, in the small business, in the lower administrations; but where things are really at stake, we have to look to capability and knowledge, not ambition and alliances. I assure you, Liszendir, you should be all done by the time of your fertility. The reward for successful accomplishment will be, of course, your choice of mates from the whole horde. Do you understand? Choice comes out of position, and position out of deeds."

Liszendir looked puzzled at the short time Hatha was talking about, and in regards to her future degree of choice, she indicated nothing. But Han reflected on that for a long time. Choice, indeed. In her system, the one she had grown up with, such choice was deadly to the race, it held the potential of disaster for them. But more importantly, he saw something else, which he was sure Liszendir did not see, for she was no politician: Hatha was after far more than just the conquest of the inner worlds, all for the glory of the high triad, whatever that was. He was, first and foremost, after power within the Warriors, and what he had in mind for Liszendir was the training of a corps of shock troops to be used upon his own people. And more flowed out of that realization: the factions surrounding the central authority must be very strong in their own right, or Hatha, the wily old beast, would have moved already. Han felt mixed emotions. It had been easy to hate Hatha-Hath'ingar, back on Chalcedon, at Aving's castle, where he could be cast in the role of a personal devil to himself and Liszendir. But on closer inspection, Han saw that the evil in Hatha was mostly an evil as defined by Han in personal terms. He could never like the hetman, or follow his goals voluntarily. But he could not help admiring, cautiously, his capability and wit. He was sharp.

IX

Excerpts from *'L Knun al-Vrazuus, The Doctrine of Opposites:*

"The reasons for change, the true reasons and not the illusory ones, and the direction of events in a given system are, to the novice, the uninitiated, paradoxical and multifaceted beyond enumeration. Moreover, the following course of events is most often exactly the reverse of what the untrained expect. Thus we observe the phenomena that, (1) the amount of administrative effort increases as the function becomes defunct; and (2) that the severity of military training increases as the possibility of war becomes more remote. It follows that the first level of adepthood will be to see beneath the illusion, which is generated by poor approximations of theory; the second is to learn to conduct oneself as if one did not see these contradictions, while all the while unraveling them so that others, not so perceptive, will not become meshed in their tangles."

—Borzalhai, Rithosi *mnathman*

"The only constant aspect of change is the fluctuation of its rate."

—Weldyanzhoi the Great

> *"Water is soft and has no will save that to be
> low and level. Yet, given time, water levels the
> high and distinctively individual mountains and
> disperses their substance to the winds and the
> bottoms of the seas. Space is of similar nature,
> even more devoid of will, yet it absorbs every-
> thing and manipulates it so perfectly."*

—Jwinverlis the Blind

> *"Humans invariably elaborate upon that
> which they lack, in their myths. Ler do not, as
> a rule, but the reason lies not in substance, but
> in culture and certain disciplines arising out of
> it."*

—Shennanskoth (*Kadhos Liszendiruus*)

On the next day, Hatha disappeared, which left Han with
nothing to do, except sit and think, or wander around the
place where Hatha made his headquarters. He tried to visit
other parts of the building, but guards and locked doorways
limited the room he had to move around in to only a few
chambers. They were all singularly bare. He was definitely a
prisoner, even if he was not having his face rubbed in the
fact any more by more obvious methods. Nor did he see
any sign of Liszendir, either. She was either in another part
of the building, or gone with Hatha, wherever he was. This
all left Han with considerable time to think things over, resort and reclassify facts in his mind, and neither the facts,
nor the conclusions they led to, were very comfortable to
live with. They suggested a certain direction to the flow of
events which had definitely disturbing aspects, far beyond
considerations of personal safety.

Han considered the threat of the Warriors and their massive warship. It was true it was a monstrous war machine,
which now effectively cowed and dominated two planets,
Dawn and Chalcedon alike. But Chalcedon had no ships of
its own, and on Dawn, nobody outside the Warriors had
anything more destructive than a crossbow. Under those
conditions, he reflected, he himself could probably rule the
two worlds with no more than the weaponry installed on the
Pallenber, which was, after all, a rather small ship. So, too,

with surprise, the Warriors could very easily make a further early conquest or two, but once the mercenary men-of-war located them by the pattern of their raids, and the leaky emissions of their warship, it would be settled in a hurry— that much was obvious even to someone who had neither military training nor interest in it in particular. Hatha didn't see the obvious, which meant he knew nothing about civilized worlds, except by hearsay or deliberate misinformation. So, after discovery, then what?

There was another aspect as well: all the technology represented by the warship strongly smelled of cultural grafting, the imposition of high-level machinery upon a relatively low-level culture, and recently, too. The warship was a powered ship, so it had to be refueled eventually. Who would do that? Han had seen no evidence whatsoever of facilities which could either fuel or repair a craft like that. Or perhaps that was intentional—no repair facilities, and just enough fuel to get them into trouble. And he considered the fact that Hatha had a spaceship which could cross space and devastate a whole planet, but he knew nothing about orbits, minimum-energy curves and geodesics, and sat grounded on a plain, visible from orbit, and had not a care about defense or detection. And the ship was in such shaky condition that it could not land unpowered, nor could it be fixed. And it was deteriorating fast, judging from what he had seen. All these things hinted strongly at some unknown and unseen agency highly skilled in the manipulations of primitives, and skilled at hiding as well, at least from the primitives themselves.

That thought led Han onwards to the anomaly his instruments had suggested in the Dawn system. That, too, smelled. But it had been a subtle indication, possbily questionable, unlocatable. And the instruments could have been decalibrated by some inadvertent act of Hatha's when he was flying the *Pallenber* manually. But for a moment, he could have been almost sure that there was something. It was true—it would take years of measurements to pinpoint the location, and actually find out what was causing it. By then, it would be too late, of course. Hatha now had two ships, and two ships was a fleet, in these parts. It was very slick, if the anomaly was, as Han suspected, another ship, hiding in the Dawn system somewhere with drives on standby and highly shielded. Han saw it as a problem in cryptology, with which he as a trader was familiar, at least with commercial applications of the arcane science. And he knew very well that the first principle of cryptology was that no system is secure perfectly, nor is it intended to be; the purpose of a system of concealment is to slow detection down until the moment of exposure is well after the actions concealed by the system. So cryptosystems slowed eavesdropping down, and then you could run an operation, capture a market, get in and get out before anyone else knew about it, or could take advantage of it. And the same principle applied here. It was hidden, well enough, and by the time anyone could read the truth in it, it would be much too late.

There were more mysteries. Dawn had a powerful magnetic field, which was good in view of the radiation being put out by the hot star that was Dawn's primary. Otherwise, Dawn, even with a mild climate and normal rotation, would be quite uninhabitable. But planets with measurable magnetic fields switched polarity periodically, and by Kahn's Law, the stronger the field, the greater the rate of change of polarity. Neither the ler nor the humans on Dawn would ever be aware of it, because they did not have compasses. And he didn't know if they understood electricity or not. He suspected not. But the rate for Dawn! It must switch poles on the order of every few thousand years, or possibly even on the order of every few hundred. Han saw what had been happening on Dawn, from that.

It went approximately like this: Sanjirmil's followers stole the ship, and fled to the edge, looking for a planet where they would not be located for many years, years beyond counting. They happened on the world Dawn, and settled on it. Some years later, cruising about, probably on the lookout for other planets, they detected a human colony ship bound somewhere. This they captured, probably with the motive of slave-taking in mind, and nothing more than that. It would not have attracted much notice—many of the early ships were lost, and never seen again; a certain attrition rate was part of the risk. They returned to Dawn, to institute their new slave-based society. Then perhaps the original ship malfunctioned, or they forgot how to fly it. Individual ler would probably not forget, but the society could over a few negligent generations. So the ship became a holy relic, and a period of long quiet ensued. The humans were either enslaved and domesticated, or turned loose on Dawn to fare as they could. Who would care? They couldn't get off the planet, even if they thought such a thing were possible. And every few generations, the human and ler populations of

Dawn would get a massive dose of radiation from their primary, when the planet's magnetic field was switching, and all barriers were down to charged particles. Effects of this would show in the humans, but the ler would begin to show effects immediately. It would probably run their already-high mutation rate completely off the scale. And long before, they had abandoned the wide-pool braid system, which would certainly have delayed any change, and might have saved them. So instead of advancing, or maintaining certain superior traits, they were devolving, and as far as Han could tell, were actually below the human norm in abilities. That, of course, would make no difference to the slaves—they had been conditioned to believe in ler suepriority for thousands of years, and would have never had the opportunity to see anything different. But for the ler, they were back to city-states and bands of nomads, and they had apparently lost the ability for Multispeech. A few more thousand years and they would be back to body language, grunts and squeals, and would lose what little civilization they had. That would have been bad enough on a planet which had run its own evolutionary sequence through time to the point where complex organisms like man could survive, even in the wild state, but this was not possible on Dawn—the ecology was simply too primitive, and very likely wouldn't improve much, even in the very long run. There was potential for a circular, man-only system, but that wasn't a very pretty one any way you figured it. And what was happening to the humans, while the Dawn ler were devolving?

But now there was a kink in the program: the ler on Dawn, a culture hardly above the ability to forge spears, were operating a monster warship which dropped meteors as weapons. All this very definitely pointed to an agency or persons standing behind the Warriors and using them as a screen. But who were they, if it was indeed a "they," and what was the underlying purpose, the one which was being screened, not the screener? Han, since Chalcedon, had wanted to hurry back to Seabright, and tell Hetrus that his suspicions were wrong. Now he felt an even more urgent need to hurry back and tell him that he had been, in essence, right. But, as it appeared, there was for the present little chance of telling Hetrus anything.

In the afternoon, Hatha and Liszendir arrived from wherever they had been, and both of them seemed pleased with themselves. Hatha disappeared again, almost immediately, but Liszendir hurried over to Han. She spoke in a low tone, very fast.

"I can't say this except quickly, nor can I explain much. You will have to take it on faith. He will be back—he is not gone for long. Three things: one, this triad-oversex thing is a nightmare. They have no sex as adolescents, and in fertility, the offspring are raised by the predominantly female triads. They think no sex increases your strength. Vital-fluids doctrine, if you can believe it. Even the worst humans have given that cult up in disgust. Second: if Hatha offers you a female human, or offers you a choice of one, take what choice you can. He thinks that what we did was mere hunger, sensual gratification. He must not suspect anything more than that. Act like some barbarian lord: he will approve. And you must not think in reference to me or what we have done. Think of it as if I were helping you become woven, as you will do for me someday, I hope. You must remember that she will, however strange, be of your own kind, and I wish it of you. Understood? Good. Third: there is something very wrong here. What is the word you use? Synchronization? They do not have it here. Things are badly distorted somehow. I do not understand what I have seen, but it is coming. And I do not like the outline that is taking shape."

Han knew he had to make his decision with her now, no second thoughts, no turning back. And what they had done, what they had been, would never be again. It was like the conditions which set up a total eclipse: they approached maximum, they culminated, the bright spot of the returning sun appeared, and the eclipse was over. They had, now, only the residue to live with: memories and commitments, to be discharged in ways outside the body and beyond the heart. He answered, "One—it figures. Two—I will do what I can, but if I have changed you, you have changed me, too. Three: I know." They had no more time: Hatha could be heard approaching around the corner. He came into the room.

"We have had a most interesting tour. I must say that this girl is flexible and alert far beyond her years and sex. I will be overlooking much for her services. And you have a part in this as well—do not dissemble! I can detect your influence, and much to my surprise, I find it generally beneficial."

Han answered, neutrally, "That sounds wonderful."

"Now, Han, you and I," Hatha said, waving Liszendir off, have an area to explore. Have you thought of some way you might be of service to us, while you have been waiting?" Liszendir left the room through a door to the rear.

"Well, in fact, something has been on my mind, since we came to your camp, here. I think, if I may speak freely, that your defense system could stand some improvement, otherwise when your conquest starts, you're going to be wide open. Those meteors may be fine against a planetary population, but against armed ships who can see you before you see them . . . Do you see? I'd like to see your ship, your equipment, how your people operate it. Perhaps I can suggest some ideas. You are going to have to keep your hindside covered." He thought, if what he suspected was true, that that small action would change little.

"There is warrior's wisdom in what you say. I, too, have thought on this, since you brought it up yesterday. So then! Matters shall proceed! We will go to the ship!"

"Now?"

"On the very instant. Come along. We will gather some rations along the way."

Hatha turned and barked an order to a subordinate who apparently had been waiting just behind the main door. There were sounds of departure, and only minutes later, returning. The functionary reappeared, saluted, and left. Hatha motioned to Han, and marched off through the door. Han followed, and outside, saw Hatha disappearing into one of the shuttles from the warship. He caught up with him, the door closed, and with no preliminaries, Hatha activated the shuttle, and began flying a course towards the warship.

They arrived in a reception bay similar to the one through which Han remembered himself and Liszendir marching. How long ago had that been? It seemed like a very long time, but he could not scale it to any time frame with which he was familiar. Six months? A year? It was much like before, but this time they began to follow the maze of corridors upwards, and the surroundings began to take on a more operational look. Finally, they arrived at a large room with a low ceiling, curiously low, which had the distinctive aspect of a command center. It was almost completely filled with panels and light displays, now mostly deactivated. A few screens, apparently cathode-ray and not microvision, were mounted on some panels. There was only a handful of people

in the room. These were all seated before—Han could not
believe his eyes—what appeared to be radar scopes. It looked
crude.

The operators came to attention as Hatha entered the
room. Commanded, they explained their equipment and duties, and as they became more involved in so doing, warmed
up, and spoke freely, and with considerable pride. Han paid
close attention to them as they discussed their detection
system, of which they were knowledgeable, at least in how
it worked. They thought it was the best in the universe. Han
thought otherwise, but he kept his thoughts to himself.
Range-azimuth radar scopes, coupled through receivers and
amplifiers directly to steerable mechanical antennas mounted
atop the warship. Incredible! It was like a class in ancient
history, with a neolithic farmer explaining how a broken
branch could be used as a plow. Yes, the women went in
front. They could pull, but steering was a finer art.

After a time, Han was able to understand enough of their
system to make some suggestions for some slight improvements, which would not, considering their equipment limitations, materially increase their capabilities, but it would
seem to. He also busied himself jotting down some notes for
a set of operating instructions, since the operators were, for
all their pride, manifestly too ignorant to make them for
themselves. Han also agreed to train additional triads, who
would be required either for use or backup duties, when the
new system was implemented.

"Now," he said. "How about communications? Delegation
of authority? Identification? Rules of engagement?" The answers he got stupefied him. They had electrical communications within the ship, but outside, on the plains, they used
couriers and heliographs, whose light source could be
supplanted with lanterns when the light level was low. These
last used a complex, highly redundant code which the Warriors considered a paragon of secrecy. Han suggested some
improvements, but for the present, no really radical changes.
A simplified code. Better heliographs with a narrower beam.
And a powered light line direct from the ship to Hatha's
tent complex. And yes, a duty officer with some authority.

To Han's surprise, Hatha readily agreed, vastly impressed
and not at all discomfited by Han's suggestions and evaluations, which Han himself thought were all rather overly
obvious. As they toured the rest of the command room,
Han found another piece of the puzzle he was working on.

They had only simple detection; nothing that could even be called modern, by the remotest stretch of the imagination. And the command room had the same air of hasty improvisation and newness as the part he had seen earlier. That was interesting indeed. When the ship was rebuilt, whoever did the work left out—was it on purpose?—the very thing they could have used right here on their own planet. But he kept those speculations to himself. And he was not quite up to pressing too closely into origins, not unless he had some further sign from Hatha. He pronounced himself satisfied with his tour, and began outlining projects which Hatha would need to oversee or at least approve.

Hatha appeared to be both astounded and grateful. As they returned to the shuttle, he fairly bubbled with enthusiasm.

"Ah, yes, cooperation and progress! My boy, if all took your attitude we would be spared the onerous and time-consuming tasks of bombardment, siege, reduction. You are a very storehouse of valuables, which you volunteer. Rewards and honor! I hope we will see more of this. As you see, things are in need of improvement. True, work has been done, but it always seemed, somehow, unfinished, do you know? I am no technician, I do not know these things personally, but I have always felt that somehow, some quality was . . . not right."

"I thought you were going to sell me."

"That was a hasty remark engendered by the events on Chalcedon. Actually, aside from your knowledge, you have no great value in particular. No offense intended, but you are too close to the wild stock to be of any value to those who make a specialty of refining pure strains. Our domestic varieties are highly refined."

Han thought ruefully that here, in Hatha's remarks, was part of the reason why they were going downhill steadily on Dawn. The ler were devolving on Dawn, and the humans, whatever they were after an unknown number of years of selective domestication, were, if Han knew anything about slaves, probably glad enough to get the next meal. Hatha interrupted his train of thought.

"Understand, I am no breeder myself. I consider it all a waste of time, to labor over an essentially alien species while one's own seems to get nowhere, no matter what we do. And matters have not improved with the ship, either."

"How long has this domestication been going on?"

"Since the first, when the humans were captured. At first, with the raids on Chalcedon, we thought the new blood would build up the stock types we had; but most knowledge-able breeders now hold that the new acquisitions will only lead to new types. When they got the captives back here, they were definitely different, compared with the old types, even where there was a superficial resemblance. And of course, none of them have been as flexible as you."

Han bit his tongue again. More flexible, indeed! A batch of farmers and small tradesmen and children, sifted for their physical characteristics; they would be both ignorant and terrified. How could they be expected to know anything about spaceships, and even if they had, who could have been expected to volunteer anything? But something else was apparent here, something that measured how far down the ler on Dawn had gone: they would not have made the mistake of thinking the new captives looked like the old if they had retained the eidetic memory which was character-istic of mainstream ler. Indeed, it was one of the main reasons why ler navigators flew space manually—they could compare two views of the sky from different points and make up a mental stereo image in their minds. Given two positions in space, the ler pilot "saw" space in three dimen-sions in a plane at right angles to the line of movement. But neither Hatha nor any of the Warriors, apparently, realized this. Nor did Hatha realize how much he had given Han. The Warriors could be outwitted.

"Well. I promised you reward, and reward you shall have, if you will." A calculating gleam came into Hatha's eyes. "I will set aside some quarters for you, a place to work, and assign a clerk or two. But, best of all, you may, at my expense, select a female of your choice. You see! Already you rise in status! I grant you choices even many of us do not have."

"How shall I exercise this choice? I have seen few humans, the old people, in this camp."

"There will be no problem at all. Because you have not seen the *klesh* does not mean that they do not exist. Ah, humans. If you lived in a cave, you would deny that stars existed. But more seriously, during normal times, there would be few, at least so that you could see them. But it happens that now, this season, we hold a winter exhibition of our art—our only art form, by the way. Would you say sub-racial types, or breeds? Or perhaps tribes. But at any rate, come along! Exert choice! Be discriminatory!"

Han entered the shuttle with Hatha. He suddenly felt uneasy, apprehensive; he did not think that he really wanted to see the product of several thousand years of forced breeding. What would *klesh* look like? Would the Warriors have aimed for beauty or function? And, more importantly, in whose terms? Han expected to see, at least in part, freaks, mutants, deformities, teratological amazements. But he went. They flew to an area north of the ship, quite far from Hatha's own place. Night was already falling in the short day cycle of the winter of Dawn; below, as they flew, Han could see a large complex, partly by its shape, partly by scattered lights around it. It seemed rather better lit than most of the camp. Hatha waxed proud.

"Here you are lucky indeed. This is a yearly spectacle of interest, education and enlightenment to us all. It goes on for many days. I suppose that for us the timing is fortuitous. If we had come here days earlier, all we would have had to pick from would have been agricultural specialties; good enough for work and production, but surely nothing there for the man of discriminating tastes. But now; now we arrive just past the peak of the exhibition. On display now are examples of *klesh* bred purely for purity of bloodline and beauty. Control of genetics. Marvels. True wonders!"

They landed. An attendant triad bowed respectfully to Hatha as they emerged from the shuttle and started toward the complex. It seemed to be a kind of tented structure, but as they went inside, it did not resemble a circus or carnival at all, as its outside might have suggested. It seemed plush, neat, even luxurious. Hatha was expansive.

"These on display now are, ah, ornamentals. They generally have no duties, no responsibilities, except to be cooperative and well behaved. Of course, some have functions— but now these are but shadows of the original purposes. Most are quiet, although some types tend to unruliness. You will doubtless find this entertaining, pure edification."

They went into the first section. What Han saw there completely dislocated his sense of reality. The displays were open cubicles with a portion in the rear closed off. They were furnished with rugs and cassocks, and those inside were prevented from wandering by a mesh of fine wires in the front. The specimens were labeled, on boards at the front of the cubicles, in an arcane terminology Han could not decipher. Also, attached to the boards were elaborate knotted designs, which Han presumed were symbols for various prizes and awards. Inside the cubicles sat or paced males or females, naked but neat, clean, and seemingly unconcerned, either with their situation or their nudity. The faces exhibited curiosity or animation, but in them there was no resistance, no calculation or hatred. In this particular section, all appeared to be redheads who bore an astonishing resemblance to one another. It was much closer than tribal, at least in the sense Han understood the term, and indeed, the individuals looked more like each other than members of most families. He had to look closely to see differences. But they were there. To the creatures themselves, they probably saw the differences as glaring, obvious, and certainly, the personalities would vary wildly—seen from inside the breed, as it were. These had dense, deep-coppery hair which fell free and more or less straight to their shoulders. Their skins were creamy and light in tone, smooth and hairless except for the pubic region and, oddly enough, the lower legs, which were, from the knee down, heavily furred with the same coppery red hair, males and females alike. They were, as a group, rather small-boned and delicate in appearance, and they all had deep, sea-green eyes, of an intensity of color Han had never seen before. Hatha commented knowledgeably, while Han stared.

"Here you see the best examples of the *Zlat Klesh*. It is an old breed. I am told it was difficult to establish, and is still difficult to maintain according to breed standards, which exclude blemishes and freckles, as well as a certain heavier bone structure. These things tend to recur in Zlats. But as a group, these are generally fine examples. Zlats are not to my taste, of course, but everyone has his own preferences."

Han felt a hundred emotions boiling within himself. Impossible not to feel rage at this slow atrocity generations long. He looked at the smooth faces, the small, delicate nostrils. The males were bearded in pleasing patterns. The females looked pampered and untroubled. Most were young adults, approximately Han's age, or comparable with it, but a few were older. One distinguished-looking male in particular was middle-aged, but in perfect physical condition. His mustache dropped with flair and charm; patterns of iron gray streaked his hair and beard.

"I confess, Hatha, that it shocks me to see my own kind

here. It would shock me to see her displayed like this."

"So, indeed. But by expressing it as you do, you pass another test. Not many of your kind can see this, and fail to run crazy. But to what end? These imagine no rescue. They lead lives of pampered boredom. It is also so with the others." The voice was coldly rational.

Han stifled an urge to attempt to strangle Hatha. He had seen him in action, against Liszendir, and he knew that he could not hope to best him barehanded. Futility. Frustration.

"I can't read the signs. Who has won what?"

"Ah . . . Let me see. This one, here, for example, is unbred, a young female, as you can doubtless observe for yourself, and in late adolescence. Fourth place in her class— unbred females. Not so good, for a first show. The fault is delicacy—she is just a bit too fine-boned, I think. Now this one over here is a first. You will notice that she differs chiefly in . . ."

As Hatha went on, describing the virtues of another Zlat female, Han looked at the girl who had placed fourth. She was sitting relaxed on a cassock to one side, looking at nothing; she seemed to be dozing. As he watched, she became more alert, possibly sensing that she was being watched, not just idly glanced at. She arose, moved gracefully over to another cassock, which served as a storage area, opened it and removed a complicated object which she began to handle deftly, manipulating it into another configuration, which required considerable effort and concentration, but whose results seemed to please her. He looked closer at her.

Her face had an oval shape, with the slightest hint of cheekbone showing below her eyes, which were deep and thoughtful. They slanted slightly, which accented her face beautifully and subtly. Her mouth was finely formed, small, with rather full lips, slightly pursed. The upper lip was fractionally more full than the lower. He looked again. She had a beauty that was mind-wrenching. Han let his eyes fall downwards, to the body. Like her face, it was small, delicate, finely formed and outlined. Her breasts were small, round, accented with delicate brown nipples. She looked back at him and smiled vacantly. Then, recognizing him as a human like herself, although very different in appearance, she looked curious, friendly. Han turned away, entranced and sickened at the same time.

Hatha had turned back from his explanation of Zlat virtues. He had been saying that Zlats had been originally bred to perform fine-detail electronic assemblies. Han heard, and noted the fact, but it was just another piece of data.

Hatha was inexhaustible. He walked Han for miles, or so it seemed, through exhibits of every type Han could have imagined. There was more variety here than one could find in a hundred years on any one planet; sifted, classified, bred, rebred, inbred, to produce pure specimens, far beyond any concept of race. That staggered Han; back in the normal world, one hardly ever saw any person near a pure type, so mixed had people become in the course of long years and many migrations. But these were races, which, strictly speaking, had never existed. Only here. Han recalled his first sight of the warship; this was a sight which paled that into utter insignificance. Finally, mercifully, Hatha reached the end of his travels. There was more, but there was only so much one could take in at one time. The variety was staggering.

Hatha announced, "This is by no means all. We have only been slightly more than half. But it may serve. Did you see anything that caught your fancy?"

"Oh, many, many. It is hard to choose."

"Indeed it is. That is why only the high have it. Strength and fortitude! But was there anything in particular?"

"Only one?" He had a rash thought of asking for all of them. But that would solve nothing. They wouldn't understand what he expected of them, would probably resent it, and certainly would not be able to get along with all the other breeds. The race issue had caused humans problems since the dawn of civilization, and that had risen from racial differences which were, in some cases, subtle, accidental, or even imaginary. Han could easily imagine, from that, the kinds of prejudice which one might find in artificially bred populations of pure types. But he could not know how they would act together.

"Only one."

"Well, if I must . . ." He thought back, verifying an earlier impulse. Yes. It was still true. He had seen here girls more sexually attractive, more lovely, more almost anything. But one had possessed a quality that combined them all, and yet under the blend remained visible as a person, something more than just a body, or a face. "Of all we have seen here today, I think the one that enchanted me the most was the first one we looked at, the young female of the Zlats. The fourth class."

"Indeed? A Zlat? A fourth? You disappoint me in some ways; but in others you exhibit a refinement in taste, in which I will admit to a certain deficiency. Now, then, so be it. We shall go and conclude the arrangements. But as we go, let me tell you what I know of the breed, which I suppose is little enough. They are generally intelligent and quick, and are still occasionally used practically, for performing fine-detail work, at which they excel. The only fault here is perhaps lack of persistence, which I suppose arises from lack of practice. Also, they are affectionate and dependent, becoming tense only in situations of sexual rivalry, at which the females are as belligerent and demonstrative as the males. They are known to require considerable care, grooming, and so forth. Fourth class! You must see something I miss. But well enough—Zlats are all supple and responsive. And a fourth will lower the cost as well, for which I, with limited resources, thank you. Your taste may very well carry a component of tact, eh? Also, you will not have to compete with other prospective breeders, as a fourth would not be in great demand for breeding stock, even as a speculation."

"Does she know the nature of her award?"

"No. She does not read or write. But that will be no problem; she will be very adaptable, if what I have heard about Zlats is true. By the way, do you plan to keep her as a brood female—for breeding? Do you intend to become a Zlat fancier? If so, I would advise a better specimen, even though such advice will cost me dearly. Thus I demonstrate my altruism and camaraderie."

"Well, no . . . I was thinking of perhaps a more selfish approach . . ."

"Never mind, never mind, my young buck! No confidences! I understand perfectly. Ah, were I a youth again! How the juices flow! Well, then: matters shall proceed as you have chosen. Come along, now."

They went back to the area where the Zlats were displayed. Han looked for the girl again, but most of the specimens had retired for the night, apparently, to the closed-off portion in the rear of the stalls. It seemed that a very long time had passed—Han became conscious of the passage of time again; he realized that he had completely lost track of time while they had been in the exhibition. After a lengthy search, Hatha was able to locate the manager-keeper, who was well into his years. He wrote out a note with a great flourish, and in return, the manager-keeper gave

Han a folder, inside which were printed lengthy instructions regarding the care of Zlats, all written in an elaborate script and arcane breeder terminology which was far beyond Han's current level of comprehension. Then there was another form, in several copies, which the keeper-manager filled out, retaining one copy for himself; it was apparently a kind of registration. Still other paperwork appeared, which listed in considerable detail the girl's ancestry backwards for twenty or more generations, with amplified and expanded sections dealing with champions in her line of particularly high honors, and fortuitous crosses between specific lines. No doubt about it—the girl might very well have only earned a fourth place herself, but she was certainly a Zlat beyond any shadow of doubt. Han looked through the wild squiggles of the letters, and finally pointed to one.

"Is this her name?" Transliterated, it probably would have taken forty characters to spell out.

"Only in a sense," answered Hatha. "That is a registration name. We would not use that in speaking with the girl herself; she wouldn't recognize it has having any connection with her. She wouldn't respond. Now, what do they call her, colloquially? Let me see . . . Ah! Here it is. Usteyin. That's her name."

"Does she talk?" Han felt completely insane as he asked the question.

"Oh, yes, indeed. Speak slowly, clearly, as with a child."

The party returned to the area where the Zlats were on exhibition, finding the girl's cubicle without difficulty. The keeper-manager, Han could see, was concerned for, and even fond of, his charges, and would brook no mistreatment. As they went, the ancient Ier admonished Han vigorously and definitively as to care, exercise, diet and kindness.

"These Zlats are a sensitive lot! But treat them right, and they are wonders, absolute paragons. They can do almost anything, except, of course, feats involving gross strength. I myself prefer the Haydars. Noble beasts, indeed!" Han remembered the Haydars well. They had been striking people. They were a lean, tall, attenuated people with olive skins, long, powerful limbs and great, bladelike noses. Their hair was oily black, dense and curly. Deeply set under heavy foreheads were sad, sad eyes whose pupils were almost completely black. Hatha had told him that they were hunters and trackers. It was only later that Han began to wonder what it was the Haydars had tracked and hunted, on this

planet with no native animal more highly evolved than oversized toads. Of course . . .

The girl Usteyin was indeed asleep. Han watched her for
a moment, repressing an urge to gather her up, embrace her
on the spot. But she was a stranger, completely, more of a
stranger than Liszendir. Her form was girly, attractive, familiar. But she was a highly cultured product of a society
more alien than anything of either Han's or Liszendir's
societies. She lay in a small bed in the back of the enclosure,
wrapped up in a soft, light blanket. It looked hand-woven.
Her mouth was slightly open; she was breathing deeply,
slowly, and apparently was dreaming of some pleasant circumstance, for a soft smile was drifting across the oval,
exquisite face, the rosy, pursed mouth. Something tugged at
his mind, something about the face. He couldn't place it.
Han signaled the keeper to wait to awaken her until the
dream was over. Presently she shifted position. An idle
thought flashed through his mind, a remark of the classical
writer, Durrell—"unfair to watch a sleeping woman."

The keeper woke her up, gently. At first, she seemed
frightened, as Han expected she would, by the numbers of
people in her cubicle, but the keeper patiently explained what
had transpired, and as he did, she relaxed, brightened up,
and even became excited and animated. Han resisted an
impulse to go completely mad; this lovely creature was
actually happy to be sold. She asked, timidly, of him, if she
could take her few little things with her. He agreed, heart
pounding.

While she gathered her few belongings up, the complicated
gadget or thingamabob, a small pillow, the blanket, a small
bag, presumably of toilet articles, the keeper divulged some
more information about the breed.

"Now, these Zlats: records only go so far back, but with
these we have accurate records farther back than most. They
are one of the oldest types, and their roots go back almost
to the beginning, the first humans on Dawn. They, like us
all, have had their ups and downs. But for the most part,
they are rather docile—she will not try to escape. You must
treat her with care: her bones are fragile and will break, if
she is handled too roughly. She will also need some protection from the worst airs, and considerable grooming.
There is a good description in the papers I gave you, but
they do not ever capture the dimension of one's responsibilities."

Han thought about the remark about not trying to escape. No, he could see that easily enough. Escapees would have been hunted, and he did not care to speculate upon their fate. So they would learn, over the years and generations, that escape was not an option for them. No out. They would develop a peculiar outlook, a psychology, which no other creature would have: they could not escape—but would have to face things as they came. He looked back to the girl, who was happy, excited. She had rolled her possessions into a neat ball, and stood quietly, waiting. Han reached to her, took her hand, the first female human hand he had touched, it seemed, in years, centuries. It was soft, delicate, warm; the nails were exquisitely manicured. She followed them quietly back to the shuttle.

Outside, it was completely dark, for night had fallen. Han again thought of the passage of time: they had been in the exhibition a long time—it must be very late. A snowstorm was trying to start up, blowing gusts of fitful, dry, gritty snow. As they walked to the shuttlecraft, he noticed that her teeth were chattering. He took her blanket, a soft, delicate thing much larger than it seemed, unrolled it, and wrapped her in it, while she looked at him with wide-eyed wonderment. He looked down at her bare feet, as finely formed as the rest of her, leaving footprints in the new snow. Her toes were red with the raw cold. She did not complain.

In the shuttle, Han suddenly felt the weight of fatigue begin to fall on him, a heavy curtain, a fog. Through this fog, he heard Hatha, vaguely. Hatha was telling him that he should busy himself with his new pet and get to work on the procedures to be followed by the watch aboard the *Hammerhand*. At the hetman's headquarters, Hatha conducted them to a set of rooms, comfortably furnished, and departed.

X

———◆———

"Civilization is a thing which man does not really want; it is also a thing for which he can demonstrate no clear-cut requirement. Therefore, by the most simple and innocent probings, we are brought to those disturbing and terrible questions which always seem to begin with 'why . . .'"

— *Roderigo's Apocrypha*

"You may expect everything or nothing, as it suits you, but both are equally false. Only one thing true—something will happen to you; events are imperishable.

— *'1 Knun i Slam (The Doctrine of Submission)*

Several of the short and dark days of the winter of Dawn passed, while Han tried to accommodate himself to his new reality; a task which was complicated greatly by the fact that he did not know very well what reality he should try to adhere to. He tried to examine his present context in the light of past experiences and found that impossible— the past would not fit the present, and neither would engage with any future he could imagine. Most of this was engendered by the quiet and almost unnoticeable presence of the girl, Usteyin, for she, as nothing else, reminded him of how far his adventure had diverged from his original position. What had started as a relatively simple journey had become impossibly complex, a total wilderness in which issues of morality, emotion, loyalty and the very personality were all blown this way and that. So long as the flow of events had been simplex and serial, as he and Liszendir became drawn deeper and deeper, farther and farther out, he had maintained some balance. But now, it all returned. His system, he realized, had been jury-rigged and jerry-built. Or was it jury-built and jerry-rigged. He knew the ancient formula, but he could not get it straight. He suspected that it did not really make any difference. So, with the undeniably human girl, he came back to the roots of things. To a reality. But it was a reality that made no sense.

As for Usteyin, she had installed herself with a minimum of fuss and was indeed as advertised, docile, quiet and neat. Han was mystified by her in several ways—for although a young girl, barely adult, if that, she was completely self-sufficient. She had a sense of self-possession that was beyond anything he had ever seen or heard of. He thought that if by some chance he could maroon Usteyin on some obscure asteroid, she would continue her routine until her supplies gave out, and face the void calmly, as if it were nothing more remarkable than awaking from a nap. He had watched her as she slept; she slept like an animal, lightly, with little movement. She dreamed, for he could watch the changes of expression moving over the exquisite face, but they moved with a slow, steady rhythm that resembled no one he had known. She had a reserve and a sense of self-discipline that made Liszendir look like a wild barbarian by comparison. She responded to Han directly, without artifice or mannerism, speaking in simple, short sentences, in a girl's clear voice, but one which was absolutely steady. Whatever she thought she was, she was absolutely sure of it. Perhaps she really did think of herself as nothing more than an animal, a pet, a breed. But he could not tell—she was completely opaque and revealed nothing. Han could thank Liszendir for teaching him that such behavior was indicative of depth, just as overly demonstrative behavior was indicative of great shallowness. If this was true, the girl Usteyin was an ocean.

As he saw more and more of her, he became more convinced of his original impression of her—she did have a mind-wrenching beauty, and was as different from Liszendir as any living person could be, and still remain a person. He visualized Liszendir as a picture in monotone. A picture in great detail, a picture filled with a thousand details, highly erotic and suggestive in the mind of even more than the body could accomplish. But Usteyin was something done in full, broadband color, a dazzling figure whose brightness concealed—something, everything. He viewed the prospect of any further relationship with her with misgivings. So, indeed, had he been advised to take his choice, and so he had done. He could not see any materially different result; and the few days only served to allow him to realize the depth of the problem. And he did have a problem. Owning her had been as simple as just asking. But in reverse proportion to what he really wanted of her, he felt as if he had set an impossible task upon himself—for to truly possess her as he wished, now, he would have to know her, and she would have to know him.

Han considered cultural shock, but as a meaningful symbol it fell far short of the reality. Already, there were subtle hints that within her, a delicate balance was being upset, slowly, to be true, but nevertheless, upset, completely. He had come to want her more than any other girl or woman he had known, but he did not want it at the price of ruining her forever, by destroying the very basis of her intangible appeal.

He considered that a person who had never had any money could suddenly become rich, through a lottery, or some similar circumstance. Likewise, a farmer could move to the city; a person from a backward and rude planet could arrive on a developed and sophisticated one. But all those were of one range. The next level down was that of a slave become a freedman, or perhaps a responsible member of society. Then, below that, was Usteyin, who did not even think of herself, as well as Han could determine, as a person.

This was doubly ironic, he realized, because as a result of the heavy bombardment of charged particles Dawn received periodically, when the planet's magnetic field reversed polarity, the renegade ler who ruled most of Dawn were sinking, losing abilities, and some of the humans were undoubtedly advancing, or at least holding their own. Han strongly suspected that given equal conditions, Usteyin was probably vastly more capable and intelligent that even the better Warriors. He could pursue more paradoxes—for in comparing Usteyin with Liszendir, he could see that Liszendir, while denouncing civilization, was completely civilized, and Usteyin not. Yet in another sense, if civilization was an exercise in self-control, then it was Usteyin who was the furthest along of all of them.

A pet. But a highly refined pet. One did not hitch a thoroughbred horse to a plow, nor did the lapdogs of a previous age pull carts and sleds. She was not a drudge, a scullery maid, nor a concubine. It had been the most quixotic of hopes to take her at all. And to maintain such a self-view required a balance equal to that of the finest chronometer. He feared damages to his own ego if he treated her in error; but he feared even more for her, if he tried, too abruptly or too coarsely, to turn her into a human being, a person, overnight. And he found that the longer he had her in his presence, the more he wanted just that: she would do something to his life forever.

He was suspicious of the word "love." So he had been, long before, and since Liszendir, doubly so. She had been right, of course—there were an unnumbered quantity of things, states, relationships that all fell, in human society, within the large expanse covered by the symbol. It was as if someone asked if the city Boomtown were located in the universe! But he saw in himself a continuum here, beginning with a native selfishness and an idle concern for sensual pleasures, which had been fun, never regret it. But he had reached a deeper level with Liszendir, a mutuality that was far different. And with Usteyin, he could sense, somewhere out of sight, a deeper sense of commitment, in the same degree of logarithmic scale. It did not change or degrade anything which had passed between himself and Liszendir. He realized with a sudden pang that it indeed was past-tense, now. Rather, it brought it into more meaning.

His mind went off on another tangent: what about the other *klesh*, any of them, the Zlats, the Haydars, and the Marenij, who resembled the Zlats in build, but who were slightly taller and who had gold-olive skins and fine, silky, pale-blond hair. The girls had been breathtaking, simply unbelievable. He had read the material in the folder, eventually deciphering it out: the Warriors who were fanciers of *klesh* thought that they were, by breeding, working back to the original human types. But you could not work backwards this way, and they had instead created, unwittingly, several hundred types of races, each with its own strengths and shortcomings. Han had no doubts that immeasurable harm had been done in the weeding process over thousands of years. But it had also brought some qualities into piercing, burning focus; all the *klesh* would have to have something to survive. And from what he had seen, the Zlats were the furthest along of all. If they all could only be brought back into the common stream of humanity . . .

As for Usteyin herself, she seemed content in her new home. He had no idea what her old one had been like. She gave no indication of sadness at leaving her past, whatever it had been. She was clean, fastidious, neat, and took care of herself with the seriousness of some ancient courtesan, although much of the effort she expended was, at second glance, completely asexual in nature, and very probably served to pass time. She had a small bag of toilet articles, a comb, a simple brush, a miniature file, a crude toothbrush. She spent the days grooming herself, sleeping, or occasionally manipulating the gadget that looked like a tangle of fine silver wires. More rarely, she sang quietly to herself, aimless and endless songs in a dialect Han could not follow. In these times she seemed to be oblivious to everything, withdrawn into some private universe whose dimensions only the Zlats knew, and perhaps only she knew them accurately. Han let her sleep and make herself comfortable when and where she would; at night, she curled up in the corner by his bed. And slept lightly, for many times he was awakened by a sudden noise, or a shout from outside, and looking about in the darkness to locate the source of whatever woke him up, he would glimpse, in the corner, the sheen of her eyes, wide open. But in a moment, the sound of her breathing would become audible and regular again. As soon as he realized what he wanted with her, he wanted to begin immediately, but thought it best, for the present, to let her establish a routine comfortable to her before he started trying to unravel the fabric of probably six thousand standard years of intensive breeding and an ingrown, introspective culture; and a score of years on her own.

He had not been able to locate Liszendir, or find out anything about her, during the days in which he and Usteyin were left to themselves, and he had begun to worry about her. But finally she appeared. His feelings were mixed—relief that she was present and in seemingly good shape, and acute embarrassment over the presence of Usteyin. But he could sense in her eyes as she came in that whatever had been between them, it had now evolved into something different, and there was no jealousy in it. Rather, something comradely and responsible. Han followed the hint closely, for he felt the same way.

"I have come because we can meet and talk more freely now. I have some interesting information. Apparently, we are now to be trusted somewhat by these clods; I am doing what I can. They think I am teaching them great secrets, but in reality, I am only giving them beginner's-level exercises. I feel guilty, because they will be deadly enough here, but it will be child's play if they try to use it back in a ler civilized place. Some of them, it is true, have a high degree of native skill, but it seems to be caught by accident and personality and circumstance. Hatha, for example, is not a member of a class, but an individual in his skill, which by the way increases my professional regard for him, though I detest him and everything he stands for, just as before.

"Also, Han, your behavior at the *klesh* exhibit was a factor in this. Hatha was astonished! He actually respects you! It is the talk of the camp. So here I am. I came to tell you to stay on the course you have chosen. And to see the girl."

Han called Usteyin. She appeared shortly, and stood quietly, obediently, while Liszendir looked her over carefully. Now that he could see the two of them together, it reinforced his impression about Liszendir being monotone, monochromatic, while Usteyin was something in color. But there were other differences now apparent. Usteyin was slightly smaller in size than the ler girl, and considerably more delicate in structure, yet through some process Han could not fathom, she seemed to be the stronger of the two. It was Liszendir who had to exert some effort to keep her face expressionless.

Finally, she spoke. "I understand completely. In a house full of everything you could desire, you chose better than you know. She is far more than a pretty face, a young body, even though even to my eyes she is lovely. And you and I know how it must be with us. No bitterness. No recriminations. You must do this thing, for it has been set long before you ever saw me at Boomtown."

"It is a thing I have wrestled with deeply, Liszendir," he said, avoiding her eyes, still as full and liquid gray as they had been in the bright sunlit room where he had first seen Liszendir Srith-Karen.

"I know what you feel. But you must not project traditional human emotions, out of what one of your Boomtown secretaries might think, seeing you with some new lover, onto me. I feel no jealousy or envy. I wanted you to do this, and I know that were things reversed, I could not have done so well. Indeed, I feel as Hatha; in Boomtown, my first impression was of a lazy human fool. I see deeper now. Our peoples misunderstand much about one another; we should get back together somehow. It has been too long."

Han did not say anything. She went on, "You will save this one, she will be your life, and you will come back, or send back for the others. I see this. I visited the *klesh* exhibition also. It was disgusting—not the people themselves, but in how they came to be what they are, and what they are. But every human on Dawn is worth it. As for me, I have not found one ler on the whole planet I would lift a finger for. They are both inferior and evil—let them devolve back into the chaos and bestiality they deserve.

"I did as you suggested, and as I felt the pressure to act. It was like feeling the cleavage in a piece of wood. I knew which way lay the grain, and which way lay the knots. I must have learned how to think that way from you."

"You did well, completely. You know that you were not being rewarded; you were being tested. And in passing it as you did, you have astounded Hatha so much that we now have room to move about."

"Liszen, I have not forgotten . . ." At the use of her love-name, he thought he saw a quick shadow flit across her face.

"Nor have I. Nor will I ever. But you know we could not spend our lives together, that I must someday weave with others. I want to; even when you were within me, I knew what I would have to do. Even your name was an omen. It means 'last,' in the mode of the power of the water, which governs the emotions. I can tell you that, now. You know ler too well to have anything like that concealed any longer. And she? She should be obvious to you, even if you are not trained in such things. Look at her color: red hair. She is powerful in the air elemental, she radiates it, she is a living spirit of the power of events, the onrush of things. I am Liszendir-the-fire, a creature of the will, but it is so strong in her that she would blow me out like a candle. She is small and fragile, but she bears the weight of the universe behind her.

"So, now, Han. You know what must be, with me. You

knew long before you asked me if ler kissed. So would you
stand outside the *yos* of my braid and bay at the moon? No.
And I would not stand outside yours either. And if I can help
with what will be your most difficult task, I will. Ask it of
me, for what we made between us with our bodies was
hodh, and afterwards we are closer than parent and child.
Will you have enemies? Let them tremble in the night, for
I will lay hands of fire upon them. And wilt thou lovers?
Then I will warm them with my heart as I once warmed you.
It is all now far beyond what you call love and sex."

She turned and left.

Han turned to Usteyin and looked at her for a long time.
He regarded elementals as rank superstition, but there was
an undercurrent of sense in what Liszendir had been saying,
something which could not be denied, however rationally
one pursued it. Usteyin finally spoke. It was the first time he
had heard her speak directly to him, in confidence. Her voice
was lower, and had a slightly throaty quality.

"Who is that lady?"

"She came here with me. From another world."

"Did she own you?"

"No. We were both wild." He had to use the word. There
was no word for "free" in the distorted ler Singlespeech of
Dawn.

"I fear her greatly. Females are cruel. She is warm one
way, I see that, she has known love, but in another, she is
cold, like ice, like the wind of the south, now. Like the
darkness out of the south. She came before you, to the place
of show. I thought then she must be from some far place.
She looked at me with hardness, with eyes of wands."

"Usteyin, what do you want?"

"Want? I do not understand."

"Desire. Ambition. Need. Before you were in the show."
He paused. "Plans. Hopes."

"I . . . want to have some honor, that I may mate. If not
that, a kind home, where there are people who will treat me
well, even feel warmth, protection." She paused, thinking.
"But I know from the way the people acted when they were
deciding who was best that I did not fare well."

"Is that all?"

"All? Is there more? To have hope, an alien thing, one
must be either of the people or the wild. I am neither. I
would see that my life is good as it unfolds, but I am prepared that it be otherwise. There is no past, no future. Those

are things-not-real which unwild creatures tangle themselves into."

"They told me you were not high, this show, but of what I saw, I wanted you more than anything else. Above all."

"Above females nearer to yourself?"

"Yes."

"Then I am happy. It is good to be wanted, even more to want, and find that which is yours."

"What do I look like to you?"

"When I saw you first, I was very surprised; wild *klesh* never come. I thought you were a person from far away. But I saw your hands, your face, the fear on it. What was that from? You are *klesh*, even as I, yet you must be a great one, just so, to walk with the people as one. *Mnar*, I thought, but I saw then that it could not be so. You look like them a little, but only at first."

He could not explain everything. Not yet. She waited a moment, then continued.

"Sometimes we see wild ones. There were many, not so long ago. I did not meet any myself, but I heard tales. It was very hard on them; they pined, they languished, they refused to eat. Many fought constantly, and some were killed. What do the people wish of you? Will they mate you?"

"No, I don't think so, at least not the way you mean. They wanted to, at first, I think, the fat one who was with me. But later he changed his mind. He said I was too close to the wild to be of any value to any breeder. No demand. They can get all the wild ones they want, here. I work for him. He was pleased, and so gave you to me as a present."

"Me?"

"Yes."

"Will you let me mate? I desire it very much." She said the last with a coy glance from under her eyelashes in a mannerism that was something more than a flat statement. To be sure, he wanted her—but he had hoped to put the issue off for some time, start changing her first. He realized that he should have known better. She had seen through all that with insight, and had gone directly to the point. He decided to be honest, and step ahead.

"I had hoped to win you for myself. Perhaps not immediately, but when you wanted, later. For a long time."

She did not answer him, but instead looked downwards to the floor, shyly. He looked at her eyelashes: they were long, feathery, the same deep coppery color as her hair. Suddenly she became, without doing anything, very desirable. Her posture relaxed imperceptibly, suggesting confidence, submission. Han felt his hold on his old resolves growing slippery, hard to hold. The moment was now, approaching like a thunderbolt.

Han said, softly, "I wanted to wait, because I didn't know if you would want me, or one of your own kind more."

She looked up, demurely, her eyes moist and shining under her lashes, her mouth soft. "Another Zlat would have been fine. But you are beautiful to me, because of your strangeness, because of something I saw in you when you looked at me there, the first time. Something I have known only in stories, not something I would expect to see. Why did you not speak of this earlier?"

She stood quietly, looking into nothing, expectant. Han could see the pulse in her fine, slim neck. It was racing. He turned and locked the door. When he turned back to Usteyin, she reached up, hesitantly, and stroked his beard, softly, tenderly, her eyes glassy. Han felt fire. He could not speak now, and he knew that he could not even begin to say, "No, later." Whatever was coming, let it come, he thought, feeling his own pulse going up, feeling the lightheadedness, the sense of falling without vertigo. He touched the clear, creamy skin, brushed against her dense, fragrant hair. Time changed to Usteyin's concept of itself: it ceased to exist.

Usteyin was a complete beginner in lovemaking who knew almost totally nothing. She was artless and seemed to be guided only by the things she felt, and tales she had heard. It was, in fact, difficult for them at the first, for as Han recalled, she was "unbred," to use the phrase of the *klesh*-breeders of Dawn. But she made up the lack of knowledge and experience with a naive enthusiasm, and an ability to learn, which Han found to be both disarming and disturbing. He treated her with tenderness and patience, and she responded with a fierceness and an immediacy; Usteyin could not live for maybes or laters. She lived now, and it was reach it now first. Other times would be other times. Foreplay, apparently, was another of the things she knew nothing of. That, for her, now consisted, so it seemed, of a few fleeting gestures. Then to work. The spirit of it was not one of selfish gratification, but one of the fear that it would never be again, and so it was to be experienced to the fullest. He thought afterwards, as they lay close together, that she had volumes to learn, and that he would enjoy being the instructor.

She made a motion to return to the corner where she made her bed, but Han stopped her gently, asking her to stay where she was, close to him. Wordless, she curled close beside him, seeming almost to glow in the dark from some inner sense of happiness. It was something beyond her wildest dreams. As he moved his shoulder to make room for her, he winced. However delicate and fragile she looked, it was not apparent within an intimate embrace; she was both violent and strong. At the height of her own feelings, her muscles had rippled like hot wires. And she bit. He gingerly felt new tender spots along his neck and shoulders. He winced again. Yes, that had been in the sheaf of instructions, too. Zlats were passionate.

When he awoke, it had become dark, and was late at night, the long night of the Dawn Winter. The lamp was on, and under it, Usteyin was combing out her hair. She sat in her corner, her blanket draped over her legs. The lamplight cast golden planes on her skin, rippling fiery highlights in her hair. She noticed immediately that Han was awake, and looked to him expectantly, then away, in the shy, submissive gesture he had seen her make before. But now he knew what it meant.

She said, her voice soft, "You and I, we must do that often, as much as we can. I am afraid they will take us apart. I expect it. But I would have this last forever."

Han watched the girl, and did not speak, for some time. He found himself feeling much the same, and he could not explain it to himself; but however it was, this girl had become priceless, the end of all searching. There was no reason for it—it simply was, and he knew, from long before Liszendir, that a love (however broad and meaningless the word was in general usage) which could be explained wasn't much of a love at all. If you could say "Because . . ." then it was already over, a thing of the past. He said to her, "So I would have it too. What do they normally do when it is just two Zlats, your own kind?"

"We stay together only long enough for the girl to conceive. Sometimes days, sometimes weeks. But not long. But with you and me, I don't know . . . they did not put us together to breed more Zlats, so it could be shorter or longer. Who knows what they want of us?"

Han felt icy. The Zlats, and all the rest, were pets! They would be very fertile, bred for it. And no contraceptives; they would be light years away. He had forgotten, in his long time with Liszendir, when they didn't have that problem. He looked closely at Usteyin again, sitting quietly under the lamp; the exquisite figure, the deep, thoughtful sea-green eyes, the spirit, the strong emotions . . . no. He was sure. He would see this thing through to its ultimate end, whatever came. He felt a sudden surge of possessiveness, something alien to him. Yes, he thought. To the end. In civilization, on Dawn, or in Hell.

"Usteyin, we have much to do."

"I know."

"Not only more than you know, but more than you can know, right now," he said, paraphrasing Haldane's law. "But aren't you hungry? Come on. I will find something for us."

Her reaction was not what he expected. "You would share your sleep with me? Your food?" she asked suddenly, and began crying. He went over to her and put his arms around her, saying nothing, letting her calm down of her own accord and at her own pace. Even such simple things as that were more alien to her than she could be to him. Or so he thought, at least for the present. Again, he reflected that he had a lot to learn, as well. She calmed down quickly, showing the same speed of realization and readjustment that she had displayed before.

"Now I understand more. We are people, you and I, in the place where you are from. Not them. You see me that way, not as an unwilling Zlat, or any kind of Zlat. Do you want that? They will probably kill us when they find out." She said the last bluntly, unemotionally.

"Yes, just that. We are people. Back in my place, the world is filled with people, just like us. There are no *klesh* there. We are the people."

"I . . . I fear that greatly. I cannot see it. I am afraid of the wild."

"It is not all that wild. Better than the people here have."

"Then you must tell me, and I will understand. About a place where the *klesh* are people. I have heard this tale before, in parts, but I did not believe. That is the kind of thing that we tell ourselves in our stories. Thus have some of the

wild females talked, sometimes in words I did not understand at all."

"That is *klesh* speech from the other place. Our speech.
There are many different ways of speech."

She laughed. "So you think. Many, all different, like the
klesh here, but I know that we are all the same under the
skin, and so I know that however we wish to say our needs,
so it can be understood by all, with a little trying." Then
she suddenly became serious again. "But you must return me,
send me back. I do not think I can do this thing. I will fail
you. Send me back, now, while the desire is still deep in your
eyes. I do not wish to see the other."

"The other?"

"The anger you will feel when you discover that I cannot
follow you, that I will be too weak."

"Oh, no. You will do well." He was not saying it to calm
her fears, her sudden loss of confidence. It was true. Han
had never met any creature that learned as fast, adjusted as
fast. It was almost as if she had nothing to reject, which was
probably quite close to the truth, at least as much of it as he
could see, as much as anyone could see. "Come, now. Share
food. We will talk. You first. Tell me everything."

"Everything?"

"All of it. I want to know."

"And you will give me your everything in return?"

"As much as you can take."

"There is darkness and the night in your words, behind
your eyes. But I will come, and I will take it, gladly, for
this is a thing far beyond even the make-believe stories of the
Zlats."

Somehow, he had imagined that she might eat with her
fingers, but she did not, using the utensils with deft accuracy.
Familiarly. But she ate fast. She said, "Food is a serious
thing. That is why I was surprised you would share, even
after what we had done. It would not be thus with a Zlat
male. We are always hungry."

"You must keep a little of that. If you eat too much you
won't be pretty any more."

"Ugh. Yes, I have seen a few fat *klesh*. They are not so
pretty."

After they finished, Han gave her a cup of hot beer,
which she sniffed at suspiciously. She said, "There is people
magic in this. It is forbidden."

"I know. It is good, and it is not forbidden any more, to us. Not to you, now."

"Do you really mean to keep me, yourself, always?"

"Yes, I do, if you will stay."

"You would let me choose?"

"Yes. Not here, but in my own land, my country. You will be free there, even of me, if you wish it, though it pains me to offer it to you."

"It is no matter. I will not exercise such a choice, either here or there. I have only one life to live, I only want one such a love as this. It is so much more . . ." She stopped and thought for a moment. "Besides," she said, with a flash of sudden shrewdness, "we are not there yet."

"That is so. Now we wait. Tell me now of the Zlats. Everything. Come, let us sit together."

She joined him, sitting closely beside him. At first she began hesitantly, as if she were revealing deep secrets, but gradually the hot beer worked on her inhibitions, and the tale began to unfold.

It was a simple story, really, and they had forgotten much. The way Usteyin told it, before there had been chaos, in which humans were as wild as any other creature. The people, the ler, came, and set things in order, then producing the breeds. It was a narrow, narrow world, but within its limits it was relatively secure. She knew that there were still wild humans, but she did not envy them. She had never even thought deeply about it before.

The Zlats, of course, were the only breed she knew well. They seemed, to Han's ears, somewhat more advanced and sophisticated than most of the others, but even then, they had so little of what might have been called culture that he could not compare them to any society he knew. They were something even below slaves, and were not used to any practical purpose. They did not have religion, nor did they have any sort of underground. Keeping them separated for most of their lives, over thousands of years, had ensured that there would be none of that. They bred only when allowed to have a few days together, and the rest of the time they were carefully segregated. Children were raised by their mothers, and after a certain age the boys were raised by the males. Usteyin knew about sex, about the love of the parent for the child; and she knew many stories about men and women, but they were not real—they were for the quiet times only.

That was what the tangle of wire was for: it was actually a mechanism which could be put into an almost infinite number of possible arrangements and configurations. Those, and the way light fell on it, and the motions she used to set it, were all elements of a symbolic system, probably closer to an abacus than anything else, but it was a system that coded relationships, emotions, events and desires, whole realities. She could tell to herself an infinite number of stories on it, learning the proper motions and settings from others, when they had their rare personal contacts. She was proud of the one she had, for she had made it herself, when she had been young. The word she used, however, was "grown." She had grown it. But she was afraid of it, too. "You use it too much, the story-block, and it catches your mind. You stay down there, in the wires and the beads; no one can get you out of a story-block, except yourself."

The only other thing she did was hand-weaving, by an unusual method which did not use a loom. Her blanket, which was as fine a thing as Han had ever seen. It was her only item of property, so to speak, and was both cover, house or place, and clothes, when the weather required them.

She knew about the other kinds of *klesh*, but in an odd and abstract way. She would have said more, but she began to grow sleepy, and like most of her kind, when she reached a certain degree of drowsiness, she simply went under, like a lamp being blown out. Han carried her to the small bed, placed her in it, and covered her up with her own blanket. As she settled into her new position, a soft smile grew on the delicately formed face, and she murmured something in her sleep, too quietly for Han to hear. He was not sleepy, not just then, and turned away to think.

Han reflected on Usteyin. She lived, exactly in the present. She did not measure herself, as did Liszendir, by a set of traditions, or like a civilized human, by an unconscious set of cultural values, but solely by an unknown sense of interior balance. Han could see that she did this: he could not see how that interior balance was structured, and he imagined that he would never be able to glimpse it, even for a moment. To grasp it, one would have to strip off all civilized values, then program oneself to think of a personal image something more than a wild animal, but less than a slave, for at least slaves had functions, duties, and contributed something, even if that something was unwilling support of the rest of the society.

But she was fully human, not ler, and not an animal. And as such, she had vast reserves of curiosity, of mind, which would be used for something. So far, all he had seen was her incredible flexibility. Liszendir had made Han partly ler as far as she could, to make herself comprehensible to him. Usteyin simply absorbed everything, integrated it, and pressed on in her eternal present.

Abandoning that train of thought, he picked up the folder concerning the care of the Zlats, and read the crabbed characters until his eyes burned. After a bout of struggling with the boring expostulations, the overaccurate language, the many injunctions, he finally felt sleepy, and turned out the lamp, getting into bed beside the sleeping girl, warm and soft in complete trust and relaxation. He thought about her in relation to all others he had known. He was no stranger to girls, not at all. But there was something different here, some inner essence that the others had simply not had. Her beauty was manifested in body, face, skin, carriage. Yet for all of that, it was not a mask to hide something less inside, but something which escaped from the inside despite all the limitations the physical body placed on such expressions. There was something sweeter just out of reach. Was it her scent, disturbingly like a child's? No, something abstract. Something about time. Time. Wife? Lover? Family. Children. Red hair and furred lower legs . . . almost under. Time. Sense of time. Children.

Then his eyes opened wide. He had it. The answer. He knew who was manipulating the Warriors. And why. And all the proof required would be a few answers from Hatha. Simple questions. It was all so clear. And for an instant, invisibly tiny, unmeasurable in time, he glimpsed a fraction of the reality that was Usteyin. He slept.

XI

*We have learned one thing about nature: that
it is a great generalizer—it forces its component
parts to be multiplex or perish, all in degrees
commensurate to their ability to influence other
parts around them. Artificial things do not show
this trait; and this applies to the living as well as
to the nonliving, if you prefer that level of distinction. So it is that within a narrow range of
specifications, we ler are indeed superior to the
old people, the humans. Yet one cannot escape
the weight of evidence—whole for whole, ler
and human are approximately equal—different,
not better or worse in either case. No ler sur-
prises a human, after the initial shock of ac-
quaintance, but humans continually surprise ler,
just as they do each other. We prefer our own
carefully structured society. But we, I assure
you, stand in considerable awe of people who
live closer to chaos than do we, and do not fear
it, as we do very much.*

—Klislangir Tlanh

Han soon began to be worried about Usteyin, and Liszendir as well. If his guess was anywhere near correct, even
partially correct, they were all in great danger, much greater
than anything Hatha could do to them. In fact, he was beginning to feel a certain pity for Hatha and the whole crew
of the Warriors. They, in fact, were being used, and much of

their potential for future evil was reduced by the same amount. And, to continue, if the suspicion was right, then they were a disposable tool as well.

He countered these thoughts with reminders of the miseries Hatha had caused with his vainglorious raids—the broken families, the sundered friends, the deaths, the appalling view one had to take, to survive at all, once on Dawn. And the meteoric bombardment was a horror beyond most weapons, for realistically, it could be used only against populations. A terror weapon, solely. Aving's cold remarks about livestock, and of course the history of the Zlats, and all the other *klesh*. If by magic he could forget the rest of the universe, judging solely from Dawn, he would have to agree with Liszendir's fierce condemnation of the Warriors —let them fall to their fates, except that he would attempt to get the humans off the planet first. But conditions were not like that, and there was the issue of the real villains, who would have to be neutralized before they could do anything, because he was sure that whoever and whatever they were, they had the means to eliminate any threat from the Warriors, should one appear. One did not, however advanced, work on nuclear weapons without fail-safes, and to manipulate a whole culture was potentially even more dangerous. To do what must be done here, he would need both ships and Hatha's cooperation. And he would have to do it without Liszendir. And he would have to get it quickly, for he had heard rumors among the guard staff to the effect that recruiting was now going on for a new and more extensive adventure than any they had previously had.

Again, he set out, looking for Hatha throughout as much of the rambling quarters as he could move around in; but he looked in vain, and found no trace of him. Hatha was gone, and apparently so was Liszendir. After wasting the greater part of the day with guards and clerks who either knew nothing or would admit to nothing, Han finally located a subordinate of the hetman's who still possessed a little initiative, who agreed after considerable persuasion to send a recall out by heliograph. But he could not promise that it would be answered. "The hetman," he said, "comes and goes as he chooses." Han gritted his teeth with impatience; it might take days to find him, and what he had to do could not be done with anyone else. The rest of the ler Warriors around Hatha neither trusted Han nor would they pay any attention to him whatsoever. Why should they, he reflected. Han, like Usteyin, was not a person. He was, in fact, now no less a pet than the girl.

He returned, enthusiasm blunted, to the little quarters where Usteyin waited. As Han came into the room, he saw her sitting quietly in her corner, as he had come to think of it, going through her morning routine: a thorough combing-out of the fine, copper-colored hair, to be followed by a short nap. He went over to her and settled down beside her. We will, he thought, still have some days left together; and then, either many more, or none at all. He touched the girl's hair lightly.

"Show me how to do this, with that." He pointed to the little comb, seemingly undersize, which she used so expert-ly. Usteyin slowly handed it to him, a wondering expression on her face. He continued, "And I will show you some other things, which I hope will make you happy. Others . . ."

Hatha did not appear that day, nor the following one. So, having caught a moment of time, they had time to con-sider, to decide, and to try the feel of it on for size. It fitted them both better than either would have hoped.

As he spent more time with her, he learned something else about the girl Usteyin: she learned fast, blindingly fast, much faster even than he had suspected at first. He had a lot to expose her to, and he went slowly at first. At times she balked, or would cry in frustration, but she would recover, immediately, and they would go on. Gradually, Usteyin learned all about a world she had suddenly been born into. But if Han had worried at the first about turning the uni-verse loose on her, it was now the other way around—he worried about turning her loose on the universe. And once it was brought out of her, into the open, she had a matter-of-factness that was even more abrupt than Liszendir's.

"So if you catch the fat one again, then we may go back to your home, to the wild-ones-who-are-people? And you want me, a Zlat, for all time you can see? Do you not have others whom you would want more?"

"Indeed I do not."

"It is a hard thing to see, for me. Your world. I will not know how to behave with decorum."

"I will show you, and you will act as you wish. Do you want this thing?"

"If you were offering to send me there alone, I would say no. But I will go with you, and I will stay. Do not fear! I have made my mind the same way you have made yours. I feel something with you I did not know even existed for creatures of the world. Only in story-blocks. But I ask one thing of you."

"Ask, Usteyin."

"Please do not make me take the hair off my legs. That is the most prized Zlat trait. I will cover myself, if that is your way, curious though it seems. Do your women not think they are beautiful, that they have to hide what they are, and then show only certain parts? Would you cut off the hair on your head?"

"No. And you can keep it. I have grown to like it, too." He stroked the fine, silky hair which covered her lower legs to the ankles. He had, he admitted to himself, indeed grown very fond of it. As he sat, absentminded, he noticed her looking at him, expectantly, shyly.

"Now come closer to me, here. I wish to nibble on you some more," she said softly. "Of all the things we have done together, that is the sweetest."

So the days and nights passed. And he did not grow tired of her. She had aspects, sides, angles which he had not been aware of at first, but which unfolded, like some vastly accelerated recording of a plant, developing. But the day came when Hatha returned, and their time was over. Han was notified as soon as he had come back into the compound. It was suppertime, and Hatha summoned him. Han asked to take Usteyin, and to his surprise, Hatha agreed, although with a cynical leer Han found disturbing, and dangerous.

Liszendir was waiting for them, in the hall where they were to gather. Han looked at her closely: she appeared to be tired, drawn, overworked. Whatever had been happening, she was being pushed close to her limits, somehow. He did not think it was physical, but something deeper. The strain of cooperating with the Warriors was beginning to tell on her. And as far as he could see, she did not know what he thought he knew, which made this temporary cooperation much easier. And she did not have an Usteyin.

Hatha would not hear any talk until the meal was over. He was, he announced, a bit worn himself. Han restrained himself, with difficulty; but at last, the moment came. Hatha spoke.

"I see that you have done wonders with your new friend. I, too, can no longer bring myself to refer to her as a mere possession, a pet, a breed. You have undone in a few days what it took us thousands of years to do. She is now human. You will realize what this accomplishment means. She can never go back to the Zlats, or even be allowed near one again. She knows entirely too much for her scope. Yours I overlook, for it arose in an erroneous society; but hers is new, special. So if she went back, I think she would very likely become, ah, fatally unhappy with her place." It was a reminder and a threat. He was in very ill-temper, tonight.

But Han went ahead anyway. "There are many things which have been bothering me, since I came to this planet Dawn."

"Some valuable, some inconsequential rubbish." He scoffed.

"May I ask you some questions? I suspect something. And if I am wrong, then I will keep silent forever; but if I am right, even partly right, then you yourself will not wait for me to ask for action. You will demand it!"

"Indeed? Well, then—proceed!"

"How long ago was the *Hammerhand* built?"

"Not so very long ago. That is no secret. About twenty of your so-called standard years ago." A relay closed in Han's mental picture. Step one, verified. The rest grew brighter and clearer by a degree.

"How did this happen? Did you just think it up, or did someone suggest it?"

"It was acted upon in the great council. Some of us, who were junior at the time, thought to enlarge our scope, to assume our rightful place in the universe."

"Who brought it up?"

"As a fact, I did."

"Where did you get the idea?"

"To be more truthful than I prefer, it came from a valued associate. But it was I who acted decisively."

"And you did well. Who was the valued associate?"

"Aving, in company with his three sons." Relay two closed. The image was coming into shape fast now.

"Did you know Aving before this?"

"Ahh, this is nonsense. I grow tired. I have not been so shabbily interrogated since I was a buck."

"If you will grant me the liberty of asking a few more questions, I will do you and the Warriors a service that you will judge to be greater than Aving's."

"How could that be? You are nothing but a wild *klesh* and a prisoner. But go on a little more. A little. Only a little. Now, Aving. No, I did not know Aving, then. The position he held had been vacant, defunct. He took it over. I assumed he came up from the ler folk of the upper troughs. They are, by and large, an unassuming folk, and such ambition would be rare, but valuable. He came here."

"Did you check his origins? Do you know, personally, where he came from?"

"No. I would have no reason to. He was ler, he came to the Warriors."

"Has anyone ever seen him or his so-called sons unclothed?"

"Ridiculous and impertinent! No. Their Triad . . . No. I do not know."

"If you look as you may, you will not find one who has mated with any of them."

"That would take days. And for what? We are a restrained folk, compared to you, or to these overcivilized ler of which this girl, Liszendir, is a specimen."

"This is my suspicion: Aving is not a native of Dawn. He, if you can call him that, if his people even have sex as we know it, and gender, is very likely neither human nor ler. Check with your oversexes. They will have had no contact. Aving has set up a vile thing here; he is a spy, and worse. He is using the Warriors, your culture, to perform his own ends."

Hatha was on his feet instantly. Mad, raging. This was perilous, now, if he had not planted the tiniest seed of doubt. Usteyin already had heard his suspicions, and agreed. In fact, she had been able to fill in considerable detail. He glanced at her: she was rigid, tense, waiting. But Liszendir was just catching on. Yes! She saw it, too.

"What is it you say? Do you seek to sow dissent? I will put you in a cage! I will . . ."

"Wait! Who rebuilt the ship?"

"Guards! Guards! Here! . . . Who built the ship? That makes no difference! I will . . . Aving and his sons built it." He paused, reflecting, suddenly sober. The guards rushed in. He waved them to a halt.

"And they took it off-planet, didn't they?"

"Well, yes, after some local repairs. They said they needed weightlessness, to make the changes."

"Could you ever see the ship from the surface of Dawn?"

"No. They said they were to fly to the gas giant—the one we call Pesha. For certain tests."

"How did you explain their knowledge?"

"We accepted their word, their Warriors' words, after they had been initiated. They said that the family had been studying the holy books, the old manuals, and that they had discovered a new way out of the old. Well? We could not use it for much as it was. They seemed . . . But they were gone for a year. A Dawn year. I had not looked at this in this way before. But I fail to see, even if what you say is true, how this affects things. It makes no difference. We have the weapon, we have used it, and we can use it in the future against whomever we choose."

"Hatha, a weapon is only as powerful as the uses to which it is put, and the defenses used against it. Arrows daunt those who have none, but those with armor and shields merely laugh as they cut the archers down. Liszendir tells me that your ship once had extensive detection equipment on it. What happened to it all? I saw none, on that tour you took me on."

"They said that it was not necessary." He was still not convinced. But he was wavering.

"Listen. I will tell you something you do not know. In mine and Liszendir's ship, a little ship, which you fly manually, knowing nothing of what it can do, I could detect you long before you even were aware of my existence; and then I could inflict enough damage on yours to immobilize that monster out there. Mine and hers! And ours is the smallest one made with arms! Do you know what would happen if you took the *Hammerhand* into a real battle? They would carve you up like meat! Conquest! You fool, you'd stir up a war for someone else's profit, and pay all the costs yourself. Oh, sure, the first planet you hit, you'd probably win. But then the armed ships would come, from the other worlds, and ler ships, too, filled with warriors who give no quarter, once you use a projectile weapon against people, a planetary population. Who was it that told you to capture wild humans?"

"It was Aving . . ."

"Of course. He wanted the Warriors to be seen. Identified. Reported. As they were. Otherwise, how would anyone know the Warriors were ler? Did you know that while you were lurking around Chalcedon that Aving was back in *our* civilization, visiting?"

"When?"

"Before Liszendir and I came to Chalcedon. He made

sure that the news got back, and then he killed him, Efrem."

"That's impossible. I don't understand. How could he get there? He was here, in the camp, when we left on the raid. And I commanded the only spaceship on Dawn."

"Crap. *Khashet* manure. He waited until you left, then went to his own ship, shadowed you. While you were playing around Chalcedon, he was waiting somewhere nearby, waiting for a response. Then, before you left, he returned here. He left Seabright after us. But we detected his ship decelerating for Chalcedon, so he had passed us in midflight."

Liszendir broke in wildly, "Yes! Yes! It was he who we ler did not know, who wanted only two of us to journey to Chalcedon, not a fleet!"

"We shall see if Aving will admit to this."

"No. I have a better idea. Take your guards with you, and go to my ship. We will fly, and find the anomaly I saw as we flew here. Then you will see, and then you can come back here, get the big ship, and treat it to the sting of its own lash. Only let us all stay together, now."

"And if you are wrong . . . ?"

"No, I am not! And there is more. They would incite a war, identify the tool, and afterwards see all the evidence destroyed. Do your people know how stars evolve?"

"Evolve? No. Are they not eternal?"

"Great gods of history, Hatha! Your star out there is too big. It's going to explode, and I'll bet within a few years. Before anyone could work back to this isolated planet, and uncover the truth. That would seal up the evidence for sure. Aving would know; that is why he chose this planet as a base of operations. It had everything he needed—a steerable, primitive culture, complete ignorance of the inner civilized parts of this part of the galaxy, and something which would eradicate all the evidence that anything had ever been done here. And you had a spaceship you couldn't, or wouldn't, fly. A little cosmetic surgery, small price to pay, and he was in. What he couldn't know was that the ler here were devolving into a more primitive form, from the repeated bursts of hard radiation that gets in when your planet, Dawn, reverses polarity of its magnetic field. They might have known a few things, but not that kind of detailed information, to compare, which Liszendir would see instantly, and even I caught after a little time. You talk about superior types, Hatha, but I'd be willing to bet that the Warriors are no better on the whole than the wild humans of the Leilas area, and your pets may very well be superior to you. The only thing that would keep them from taking over is the ingrained belief that they themselves are not people, but animals. How could they think otherwise? They have no native primates, or even mammals, on Dawn with which to compare themselves."

Liszendir said sadly, "It is true, every word of it. I see its sense, now. You have lost Multispeech, this I know, not just forgotten it, or let it fall into misuse. Your people are indeed devolving; you don't even know what standards are except for the physical ones you impose on your pets, like this girl, Usteyin."

Hatha's face was blank, and his only response to this sudden revelation was to turn and gaze at Usteyin. When he did speak, it was towards her, but the tone was abstracted and distant, as if he were ruminating to himself.

"I have not believed them until now, of course, but we have several legends which speak to that effect—that the people of the past were somehow greater than we are today. This is the root of our desire to annex the older worlds and bring them to the realization of the great truth. And we have other legends, too. About the Zlats, in particular. It has been said that the Zlats have supernatural powers, that they are waiting, biding their time, until the day when they shall all speak a great spell in unison and in an instant they, not the Warriors, will be the masters of Dawn. When did it arise? I cannot say. I have heard that they know something which cannot be realized until they are all together; hence comes the prohibitions about gathering more than a few together."

Usteyin looked directly at Hatha. "So I have also heard. But I can give you no knowledge of how it would be done, for I do not know myself. That has never been said. Only that we would know when the moment had come, and we would know what to do. Then. I have always felt it just a story, that we would never do it. Just a story. And win or lose here, in this, I foresee that it will not come to pass. You will escape us. But we would have treated you with some honor, for though we hated you deep inside, we were also grateful, for without the Warriors, there would have been no Zlats, no what-we-are."

Han said, "I have nothing from you to be grateful for. You have favored me, but you have brought misery to uncounted millions, and ruined your own people as well. I

would wish my own revenge, therefore, but I will not have
it, because there is a greater danger, and I would not see
any people be used as you have here."

Hatha asked, "Everything but reason. Motivation. Why
would they—if there is a they—do such a thing as this, a
task which at best would take years?"

Liszendir answered, "They are probably an old race, and
are now declining in numbers. They will have exhausted the
energy potential of the worlds they control, and would seek
others. Only they know that now they cannot conquer by
force. But we both are still expanding, full of low-energy
demands, since the first runaway days. They will take us
who have saved, and live like lords after we have worn ourselves out fighting each other. It will be like nothing you
can imagine."

"One more thing, Hatha." Han said, getting to his feet.
"The gun."

"Gun?"

"The one you had on Chalcedon. Where did you get it?"

He looked like a bear at bay. He moved from one foot to
the other, uncertainly, vaguely. "The air gun came with the
ship!" he blurted out.

"There is one on my ship as well. Liszendir and I took
it from a murdered man's room, in Boomtown, on Seabright,
which you have never seen. Who put it there?" At the last,
Han was shouting; the guards looked nervous, jumpy, hair-
trigger. Never before had they seen Hatha, the great war-
lord, the hetman, addressed in such a manner. Han continued, "Go to the *Pallenber* and look in the locker in the
rear of the control room."

During the last exchange, Han had been slowly moving,
almost unnoticeably, imperceptibly, closer to the guards,
away from Hatha. No one had noticed, except the glittering
bright eyes of Usteyin. Even Liszendir was fooled.

Han asked, softly, "Can you trust these guards, who have
heard what we know? How do you know who is a creature
of Aving's, and who is one of yours?"

"I will have them strip, now; then . . ."

But Hatha was unable to finish what he had intended to
say, just then, for one of the guards had dropped his ornamental sword and his crossbow, and was displaying one of
the deadly little gas guns. Two others followed suit, almost
in unison with the first. They immediately shot the other
guards in the room, who were presumably real ler. As soon

as they had done this, they turned to the others in the room, but it was too late, for Liszendir and Hatha had overturned some tables, and ducked behind them, knowing that however deadly the little darts might be, they had no real penetrating power. And Han had been close enough to one of the phony guards to strike him with an elbow chop, which, to Han's surprise, doubled the creature over. It appeared to have died instantly from the blow, which Han had not thought deadly. Using the fallen one as a shield, and grabbing the fallen gas gun, he shot the other before it could get a shot off. It fell, grimacing horribly and convulsing. Whatever was in those poison darts, it worked as well on the guards as it was intended to on humans and ler. From his position, he could see Liszendir's pale face, grimacing with distaste at his use of a projectile weapon. But this was no time for her mannered niceties!

By this time, which seemed to Han to have taken an eternity, but which was quite short, all of them had gotten under cover, except Usteyin, who had vanished. Where was she? Han could not go looking for her, for the remaining phony guard was hiding in the doorway, and he had them pinned down. He was screeching in a loud, piercing cry, in a language none of them had heard before, presumably calling for assistance. It was liquid, trilling, suggestive of birdsong, but in a much lower register. But it carried well. Han called out to Liszendir.

"I was right! They are not ler. They do not have a rib cage, but something like a cartilage tube. Hit them in the middle! They break there."

The remaining phony guard was still in the doorway, still screeching. Han thought desperately. That one must not get away, and we must get him, somehow, before he can get reinforcements in here. Hatha added to the din by bellowing like a bull, calling for his own reinforcements, if any of them could hear him. It probably did no good, but it added to the confusion, and lent Han some spirit. Suddenly, the trilling, liquid screeching stopped abruptly, as if cut off. Hatha continued for a breath or two, then he, too, fell silent. Han looked around, cautiously. Where the hell was Usteyin? The one guard seemed to have also disappeared. Han took a chance, and ran to the doorway. The guard was slumped backwards, behind the edge, and standing over him was Usteyin, holding one of the ornamental swords, which was dripping with a brownish fluid, rather watery, which was not blood, even though it obviously served the same function. She had wormed along the wall, gotten out of the room somehow, and stabbed the creature from behind.

Han looked at her for a moment, amazed. She looked back, and there was a feral, wild light in her eyes he had not seen before. It faded, even as he watched. He turned from her, and called to Hatha.

"Hatha, what did you do with that crossbow? The one Liszendir and I had when we came to Aving's castle. Where is it?"

"In another room, here. Three doors down, on the right. I kept it. I was going to send it back to the warship, but never got around to it."

"I'll get it. It is better than the ones your guards carried. Stay here. Strip these bodies. We will need the gas guns. Yours, too."

Motioning Usteyin back into the relative security of the room, Han made his way down the corridor to the room Hatha had indicated. His skin began to crawl. Damn! It was dark in here! How many more of them were there? He began to feel along the back of his neck the aim of a sniper. But the dart did not come. He made it to the room. There, on a table, was the crossbow, still disassembled. He picked it up, and ducking beneath the table, assembled it, cocked it, and loaded it. The quiver of iron darts was still with it. Then, hurrying back up the hall, he joined the others, who were waiting in the doorway. Together, they made their way towards the outer exit from the building. Nothing happened, until they reached the door to the outside, suspiciously standing wide open. Hatha started into the opening, but Han pulled him back. Just as he did, a sliver pinned one edge of Hatha's cloak to the frame. He returned to a hiding place, pasty-faced.

Han wriggled to the opening, lying on the floor. Outside, the winter darkness was complete, as he had expected. He could see nothing from where he was without exposing himself further. But the angle at which the dart had struck suggested a direction, just out of sight. Han motioned to Liszendir; she came up to kneel beside him.

"Can you get across this doorway, very quickly, too fast for whoever that is out there to get a good shot at you?"

She nodded assent, tensed her muscles. Han got ready. "Go!" he whispered. Liszendir flipped across the opening. A sliver of something struck the wall behind her, with plenty of 100m to spare. Their reactions were slow. Han thought that he could have beat their aim himself. But he saw the sniper. He took careful aim and fired. There was a howl, and a figure burst out of concealment, staggering, making a weird howling noise. Before it became completely still, another came running from the right, to help. Han recocked the crossbow he had just used, and shot the second one. This one fell silently and lay still. The other was still as well. It seemed odd. They were killers, but they died at the slightest blow, the lightest wound. He could have sworn that the wound would not have been mortal. Curious . . . He got up and ran recklessly out into the night, looking around, followed by Liszendir.

It was a clear, very cold night, without fresh snow or cloud cover; frosty starlight spattered the Pannona Plain with weak light, bluish in tone. Han caught a hurried movement out of the corner of his eye. He turned, and saw still another one of the phony guards drawing an aim on him. He bent over, falling, knowing it was his only chance. The first shot missed, and Han kept moving, trying to recock the crossbow as he went, knowing that he would probably not complete the act. No thoughts at all passed through his mind; just a sudden sharp pang. But the figure did not take advantage of this, but instead burst out of hiding, running, trying to get away. Of course! He was the last. Before Han could load and fire, the figure suddenly performed a wild somersault and sprawled on the cold ground, biting the icy dirt and convulsing into impossible, topological shapes in his frenzy. Then it gave a tremendous heave, and became still. Han looked around. Liszendir was standing, slightly behind him, with a gas gun in her hand, and in the weak, faint light, a wry expression on her face.

They looked at each other, and she said, in a low voice, "I menaced him with this, to give you time to reload. You would have gotten him, too, had he tried to shoot, because he would have had to choose between us. But instead, he tried to run. He would have gotten out of range for you. So I did the deed. All laws must be broken, at least once. There is not a single one that does not have an exception, in some circumstance. Remember what I told you about your irrational decimals being the only rational parts of the universe? Well—I have met one face to face." But however casually she uttered the words, there was a price, within her, to be paid. Now she, the cold one who had avoided passions

in her youth, had broken two prohibitions. Han touched
Liszendir affectionately on the shoulder. She had turned
away, but she looked back. "And now I shall be known as
Liszendir Oathbreaker, for all time. No one else has gone so
far." Han could not answer her. Suddenly the illusion of
closeness between them, which had been growing since they
had boarded the ship, together, at Boomtown, vanished.
This was something she could not share. An edifice in Han's
mind, which had seemed as solid as the mountains far to
the west, turned to fog, dimmed, and vanished. Illusions,
that was what they had been to each other. Phantoms. But
that was what defined the deepest feelings, loyalites. Then it
stabilized. Liszendir receded with the speed of light, in
his mind, shifting all the frequencies to the red. Then became still. She was now of the past.

Han left her, and went over to the last guard. He removed the cloak it wore; felt the body, which seemed to be
losing heat more rapidly than it should, even in this cold
air. He could sense some difference in the creature, but exactly what he could not determine. It looked ler-like enough,
but that was probably cosmetic surgery. He pushed experimentally at the area where the ribs would have been. It
gave oddly, as if it were not bone, but a tube of cartilage,
flattish, of one piece. Odd . . .

He rejoined the others, who were coming out into the
open. He said, "To our ship, quickly. We can fly it over to
Hatha's. We need to get both of them off-planet, into space,
right now, before we run into any more of these."

But apparently there were no more of the creatures in
the immediate area, for they had no further incidents. They
made their way to the *Pallenber* without seeing any further
evidence of them. Still, with as much hanging in the balance
as was here now, they could not waste time, nor take any
more chances. Hatha had recovered, and was in his characteristic temper, fuming and enraged. While Han was sealing and activating the *Pallenber*, Usteyin came to Han,
where he was working in the control room. She was still
carrying her small roll of possessions with her, and she had
also kept the ornamental sword.

"I have never done such a thing, never dreamed of it,
never tried to set it in the story-block. But he—that thing
was trying to kill you, you more than all the rest of us, for
you had found it out, and it knew that only you could find
its masters. Myself—so what is termination but the end?

Our regrets and pain are short; but to lose you is a price I will not pay." She was shaking and her eyes were overflowing. But she gained control of herself, and placed the sword to the side, repeating, "I have never dreamed of such a thing," half to Han, and half to herself.

Han lifted the *Pallenber* off, hoping they were making as little noise as possible, and flew rapidly over the short distance to where the *Hammerhand* sat in the frosty starlight and the silences of the winter night, grounded. Han found one of the shuttle bays open, yawning, and without hesitating, flew carefully into it and landed. Hatha was waiting at the outer lock, and they had hardly stopped when he had bolted out, running with an agility that none of them would have credited to his bulk, until they might have recalled his abilities during the first fight Han and Liszendir had had with him. It seemed that he was there, and back, before they had finished recollecting that first scene. He returned to the control room, breathing hard.

"There is only a small crew aboard, a duty watch, but it will be enough. I told them everything, and to go as it is, now." Even as he was speaking, the warship began the rumbling, rocking motion Han remembered. Hatha watched for a moment in evident satisfaction, and added, "A runner is already on the way to the rest of the senior Warriors with this tale. We must alert the camp."

Han turned to him. "Go back. Have them leave the meteors here. It will speed takeoff. Go to the place where you get more, and gather some large ones. Bigger than these. I think that these may be too small for what we will have to do."

Hatha sprang for the lock again, shouting over his shoulder, "So it is! I will tell them. We will meet them there!" Then he disappeared, reappearing after a short interval. He locked down the outer door, and said, "All is ready. They will be awaiting us. Now let us go!"

Han had the *Pallenber* ready, and without effort, they lifted off the floor of the bay, glided outside, and took to the air. Han switched the screen to ventral view, and they watched the huge bulk dwindling on the darkened plains below, until it was at the edge of visibility. Before it merged into the dark background, they could see that it was moving, hovering uncertainly, finally moving off at right angles to their course.

Once they had risen out of the steeper gradient of Dawn's gravity well, Han set an automatic course in to bring them up out of the orbital plane. Usteyin stood close by him, her eyes wide, entranced, staring at the instruments, the controls, the screen, now switched back to look into the endless night of space. Han watched her closely; what could she be thinking, how would all of this seem to her? She moved closer to him, touched her arm against his.

Hatha watched the screen for a time, also. Then he turned to Liszendir. "What he says fits together well enough. But I am still not satisfied with the reasons why these creatures from the void chose Dawn as the place to begin their aggression. You tell me why. You have odd insights into things."

Liszendir was standing towards the rear of the room. She answered, absent-mindedly at first, "Oh, I suppose they thought to start at the weakest point. You know, no one ever attacks anyone else for a reason, but because they think they can get away with it. They have reasons enough, but they are only for questioners among their own, and others. They are most assuredly not the real reasons. This is true on the individual level, on the level of tribes and nations, and between planets. True of ler, too, and I would project all sentient life forms. They doubtless think all of us primitives, but the problem in dealing with primitives is that on the average, the individuals of a primitive culture are more capable than those of the superior culture, culture differences notwithstanding. Aving only saw mine and Han's problems, our blunders, our stumblings. He was perceptive, there, and saw far into me, and my own thoughts of lacks in my life. He thought we would bumble it up good! But the further in we got, the more we learned. You played a part, too, Hatha. We are all in a chain of causality that has not yet ended, nor whose end I can see."

Han and Usteyin were not listening too intently to the conversation. Han was, now that they were out into deep space, programming and running the detection sequence, hoping to get a more accurate position on the anomalous emissions he had seen when they were flying from Aving's castle to Hatha's camp. Usteyin watched with great attention, as the panel lights flickered on and off, many colors; while on the various screens to the side, numbers and letters appeared briefly, vanishing seemingly as fast as they appeared. Other screens displayed possible configurations, arrangements of points. Nothing seemed stable for any length of time. Occasionally, there would be a hint of a promise of something definite coming into view, surfacing out of mountains of meaningless data—facts; but nothing of any definite shape would hold, longer than a few seconds. Han explained as he went to the girl, knowing that it could not be making very much sense to her. After all, the symbols and numbers could mean nothing to a person who couldn't read and write, nor count past five. After a frustrating period of time, he stood back from the panels in resignation.

"It's the same problem as before. I can definitely tell now that there is something here," he said, pointing at various indicators, meters, data, "but I can't pin it down. We'll have to keep taking readings from different positions until we get a better fix. This could take years."

Usteyin looked at the ship's detection equipment and computation panels with something between curiosity and, impossibly, recognition. She watched it closely, as if she were working some puzzle out in her mind. Then she abruptly turned and grabbed Han.

"Why didn't you tell me before you had a story-block? You kept a secret, you pretended you didn't know what mine was. Why did you do this?"

Han looked back at her, understanding nothing. "What are you talking about, Usteyin? What story-block? I have nothing like that tangle of wire you use. I don't understand what you mean." He felt completely blank.

She darted to her blanket roll, dug out the small bag in which she kept all her small things. She reached within, deftly, and brought out the complicated tangle of wire Han had seen her use before, as she said, to tell stories on. She unfolded it to full expansion. Han peered at it closely, trying to make something coherent out of its randomness. It was still a seemingly random tangle of hair-fine wires, silver or platinum, tied at the junctions of the wires, and strung with hundreds of infinitesimally small beads. She held it up to him proudly, but she would not let him touch it, when he reached for it, to bring it closer.

"This," she said, as if explaining something very obvious to a child who was refusing to cooperate. "I told you before. I tell stories on it, to myself. We Zlats all have them. But this one of yours—I know it is a story-block, too, but it is so big. You cannot carry it around with you. And what is wrong with it? Why won't it read back? Can't it tell you the

things you wish to see?" Concern replaced the tone of mild
irritation which had slipped into her voice.

"Tell me again, Usteyin. Slowly. I am just beginning to
see what that is."

She shook her head, as if clearing cobwebs, a gesture of
impatience. How could he fail to see this, he who had seen
so much, of herself, and of other creatures. "This is mine. I
made it, grew it, when I was very young, a tiny girl, with
my mother. We all have them. Zlats. No one else. I know.
When I wish time to pass, when I need to know a story, I
take it like this." She held it in a peculiar gesture with her
left hand. "And I make it tell me stories. Like this." She made
a quick series of flickering motions with her right hand,
hardly touching the tangle. Some of the beads moved, changing position. The deft, sure finger motions were almost too
swift to follow. She did something else to it, tensing it with
her left hand, and it responded, very subtly, shifting in some
way, becoming . . . another random tangle of wires with
beads strung along them. "Can't you see it?" she asked. "That
was the tale of Koren and Jolise; they are Zlats who have a
great love story, they stole the jewels and ran away to . . ."
She trailed off, watching Han's face, closely. "No, you don't
see, do you?" Her enthusiasm turned to disappointment.

Han stared at the tangle, dumbfounded. "No. I can't see
it. I don't know how. How many stories does that thing
have stored in it?" Han began to imagine that it was a symbolic kind of memory bank.

He was wrong. Usteyin said, "There is no end to stories
you can tell on a story-block. I made it well. I know. I may
be only a fourth, in my first show, but my story-block is the
best one the Zlats have ever made. You see wires, beads,
how they are in relation to one another. There are the motions, the way you hold it, the way light strikes it. I can
always invent more motions. No end. It is all me when it
speaks, hands, motions, eyes, me, the story-block. I see in
it, all at once, when it does the change." Usteyin stumbled
for words, hesitating, growing suddenly shy again. They obviously did not understand story-blocks. She took a deep
breath and began again. "All at once, no-time. Then I remember it as it happens, afterwards. In there, there is no
time, so I have to put that in myself, afterwards. After it
changes. It comes . . . sideways. I string it out in my head,
put the story in the way that we see things as we live.
Time is an illusion to us, not real. Everything is instant. But

we do not live instantly, so I make it fit my rate, how I move. Do you see, now?"

They did. All of them stared at the shining tangle in Usteyin's left hand. Han felt superstitions crawling about the control room, ghosts out of the far past, oracles, magi, bearded gurus walking out of the forest, yogin who could move from one place to another. Milarepa, on old earth, the Tarot, the Cabala, the I Ching. Witches. This copper-haired girl who had no clothes, who could not read and write, who had not known how to make love, who did not even consider herself a *person*. Liszendir's matter-of-factness broke the spell.

"What can you put into it to make a story?" Liszendir understood what a story-block was.

Usteyin saw the expression on the other girl's face and recognized understanding. "Anything. I make up stories, I retell the old ones I know. There are many-many. I do not know them all. The Zlats have more stories than one can know in one's whole life. They are about love, excitement, lands, people, heroes. Things-that-are-not. But we cannot use it so often. It is dangerous, perilous. Too much story-telling, and reaching too far, and it catches your mind, it captures your spirit, and you are trapped there, in the wires."

She paused, looking at all of them, seeing more comprehension now on their faces. And Han, too. Now he saw. That was good, she wanted him to see it, desperately. He had to. She continued, "Now, Han, love, why won't yours work? It is broken? Has he," she gestured with her bright eyes at Hatha, "tried to use it?" Hatha was lost. He saw, but it was far beyond him.

Han answered her, "No, it works well enough, but it can't tell me what I want to know." How could he tell her that the threshhold level was too low, and that the detection equipment could not locate it out of the noise of the background? Or that the data was insufficient? He said, "I can't get the settings just right. It is too subtle for the equipment."

"I will fix it later," she said, pleased that she could see what the problem was. "I am a Zlat. I can do such things. Yours is strange, but a story-block is a story-block. I will move some time, and you will be able to do with yours as I do with mine, although I wish there was some way I could make yours easy to carry around, like mine. But why is this story so important? I could see part of it; I watched, I knew. But it was about . . . things, where they are. Rocks or things in different places."

"Can you run that story on your story-block?"

"Oh, yes. That is an easy one. Wait." She took it up again, shaking it. Han winced; he knew what she was doing: clearing the memory. "One more thing," she added. "Show me your starts again."

"The whats?"

"Starts. The things you begin with. The pretty lights, and the pictures."

Han silently complied, running through the detection sequence again for her. As he saw it, the results were neither different nor better than the first time he had run through it. Usteyin watched the instruments intently, singlemindedly, ignoring everything else in the control room. He stood back. Finally, she looked back to him.

"Is that all? What a curious story. I could almost do it without this. Now . . ." She paused, looked deeply *into* the glittering tangle of wires, and made a few quick adjustments. It moved, sprung, a few wires shifted position. She manipulated it again, and it responded again for her. She looked off into the viewscreen, into space, reflecting. Then back at the story-block. Then she looked up, and laughed, lightly. "How strange! You are a very curious person, Han. You must teach me these stories you know. They are like nothing I ever knew from the Zlats. They are short and easy to set, but they are full of odd jumps and shifts. And I do not understand all that I see, there . . ."

"Tell me what you see, just as you see it."

"There are three things, they have light of their own. One is that." She pointed at the star, filtered by the compensations of the screen. She apparently did not recognize it as the swift sun of the planet Dawn. "That one. It is very bright. Then there is another. We can't see it now. It was where we were, but it has moved, far away. It starts and stops. And there is one more. It is . . . ahh, what? Wait. It is big, but not big. I see it both ways. Hazy. I can see through it. It looks big one way, small the other."

"That is the one I want. Where is it?"

"Show me the world. I will show you where it is."

Han moved some switches, changed the display to read out a map of the planet Dawn. A globe appeared, then a picture of a map projection, then stabilized. It was Dawn. She pointed to the south pole, after looking at the map for a

second. She said, "You want to find this one very much. Go
to this place." She suddenly giggled, a very little-girl sound.
Then she recovered. "I am sorry. But it is a very silly story."

Hatha interrupted, "What is this mad *klesh* saying?"

Han answered, "She's telling you where Aving's ship is.
At the south pole."

Hatha looked at them as if they were all insane.

Usteyin was excited. She had pleased them! She looked
sidelong at Hatha. "He wants to go to it, to break it. But he
must now go! There is more!"

Liszendir was staring at the story-block, and Usteyin,
open-mouthed. "Can you see the now with that thing?"

"Oh, yes. No story has end or beginning, like the all. We
just start and end where it suits us; after all, we do not
want to see everything—our minds are too small. I stopped
it, but wait: I will finish the sequence." She had not yet
cleared it. She turned her attention to the story-block,
tensed it once more, and looked at it for a long time. She
stopped, then looked back, as if she had made an error.
Then she exclaimed, "Oh!" and hastily cleared it.

She started speaking, rapidly, shaken by what she had
seen within the tangles of wires. "There is evil there. Bad
things. I stopped it. I do not want to see them. They are
like worms in a manure pile. Moving. Angry. They are
watching . . . us. They can see us in some way I do not
know. If we go near them they will hurt us, with white
fire. It is very strange. They look like people but they are
not people. Not any kind of people; they are something else.
They can see me and my story-block, but they cannot reach
me." She looked around, wide-eyed. She moved close to
Han, huddling against him.

"Do not let them take me to that place!" She began babbling uncontrollably. But Han noticed that whatever was
the degree of fear, or even mild hysteria, that she felt, it
did not break the grip with which she held the device, nor
the angle at which she held it. She grasped him tightly with
her free hand.

Han stroked her hair, comforting her, calming her down.
Reassuring her. Then, as she subsided, he turned to Hatha.

"They have weapons, Hatha. Beam radiation weapons.
They'll fire on us, if we get within range."

Hatha said back, "I care not. Let us go to my ship,
where it gathers meteors. I will go back and punish them
with something even their fire cannot stop."

Liszendir came closer, watching Usteyin, the story-block.
She sighed, in resignation. She said, slowly and sadly, "I
finally see what she is and what she can do. But I cannot do
it myself; no ler would ever be able to use that thing.
There is no mystery to it, no occultism. She has a feedback
loop in that tangle. Human minds are structured to use it.
It multiplies your consciousness through an odd sort of mo-
tional symbolism."

Han looked at Liszendir as if she had suddenly become a
stranger, a most completely alien being. "What do you mean,
Liszendir?" He had never seen such an expression of sadness
in her face.

"Can't you see it? That thing, plus hand, eye, mind, and
probably different kinds of light as well." Usteyin nodded,
agreeing. "It's not electronic, it's not magic. It isn't even
mechanical in the strictest sense. It's like the thing you count
with; primitive people use them. Beads on rods. An abacus.
But that thing doesn't stop with numbers: it symbolizes
whole realities. It's a macroscope and a computer all in
one. Don't you see what you have brought to yourself,
what you have loved and won, at my insistence? You can
hide nothing from her, in time or space."

Usteyin collapsed the story-block. She released her grip
on Han, and moved close to Liszendir, looking into the
other girl's eyes deeply. "You know, so then you know that I
have seen the thing that you and my Han made together,
before-time." Liszendir flinched, but Usteyin was not angry
with her. She put her free arm around the ler girl, spoke in
an affectionate tone. "But you are a good person, you are
innocent. You thought that your life had not been passionate
enough, that you had not had a great love. Yes, I looked. All
the way back, you and Han alike. I know. But we do not do
that often. It is not good to look at your own life from outside. But I had to know."

Liszendir asked her, in a tiny voice, "Did you see this,
before?"

"No. How could I know? We do not look at our own fu-
tures, for we do not want to know. It is the only story we
have. And one must have the starts. But then he came, he
bought me, he made me his own. It was so strange that I
had to look. I did not dare for a long time. But yesterday I
did. Your life is so different from mine. To me, we are none
of us yet the real people, we are just all poor creatures acting
out what has been preplanned for us, flowing in current, but

to you, you are a kind of ultimate. I see that I was wrong, you too. Creatures fade into the other, and there is no ultimate. We are all related. And you have known many loves, many ways, your body is a fine instrument to you. And you will mate with two more, in an odd ritual I do not understand. But I have only one. And I will have an even stranger life than yours, and now I understand it less than I do yours. But it will be far more than the Zlats could imagine—maybe not so adventuresome, but much sweeter. There is much peace there, and I fall into it, pretending I am flying. You will not change, but I will. This is fixed, like rocks, like the old stories of the Zlats. But you should not fear me, Liszendir Srith-Karen of a many-many generations of Karens. You prepared him for me, and it is a gift for which I will be forever in your debt."

XII

> *"All religions originate in discredited sciences."*
>
> —Holden Czepelewski, *Cahiers*

> *"Truth, such as we find it, appears in mythic stories, while recited facts fall into mere opinions. And the more facts are enumerated, the more opinionated and erroneous the matter becomes. At the level of pure facts, there is nothing but chaos. Ah, to be sure, facts are real; one should respect them, but one should beware of them greatly, for it is the feel of the flow that makes the dancer beautiful.*
>
> —Brunsimber Frazhen

Han turned away for a moment, and began programming a course that would bring them to a rendezvous with the larger ship. When he turned back, one of them was smiling affectionately, and the other was still staring off into some personal noplace, blankly. He wanted to break the stasis of this scene, somehow get things back into some framework of motion, at least of the illusion that they were moving, but he could not bring himself to it; he sensed that the slightest tap from him might prove to be a blow which shattered.

Hatha broke the silence by asking, "If what my eyes and ears tell me is true, then I take it that she, or any Zlat for the matter, or even any human, if trained, can see through that tangle, that wad, into anywhere?" He stopped, searching for a word which didn't exist. "Anywhen? And how did they get them?"

Usteyin answered, "It is just as you say—anywhere and anywhen. But where we were, on the plain, as what I was, I did not know many things, and those things of the outer world I knew, I did not care about. If I do not know you because you live in some far place, I would not ever have a reason to see to that place, to see you, how you are. No. We did not use them for that; we used them to tell stories on, to make us proud, to give us identity. We made them ourselves, from the first. That is one of the stories—how the Zlats made story-blocks. It was our specialty—in the old days—but the things we made fell into disuse and we had no work, no place. So we made something for ourselves—I call them story-blocks to you, but to another Zlat I should say 'the last gift.' We used to make big ones—like this one on this ship. We had no power, no machines—so we made one that needed no power but that of the spirit, and no machine but the hand."

She smiled, as if to herself. "I used to think that all these things were just make-believe. But now? Perhaps all the time we were looking across time, across distance—to the long-ago or to the yet-to-be. That the story of Koren and Jolise, remember that?—is perhaps real, somewhere, somewhen. I do not know that. I do not want to know whether it is real or not, for just as this can show beautiful things, it can show things of terror and evil."

Han asked, "Could I learn to use one?"

She reflected for a moment, then said, "No. I do not think so. Not because of what you are, but because you are too old, you know words too well. You have to start before you become too tied up in words. Very young. Not yet walking well, that young. And them, the ler? Not at all, never. They do not have the mind for it—they cannot let go. Now you are changing me to your life, you have told me, shown me, and so as I learn, then I lose this. After a few years I will no longer be able to use it at all, it will be just a tangle of wire. Do not be sad! I want this or I would not have come with you. Since I am with you I no longer need stories, I live one, ever so much more than what you see in here."

She looked at Hatha. "So under them, we just had time, time, which we called an illusion. It had to be so, to use the story-blocks. No time or it won't work. That is another reason why you can't use one—you see too much time, and *they* see nothing but time. You, Han, see that everything has a connection, one thing makes another. She, Liszendir, thinks that things happen on their own. Both are wrong."

Han felt out of his depth. This girl who had been a pet a few weeks ago was calmly discussing the dimensional continuum of time and space—and dismissing it, in the speech of an eight-year-old.

Liszendir said, "I don't agree, and I will not change, but she means that 'causality is an illusion of time, chance is an illusion of ignorance, and time itself is an illusion of . . . ah . . . length, perhaps, is the best word'."

"Yes, yes, you see it!" she exclaimed. "That is how it is. It does not move. I lack the words. We move, in here, in our minds."

Hatha scoffed, "You may believe in fortunetellers all you wish, but I have always run them off whenever I found them skulking about the camp. This is nonsense! She is a *klesh*. She knows nothing."

The girl turned on him with a voice that carried venom. "It is because I know what you call nothing in your vanity that I can use this and see through all your schemes. A higher people keeping pets. What foolishness! Your pets are higher than you, keeper. And what you think you know is less than nothing. Trash in a pit. Broken bits, shards of a jar you will never see as a whole nor use for water. This is not magic, fortunes, divinations. This is a tool which helps me to see—what is, what was—and what is to be. Do you wish to know what else I have seen in here? That you will never see the sun rise over Dawn again, that is what I have seen."

Hatha retreated from her, illogically, in view of what he had said before. "Stay away from me, Zlat witch!"

"I do nothing to you! You will do it to yourself!" She was angry now, and despite her small size, and lack of obvious weapons, she had suddenly become a figure of danger and malice, something not entirely controlled. Han reached for her, touched the soft girly skin of her shoulder. At his touch, she began calming, returning to her earlier state.

He said, "Wait. Do not waste this on him. Let him go his way. If you must use it again, then use it to tell me one more story. He will want to see it, too."

She turned, calmed. "What is it?"

"The bright one, the star. Tell me its story, and where we are in it. I will show you the starts."

"Once more, no more. I cannot use it again, after this. I have already used it too much this day. I fear it now. Let me tell you something about it, how it is used. Now if I wish to make a story about just such a place, exactly such a person, at a special time, it takes many starts, many motions, many settings before I move it. The more detail, the more I have to put in, and the less it gives me back. To watch one grain of sand fall, in one place, at one time, it would take me a year to set it just right, maybe longer. And who would wish to see it? But at the other end, if I wish to ask it, 'What is the meaning of life?' then there are no starts. Just tense it and look. Many starts, short story; few starts, long story. And the last one is the longest of all: it never ends, it lasts forever. And since there is no time, that means you are trapped in that, where the illusion won't work. So we never ask that; that is the one answer that traps you for ever. Your spirit is lost. You can't get back yourself, and no one can get you out of it."

Liszendir added, "Irrational numbers, again. The realities that device symbolizes are all irrational numbers, nonrepeating decimals. But in her system, she has a way to cut them off at any point, except in certain questions. Without the cut-off, you have to keep considering the operation. I see why it is deadly. Never mind that I can't use one—I wouldn't think of even trying."

"Yes. And it jumps at the first, the first part sets everything up, even the end, of each story. You need do nothing at the end. But I know that is because it was there all along, the jumps because in reality it was smooth, but all that went before has to be compressed at the first."

She finished, and turned to the panels, expectantly. Han began the sequence, a complete data acquisition sequence for the primary of Dawn, all-instruments mode, all sensor. He did not understand how she could derive any meaningful ideas from what she saw, for much of it was being displayed in a set of symbols which were strange and unknown to her; but on the other hand, perhaps Usteyin, as she had suggested had been the case for the story-block, didn't see data at all in any kind of symbols, but gestalt patterns of flow, vectors, directions, intersections, and could insert her own symbols for specific items. It did not seem to make a great deal of difference to her.

"Again, please."

He started the sequence over again. Yes. Now he was more sure; that was the way she saw things, probably the best possible way, except for the fact that it must be non-verbal, nonsymbolic as he understood symbols, and being thus, could not be explained by her, any more than a two-year-old could explain how he walked.

"Enough. I can do it. Now I need light, strong light. Can you make the window brighter, give me daylight? This is a hard pattern, I will need hard light for this; light is a thing in this, too. It controls accuracy and the rate of movement." Han adjusted the viewscreen, keeping the bandwidth constant, but lowering the filtration, as he turned the ship so the star came to rest at the center of the screen. Usteyin was already at work. She said, absent-mindedly, to Han, "Yes, that's right, just right . . ." and trailed off, muttering to herself, absorbed in putting the settings into the story-block.

The glare of the star flooded the control room, erasing color and making contrasts strong, glaring black and whites: in this light a petite witch with burning white skin and hair of space-darkness held up a glittering miniature silver galaxy, her body oriented exactly ninety degrees to the light source, eyes focused intently, mouth slightly open. She made the setting motions for a long time with her free hand, occasionally moving her lips silently, as if subvocalizing something; Han could not read her lips. Then, without waiting, she tensed it: he could sense movement, within it, something shifting, moving, falling into a new configuration. Beads moved, a wire shifted its orientation. Usteyin gasped once, cleared it with a sharp motion that implied pain, and looked away quickly. Han darkened the screen, and Usteyin, moving like a zombie, carefully collapsed the story-block and stowed it away in its place in the small bag. She stood up, but did not say anything. She looked dazed. Han touched her. She did not respond. He took her with both hands, shook her.

"Usteyin! Are you all right?"

The voice seemed to bring her back. She looked at him, nodded. "Yes. But almost not. I had to make myself get out; I have used it too much, tried to see too much, too far. No more."

"What did you see? What about the bright one?"

She hesitated for a moment before answering, as if trying to recall the exact flavor of the experience. Then she began. "It was long ago, very long ago. There was darkness. Stars. All far away. Emptiness, loneliness, the void felt tension. There was something there, but it was weak, spread, all over. Then it came together; it looked like smoke, boiling, moving, upwards, like for smoke, but inwards, to a point. Knots formed in it, things that glowed, lit up, caught on fire. Many of them. Then the air cleared, the lights became bright, hard fires, and then they began to move apart. This one I saw. It was larger than the others, and it had little cold knots all around it, which did not glow. It took longer . . . but then it grew quiet. I came closer to it. The rate of allmotion that you call time speeded up, raced, slowed down. I was to understand by this that many-many years passed. The thing grew slowly, it stayed much the same outside, but inside it was all sick, heavy, toppling, like when you stack rocks to see how high you can get the pile. Then it became bright, and time slowed greatly, so I could see it, but even with that it was too fast. It became large, bright, like this." She made a ball of her hands, and then opened them rapidly, spreading her fingers and moving her hands apart. "There was only a little thing left of it, but it was very strong. I could feel it, pulling at me."

"Where are we in that story?" Hatha asked.

"Near the end. I saw us, we will be gone, then. You want time, how-long. Go to the land where we were before. The sun will make the full circle of the two winters five times. No more. They will see it, too. It will be morning, the late spring of the north-winter. Early in the morning. There will be no clouds, they will see . . . . and . . ." She stopped. "What does it mean?"

Liszendir said, "You see and you do not know?"

"I see many things I do not know. That is how you get trapped in a story-block: you keep saying, 'What is this, and this, and this?' This last time, I saw others like the bright one, like, and not like. How they become, what they become, what all of them mean . . ." She trailed off, became still, glassy-eyed, staring into some interior noplace.

Han took her again, shook her roughly. At first, it seemed to have no effect, but by the second or third, she was out of the trance, returning to reality. As she recovered, she quickly touched Han on the face, chest, shoulders, then turned to Liszendir and touched her, also. She sighed, deeply.

"Yes, here. Back where I am, where I belong. Do not ask me to look into it again, in these stories you have. Please."

Han turned to Hatha. "She has seen the future and the past. Your star. She has seen it explode. It will supernova in five of your years. You will have time to get the people off Dawn and get away, but no more. And far away. That thing will poison everything within many years' travel of Dawn, moving outwards almost at the speed of light itself. And we will have to come back and get the humans, too."

They made their rendezvous with the *Hammerhand* on the other side of the Dawn system. And its new weapon, a huge clod of nickel-iron almost as large as the warship itself. At first, the scrub crew operating the warship had been reluctant, even hesitant, to make contact; but, thankfully, they had been finally convinced by the sight of the smaller *Pallenber*. Somebody aboard that monster evidently remembered. They landed in one of the bays, which was opened for them, and then closed over them. The outside sensors reported normal air pressure was returning to the bay. Hatha prepared to return to his ship. At the outer lock, Han and he had a few last words.

Hatha spoke first. "Well, now! All ends here, so it does. It would seem that you have managed to elude me at every turn, so after so many times, I finally admit to a bit of learning. Usually, with a captive, particularly a captive spy, I have found that the value of the individual decreases with time, from the capture. But you and Liszendir fared just the reverse. I had to conclude that I was wrong earlier, or that you two were not spies, but something else entirely."

"We were not spies, at least as I would think of them. We were not sent out to penetrate anyone's realm and send back secrets, but rather just go and have a look at what had happened. Hetrus, the human who seemed to be in charge of this, apparently smelled a rat, either in the planted trader, Efrem, or in the reported circumstances, or perhaps both.

But however it was, you would have done better to let us alone, on Chalcedon. Why meddle? Nobody there knew anything; I found that out, after you took the ship away from Liszendir. Things would probably have gone much as Aving had hoped."

The reminder of Hatha and the Warriors having been used as a disposable tool stung, and Han intended it to. That would not repay any of the Warriors for the generations of *klesh,* but it would be a gesture.

But if Hatha felt any direct resentment, he kept it to himself. "Possible, possible," he said, noncommittally. "But now we must go our ways, I to smite the aliens, and you back to your own planet, with two girls."

"Yes, back. But were it not for the fact that you will have to get your own people off Dawn before your star blows, I would fire on your ship myself, for what you tried to do, regardless of the source of that motivation. But I will not. Your ship has its uses. And when you have done it, then save your people. But time is precious. And be warned. Liszendir and Usteyin and I go, but we will all be back, within a Dawn year, and this time at the head of a fleet. We humans will take our own back, all of them, and I swear that if one Warrior so much as raises one spear against us, I will polish Dawn as smooth as a steel ball. And they are not to be harmed or carted off to another Dawn."

"All? Even the pets? Some have treated them kindly, and feel affection for their own."

"Every single one. Leave them and go your way, follow the teachings of Sanjirmil or the devil. But take one, and we will hunt you to the ends of the universe, for we have Usteyin-who-sees. She can find you, even if you hide in the core of a dark star."

Hatha looked around, idly, a gesture of resignation. "Very well. I suppose I would feel the same, were things reversed. So it will be! I will do as you ask. And have no fears, if I do not return from this expedition, now, for it is a possibility. When I sent the messenger off, I told him what might be. And without a ship, they can of course go nowhere." Here, he brightened. "But now, we have a mutual enemy."

"I will follow you down. Come onto Dawn from its north, out of the sun; follow the curve of the planet around, and drop your meteor as you move away. You should have a chance, because they will have to shoot at it first—I don't think even the weapons they have will deflect a mass like that. We will make sure nothing is left, and then go get Aving's castle. And Aving, hopefully. And so, good fortune."

"I will say one more thing: you have garnered more choice and kept it, than I would have reached for. And you have done much, with very little. I know you are no spy, no militarist. Such a one would have spent his energy on resisting. But I see much, at this late hour, and even a little bit of what that Zlat girl sees, and why. Go! I will await you on Dawn, a year hence, in a ship without weapons." He turned and left, with neither further word nor gesture. As Han was closing the outer lock, he caught a glimpse of Hatha, hurrying through his own lock, in the cavernous bay.

He returned to the control room, where Liszendir and Usteyin waited, Liszendir looking for him, and Usteyin gazing at the screen, which was once again displaying a view of the stars. Hatha had opened the bay, released the *Pallenber*, and they were drifting free. She turned to Han as he came to the panels.

"Now what will we do? Go to your place, your world?"

"No. We must finish a thing here, complete the affair with Aving. Then we will go, but we will come back, to take all of them on Dawn to a place where they can be people again."

The *Hammerhand* had already started moving, heedless of energy, on a manual course straight for Dawn. The large meteor, or small asteroid, however one wished to look at such an ambiguous object, trailed behind, sluggishly, reluctantly, as if it did not wish to leave its old comfortable place in the void. Han watched for a moment, then set in a course and let the *Pallenber* fall towards Dawn on a geodesic, down an invisible curve no one of them could see, except the ship's computer, or perhaps Usteyin, and she would not look. As they began their fall, Han showed Usteyin how to use the screen and make the adjustments. As with everything else, he didn't have to repeat anything he showed her.

Then they were over Dawn, catching up with the warship, which was close to the surface, near the upper atmosphere, skimming, accelerating, the meteor still trailing behind, but beginning to show some motion of its own. Then, as they watched, under magnification, the *Hammerhand* began a long, shallow tangental curve outwards, away from the planet. The meteor dipped briefly into the atmosphere, flaring greenish fire, and curved back into space, and then down, on a course which would intersect the south pole, now covered

in complete darkness and ice. Nothing showed at the pole
except the unrelieved blankness of the ice cap, lit only by
the weak light of the stars. Han knew only that they were
down there. What they had or how they managed was beyond him.

Seemingly from nowhere, a pale bluish beam appeared
from the polar area, waving around uncertainly, seeking. It
played briefly upon both objects, one moving away, accelerating, and the other incoming with unmistakable intent. It
hesitated, flicked back and forth, and selected the incoming
meteor, becoming a narrow lance of burning white light that
set off alarms all over the *Pallenber*, a searing, purple-white
dazzle that left painful afterimages. The meteor simply vanished. It was gone, as if it never had been. The light became
the pale, broader beam again, almost invisible until their
vision returned. They could see a fine cloud, looking like dust
at this distance. That was all.

Han began activating defense screens, fields, sealing off
sections of the ship. He also opened the weapons bays, although he suspected, with a certain sinking feeling, that nothing he had could match that terrible beam. But Hatha had
also seen what had happened to his meteor, and had taken
an action of his own. By the time the pale guide beam had
found him again, he had reversed courses in a hairpin maneuver and was falling directly onto the pole, apparently under full normal-space drives. The warship was completely
dark, and it seemed to be flickering.

Han said, "Suicide dive. He's got all his power off except
the parts powering the drives and the defensive fields. He
wants that ship badly!"

The aliens recognized what was happening too late. Again
the full power of the beam flashed out, to skewer the on-
coming ship and blast it into a cloud of dust. It had no effect.
It glanced off the blurred warship without visible effect,
showering the darkness with glittering points and streaks of
light. Suddenly the screen began an odd, pulsing motion, like
ripples spreading on the surface of a pond, the same motion
Han and Liszendir had seen when approaching Chalcedon.
Both of them recognized it simultaneously. They knew
what the aliens, Aving's people, were doing. They had turned
the full drive on and were readying their ship for flight, with
a peculiar drive that distorted his screens. Then that was
why they had seen this near Chalcedon—Aving had stopped
off to see how things were going, in secret, before returning

to Dawn. At the pole, something was moving, the ice cap
was breaking up, something was coming upwards, out of the
ice. Still firing—although they could not do both well, for
every time they fired with the intense beam, the disturbance
in their screen gave off extra pulses, as if operating both the
drive and the weapon made them interfere with each other.
With all shields down, detection gave him an honest reading
now, pinpointing the source. The power plant was like the
one on Hatha's rebuilt ship, but much more powerful, not
even reasonably comparable in relative strengths. Han expected that. Give the natives rifles, but keep the Gatling
guns for yourself. And it was large, as large as Hatha's ship,
perhaps larger; something as yet invisible, down there in the
ice, struggling like some insect to get out of the way.

But it was too late. Before the alien ship, still unseen, only
a suggestive motion below the surface, could emerge, the
two objects merged. Han seemed to be seeing it in slow-time,
the action fantastically slowed so he could see every detail.
They moved together, embraced, intertwined; the mass did
not explode, but simply glowed redly, and sank from sight,
one undistinguishable, unrecognizable mass. The glow disappeared in a huge gout of steam, fog and cloud, and the
pulsating disturbance on the screen faded away to nothing,
was gone. Detection showed one remaining source of drive
energy in the Dawn system—the star of Dawn, now invisible
behind the bulk of the planet, only showing shreds of its
swollen corona behind the curve.

Liszendir had watched the entire event without comment
or reaction. After a long silence, she finally said, in a calm
voice, "You may think I might see this as only evidence of
further dishonor and perfidy on the part of Hatha. Not so,
not so at all. The law says, 'Use no weapon that leaves the
hand.' So in the end he did not; it did not leave his hand.
Nor does suicide distress me, for it is only an act, and the
value of an act lies solely in its purpose in the present and
immediate future."

Han looked at her from the instruments, slowly. He said,
"I see that. I also see that in his system, a noble had choice—
the higher the noble, the greater the degree of choice. This
was an article of faith, so that when he arrived by his own
acts into a situation which left one no choices, then one was
no longer noble, could not be. He also faced some interesting
explanations upon his return, for in the same system, the

free chooser does not allow himself to be used as an ex-pendable tool."

Usteyin added, somberly, "So it is done. They hurt him, just as I said they would. As I saw."

"He hurt them far worse," Han answered. "Now the mas-ter plotter is found out, and he is trapped, with no place to run. Look at what he faces: he cannot stay on Dawn. The Warriors will be hunting for him, even now, and even if he escapes them, he has the nova to worry about. And of course, the only ship that would take him anywhere is dis-posed of, gone, ruined, destroyed."

"No. Not that way of hurt, not the body. I mean they hurt him when he finally realized what they had done to him first, and then to his people. You told him before we came onto this ship, but he did not really examine it in his heart until he was back on his own ship, off this one. For us, he kept a front. A story, if you like. Then he thought. And what he did was planned, not an anger-thing. Those things could deal with the weapons they themselves gave him, those rocks, but they were paralyzed when he used the ship as a weapon, a simple thrust. He knew they would be, that they would think he would save the warship at all costs."

Liszendir said, "And so I have lived to see the end of a legend, the end of the tale of Sanjirmil. Somehow, I wish I hadn't, that something better, or the unknown, could have been for them. . . . But now it is over, and we can go home. We are free."

"We are free, and now we have choice," said Han quietly.

"What choice?" Both girls spoke almost in unison.

"We can go back now, or attend to some other unfinished business."

"What could we have that is unfinished, here?"

"Aving. Have you forgotten? I know Aving was not on that ship below the pole. He could not be—he would not be able, even on a place like Dawn, to go and come unnoticed in such a ship; it was as big or bigger than Hatha's. No. The only time he could board it was when Hatha was away, and the season kept everyone else indoors, at night, so they would not see. And he couldn't live at the pole, either. So Aving has not yet been caught up in the ruin of his adventure. He will have had communications with his ship, and now he knows it is gone. They cannot answer his calls, the equip-ment will be silent, and so he will have guessed something. If we can bring him back, dead or alive, we can prove what we say, for however much he may look like a ler, I will bet everything I now have that he will be different inside. And more: we do not know that he can't communicate with his homeworld. He may even now be calling for help. We don't know where it is, or how far. It could be hundreds of lights away, or over in the next system."

Liszendir looked grave, thoughtful. "Yes. It would almost have to be as you say. But what you are thinking, Han, that is more dangerous than anything we have done yet. Think: we came to look, and we were dragged off to the ends of the universe, hunted, beaten. If we go looking for trouble, to seek one out like that, ah, now, that is a fine peril. And I do not wish to be hauled off to any more planets, save my own, which I will allow you to do."

Usteyin was equally concerned. "I agree with what Liszendir says. And more. Who will do this thing, capture or kill this creature? There are only three of us; you two are fighters, that I see, but I am not, even if I have ended one of those things."

"I do not mean that we should go back there blind. But we should at least go and have a look at the castle. We know he has no ship, and we can reason that he has no weapons heavy enough to do us damage at the castle. We would be able to detect the power source, if one were there. And if he has gone, then we can't spend the rest of our lives looking for him. But I do not want to leave him here."

Liszendir moved around Han, and set the course in herself. "All right. I see it. You are right. I do not want him loose either."

Usteyin looked at both of them. "I do not like this at all, but I have no way to stop you, and I see there is no way to get off this machine. I am not brave. I have fear of beings who could use the people so."

"Not brave? I don't think that's true, Usteyin. And if you lack it, you are going to have to learn it soon. Because if any of us have to go into the castle, it will have to be you and I. Somebody who can fly the ship has to stay in it, and that is Liszendir."

In a short time, they were approaching Aving's castle from the south, flying the *Pallenber* down in the upper atmosphere. As they passed over the location of the city Leilas, Han and Liszendir looked below through the ventral pickups for signs of life. There were none. Leilas was buried under snow. All they could see, even with low-level augmentation, were patterns of different tints of snow and rocks, the random traceries of hard winter and night. Soon after, they were over the top of the northern trough, dropping lower and lower, decreasing their speed as they came closer. They passed the castle, carefully watching for any sign of life about it, but there was nothing. In the twilight of the north-winter, the castle sat on its outcrop, dark and empty. It had been abandoned.

While Han and Liszendir were looking at the castle and the lands around it, Usteyin was looking ahead, northwards, on the main viewscreen. It was not long before her sharp eyes saw something far ahead on the gently dipping slope of the northern end of the trough: small knots of people, fleeing north, to the polar summer, and perhaps another way out, or back, or into obscurity. Or just away. She called to Han and Liszendir.

Han flew closer to the straggling knots, to get a better view of them. Yes; they were fleeing, all walking away from the castle. He could not make out any features on any of them, but something of the way they hurried, the way they scattered as they heard the approach of the ship; those ways were not the way of an Aving. Liar and deceiver he could be, but he would neither scuttle nor cower, even in defeat. He also felt with all the strength of a hunch that Aving would not be one to run, if he ran at all, into isolation—that would make him all the easier to spot, to hunt down. No—he was not with these. He would be back at the castle, hiding, or perhaps in Leilas. He turned the ship around and headed back to the castle.

The strength of the hunch waned as he came closer to the castle. It had been a foolish idea to come back here at all. They would never find Aving. The sly fox had too much of a head start on them—even if it were only an hour, it was enough. They could not expect to locate one creature from a spaceship—this was one time when machinery and technology could not help them, and they did not have time to go down and search the whole planet on foot. But a trip into the castle might be worthwhile, for artifacts, if nothing else. Proof. They flew around the dark hulk several times, but they saw no sign of life on it, not even smoke. On an impulse, he flew right up to the castle and grounded the ship inside the courtyard, although there was barely room for it. It was a small ship, yet inside the walls, it seemed improbably large. The *Pallenber* settled into the snow, gingerly, tentatively, protesting the soft, yielding surface under its landing legs.

The ship quieted, became silent. Han set the controls on standby, and began getting ready to go out. "Liszendir, you stay here. If anything goes wrong, if we don't come back, you will have to get the information back into the Union. Take off and fly it—you know how. And burn this place to a cinder before you leave, if it comes to that. Forget your inhibitions once. You can go straight through on Matrix-12. I've already set it up. Just punch it in."

She became obstinate. "This is not right! You and I should be going in there. If you must."

Usteyin began wrapping her blanket around herself. "I fear this place, and I fear to leave the ship, for it is the only place, save our little room in the camp on the plains, where I have felt my reality so strongly. But I must go with you, even if all I do is carry things. You understand me, Liszendir, and you will not be offended, but my life with you would not be so much as with him."

"I am not. Now go! Let it be done and let us leave this place."

Han gave Usteyin one of the gas guns, showed her how to use it. She listened patiently, grimly serious. For himself, he went to the locker and removed two weapons, just in case. One was a flash gun, which generated a narrow beam whose wavelength was in the near infrared. The other was a devilish reactionless pistol that fired tiny rocket-powered projectiles, guided by a fine attached wire. The projectiles were also explosive. He found also some extra clothing, and offered the things to Usteyin, for it was cold outside. She refused them.

They left the ship, climbed down the ladder, and stood for a time in the courtyard. They could not see the sun; it was now below the horizon, below the walls, and behind the mountains. But its glow spread a diffuse, weak light all over the northern sky, fading overhead into an overlay on the darkness, of a color suggesting blue flame. The stars shone brightly, what few there were. The courtyard was all shadows, suggestions of shape, in the strange twilight, made by the erratic sun of Dawn, halting, standing still in its yearly spiral sunset.

Overhead, in the depths of the eerie, darkened sky, a faint, almost invisible flickering began. Both Han and Usteyin stopped and looked up: it was an aurora starting up, now too weak, too undefined for them to be able to make out any details or colors of it. Standing barefoot in the fine, powdery snow, her blanket wrapped around her, Usteyin tilted her head and smelled the icy air, her delicate nostrils flaring; in a situation of both suspicion and possible danger, she had reverted to patterns of behavior that stretched across time and space to the dark glacial forests of precivilization old Earth. Then they walked through the snow, hearing only the whisper of it underfoot, to the great hall entrance, which hung open, ajar. Waiting another moment, like burglars, they stepped cautiously into Aving's castle.

Inside it was as cold as the outside. Usteyin whispered to Han, "They are all gone. There is no presence here. The people left before the ship was destroyed—they have been gone for hours. This place is cold, dead."

"How could that be? They should be only about an hour ahead of us. This place should still be warm."

"Remember? When I used the story-block, on our ship? I told you that they could *see* me, with some sense I do not understand, not-sight, but something that acts like it. Perhaps they gave the alarm then."

But as they passed through the darkened castle, Han could see that she was right—there was no one in it, and it had been empty for hours, much longer than from the time the alien ship had fallen to Hatha's dive on it. But all through the castle there were signs of recent and hasty abandonment: an astonishing variety of junk and trash was strewn all over, and some ways into the castle, they found some bodies. Some were ler, some human. None were of the aliens. There had been fighting, but over what they could not see—perhaps over the spoils, or something else.

As they made their way to the central hall, and found the corridor Aving had used to come into it, Han told Usteyin, "When Liszendir and I came here before, they had a musical troupe here, in this hall, playing for dinner. At the time, I knew nothing about *klesh*, I thought the players were all members of a family, or something like that—a caste or tribe. But they all resembled one another about to the same degree that you Zlats look like each other."

"Music? They were actually doing something? You know that most of the *klesh* have long since lost their old functions; they no longer do the things they were specialized for. I do not know which those you saw would be."

"I don't think there have been any of them among the bodies we have found. They were light in complexion, not especially pretty in the faces, and stocky. They had brown hair, with some curl in it, and big noses—not as large as on the Haydars, but large just the same. Larger in size than you, but shorter than me."

"Ah, ha! Those would be Peynir. I did not know there were any left. We all know, in a general way, about each other; the Peynir are supposed to be almost as old as the Zlats. There are *klesh* and then there are others."

Farther up the corridor, they had better luck. In a room at the top of a flight of stairs, narrow and littered with papers, they found a communications device, or at least what appeared to be a communications device. There were several meters and light indicators on it, but what gave it away was a small, oddly designed microphone and earset, still plugged into it. The rest of the box, or console, made little sense, and they did not touch it or attempt to manipulate it. There were various knobs, push-places, transparent windows which must have been indicators of some type, but which now were indicating nothing. They could not even find the power pack for it. There was some writing, but neither of them could understand it; it seemed to be made up of narrow lines with infinitesimal, subtle variations in thickness.

Han said, half to himself, "The Warriors had radar, of all things, the oldest kind, with steerable antennas, physical things, but they had no radio. That is like us having voices, but only using them to find out where things are around us by listening for the echo. So Aving could use any number of ways to transmit to his ship, any wavelength: no one on this planet would hear him. But the best way would be the longer wavelengths, very long waves. That way, he could bury the antenna underground, and they would be able to send back and forth even under the magnetic storms."

Usteyin whispered, her breath steaming in the cold, "I do not know what you are saying. It appears that this Aving was a wizard, and you are one too. A greater one, for was it not you who saw through his deceptions? But wait! Look out the window."

Han went to the narrow window, the only one in the room, and looked out, around, upwards. This room faced somewhat to the north, and on the horizon, he could see the sunset unmoving northern sun, in one corner. It was on the horizon, just below it, but there the sky was tinged with pale rose, lemon, wild blues that carried strong greenish overtones. What caught his attention more was the strong flickering that came from overhead. He looked up. Yes. It was a strong aurora.

Usteyin came to the window and joined Han there, looking upwards, momentarily entranced. It was the strongest aurora Han had ever seen, vast curtains converging on a point in the zenith which seemed an infinite distance away, vast curtains that moved and rippled along their lower skirts, and which were lit up, from within, from the sides, from below, by particolored beams of colored searchlights, or bonfires. The outside had become lighter, noticeably. Usteyin stood, face upturned, beautiful in the flickering light, unreal, twin plumes of breath-steam flowing out of her delicate nostrils, the light painting wild iridescences in her hair.

She came down from the window. "That I have seen before, many times, but never so bright or so easy to see! Nor so wild. Now let us leave this place! There is no one here."

Han reluctantly came away from the window also, and scooped up some things that appeared to be books or manuals. He had no idea what they were, but he thought, irreverently, that if he were going to be a burglar, then he had to burgle something, anything, and they had seen nothing else. Usteyin picked up nothing; she had seen nothing she wanted, even for burgling. It was clear to Han that she did not like this place, nor her being in it, not in the least.

They made their way back to the *Pallenber*, through the empty and silent cold halls and corridors, seeing no more than they did when they had first entered the castle—bodies, rubbish, abandoned rags, dropped weapons. All the way back, they went quietly, moving from shadow to shadow, feeling as if any moment there would come a sudden shock, a cry, the bite of steel, a sudden stab of bright pain, then darkness. But there was nothing in the still darkness except the pounding of their pulses. In the courtyard at last, the ship still bulked over them. All appeared secure. The lights were still on, the port was still open. There was no change, except in the sky above, where the aurora still held court, playing, dancing. Han looked at Usteyin. There was no more awe on her pretty, serious face; just apprehension. He sighed in a minor kind of defeat and resignation; Aving had indeed escaped them, probably for good, for they could not very well sift the whole planet to find him. He could be anywhere.

They climbed the ladder, Han first, Usteyin waiting below, gas gun at the ready, in case. She was jumpy, suspicious, although Han could see no reason why. She kept looking around, as if there was something wrong somewhere in the scene around them. Something out of place. But it might take weeks to find that as well. Han made it to the lock, and covered Usteyin while she climbed. They were on the point of going within when she suddenly stopped, taking a deep breath of the icy air.

"Wait. Just one minute, for me. I want to take one last look out on my world, for I will never see it again."

"All right. But hurry—it's cold. When you pass the second door, press the black button; that will close the lock port doors and retract the ladder."

"I'll just be a minute."

Han went ahead. Usteyin might not mind the cold, but it was beginning to bite into him. He didn't know how she stood it, and walking around in that place barefooted, too! And that had been odd, what she had said about not coming back to Dawn. Of course she would come back—they would have to, to see to everything, when they came back for the humans, and the klesh, to take them to a place of their own. That was a shame, in a way—that Dawn would end in five of its years, burnt to a cinder, scattered over the void, later to be incorporated in some other star, some other planet, recycled. He had been himself appalled by the visage of the planet, its terrible weather and seasons, its impossible geography, but there was something there—in a universe of marvels, Dawn was something special, one of a kind. A place of terror and isolation and ignorance, but a place of heroic beauty as well. The Warriors were not all to blame themselves, nor could it all be laid to Aving's manipulations—the place itself acted in an underground way in the mind, conjuring up visions of heroism, of greatness.

Han went ahead, entered the corridor, and started to enter the control room. Just as he opened the door, he heard a squeal from Usteyin. He stopped in the doorway, holding the panel half open and looking back to the lock, and called to her.

"What is it?"

"Han! The snow! That is wrong. I knew something wasn't right! You and I, we came and went: four tracks of footprints, yours with shoes, mine without. Four! But there are five. Did Liszendir leave the ship? No! Somebody came here. To the ladder."

Han knew, before he heard the voice from the control room, the voice he had heard before, the voice which did not belong, by any stretch of the imagination, to Liszendir. It was not a human voice, not even ler-human.

The speaker said, "I hold a flash gun on your ex-lover. Bid the *klesh* girl come in, and enter yourself, leaving your weapons by the door. And do it quickly, for we have far to go and little time remaining to do it in."

He turned and called to Usteyin. "Come in. Cycle the door." He was thinking as fast as he could, for some way. There was none. Better to follow this line, inside the ship, a little longer, than face a certain end, freezing in the castle— if any of them lived beyond the threat. With three of us, there may just be a chance, he thought. He did not see one at that moment, however hard he tried.

XIII

"Characters in a story or tale are, in four dimensions, equivalent to, in two dimensions, the waves on the sea, the ripples on the pond, the waving fields of grass, the snowdrifts, by whose motion and shaping we become able to discern the shape of the wind. It is hard to make up that shape in our minds, just so, but even harder to see the shape of the winds of our own lives, which are displayed by type in the various tales.

—Zermanshan Tlanh

Usteyin came into the control room, both excited and apprehensive at the same time, saying, "Han, there are extra footprints out there in the snow, not ours, I think . . . Oh!" She entered the room quietly, closed the door, and stood beside Han, slipping the blanket off herself.

Aving said, "This is a flash gun. It is very good for close work, such as we have here. I have it set on maximum dispersion. It does not completely kill humans or ler at the first shot, but it does incapacitate with severe burns, which produce fatality, later. I know that this one, this girl, is trained for combat, so that by neutralizing her I can easily keep you two in check. Unlike Hatha, I waste no time on tribal-level status-measuring mannerisms and appreciations. She is completely expendable, as are the *klesh.* I know that you will not sacrifice both."

He paused briefly, letting that sink in. They did not doubt him for a minute. Liszendir sat quietly in the pilot's chair,

251

saying, doing nothing. But the expression on her face would have curdled fresh milk in the next town, as Han had heard said. The next town? The next planet.

Aving, seeing that they understood, continued, "So, then. The program is simplicity itself. You will fly us to my home-world, where you will remain, in one mode or another, as circumstances dictate, while the overcouncil approaches this problem from another angle, to see if anything can be salvaged from this wreckage. And I do not sleep. So, then. To work!"

Han desperately wanted time to think. He asked, "So we were right about the situation here on Dawn?"

"Yes. The Warrior-ler did not see it at all. Whatever abilities they may still have, they are not devious, like all primitives. But we had not reckoned on the abilities of some of the old people—yourself, for example, or that Hetrus on Seabright. He saw far into it, at least by suspicion. I was able to influence events there so that two relative incompetents would be sent. Naturally, you would either see nothing and report the same—or find out something, and vanish without a trace. But you, like Hetrus, have proved to be resourceful, and the ler girl has contributed all out of proportion to our perspective on the ler. You do not see well ahead, but you find ways out. That kind of thinking has managed to create complete disruption of the plan here, and in fact has nullified the future uses of Dawn as a staging base for further operations. You have guessed, I suspect, from your instruments, that that star out there is very sick. By the time we could recover momentum here, a factor in events as well as bodies, there would be no time left to establish an orderly progression of happenings. We do not salvage lost causes."

"What was that progression?"

"That is no interest to you, now."

"Satisfy my idle curiosity, if you will."

"Well, there is no harm, I suppose. That, too, was much as you have probably suspected. We hoped to instigate a war between the humans and the ler—you know, 'no fight half so vicious as between members of the family,' I believe you say. We hoped that such a conflict would weaken both to the point where we could move into the area and take each world, one at a time, until the strength of the remaining would not matter. We are on the rim and must needs expand inwards. We prefer our worlds already civilized for us—we do not imagine ourselves a race of pioneers, living among the beasts of the wild and hewing forests."

"Is your appearance a true one, or is it disguised?"

"The basics are as you see. Only certain details have been altered to fit into the Warriors' surround. But during this project, which has already occupied several lifetimes, we discovered that we look rather more like ler, so it is easier to masquerade as one; but in patterns of thought, we resemble humans, the old people, more, if you can sense the difference between the two types. Except more so! Much more so. But all this wastes time. We can talk on the way, if you like, but be seated and let us be on the way. Or stand, if you prefer. Only remember that she will be the price for creating any suspicion in my mind!"

"I will stand. I will tell Liszendir what settings to insert, and she will do it." More like humans in the way they thought. . . . That keyed something. Yes. Han did have one idea. It might work, yes indeed. In fact, the more he thought on it, the more sure he became that it would work, or at least cause enough distraction for him to get that flash gun. Then Aving would see who would burn. They could not afford to take any more chances. If they got any more of their own. But this . . .

Aving said, as Han moved closer to the panels, "Don't you want the course?"

"Not now. Have you ever flown on a human ship before?"

"No. Nor ler. I used my own craft to make the voyage to Seabright, and other places."

"Let me explain, then. I do not want you getting suspicious over any act that I might perform. When we traverse space, we use a set of preset points in space whose locations are known in the ship's memory. I did not know of the location of your planet, so I shall have to set the course manually. Both end-points of the transferral coordinate, because Hatha brought this ship here in the hold of his warship. This process will require a calibration routine, for I shall have to determine my location exactly, bearing Heisenberg's theorem respectfully in mind. This will require some time and work."

"Very well. But perform it with dispatch and use no tricks. You know the penalty. First this one, then the fire-haired *klesh* girl. You do not wish them to suffer? Then haste. I feel the pressure of time."

Han nodded, grimacing inwardly to himself. If he was wrong . . . "Just so. Now we will enter space." And as he set the course in for the point he wanted, he glanced covertly at Liszendir, and then Usteyin. Not a flicker of recognition was stirring in either of their faces; both were passive, resigned, apprehensive. But nothing else. What he had in his mind depended on that—they must not recognize what he was going to do until he did it; otherwise, Aving might suspect something was coming that was more than it seemed.

The ship reached the point Han had programmed in, and the drives shut down. There remained a minor manual correction, which Liszendir did herself, bringing the *Pallenber* exactly into position, between the planet and its primary. The star glared whitely through the main screen, an obsession, a fire that drowned out all the rest of the stars in the darks of space.

Now. He turned to Aving, saying, "The girl will now have to hand me a certain object, which I will use to make an exact calculation. It is there, in the small bag. May she get it out and give it to me?"

"What does it look like?"

"To you, a tangle of wire."

"Are you sure. . . ?"

"Do you know anything about navigation, astrogation?"

"No. That is for the crew. Mere mechanics."

"Yes, then. I am sure."

Han turned back to Usteyin. Now she would have to be completely straight. One slip . . . Usteyin still had not caught on. Only concern showed on her face.

"Are you sure you want it, Han? It is dangerous, and I don't understand . . ."

"Never mind, never mind. I need the block, Usteyin. Please give it to me. I know what I'm doing." Han felt a slight sense of irritation, of anxiety; this was tense. If she said one word about the story-block's real purpose . . .

She didn't. Usteyin moved to the bag, reached within, very carefully withdrew the story-block, opened it to its full size, and handed it to Han, with a reluctance that could not be hidden. "Here. But you must be careful. When somebody else uses one . . ."

Han cut her off. "No matter. I know the cautions." He took the device, risking a quick glance at Liszendir. Something was in her eyes; yes! She knew. And at Aving. Suddenly, he was very interested in the story-block, watching it with eerie intensity. Han ignored the alien, held the story-block up to the star, so it would catch the light, looked into it, hoping his pretending would seem reasonably enough like some astrogator taking a measurement.

Curious, he thought, as he held it in his hand, watching the play of light among the wires, the junctions, the positions of the beads. Odd, that you could use a thing like this to symbolize anything. What was it Usteyin had said? Non-verbal. Yes. No words. He wondered how her perception of it was; he stared into it, looking for something suggestive, a symbol, an inkblot, an optical illusion. Nothing. It was just a tangle of wire, just a tangle of wire, but you could follow the lines of it indefinitely, it was hypnotic, relaxing, he felt muscles in the back of his neck relaxing, tiny strain lines in his face loosening. Yes, it could at least put you to sleep, if you weren't careful; must speak to Usteyin about that part of it. What time was it? Time felt odd, like it was not passing right. He looked away, feeling a reluctance to take his eyes out of it. He looked back. He had not registered the time on the panel chronometer, except the second hand. That had stood out, starkly: it was ten seconds past. Ten seconds past what? Nothing. It didn't matter. There was no time, time was an illusion, he would see that here, just a little more, the effort that was not effort, the unpremeditated act, the sudden sneaking up upon reality, reality.

There was motion, movement, the control room, the ship was shifting, flowing, melting, no not doing anything, he was moving, evolving, changing, the streaks of light were forming themselves into shapes, suggestions, fast, fast, he knew his mind was doing it; slow it down, timeless, timeless, bring the rate down, untryingly trying, effortlessly efforting. Efforting. Not-word. Ha ha. Funny, words. He had no need of them, it was so easy, just beneath the surface, reaching for it, the water changed the apparent angle, things were offset, groping in the water . . . water, silvery wires, swift flowing water, water falling to the bottom of the sink, the well, the pit, water seeking its level, water wetting, soaking, sea-changes, there was a sea on Seabright, something was urgent, he had to do something. Water, that was it. He was water, flowing, penetrating, moving into every space, every void, space had taken the place of water in the old symbolisms, he was water, he was space he could seestars, allonething seerseen seerseen-mediumoftransmission lightwavescrawlinglike worms stars-stars and therewassomething more reaching reaching

STOP. nodeceleration. Juststopinstant. Alone. No. Not-alone. Others. Nearfar/herethere. No, he said, trying to find some numbers for this, mask it with symbols, break the chain, why heHan was here in the controlroomnow, there was Aving, and Liszendir and Usteyin and himself himself-selflff. No, must get out of it, goddam deadly thing, got to get out, turn around easy and *move*. He turned around. There was no around. He looked up. There was no up. The referent universe had vanished. It was gone. How could you get out when you didn't know how you got in, how could you reach a place if you didn't know where you were. What differencediditmakemakemake? A vast joke, and that it was onhim was onlyfunny. Unimportant. Here were them all, Hatha, Dardenglir, Liszendir, Hetrus, a child with red hair, whothehellwasthat? Others. He could blank them, one by one. There was no time. Child-out. Hatha-out. some more anuncountablenumber-out. Gone. Aving, too, he wasn't anyway. Out. Now him, Liszendir, Usteyin, but not in the right positions. They were all moving around, Liszendir behind him, but he could still see herherher Usteyin in front, the stars came back into view, notstarshere, starssomewhereelse, thick, dewyspiderwebs, clouds, seas, water. He was water, yes! Usteyin was looking toward him, reaching, her face. Liszendir was pushing him, notrejecting, moving him, she had sadness on hers, but on Usteyin's there was more, he was not getting closer, she was expanding, enlarging, beckoning to him with her sea-green eyes from the edge of the universe. No. Outside it, they were expanding, filling it, filling everything, the stars became galaxies, the galaxies shrunk, diminished, faded, went out. Blackness. Then stars again, a few, then many, then repeating cycle again. Stars, galaxies, the night, starsgalaxiesnight. Flashing, flickering, then merginginto continuoussmoothgrey, The Aleph, and Usteyin was now enormous, she filled his vision, she surrounded him, he felt no fear, no apprehension, there was no danger, it was preplanned, programmed into the steadystate universe, rightcorrectproper like falling, falling Liszendir was a point, a one-dimensional object of singular purpose tremendous power, the will, fire, the magicians wand, green sprouting branch, lifegiving, Usteyin was event, air, swords, that the three of them would fall together was a property of the universe, the universe, he could go forwardsbackwards, tofro, sideside, updown the meaning was just out of reach, one more effortlesseffort nownownow its in my hand slippery slippery can't hold it the more i catch the less i have got to get it all usteyin back into being reaching she has a story block in her other hand other hand, which is the other hand from the other hand/ like a box on both ends it says open other end endless spiral. doctor, which sex is the opposite. i know i no negate gate / usteyin how her body felt when they had been one creature reaching reaching slippery a soundless flash.

He heard the air moving through the ventilators into the control room, he saw the instruments on the panel, he felt time passing at its own rate again, and he held a story-block in his hand, at which he must not look. He felt purged, cleansed, washed out, but he had seen a story, if he could just sort it out, something warm, close, he and Usteyin, and there was Liszendir too, in the future, or was it the past? No. The future. She had long, long, hair, it was iron-gray, she had lines in her face. But stop. Han looked at the chronometer. That was absurd. No time at all had passed. But the second hand had moved, to the 15 mark. Five seconds? Or had he gone all the way around the clock? No. It was now. Han felt himself beginning to shake, to sweat, instantly clammy. That thing was dangerous. Perilous. He looked over to Usteyin, looked at her directly, as if he were seeing her for the first time. She looked back at him, seeing that he was out of the story-block, free, unharmed.

She spoke, and broke the silence. "Did you make your measurement?" Now she knew.

"Yes, I did. It is very simple."

He looked over to Aving. "Ah, that was a hard one. These outer regions are the very devil to astrogate in. I think we should invent a better way to do it. Don't you have a better way, Aving?"

Aving said, "What is that thing you were just using?"

"It is a calibration device. We use it only at times when we have to make a transition with both end-points open. Machines are good, machines are fast, but they are more limited than we are. With this, we can see directly, then translate the vision into numbers for the ship."

"Are you finished? Let me see that thing! I have never seen such a device . . ."

"Well, I do have to make some more measurements, but . . ."

"Give it to me! I wish to examine it. I cannot determine how it works, there is no structure . . ." He trailed off, unfinishing what he might have said. He was staring *into* the story-block, becoming glassy-eyed. Rather more like humans, not so much like ler, Han reminded himself, still remembering echoes from his own vision, still feeling bits and pieces.

He told Aving, "It is electroptical. Look into it, watch the wires. Hold it at right angles to the star, you'll see better."

Aving took the story-block, and held it as Han showed him, never taking his eyes off it. He still held the gun close to Liszendir, but he was becoming oblivious. Han felt sorry for him, just for an instant; what was going to happen to him either way wasn't going to be pleasant, not at all. . . .

Aving muttered, almost inaudibly, "I can't quite see it . . ."

Liszendir, listening to the voice, was starting to move. Han checked her with a motion. She must not interrupt this. Aving was a fish, and he must take the hook himself.

Han said, "You need more light, Aving," and Han turned the dial controlling the filter circuits of the viewscreen, simultaneously pulling Usteyin and Liszendir down to the floor as he did. The filter circuits opened and the screen passed all of the energy in the visible band into the control room, all the output of the star within the range of visible light. The glaring, stark, white light filled the room, and in that light Aving was visible, standing quite still, holding a tangle of wire in his free hand, gazing into it with eyes gone completely vacant. The flash gun dropped from his relaxed grip, to dangle on the trigger guard from a finger. Liszendir reached up from the floor beside him and carefully took the gun from his hand. Han reached over the lip of the main panel, and returned the filter circuits of the viewscreen to a lower setting. The screen darkened, dimmed the glare of the star, and the cabin returned to semidarkness again.

Aving stood in exactly the same position, holding the story-block, still gazing vacantly into the depths of glittering wire. The three of them, Han, Liszendir, and Usteyin, all got to their feet. Aving did not react, nor did he give any sign that he was even aware of them.

Liszendir asked, with awe shading the edges of her voice, "Is he disarmed, now?"

Usteyin answered, "Oh, yes. Forever. I did not see what Han was trying to do at first, but then I saw it. A good trick, one I would not have thought of myself. Look, I will show you." And she walked over to the silent staring figure, and disengaged the wire tangle from his fingers, pulling it out of his hand with some effort. He did not want to let it go. As she did so, the figure shuddered, as if with a sudden chill, but made no other motions, and continued to stare at the place where the story-block had been.

"Good. Just right," she said, with a soft voice that revealed satisfaction, and some light anger as well. Then she went behind Aving, kicked the backs of his knees, and caught him as he fell to the floor, breaking his fall. Then she turned to Han.

"A good trick, the best I have ever seen. But you have cost me my story-block to do it—a little high for the likes of Aving." Here was the source of her anger, now fading.

"How so? Why?"

"I told you before—you go too far and it traps your spirit. That is what happened to Aving, you tricked him into it. But now the story-block has his spirit, and the next person to use it will get it back, part of Aving impressed into his selfness, his mind. Maybe a lot, maybe even Aving's self will be strong enough to trade with yours, if you look again."

"How can that be? That is just hypnosis."

"No, it is more than that, what-you-say, the way you hold it, the tension, everything is input. Ask Han. He knows now, he got a taste of it. When you do not put any starts into it at the first you are asking for the meaning of everything, you have put no limits whatsoever on it. And you go within, with your mind. Are you really inside it? I do not know, except what I learned when I was young, beginning to use one. The Zlats say you go within. And when you look into one, you get out what has been stored; and if it is someone who has been careless, who looked too far . . . Aving was an evil man, even in the little part of him that we knew; I do not know what other evils he may have been prey to. But we will not have the problem of letting Aving out into one of us. I will destroy it." And before either Han or Liszendir could stop her, she took the story-block, carefully avoiding looking at it directly, and crumpled it up into a wadded tangle, a crushed mass. Then she placed it on the floor, and stamped on it until it was completely unrecognizable.

"Liszendir, you have the flash gun. Make it narrow, strong! Burn this, melt it, now!" Her voice was sharp, peremptory. "Do not worry about that body there on the floor! It still functions, but it has no mind: and I know no way to get it back. Now, the gun! Quick! You must do this now or my resolve will not last!"

Liszendir adjusted the flash gun, pointed it at the crumpled object on the floor, matted and wadded as far as hands could make it, and fired, playing the beam over the story-block until nothing remained of it but a charred lump of melted silver, unrecognizable, smoking.

Usteyin looked at the lump for a long moment, sighed deeply, and relaxed, becoming herself again. The change in her had been so gradual that Han had not noticed it, until she returned to her normal self. "So now it is done. The body is of no more use to us, so we can eject it into the night."

"But he's still alive. Shouldn't we try to take it back?"

"No. He will die soon. The story-block got a lot of him, even things like breathing. He was more susceptible to it than either Han or myself, and he had less defenses against it—none, in fact. It was catching him before he even took it from Han. The body will go bad. So we will tell them, back in your place, and they will believe."

"Couldn't we bring him back to his senses, interrogate him somehow?"

"No. Nothing is kept. I know of no one who has ever recovered from an event like that. They die sooner or later. Yes. Look at Aving. He is dead, now. I can't tell you hows— I only know whats. Just like I said. It traps the spirit. And once that has happened to a story-block, it is no good any more and the metal must be purified by fire. It is unclean. This normally happens with one's own, you know, from looking too far. But for mine, it was a stranger who was caught. If we had not destroyed it, then the next time I looked into it, I would get Aving's spirit impressed onto mine. And my self would go inside. Then you would have Aving back, but in my body. I do not think you would want that."

"Can you get another one, from the Zlats, or can you make another one?"

"No—neither. I cannot make another one. Period. As for anyone else's, they are individual. If I tried to use another's, I might see the same stories, but they would go all wrong, and if I tried to *see* with it, it would show lies. I might try to rerun the story of Koren and Jolise, remember? But in someone else's, Jolise might try to kill Koren, in some terrible way. The pattern of strong emotion would be there, but it would have been shifted into a different particular expression. Do you see? In a story-block, there are no whats, only hows. I supply the whats."

Usteyin bent to the body of the alien, began trying to drag it to a place where they could jettison it into space.

Liszendir moved to help her. It was not heavy, and they dragged it with little effort. Han showed them where the disposal bay was, and Aving vanished into space.

At last, they returned to the cabin, to the panel, where Han inserted the course, a matrix-12 course which would route them directly through to Seabright. As the *Pallenber* began to move in normal space, orienting itself, Han showed the initiate handle to Usteyin, a rough-finish simple gray lever-type device, offered it to her.

"You turn it. Just hold it firmly, turn it by rotating your hand, as if you were bringing your thumb up."

She looked shyly at Han, and then at Liszendir; reached for the handle, hesitantly, then grasped it firmly, and turned it. Normal space in the vicinity of the planet Dawn vanished, and they were on their way back. Usteyin still, for a time, tightly held the gray handle, as if she feared that if she let it go, the magic would end. Finally, convinced that it would not, she released it and stood back, smiling an odd half-smile to herself.

XIV

Epilogue

———◆———

"Ends? What ends? I know only beginnings!"
— *Valdollin Tlanh*

    On the planet Kenten, the first home of the ler after they had left Earth, it was spring, early spring, the particular time of the year when things are just starting to become tinged with green, and some days may be balmy, pleasant, but in the dregs of the day, the old winter is still hanging on, hoping against time that it still can make its presence known.

    In spring, then, in a small town located on the shore of a small sea that connected two larger seas, Han walked back to the teahouse where Usteyin awaited him, savoring the wet rain, the damp air, the suggestion of sea-odors, feeling the cold, and reflecting on all that had been said in the final report on Dawn, which Hetrus had arranged to have forwarded to him there, through the local post. This town was called Plenkhander, in accordance with the ler custom which decreed that the smaller the town, the longer the name.

    But he was not so concerned with the report, which at any rate was no more than a courtesy; Han's part in the events on Dawn had ended, by his own wish, and Usteyin's, and instead of going back, they had all three come to Kenten, to

Yalven province, to Plenkhander, to see Liszendir woven, and
to fit themselves into a more normal life again. He reflected,
as he passed rainstreaked shop windows, that adventuring
was all right, all well and good, for those who sought it out,
but he had not, however it had come off, and for the moment, he did not want any more adventures of the sort that
saw one carried further into the unknown with every minute
of time. He realized that this was, of course, just an extreme
parable of life itself, always into the unknown, no matter
if you spent your days in a shop, selling cookies, but he had
wanted time; and they had given it to him. They had come
to Kenten, left the *Pallenber* at the main spaceport, and
journeyed here.

As Han had expected, Hetrus had wanted them all to go
back to Dawn, and lead the operations there. But he had
refused, and he was glad he had done so, for not only did
Liszendir have her problem, compounded by the fact that
her age group had already made most of their arrangements, but she also had Usteyin's problem: she had a whole
world-idea to learn. So Hetrus had paid them all, hand-
somely, for all they had done, given them the ship (they had
earned it, he said), and left them alone.

He had heard that ler planets were, as the phrase was
politely put, backward, but that one word missed much of the
charm and sense of relaxed living which flowed all through
them. Time was here, one was conscious of it constantly, one
never forgot it, particularly on Kenten. He had expected
something—either vast technological progress, or at least
great intellectual subtlety, but he had seen neither. Just
people, and the basic realities of life, as might be seen at
any place and any time. It was much of what he and
Usteyin had needed.

Plenkhander was named for an ancient stone bridge which
still stood, relaying light traffic over a sluggish creek which
met the sea here, a bridge which had been standing, mortar-
less, from a time before Han's own planet had been settled.
The shore here was straight, without points or embayments,
so in a later period, they had added a jetty, and a small dock,
to facilitate trade with the interior, which loomed behind
the town, tumbling hills rising into the middle distances, cul-
minating in a sawtooth ridgeline not so very high, no more
than a few thousand feet, tree-covered to the very summits.
Farther down the coast, to the east, the mountains came
closer in to the shore, and that was where Liszendir had

grown up, in a place near a town called as she remembered it, "mill-wheel-stream."

Usteyin had been enchanted at the site of the house, and a larger building nearby which served as the school, and he himself had not wanted to leave, such was the peace and timelessness of it. It was just as she had described it—the house, or *yos*, the orchards, the farms along the slopes, the narrow beach and the sea before the house. In the foreyard of the *yos* there had been a dwarf tree in a huge stone pot. But dwarf was only a relative term, for the tree had overspread much of the yard. It was, apparently, a giant sequoia from Earth, lovingly cultivated in miniature, forced to concentrate on bulk and spread instead of height as it would have done on its own. In the space behind the *yos*, where the structure had sprouted two wings that flowed up the hill, there was another, nestled in the corner. It was a local tree, called a grayflank, which had a trunk that was veined and corded like the arm of a wrestler. It spread its branches over the *yos*, shading it in the summer with its foliage of small, rough leaves which Liszendir said turned bright yellow in the autumn. The *yos* itself was no longer the beige, off-white, parchment color of newer material, but a soft brownish-gray, streaked and stained and mossy with age. It looked as if it were part of the landscape.

The parent generation was still around, as they said it, but none of them seemed very interested in staying at home, and save for a few chance meetings, they saw little of them. As for Liszendir's insiblings, they were not yet fertile, but after the older girl had left, they had gradually taken over the *yos* themselves, and now were fully settled in their new role, painfully shy, serious, and busy as newlyweds in a new house, even though they had lived in it all their lives. They, too, spent much of their time up at the school, for they would be the ones to carry its ownership on. Which left the *thes*, the younger outsibling, Vindhermaz. Liszendir called him Vin, which embarrassed the boy terribly, but he bore up under her ribbing gracefully, smiling knowingly whenever they would hear a soft, feminine voice call for him from outside, using his love-name of two syllables.

They had visited just long enough to become acquainted, and then set out for the larger town several miles west down the coast, from which they could obtain a wider view of available insiblings. Liszendir had taken little from her home, save a few clothes, her musical instrument, the *tsonh*, made of fine, dark wood, finished in natural colors, and accented by silver keys and pad-covers. And a string of wooden beads, simple, unornamented, made of a dark, reddish wood. They were made of the wood of the tree before the *yos*, and were several generations old.   These she gave to Han, saying only that by them he should remember her. For Usteyin, a soft summer wrap she had worn earlier. They were both touched deeply by these gifts, which were not either things which could be bought anywhere.

So they returned to Plenkhander. At first, Liszendir had disclaimed the two of them, saying that she could look after herself well enough, but she did not resist when both Han and Usteyin insisted, and Han chartered a room in an obscure but comfortable hotel, for several months, with an option to renew the lease. Since then she had become gentle, even wistful, when she was not traveling all over the local area, following up leads, which were, still, turning out to be either dead ends, or past-tense, by the time she found the insiblings in question. This problem was not only one of availability, but was further compounded by a factor she told Han about only after they were safely on Kenten: her attribute being "fire," she could only weave into a braid which lacked a "fire," completing the square of Fire-Air-Earth-Water. And neither Han nor Usteyin could help her in this, for no *ler* would speak openly about the matter, even among themselves, and to talk about this with humans, the old people, was completely out of the question.

So they waited, in Plenkhander, and felt time passing in its measureless way. Here, the rain fell and blackened the trees, still bare from winter, and the wind in the night made the trees creak, and the air smelled in the soft blue twilights of sea and salt and woodsmoke; wagons and hooves rattled in the cobblestone streets, and small children on their way home played small flutes, and carried warm loaves of fresh bread flavored with onions back to clusters of ellipsoids nestling under trees that resembled plane trees or poplars. They ate their fill, slept deeply, and spent the days walking in the rich, rain-wet air, and visiting whatever struck their fancy. Usteyin did not want to leave, even after Liszendir became bewoven.

The braid-houses were, here as on Chalcedon, the low ellipsoids, loosely joined together, usually surrounded by low walls and spread gracefully under the trees, while buildings devoted to public use or commerce seemed to follow a more human shape—one- or two-story square buildings as often as not topped with low domes. The streets wound around without seeming purpose, wandering, random, as if they had followed paths before they were streets. The ler were not obvious, this Han knew well, but even more, neither were they ever in a hurry, even to get home. Rarely, a few braids lived in their shops, overhead, but this was considered low-class and on the verge of poverty, so there were few.

And back to reality, to the present. Han was nearing the teahouse, which was a low building, open, glassed in, with a low dome, which squatted or floated according to the mood of the observer, beside a ferry landing. Today, in the afternoon light, the sky was leaden and the rain pelted in Han's face, and the slate-colored sea heaved and tossed as if in some mild agitation; yet it was not dreary, apprehensive, or moody. On the contrary, Han had never felt so full of life, so involved. He looked ahead to see if he could pick Usteyin out of the crowd in the teahouse. Yes. Even from a distance he could distinguish her red hair, for, dark as it was, it was of a color no ler would ever have, and she wore it falling in cascades over her shoulders. She sat quietly unmoving in the teahouse, features rippled by the hand-poured glass panes and the streaks of rain on them, and sipped tea daintily, her full upper lip marking her face, looking out on the sea with the patience and inward calm reflections of the ler, who Han had observed watching the sea for hours if so disposed.

Han entered the tea house, shaking the rain off his cloak, and then hanging it on a peg set in the wall, secured another pot of tea from the counterman, and joined Usteyin. As he sat down at the small table with her, she turned and smiled to him with an expression at once so peaceful and at the same time so intimate and warm that he felt a sudden pang.

He said, "Have you been bored waiting? It was a very long business, picking up that message."

"No, no, I am learning to like this very much, this ler place, the way they live, not at all like the Warriors were. I fit it well. And more than once, I have caught myself wishing that you and I, we could live here. It is so . . . what? You are the one who knows words. No, I was not bored. You know that I watch the sea and spell stories in it, stories without end. We did not have seas on Dawn; only some salt lakes where nothing lived and the smell was bad. But not anything like this; this is more a wonder than the view from space. But I know there is much more to see and I want to see it all." Han looked mock-scandalized. She looked at his serious face, and then continued, "Well, the boy said they had a long message for you at the post. What do the others say?"

"That there is a planet for the *klesh,* all to itself, far away from Dawn. They had been keeping it in reserve, but this is a good purpose, and they at least will need a place of their own. After knowing you for a while, I do not worry about the Zlats adjusting. Oh, no. We are the ones who would have trouble adjusting to them! But the wild humans will come back, to backwater places, and later, they can come into the mainstream worlds, if they feel up to it. As for the ler on Dawn, I don't know. Factionalism has at last entered ler politics. One faction wants to leave them where they are and let Dawn's star take care of the problem. The other faction wants to get them off. And neither wants them integrated into mainstream ler culture. That's funny, if you think of it—I mean, they had no races as we humans do, but all the time, despite all their strictures about a wide gene pool, they were really extremely racist. Now they have a race problem as well."

"They are strange people, very strange. More so than I thought. Those on Dawn were . . . very ordinary, I suppose. Here, in their old place, this Kenten, they are deep in the way of . . . nature, but not wildness. They are warm, and treat one another well, according to their lights; yet they can be hard and cruel, too, to each other. But I am trying to imagine what a whole world of *klesh,* and wild, too, would be like. What will happen to them after they are moved?"

"I don't have any idea at all. I have never seen or heard anything like this. I suspect they will form tribes, first, oppress and exploit one another. You are a Zlat. How would you act?"

"I wouldn't know how to act on my own, in a society, at first." She said the word "society" as if it were some strange pungent herb. "We would make one, of course. Just like everyone else. We would have to, or run wild in the forest. I shouldn't want that—I would be cold, running about bare. You know that we were in some ways very primitive. I have been studying, Han, so I know what I was. But I am not ashamed. But more, we were not wild; but really a kind of privileged class, protected by a kind of civilization. On Dawn, many would have died. I know about winter." She made a motion as if she were shivering in bitter-cold airs.

Back in civilization, Usteyin had finally taken to wearing clothes, and although she was not entirely satisfied with them, and appalled at underwear, she had been dressing ler-style, in long, rather plain homespuns that covered all of her. But she had once, back in their rooms, exposed one creamy delicate shoulder and exclaimed, "A hundred and twenty generations to produce that tone of skin!" She raised the bottom of the robe as if she expected to be surprised by what she would find there, displaying her lower legs, and the fine, copper-colored hair that covered them, furlike. "And that! And now all covered up, for custom and for weather!" But at the same time she had discovered clothes with all the innocent joy of a child in a palace of toys, and however much she said that she would prefer to go about bare, she still wore them with considerable flair and pride. Liszendir had not completely approved of the styles she chose, but she had had to admit that Usteyin fitted well, and quickly. The only noticeable difference in her was her hair color and slighter build. By human standards, she was almost *petite*.

Han said, still thinking about the *klesh* and the new life that was approaching for them, "I'd guess they would form tribes at first, like kinds, but there would be some mixing, even at first, and more later on. There will be suffering and fighting and injustice. But Hetrus says that they are going to send some outside people there to keep a reasonable sort of order, at least within a certain area, and let them go into the wild as they will."

"Yes, they will fight. The males will fight over the females, and vice-versa. I would have, in my old life. In some events, I would even now." She raised an eyebrow archly.

Then they both, as if by mutual unspoken consent, fell to looking at the sea again. The subtle colors of the rainy afternoon flowed over it, changing even as they watched, but so gradually that they were not aware that a change was taking place, until it was over, and had evolved to something new. The rain stopped, and over the west a pale patch, a glowing warm tan, told of cloud decks breaking up, clearing. The sea took on a silvery surface gloss and lost much of its chop, and on the landing, a tied rowboat stopped its wild tethered leaping and began moving more sedately. The effect was hypnotic.

They began talking about Liszendir; she was, in fact, having considerable difficulty finding exactly the right braid, and was now spending most of her time traveling around to the many small villages in the area, searching. The situation was somewhat similar to an analogous predicament for a human in a society of arranged marriages; in her own village, she would have been known and it would have been fairly easy for an insibling pair to find her, go through the delicate maneuvers of determining one another's aspect, begin serious negotiations. But on her own, she had to resort to the town bulletin board, where strangers usually advertised. Han thought the custom a curious one, even verging on degrading in a way, but Liszendir didn't see it that way at all. Besides, she had to spend most of her time, now, traveling.

They had a saying—one of many, in fact, for ler culture seemed permeated with sayings. This one went: "Harder to please than an insibling." No wonder, there: they were the keepers of the nongenetic family line, the braid continuity, the continuation of the weave. The insibling females picked outsibling females for their insiblings and the males picked males, each one balancing jealousy and fear of strangers with an accurate appraisal of the needs of the braid-identity and the matching of personalities within the group. It was often a hard task, indeed, for no matter that the insiblings were not blood-related to each other, nevertheless they had grown up together in a fashion much like brother and sister, and there was considerable tension between them. So the preweaving arrangements were somewhat of a strain for all parties, and during the period, most were touchy and irritable.

Usteyin was even more astounded at the weaving customs than was Han. She observed, "I see not so much difference between how we did it on Dawn and how humans back here in civilized parts order their lives. There is a relation, a bridge between us, however strange things seem at first. But in their thing, Liszendir's people, they went further and made the family a purely social thing, not part social, part genetics; so for them, the difference between family and society has never arisen. But myself? Oh, no! I couldn't do that, no matter how well it works for them. I couldn't share you with anybody now."

Han agreed. "It's been tried in a couple of places by humans. It looks good, but it only works if you have a low birthrate and have been raised on a steady diet of sex from about age nine on. It takes a special kind of personality, too, to make it work right. They have a lot of sex, and a lot of fun, but there isn't much passion in it. That's the key. I think only one group survived any time at all, and actually made it a generation. Then that fell apart A lot of people have to participate in the system or you get ferocious inbreeding. The ler keep elaborate genealogies, but they are designed to prevent that kind of thing."

Usteyin finished her tea, arose quietly and gracefully from her seat, and stretched like some exotic, piquant feline. "Well, I'm sleepy now, and I should have a nap. Shall we go home?"

"A good idea. I was watching the waves while we talked, and it was making me sleepy, too. And more . . ."

"Oh, indeed! I would like that very much, too."

They put their cloaks on, and left the teahouse, to walk back to the hotel through the winding streets that still shone with rainwater. Afternoon was drawing to an end, and there was a tang, a scent, in the air, which promised clearer weather on the morrow. They were almost alone in the narrow lanes, for it was the end of the day, shops were closing, and the quiet of evening was settling over Plenkhander.

When they had climbed the stairs to their room, which they had shared with Liszendir when she had been in town, they found her gathering up the last of her few belongings. She looked tired, worn-down, but underneath that, there was a glow that told them what they had all been waiting for.

She smiled weakly and said, "You must wish me luck, now."

Han asked, "So you have found a braid?"

"Yes. It was ironic, that. All day, I have been across the mountains, at a place called Thursan's Landing, a fishing village. A vile place. I did not want to be a fisherwoman! But when I came back here, just now, there was a letter for me, downstairs, and so I went to see her. Imagine! After all this work, this traveling around, their *yos* is just down the beach road, hardly across the bridge. And so we made our arrangements."

Usteyin asked, "Liszendir, when you weave, do you have to do any ceremony, any special kind of act, before someone?"

She paused a moment. Then said, "If I may ask such a thing of you."

"It is no secret. For the insiblings, there is something they do something with the parent generation, the old insiblings, but I may not speak of that. It would not be for me, anyway. But for the outsiblings who are to be afterparents, there is nothing, either in religion or in law. You are accepted and you move in with your braid. They have accepted you, and that is authority enough for any hierarchy. When we are all formed, all woven, then there will be a party, friends and relations will visit, and there will be talk, singing, dancing, all night." Then she became serious. "But you know that I have never seen him, whom I will weave with. Nor do they have an afterfather yet, either, and he will be my second. But this is all I need. I was worried, deeply. I was beginning to think that no one wanted me. That is very frightening to us."

Han thought for a minute, then asked, "Do you like the girl you met? Do you think you will be happy there?"

"After adventuring, the strange things I have done, the oaths I have broken? Nothing can ever be the same for me again. But they are good people, very deep, as we say. That will be good for me; I need that deepness. I am pleased with them, at least such as I know of them. But I am finished, here. Come along. You shall see, too!"

Han and Usteyin each took a parcel for her, and together they left the room, went down the stairs, and came out onto the street.

Liszendir said, "It's not far. Practically under our noses." She was beginning to relax, visibly, yet at the same time she seemed anxious, anxious to go home. The three of them stood under the soft lights of the doorway lamp of the hotel and looked at one another. Liszendir guessed from Han's and Usteyin's faces that they were reading her with accuracy.

She said, warmly, "Yes, that is true, too. It is my home now. For forty standard years; until the insiblings weave in their turn. Here, right here, in Plenkhander." She looked around in the dim light at the trees with their sparkling drops of cold rainwater. The odors of the sea filled the air and from the beach, only a row of houses away, the sound of the surf could be heard, a light regular stroking that worked at the brown sand gently with the calming of the sea.

Han said, "It's hard to picture."

"To you, perhaps. But not to me."

They walked eastwards, crossed the ancient stone bridge, and within a few hundred yards came to a low stone wall, overgrown with vines. The *yos* lay deep in a grove of huge trees, trees with heavy mottled boles that resembled plane-trees, still bare, and was brightly lit by the door with hanging lanterns. Liszendir rang the bell, a huge pottery bell that rang with a mellow deep sound, as they entered the garden. After a moment, out of the *yos* ran a young child, obviously the elder outsibling, the *nerh,* but what sex it was could not be determined. All Han and Usteyin could see was that it was about three or four years old. It was followed by a ler female, who stood in the light of the lanterns, waiting for them. She was small and dark, pretty-pleasant but not beautiful. She looked busy, and wore her hair, considerably longer than Liszendir's, tied up in a sort of kerchief. As they came closer, Han noticed that her hands were reddened from washing, apparently, but they were strong, capable, busy hands. She would be about five years older than Liszendir.

While the child ran around them, staring shyly when it thought no one was watching at Usteyin's hair, the girl came up to them, embraced Liszendir, pressing her cheeks to the new girl's quickly, and turned to them, smiling shyly. Han repressed an urge to laugh: she had a missing tooth. But he didn't, for it added a certain charm to her face, which was painfully earnest. Her face was plain, like Liszendir's, but different, narrower, more oval, and her hair was darker. She had a soft, generous mouth and clear, direct eyes, eyes that were the color of rainwater, or the color of the sheen on the sea after a storm.

She spoke. "I am Hvethmerleyn. I am sorry you cannot meet the *kadh,* the forefather, for he is still up in the vineyards and will probably be out for several more days." Her voice was clear, a pure tone. She pronounced the "hv-" of her name with a breathy inflection that added some essence, some indecipherable attraction to her manner. "Will you join us tonight? Please stay for a while, for this is special, and we have few visitors. I would be very happy."

So they all went into the *yos* under the trees and spent the evening eating, drinking, telling part of their story over again to Hvethmerleyn, who listened to what she heard with hardly concealed amazement. If Han left some parts out, neither Liszendir nor Usteyin corrected him. And as the night went onwards, he noticed that the two females seemed to be warming up to each other well, becoming confidential, intimate. He wondered not so much how it would be for Liszendir: that he already knew, at least part of it; but rather for Hvethmerleyn. To spend your whole life with one male, more or less, and then pick yourself a second mate for him, bring her into your house, the house of your own family group . . . He tried to imagine it. He could not.

They learned that the braid-name was Ludhen. Ludh meant "wine" in Singlespeech! They were vintners! Hvethmerleyn laughed her warm laugh, and Han, now wise to some ler ways, saw, just for a moment, that Hvethmerleyn was, in ler reference, very warm, very sexy. That would be exactly what Liszendir needed, for he had begun to suspect something about her, something about a thing missing in Liszendir's life. She was pleased that Han recognized the Single-speech word-root, and insisted that he and Usteyin take a bottle of wine to remember them by. And she talked about the forefather, her insibling, who was called Thoriandas.

It seemed that Hvethmerleyn suspected that his remark about being up in the vineyards was just an excuse to go out and look for a suitable male outsibling for her. Thoriandas, apparently, had a robust sense of humor, and had promised that he would dig up the worst sort of riffraff, a drunkard and a reprobate, and probably a thief to boot. Usteyin laughed out loud.

"And what will you do with such a one?"

"Oh, I'll reform him," she answered, suddenly coy, arch, demure. "Or," she added, "I'll wear him out in the process!"

The child, Tavrenian, had proved to be a boy, and had tumbled off to bed earlier. As they talked on, Han saw that Hvethmerleyn was also getting sleepy, and he knew that Liszendir would be about run down herself. Ler went to bed early, and got up early. So they made their goodbyes, in short form, without ceremony, and made ready to leave the *yos*. Liszendir came with them to the door, while Hvethmerleyn stayed behind, sensing that they had one more thing to say that was private, part of Liszendir's old life. In the yard, it was dark and quiet, save for the remains of the dripping of rainwater, now almost stopped, and the mutter and gentle splashing of the surf behind the *yos*. Somewhere, hidden by the trees and houses, a wagon was slowly rattling along the cobblestones, blending into the water sounds in a stream of sound that fitted together perfectly.

Usteyin broke the silence, saying, "Liszendir Now-Ludhen, you have a piece of loveliness here I wish deeply we could share. But I wish you, in your life to come, the same of what we have found in ours and hope to keep for the time that will fall to us."

"Yes, it is so. This is a good place; I think I will grow into it. And it is as you say. So I will not say goodbye to you, nor will I forget. I have seen your lives, and you have seen mine, and we have all walked in one another's shoes for a time. And it ends well, more than what I once thought would never be." She stopped, biting her lower lip indecisively. Then she impulsively embraced them both, briefly, and ran back into the *yos*, stopping only in the doorway to say to them, "Many children! And many years!" She quickly disappeared within.

Outside, in the dampness of the night air and deep in the sounds of raindrip and surf, Han and Usteyin turned and walked up the path to the gate, and from there, back over the stone bridge, back to their room, through the wet streets alone, silent, deep in thoughts, occasionally touching one another as they walked.

An Explanatory Afterword
on Ler Names

As in most speculative stories, some of the names of beings, particularly the alien or the strange, may strike one as hard, odd, or impossible to pronounce. This is not the case, at least by intent, as far as the ler names used in this tale are concerned. After a moment's investigation, they should be both possible and easy to subvocalize.

All ler personal names were composed of three Singlespeech basic root-words or syllables, coupled directly together and pronounced as one word. Each root-word in Singlespeech ends in, and only in, a vowel-consonant pair. In the English spelling convention we use here, this may appear at times to be more extensive, but the units are always single phonemes. Knowing this, we may break up the name into its three parts, correctly, by finding the vowel-consonant ends of each root. An example of this is the name "Liszendir", which breaks "Lis-Zen-Dir."

Now while the generation principle behind the structure of the root words of Singlespeech was modeled on the Chinese example (i.e., few patterns of basic words, using all possible combinations), the phonetic values used to fill in the blanks were equivalent to those values in use at the time of the origin of the ler in the country where they happened to be, which was an English-speaking country. Modern English of the standard American variety is close enough. Only two consonants out of the whole thirty-six-character alphabet were not natural to that context, and they were *kh* and *gh*, added to the system to make it regular, both in a phonetic sense and a ler-qabalistic one.

Ler personal names had, for the ler, a curious duality in regard to meaning which is difficult for us to understand

fully. For us, civilized men, personal names have largely
lost their function of totem and meaning; Georges do not,
as a rule, imagine themselves to be workers of earth, nor do
Leos emulate lions, nor Leroys imagine themselves kings,
no matter how much self-esteem they may have. Our
names are derivative, meant to honor a family namesake, a
famous person, or—even sound pretty. (The girl-name Pam-
ela is reputed to have no denotative meaning whatsoever!)
So when we think of names having literal meaning, we think,
perhaps, about more primitive kinds of men, American In-
dians of the Southwest, or of Africans of the equatorial
forests.

For the ler, however, names could be, according to circumstance, very meaningful, as for the tribesman, or completely meaningless, far more so than for us, since it was
the ler custom that no child could be named for anybody.
The names were supposed to be as original as possible. If
one by chance repeated, it was strictly by chance. Ler would
not knowingly repeat a name, certainly not one used within
their local area. Because of the secret nature of the "aspect"
(Lssp: *plozos*) of the individual, a ritual part of ler culture,
and the relation of the "aspect" to the particular meaning
out of four possible meanings for each root, a person's name-
meaning could not be determined unless one knew the aspect.
Within the braid, of course, such things were known, if not
discussed, and one's name tended to form a basic guide to
character. A ler whose name happened to mean "fire-eating
devil" (*Pangurtron**) would in fact be prone to a certain
amount of belligerence and irrationality, and others would
also be guided by the meaning attributed to their names, in
like manner.

Outside the braid, however, it was another matter; one's
"aspect" was not told to anyone, except for weaving-custom,
and without the context of discourse-speech to aid meaning,
a translation could not be determined. In the case of the ler
girl Liszendir, no ler outside her birth-braid knew her aspect,
or the meaning of her name, until she was accepted by
Hvethmerleyn into Ludhen Braid (Klanludhen). That she
told the human Han first what it meant, and later that she
was fire in aspect, can be viewed as a measure of her feelings,
as it was a major sacrifice on her part.

As syllables were not repeated within names, and all

---

*Fire (*Panh*) aspect.

three parts had to be of the same aspect, the number of possible interpretations is fortunately limited; however, it is still too high to guess and beat the laws of probability, even for ler. Consequently, considerable time was devoted among the ler, socially, to determining the aspect of one's associates and friends (not to mention lovers), a practice which was countered by equally strenuous attempts to keep it concealed. Perhaps by this, some of Liszendir's actions may appear more explicable.

Liszendir's name, "(fire) velvet brushed night," carried overtones of abstraction and distance in interpersonal relations, and in fact she was rather cool and aloof, intellectual rather than intimate. While she had known lovers much the same, and to the same degree, as any other average ler girl her age, she had not had what she might have called a great love affair of passion, and felt thereupon a certain lack. She knew well enough that humans did not follow ler custom in personal names, but out of habit and to pass the time, she was not above playing a minor little fortunetelling game with Han's name, much as she might have done back in her own environment. This became more than just interesting when one considered that Han's full name, Han Keeling; by altering the -ng at the end of his last name to an -n, would produce, by accident or design by persons unknown, an acceptable Singlespeech ler name, Hankiellin. Liszendir already suspected Han of being strong in the sphere of emotions, which would fall to the water aspect (see further Tarot symbolism, the suit of Cups). That, if it were true, would make the string of roots mean, more or less, "last-passion-meeting." All things considered, it was a dire message indeed to derive from a minor session of the fortune-telling game.

M.A.F., May 1973.

DAW PRESENTS MARION ZIMMER BRADLEY

"A writer of absolute competency . . ."—Theodore Sturgeon

DAW ≡ sf BOOKS